Fran O'Brien and Arthur McGuinness
established McGuinness Books
to publish Fran's novels to raise funds
for LauraLynn Children's Hospice.

Fran's novels, *The Married Woman,*
The Liberated Woman, The Passionate Woman,
Odds on Love, Who is Faye? The Red Carpet,
Fairfields, The Pact, 1916, and *Love of her Life*
have raised over €450,000.00 in sales and
donations for LauraLynn House.

Fran and Arthur hope that *Rose Cottage Years*
will raise even more funds for LauraLynn.

www.franobrien.net

Also by Fran O'Brien

The Married Woman
The Liberated Woman
Odds on Love
Who is Faye?
The Red Carpet
Fairfields
The Pact
1916
The Passionate Woman
Love of her Life

Buy now online www.franobrien.net

Rose Cottage Years

FRAN O'BRIEN

*To Lucy,
with many thanks
Fran*

McGuinness Books

McGuinness Books

Rose Cottage Years

This book is a work of fiction and any resemblance
to actual persons, living or dead is purely coincidental.

Published by McGuinness Books,
15 Glenvara Park, Ballycullen Road,
Templeogue, Dublin 16.

Copyright © Fran O'Brien 2017
Fran O'Brien asserts the moral right
to be identified as the author of this work.

A catalogue record for this book
is available from the British Library.

ISBN 978-0-9954698-1-5

Typeset by Martone Design & Print,
Celbridge Industrial Estate, Celbridge, Co. Kildare

Printed and bound in Great Britain by
CPI Group (UK) Ltd, Croydon, CR0 4YY.

All rights reserved. No part of this publication may be reproduced,
stored in a retrieval system or transmitted, in any form or by any means,
electronic, mechanical, photocopying, recording or otherwise,
without the prior permission of the publishers.

www.franobrien.net

This novel is dedicated to Jane and Brendan McKenna,
and in memory of their daughters Laura and Lynn.

And for all our family, friends and clients who support our
efforts to raise funds for LauraLynn Children's Hospice,
Leopardstown Road, Dublin 18.

Jane and Brendan have been through every parent's worst
nightmare – the tragic loss of their only two children.

Laura died, just four years old, following surgery to repair a
heart defect. Her big sister, Lynn, died, aged fifteen, less than
two years later, having lost her battle against Leukaemia –
diagnosed on the day of Laura's surgery.

Having dealt personally with such serious illness, Jane and
Brendan's one wish was to establish a children's hospice
in memory of their girls.

Now LauraLynn House has become a reality
and their dream has come true.

LauraLynn Children's Hospice offers community based
paediatric palliative, respite, end-of-life care, and the
LauraLynn@home Programme.

At LauraLynn House there is an eight bed unit, a residential
unit for families, support and comfort for parents and siblings
for whom life can be extremely difficult.

Putting Life into a Child's Day
Not Days into a Child's Life

Part One

1913

Chapter One

'I'd give anything to go home,' Anna whispered, tears in her large blue eyes.

'All I want is to have you with me.' Fanny stretched her hand across the table and clasped her daughter's hand.

There was a warm buzz of conversation from the other patrons in the little tea shop. The tinkle of china and clatter of cutlery. At their own corner table, the pink floral design of the tea pot, cups, saucers and plates was elegant. But the cream fancies on the plates remained untouched. The tea in the cups had grown cold and was now a dull unappetising shade of brown.

Fanny picked up the teapot and poured fresh. But only she sipped a little. Her daughter didn't touch it.

'Why won't Pa and Edward forgive me?' Anna asked, drying the tears with her handkerchief.

'I don't know, both your father and brother are very stubborn.'

'What if I just go home and walk in the door, surprise them?'

'I wouldn't trust Edward, and Seamus always follows his lead.'

'They might never let me come back.'

Fanny bent her head.

'I'm sorry to have caused you so much pain,' Anna was contrite.

'I thought I couldn't live without you,' Fanny continued in a nervous rush. 'I even asked the priest about taking a child from the Blind Asylum.'

'What?' There was a puzzled frown on Anna's forehead.

'To take care of a little one would make me so happy.' Fanny looked down at the sleeping child in the baby carriage, and reached to touch her curly blonde hair.

Bina opened her eyes and stretched out her hand to Fanny.

'My little grandchild, if only …' She curled her hand around Bina's.

'Maybe you could look after Bina when she's a bit older,' Anna murmured.

Fanny raised her head up, surprise etched on her features.

'When I have my new baby, which won't be long now, I'll be kept very busy.' She pulled the lilac coat she wore across the heaviness of her stomach.

'I don't want you to part with Bina, it would be too hard on you. And what would Mike say?' Fanny asked.

'I'll talk to him when he comes home. He will understand, I'm sure of that.'

'You've a good husband.'

'I miss him. He'll be away in Hong Kong for another six months.'

'Men enjoy the excitement of sailing all over the world. His time will go fast, while your time will be slow. The life of a sailor is a hard one for his family.'

'Interminable.' Anna's expression was gloomy. 'I hate living in Portsmouth and I don't want to go back there until Mike is home.'

'But you are friendly with the other families in the naval quarters?'

'I don't know them very well, except for my close neighbours.'

'Maybe you should stay here until the baby arrives, anyway travelling so close to the time isn't wise,' Fanny suggested.

'But that means I'll have to stay in Queenstown all the time.'

'Iris and Meg will look after you. And there's something else, I didn't want to mention it but …'

'What is it?' Anna stared at her mother, puzzled.
'The Master and Mistress have finally sold *Fairfields*.'

Mr. and Mrs. Staunton, the owners of the *Fairfields* estate where Fanny and Seamus worked, had told the staff a number of years ago that they would be selling the estate. But that decision had been deferred and as time went on and nothing happened Fanny and her husband and everyone else had begun to relax, hoping that the Stauntons may have changed their plans.

'Who has bought it?' Anna asked anxiously.

'I don't know yet.'

'What's going to happen to you? Will you be kept on?'

'I've only heard it from Tess, the Master hasn't told us anything definite yet.' Fanny's lip quivered. She found it hard to deal with it. She and Seamus had been living in the stable yard all their married life and the thought of leaving the only home they had known was crushing. 'The new people will surely need horses and carriages too, and all the staff to run the house,' Fanny murmured hopefully.

'And it would be impossible to get anyone as good.' Anna squeezed her mother's hand.

'That's what we're all saying. But if we were let go, I don't know what we'd do. Your father can't live without his horses. You know how he loves them. They're his whole life. He wouldn't be able to get through a day without them. It won't affect Edward, he has his job, but we'll have no work, although the Master did mention that there would be a small pension for Seamus. But I don't know how much that will be and whether we can live on it.' There was a sudden rush of tears into Fanny's eyes.

'We have to hope that things won't be so bad,' Anna reassured gently.

'My knees are worn out praying to Our Lady.'

'I'll say a special Novena.'

'Pray she listens to us.'

'I will, Mam, I will.'

Fanny helped Anna and Bina on to the train for Queenstown, and stood watching as it chugged out of the station and disappeared into the distance, smoke drifting behind. She had a heavy heart. Saddened that her daughter couldn't stay with her at the stable yard in *Fairfields*. Since Anna had run away from home, refusing to marry the man the family had chosen for her, life had been very hard on Fanny. While Anna had eventually married Mike, the man she loved, and was living in Portsmouth in the naval quarters, she had been able to come back to Cork from time to time but because her father and brother had refused to allow her to come home, she was forced to stay with Fanny's sister Iris and her cousin Meg in Queenstown.

Needing to pick up a few messages in town, Fanny went to the Baltimore Stores. From her pocket, she pulled the scrap of paper on which she had written the various items. Her head bent as she walked, she didn't notice the man who stood watching as she approached.

'Mother?'

She looked up to see her son standing in front of her. 'Edward?'

'You're in town again. You were in yesterday as well.' There was an accusation in his voice.

'I was, and what is it to you?' she retorted.

He shrugged.

'I must buy a few things, otherwise you might have nothing to eat for your tea. Have you no work to be doing?'

'I'm on my way to a meeting.'

'Well, be off then or you'll be late. I must get back.'

'Do you want to wait and I'll take you home in the trap?' he asked to her departing figure. She waved him off and didn't reply. But Fanny was worried. She had been walking in town with Anna only a short time before and if they had met Edward then she didn't know what would have happened.

Her shopping done, she went to where she had left her bicycle, and set out for home. As she pushed up Summerhill, she realised that bumping into Edward so unexpectedly was very worrying. Goodness knows what he might have said to Anna if he had met them earlier. He had a quick temper and could fly off the handle so fast they might have been disgraced in front of other people. While she had been very short with him when she met him earlier, now she regretted that. She decided then that it would be better if she went out to Queenstown to see Anna in future.

Chapter Two

'Johnny?' Mike exclaimed, staring at the man who came towards him.

'Reporting for duty,' Johnny said and saluted, a wide grin on his cheerful features.

'What are you doing here? I haven't had a word from you in the last year, although I think I wrote you a couple of times.' Mike clasped his hand in a tight grip.

'I've been moved around, Malta, Gibraltar, and now here in this godforsaken place,' he grimaced. 'And I was never a good letter writer.'

'I've only another six months to do, thanks be to God.' They stood on the steel deck of *HMS Minotaur*. She was an armoured cruiser, and carried a complement of almost eight hundred men.

'Is Hong Kong as bad as they say?' Johnny asked.

'At times. It's the weather. The heat and humidity. And of course we've had to contend with the Chinese revolution, although it was on the mainland and didn't affect us here directly. There are elections coming up in a few weeks' time so we'll wait and see what happens, there are still powerful warlords controlling large areas.'

'China is a huge country.'

'It will take years to unify it altogether, although I don't know if the corruption will ever be wiped out. It's endemic in every part of society. And there are huge differences between the rich and poor.'

'Not that much different to many other countries, even ourselves,' commented Johnny.

'Will Ireland ever achieve Home Rule I wonder?' Mike gripped the rail tightly and stared out across the harbour.

'Better not let anyone hear you say that.'

'This is between you and I, Johnny, just my thoughts.'

'Glad of that.'

They walked along the deck for a while, silent, passing a couple of sailors who saluted them.

'This is a hell of a busy place. The streets are wild. So many people rushing everywhere. You'd take your life in your hands in one of those rickshaws, and I even saw a motor car forcing its way through the crowds,' Johnny laughed, looking back at the city which was overshadowed by Victoria Peak, the top of which was somewhat obscured today by low cloud. Below the peak were the naval dockyards stretching around the harbour, hotels, shops, businesses, banks, and the hospital, Hong Kong was a thriving exciting place.

'If you want to get somewhere fast take a rickshaw, it's the quickest. Or a sedan chair. Come in to the Mess and have something to eat, when did you actually dock?'

'A few hours ago.'

'How long are you assigned to *Minotaur*?' Mike asked as he went into the Mess.

'I'm not sure, I could be posted to any other ship without warning.'

'It's a coincidence you're here. But it's good to see you.' Mike introduced Johnny to a few of the other officers who were having lunch and then the two men sat down and ordered.

'What do you do in this place?'

'There are quite a lot of social gatherings and various clubs and hotels, so plenty of places to go.'

'I'm looking forward to the next race meeting at Happy Valley,' Johnny said with a grin, finishing off his roast beef in jig time.

'I'll be glad of your company. And you'll enjoy the Jockey Club, plenty of activity there.'

'What else is there to do?'

'Some of us play cricket, so you could come along and join in,' Mike said. 'We've our own league.'

'So it's not such a dull place after all.'

'I suppose not, although I'd rather be back in Portsmouth with Anna and Bina.'

'That's natural. I'm still looking out for some girl as beautiful as Anna, you rightly fell on your feet there.'

Off duty later, and after Johnny was settled into his quarters, the two took a stroll through the city. Walking along Queen's Road, Mike pointed out various landmarks.

'I'm amazed at this place, it's pulsing with activity,' Johnny remarked.

'There's everything here. The university is almost finished,' he indicated the building on the hill above them. 'And the trams will take you up to the Peak where the businessmen and merchants live, the upper crust you might say.'

'That's the place I'd like to go of an evening, lots of parties on up there I'd wager,' Johnny said.

'Let's go to the club for a drink, my throat is dry,' Mike suggested.

Mike was really glad to see Johnny. A good friend, he had missed his company since he had been transferred to Hong Kong. While he had served here a few years before he met Anna, and enjoyed his time in the Far East, this spell of duty had been extremely tedious, and he longed to be with the two people he loved most in the world, Anna and his daughter Bina.

His second child was due to be born soon and he would have given anything to be with his family when he or she arrived. Now he counted the days until he would leave Hong Kong to sail back, but the time went slowly, relentlessly slow.

Chapter Three

'She's beautiful, Anna, just beautiful.' Fanny cupped the little face of the baby. 'Better give her a feed, she's hungry I think.'

Anna put the child to her breast and she immediately began to suckle. 'I'm going to be so sore, I was the last time with Bina.'

'You'll get used to it.'

'I suppose I will, anyway I can't let my baby go hungry.'

'What's her name going to be?'

'I thought I might call her Eleanor, that's Mike's mother's name. He'll like that.'

'But his mother is Nancy?'

'That's his stepmother, his real mother was Eleanor.'

'I forgot that.'

'So you are Eleanor O'Sullivan,' Anna smiled down at the baby. 'I can't wait to tell him. Do you think he'll be disappointed that she's not a boy?' she asked anxiously.

'Not at all, sure wasn't his last letter full of concern for you, it seemed to be all he was worried about.' Fanny dismissed that.

'But men always want sons, and now I've had two girls.'

'Your next one will be a boy, don't fret yourself. He's not the king and must have an heir who will take his place on the throne,' Fanny laughed. 'Be happy with this darling baby. Look at her little face, the pink lips and tiny fingers. God take care of her and pray that nothing happens. Stay strong my little one.' Fanny kissed her. She thought then of her own babies she had lost. Three who had been stillborn and hadn't even lived to take a precious breath, and two who had lived some weeks and then sadly died all too soon, leaving her bereft, and not knowing why and always wondering, wondering. Eventually accepting that it was God's will, and that he needed his little angels around him. She said nothing to Anna, it wasn't something she talked about.

Anna smiled and kissed the forehead of her child. 'I love that sweet baby aroma.'

'It is your own, and you will always recognise her scent, even if there are other children there.'

'How's mother and baby?' Iris, Fanny's sister, came in.

'They're fine.'

'And you're a grandmother again, Fanny. At least your daughter is doing her duty,' Iris said, laughing.

'My sons are lagging behind. Jim is married but has no children, and Edward and Pat aren't married yet. What a family.'

'Are you feeling all right, Anna, it was a long labour, you must be tired, dear?' Iris came close to the bed.

'I am, I must admit.' She leaned back against the pillows.

'When she finishes her feed you just go right to sleep, Fanny and I will look after her.' Iris tucked the blankets in. She was a very caring person.

'Iris, we're so grateful that you've allowed Anna to stay on, I'd hate her to be on her own at a time like this.'

'You stay as long as you like, Anna, we love having you. And there's plenty of space here in the house for all of us.'

The bedroom door opened and Iris's daughter, Meg, came in. She stood by the bedside. 'I wish I was you, Anna.'

'You wouldn't at the moment,' Anna smiled.

'I'd love to have a baby.'

'You will, one of these days, as soon as you find a man,' Iris chided.

'I'm an old maid, no man is going to look at me.'

'Haven't you plenty of friends, and aren't some of them men?'

'They don't look at me …like that. Not the way they look at the others. They like to talk to me but they never try to kiss me.'

'Just as well, you don't want men who take liberties,' Fanny said.

'You couldn't marry one of them. It wouldn't be right.'

'What about Anna and Mike?'

'What do you mean?' There was suspicion in Iris's tone.

'They ran away to get married. You were in love, weren't you, Anna?'

'Well, yes.'

'And I bet Mike kissed you,' she said.

A blush stole over Anna's cheeks.

'That's not a fit conversation, Meg, particularly when Anna has just had the baby, I'm shocked to my core,' Iris spluttered. 'Away with you, do something useful instead of subjecting us to these disgraceful remarks. Go keep an eye on Bina, make sure she's all right, and after that, get down on your knees and say a decade of the Rosary as penance. I'll have you to Confession as soon as I can, never you fear, girl.'

Fanny tried to hide her smile, and kept her eyes averted from Anna's. It wouldn't do to disagree with Iris who was a stickler for conformity, or even let her see the humour in the situation. Although she felt suddenly sorry for Meg. At thirty-two, she should have been married by now and it was a pity that no man had asked for her hand.

Meg lowered her head and left the room.

Fanny felt it was a bit hard on her, but couldn't have said anything. It wouldn't do. They were indebted to Iris for looking after Anna, Bina and the new baby.

'I want to write to Mike and tell him about the baby before I go to sleep,' Anna said.

'Wait until tomorrow, love, you must be tired out,' Fanny suggested.

'No, I must tell him about Eleanor as soon as I can. Letters take so long to get to China. Will you hand me my writing things from the top drawer of the tallboy, please Mam?'

Fanny brought over the writing pad to Anna. 'Let me write it for you and then you can just sign it. You might spill ink on the bedspread if you try to write it in bed. We don't want Iris to be on the warpath.'

'All right then.'

Fanny set the folder on her knees and opened a fresh page in the writing pad. When she was finished, she took the baby, and gave the pad and pen to Anna to add her own few words.

Fanny looked down at her grandchild. 'I think Eleanor looks like you,' she said.

'Do you not see Mike in her?'

'She has dark eyes like him, and they'll probably grow even darker. But her mouth and chin are all Dineen.'

'She has a bit of both of us in her,' Anna smiled. 'Can you post my letter, Mam?'

'I'll do that on my way home.'

'Bring up Bina will you, I haven't seen her for hours.'

Fanny went home that afternoon, and Anna was left with Iris, Meg and Bina. It was a large house, with a dining room, and parlour downstairs, the kitchen in the basement, and three bedrooms on the upper level. She longed to go home to the stable yard with her mother, missing home so much and all the people who were part of her life before she married Mike.

But this was the path she had chosen. She loved Mike more than she could ever have imagined, but his work took him far away from her for long periods of time and that was something she hadn't fully understood on that day when she had promised to love him until death. The exact words they had each spoken during the marriage ceremony echoed in her mind, and tears suddenly sprang into her eyes and threatened to overwhelm.

She struggled to gain control over herself. It wouldn't do to let Iris and Meg see such emotion. They would be very concerned that there was something wrong with her, and undoubtedly create a fuss, perhaps even telling Fanny next time she came to visit. And she couldn't have that. Her poor mother was worried enough about her.

She tucked the blanket around Bina who slept on the bed beside her, and smiled down at Eleanor whose eyes were also closed, dark lashes brushing pink cheeks. She stared pensively out of the window over Queenstown Harbour, at Haulbowline where Mike had been stationed when they first met. The view of the ships which dotted the stretch of calm water always reminded her of him. To see the officers walking around the town was difficult. Every tall broad shouldered one could have been him. Even though he couldn't possibly be here, being many miles away in Hong Kong, for that first second her heart almost jumped out of her body with excitement and then she was left to endure the disappointment that it wasn't him after all.

'Anna, I'm sorry for what I said earlier. I shouldn't have, Mam was right.' Meg sat on the side of the bed.

'Don't worry, I found it hard to keep the smile off my face and I know that Mam was the same. We couldn't look at each other for fear of laughing.'

'My Mam is so serious,' Meg giggled. 'And she will make me go to Confession tomorrow, I was lucky there was none today. She'll probably tell me what sins to confess to the priest.'

'Would she do that?' Anna looked at her in surprise.

'You never know, she was pretty angry today.'

'Let's hope that doesn't happen.'

'Anna, can I hold Eleanor?' She held out her arms.

'Of course you can, and rub her back gently, I've just fed her.'

Meg put the baby on her shoulder.

'You look like a real mother, Meg.'

'I'd love to have my own baby. She's so soft and warm, the little darling.'

'You'll have your own babies soon enough, Meg.'

'Do you think so?'

'Of course you will.'

'In the meantime, I'll look after Eleanor for you, and Bina too. I love her.'

'Thank you.'

'When will Mike be back?'

'In another few months I hope, but it's hard to know exactly, it takes a long time to sail from China.'

'I wish I could travel somewhere exciting like that. Life is so boring here in Queenstown,' Meg said wistfully.

'I don't think you'd like it so much, Mike says it's a very strange place. There are nicer places in the world.'

'I haven't been anywhere at all.'

'We went to London on our honeymoon, it's a very big place,' Anna confided.

'Honeymoon? You had a honeymoon?' The other girl was agog.

'Yes of course, Meg,' Anna laughed.

'But I thought you ran away together?'

'We did I suppose, but that didn't stop us having a honeymoon.'

'How long was the honeymoon?'

'It was just two days, that was all the leave Mike had.'

'Such a pity. Was it wonderful?'

'Yes, simply magic.'

'What happened? What made it so …?' Meg's eyes were round with curiosity.

'When you love someone, it's just wonderful to be together.'

'And did he kiss you?'

Anna nodded.

'And you kissed him back?'

'Yes of course.'

'And you had a baby.'

'Yes, Bina.'

'I wish someone would take me to London,' Meg sighed dramatically.

'Someone will.'

'But when, that is the question.' Meg was glum.

'Where is Bina?' asked Anna.

'Mam took her for a walk.'

'You're both so good to us.'

'We love having you here. It makes such a difference, Anna.'

'You should cherish these days, Meg. Since Mike went to China, I've lived on my own in Portsmouth with Bina, none of the people I loved were close to me. Although there are other families there and they are very friendly, it is still lonely.'

'You should have written to me. I'd have gone over to keep you company. Even to go as far as Portsmouth would be exciting. Maybe I'll visit some time?'

'You could ...if you want.' Anna was grateful to Meg, but she wondered what Mike would think if she was there when he came back home. And did she want her to stay with them in Portsmouth? That thought was unnerving.

Chapter Four

Mike walked along the deck to his quarters. There were clouds building up on the horizon, grey blue, pink tinged in the sunset. A warm breeze blew off the land although there was no comfort in it, and waves slapped up against the side of the ship and splashed over the deck with white foaming spume. The sea was packed with battleships and cruisers of the various navies of Europe and that of the United States, interspersed with smaller vessels and local fishing boats.

They were at anchor off Weihaiwei. Britain leased it from the Chinese and it was used as a summer anchorage by the Royal Navy, and a port of call for their ships in the Far East. The weather was very hot and humid, and even now beads of sweat gathered on Mike's forehead as he pushed open the door. He had received a bundle of mail, and couldn't wait to open the letters, but before he had a chance to read the first one he was informed that a wireless message had been received from Shanghai that the Nationalist forces led by *Sun Yat Sen* had attacked the army of *Yuan Shikai* further up the Yangtze River. There was concern for the lives of all British and other nationalities and ships in the area had already sailed up the Yangtze, but no decision was made for *HMS Minotaur* to join them, and anyway her draught was not shallow enough to sail all the way to Jinjiang.

Mike opened the bundle of post. While he wrote every day to Anna, and she replied, the length of time it took was frustrating and he could never calculate what she might be doing from day to day even though she took great care to describe what happened with her and Bina. The third letter he opened told him that Anna had had another daughter. He let a loud roar out of him and punched the air, then continued to read the few words which followed but found nothing more about the birth, left wondering was Anna all right. It was common for women to die in childbirth and he had known men in the Navy who had lost their wives in this way. God forbid nothing had happened since then. He searched for a date on the page but didn't find any and could see that her mother had written the letter and Anna had added a few words. But it wasn't her usual signature but looked like the handwriting of someone who was extremely tired. But then he reasoned that she would be tired after the length of time it took to give birth. It was a most exhausting and painful process. He peered at the stamp on the envelope and was partially able to decipher the date. It was in June. A few weeks ago. He prayed she was well and their daughter too, longing now to see her. He picked up a pen and began to write.

My darling Anna,

I am so happy to know that our baby has arrived. It is wonderful, and I am hoping that it wasn't too hard on you and that you are well recovered by now. What does Bina think of our new arrival? Is she happy to be a big sister? Tell her I love her, and kiss the little one from me.

I am looking forward to seeing you all when I get back. I feel the time when we set sail for Europe will never arrive. I dream of that day.

With all my love and many kisses. Mike. xxx

On August first, a wireless message came through about eight o'clock in the evening. The cipher was decoded, and at three in the morning their ship set sail up the Yangtze as far as they could get. There was a possibility that they would have to land in enemy territory to protect their British citizens. The guns of *HMS Minotaur* were quite capable of dealing with anything *Sun* or *Yuan* could muster, but normally Britain and the other countries who had a presence there took a neutral stance. They waited for word some miles upriver and after a number of days, it was decided among the various vessels at Jinjiang that there was no requirement for a landing anywhere along the river. Then the city was set on fire by the rebels, and they abandoned it. The information was sent to *HMS Minotaur*, and she sailed back to Weihaiwei.

After that, both Mike and Johnny received a thirty-six hour pass and were glad to have some relaxation. A couple of other officers Mike knew on board were sailing in a small yacht to Shanghai and Mike and Johnny decided to join them for the trip. It was good to get away from the inflexible naval routine, and even more than that, he wanted to celebrate the arrival of his second daughter with his friends.

Shanghai was even busier than Hong Kong. It was the commercial capital of China. The nightlife in Shanghai was legendary and the clubs were popular with naval personnel. There were opium shops and a large number of the Chinese used the drug in their everyday lives. The men spent a few hours in the city, had a couple of drinks and raised their glasses to Mike's new daughter.

'This is one hell of a place, those women are beautiful, and there's so many of them around, I'm coming back here next shore leave,' Johnny said, with a wide grin.

'I'm not that interested.'

'Don't be a dry old stick, Mike.'

'Thanks,' he laughed.

'You're all sensible married men, but I'm still fancy free, the world's my oyster.'

'Most of the fellows head for here when they get a chance,' Mike said.

'Let's plan for our next leave, and we'll have a right old bash.'

Chapter Five

Meg opened the front door to find Anna's friend Ellie outside. She threw her arms around Meg and they hugged tight. Bina ran down the hall, curious.

'Bina?' Ellie gathered up the child. She squealed with excitement.

'How's my little one?' She kissed her.

Anna came downstairs and embraced her friend. 'It's so good to see you.'

'Come on in Ellie, if Mam sees you here on the doorstep she won't be too pleased.'

Ellie put Bina down on her feet, but immediately she protested, hanging on to Ellie's dark skirt to get her attention. 'It's great to take the weight off my feet after trudging up that hill.' Ellie flopped into an armchair. 'How are you since the birth of Eleanor? Your Mam was telling me all about her.'

'I'm fine now, it's taken me this length of time to get back to normal, I was exhausted after the labour.'

'You poor thing, it sounds so hard, I don't know how I'll go through it, that's if I ever find a man who will give me a baby,' she said with a wide grin.

'Any boyfriends?' Anna asked mischievously.

'Not a one. There are still some of the old crowd that we knew around, but there isn't one of them I'd take for a walk down *Lovers Lane*,' she giggled.

'You'll meet some gorgeous fellow one of these days,' Anna reassured.

'Remember the laughs we had at the dances,' Ellie said, smiling.

'Do you still go?'

'Sometimes I meet the girls in town.'

'Then there's still the chance of meeting a man,' laughed Anna.

'I miss you, Anna, it feels like years since you've been in Glanmire.'

'Five …' Tears moistened Anna's eyes.

'Not to be able to come home for a visit is awful. Everyone asks for you all the time.'

'I miss them all, and Mike is away so much it's very lonely.'

'But now you have your baby, and Bina, they'll keep you happy,' Meg added.

'I'm thrilled with my little Eleanor, she's adorable.'

'I'd love to see her, is she asleep?' Ellie asked.

'Come on and we'll see.'

Anna took Bina's hand and they all trooped upstairs and crept into the bedroom, to stare down at the baby in the crib.

'She's beautiful,' Ellie whispered.

Suddenly she opened her eyes and gazed up at the ring of faces around her.

'She's so like Mike around the eyes, but she has your mouth. So sweet.' Ellie brushed her cheek. 'Could we take her up?'

'Yes, she's awake now, and will start crying any minute. She hates being left in the crib.' Anna lifted her, and handed her to Ellie.

'Look at you, baby,' Ellie cooed, rocking her. 'You're a little pet. And you're smiling at me, look at that, big smiles for Auntie Ellie.'

'I want her,' Bina demanded.

'You can play with her in a minute,' Meg said.

Ellie sat down in the armchair with the baby in her arms and Bina leaned over and kissed her, catching hold of the baby's hand and curling it in her own.

'I've just realised something, she has the same name as myself. Isn't that wonderful, I'm so happy about that.'

'You've always been Ellie and I'd forgotten your name is actually Eleanor,' Anna smiled.

'But you called her after Mike's mother didn't you?'

'I did but it's really nice that it's your name as well.' Anna kissed Ellie.

'I'm delighted about that.'

The baby suddenly let out a cry, and her face scrunched up.

'Somebody isn't happy,' Ellie was concerned.

'She's hungry now,' Anna said.

'We'll go down and let you feed her, come on Bina.' Ellie took her hand, and Meg went ahead of them downstairs.

As Anna sat feeding the baby, a wave of loneliness swept over her, missing Mike so much, her home, Pa and Edward too. She had not mentioned leaving *Fairfields* to Ellie as she didn't want to upset her, but if she wasn't allowed to return home before the sale of the estate, would she ever see it again?

Chapter Six

Fanny took the top off the pot on the range to check the bacon. She pushed a long skewer into the meat glad to see that it was cooked. The vegetables boiled in pans alongside, all supplied from the gardens at *Fairfields*. She wiped her hands on her white apron and bent to check how the apple tart was doing in the oven. Seamus and Edward would both be in before long and she wanted everything to be ready.

She had written to her sons, Jim and Pat, who lived in America, about Anna's expulsion from home, but as Jim had explained to Fanny in his reply, there was little they could do from such a distance. Their father, Seamus, couldn't read or write so there was no point sending him a letter to explain how they felt. And as the brothers had never got on well with their brother Edward, they didn't think that he would appreciate either of them giving their opinion on something which was happening at home.

Fanny, Seamus and Edward sat together at the table. There wasn't much conversation, and all that could be heard was the sound of cutlery on plates, and the chomp of the men eating. Fanny was nervous. She had to pick the right moment to tell them of an idea which she had been pondering for the last week and which now demanded attention.

'Dessert?' she asked and served up.

They tucked into their tart immediately, and after that she poured tea and sat there, holding the cup in her two hands, sipping the hot liquid. She took a deep breath.

'Seamus, Edward …' It was a moment of confrontation. And she must grab it before it drifted away like the dry seed head of a dandelion on the breeze. They both looked at her.

'There's something I must say to you. It's about leaving here.'

'I've been looking around for a house to rent,' Edward said.

'I hope we get somewhere with a bit of land around it. I can't live somewhere with only a back yard,' Seamus added.

'Is there any definite word?' Edward asked.

'We have to be gone before the Master and Mistress go to Egypt this winter,' Seamus muttered. 'Tom was telling me.'

'But who told Tom?' Edward snapped. 'That could be just rumour-mongering.'

'There's a meeting next week, Tess told me,' Fanny added.

'That doesn't give us much time,' Edward muttered.

Fanny took a deep breath. 'Because we're leaving I want Anna to come home. I told you she has just had her second daughter and she wants to see her home once more, it's cruel to keep her away.'

Neither of the men spoke a word.

'And I want to have a little party with all of our friends, just to say farewell to *Fairfields*. We might never see it again either. We'll always be on the outside and the new owners won't allow us in the door.'

'So you go back and forth to meet her?' Edward asked.

'Yes, of course I do, she's my only daughter, and it breaks my heart to have her living with someone else instead of in her own home.'

'Where is she staying?' he asked suspiciously. 'Is it with Aunt Lizzie?'

'No, and it doesn't matter where she is. I want her home before we leave,' Fanny continued on. 'We'll invite everyone we can think of to the party.'

'They won't all fit in the door,' Seamus grunted.

'The weather is mild enough still, and they can move outside.'

'You know how I feel about her.' Edward was surly.

'You must forgive and forget. She didn't have a pleasant experience with your Robert Hobbs.'

'What do you mean?' He jerked his head up, and stared at her.

'She didn't tell me for a while afterwards, and never wanted you to know what happened. It might have come between you and your boss if she spoke out. Your sister cared about you in spite of all your scheming.' Even thinking about Robert Hobbs' assault on Anna almost made her sick.

'What are you talking about, Mother?' Edward stood up and glared at her, angry.

'I'll let her tell you herself if she wants to. And I want you here at the party, Edward, don't think you can find some excuse. If you're not there then you'll only disgrace the family. And I won't have that.' Fanny was firm. It wasn't often that she would force a decision on the two men in her life, and found herself enjoying this unexpected position of power.

'When are you having this …party?' There was a sarcastic undertone in Edward's voice.

'Saturday week.'

'So soon?'

'Why not? The question is, will you be there?'

He stared at her for a moment, and then nodded.

'And that's a promise?'

He didn't reply and left the kitchen.

'Seamus?' Fanny asked her husband.

'If Edward is there then I'll …'

'Good, that's done,' Fanny said firmly. So glad she had got around her son. While he hadn't actually promised, she knew she had him. Had him? She thought about that. Edward's sharp edged caustic nature often hurt her. His sarcasm made her feel she had been bitten. Physically. Painfully. Like a needle scratching through delicate skin, blood specking. Today, she put that aside. She had won.

As she worked around her home, washing and ironing the best linen for the House, she realised with sadness that as each day passed she was nearing the time when they would gather their pucks and leave this place for the last time. She had spent all of her married life here.

She glanced out the window. The late afternoon sunshine slanted in, tiny sparkling dust motes whirling in the beam took her mind to those little ones who had no chance in life. Were they still around her, she wondered.

'Fanny?' Tess appeared through the door. The large woman with cherry red cheeks smiled, although Fanny could instantly see that her smile didn't reach her eyes. She was the cook at *Fairfields* and a close friend of Fanny.

'I came down to tell you that there's nothing but whispers up at the House. Everyone is telling a different story.'

Fanny was very interested. Tess was her main source of information about what was going on.

She nodded, and sank into a chair. 'I just had to get out of there, so I grabbed a minute to myself and came down.'

'Take your ease now. You'll feel better.'

'Just talking to you will do that.'

'I'm glad.'

'We're all so worried.'

'What are they saying?'

'Some of them have it that the new people will keep us all on. Some that they'll bring their own staff from wherever they're living now. Others are saying that the Stauntons will bring myself and Ellie to Monkstown with them, and everyone else will be let go. The house in Monkstown is much smaller and they don't need as much staff.'

'But that means Ellie would have to do all the work, be up at dawn to clean the fireplaces, set the fires, cleaning, washing and everything else. She couldn't possibly do that.' Fanny was astonished.

'Maybe she's going to be the housekeeper, and there will be a couple of the maids to help her. She does get on exceedingly well with the Master and Mistress.'

'That's very good for Ellie, she's well capable. But there isn't room in Monkstown for staff to live in permanently.'

'They'll probably get local girls to help.'

'There are three rooms on the top floor, and you'll need one and Ellie the other, and that only leaves one more.'

'I'm distracted by it all. But at least if some of it is true then Ellie and I might have work, otherwise I don't know what I will do.' She stared at Fanny, a look of horror on her face. Then she put her hand on her chest. 'Oh forgive me, I'm forgetting about you down here.'

'When the Master first mentioned that they might sell up here, he told Seamus he would give him a small pension, so I hope he keeps his word on that. You know the Master has always been very good to us.'

'I used to be envious of you,' Tess said, smiling. 'And if Seamus gets a pension then you'll be set up.'

'I was thinking I might ask the new people for work. What's going to happen to the flocks of poultry? Sure they're hardly going to let them wander off, someone has to look after them,' Fanny mused.

'And who's going to live in your house?'

'I hate the thought of anyone coming in here.' Fanny shivered, looking around.

'We must wait until we hear the full story. There's going to be a meeting next week, the housekeeper told me, so we'll have to hold our breath until that happens.'

'Will we be asked to go up?' Fanny asked.

'I'm sure you'll have to be.'

'Anyway, I wanted to invite you down on Saturday week, we're having a bit of a get-together.'

'What's the reason for that?'

'It's mostly because we're leaving, at least some of us will be, but there's a surprise for everyone as well.'

'That's given me a lift, a party, I'm looking forward to it.' Tess was delighted.

Around the back of the house, close to the high outer walls of *Fairfields*, Fanny knelt down on the grass close to a flower bed which she had planted herself, some of the brightly coloured flowers still in bloom. Her favourites, white Queen Anne's Lace, Purple Foxglove, a rich red flowered lily, Sun Rose, and Dogwood, all growing from cuttings which had been given to her by the gardeners on the estate and which bloomed over the summer. Now she took her Rosary beads from her pocket and bending her head murmured a decade for her dear little ones who lay buried here, praying that they would never be left alone.

Chapter Seven

Fanny took the train to Queenstown the following day to see Anna. Delighted to be able to tell her that she could come home to *Fairfields*. She was beside herself with excitement. This was the biggest thing which had happened to her. Five years of loneliness which had been so insidious it dogged her every day. A sense of nothingness lurking at every hand's turn. Reminding of her loss.

'Does Edward know that I'm staying with Iris and Meg?' Anna asked.
    'No, I didn't tell him that.'
    'Thanks be to God, I'd die if he arrived up to the door and created a ruckus.'
    'He won't, don't worry.'
    'When can I come home?' Anna asked eagerly.
    'I think we'll just wait until the night of the party. I've already invited anyone I could think of so the word has gone out. Ellie danced around the kitchen when I told her you would be coming back. You should have seen her. But she's the only one who knows, I've sworn her to secrecy.'
    'I'm so happy, Mam, thank you.' Anna threw her arms around her mother, in tears.
    'It's such a relief, I can tell you. To have my girl at home with me again is going to be wonderful.'
    Iris gathered the two of them in her arms. 'I'm so glad that Seamus and Edward changed their minds, it's about time. I don't know what they were thinking.'

'Does that mean Anna will be leaving us?' Meg looked very put out.

'I'd be grateful if I can stay on with you until the party,' Anna asked hesitantly.

'Of course you can,' Iris reassured. 'We'll be delighted to keep you and the children here for another couple of weeks, at least it means that you're not leaving us suddenly. We'd be altogether too shocked if that happened, wouldn't we, Meg?' Iris put her arm around her daughter.

'Anyway, I'll have to go back to Portsmouth soon, Mike will be coming home,' Anna explained.

'And you'll be looking forward to that no doubt,' Iris said.

'I can't wait,' Anna couldn't hide her excitement.

'But at least we've got over the problem of Seamus and Edward, to be honest, I never thought that would happen, I was worn out praying,' Fanny admitted.

While Fanny was overjoyed that Anna was coming home, she still had the worry of leaving *Fairfields* and she dreaded the thought of this meeting which had been arranged for the following Thursday evening. One of the boys at the House had come down with a note this morning. She hadn't mentioned it to Anna, as she didn't want her worrying about it.

Fanny, Seamus and Edward made their way up the back stairs. At the top, they stood among the group of staff who had gathered together. She looked around the immense hallway of *Fairfields*. Admiring the warm gold of the wooden panelling. The richly coloured stained glass windows. Her eyes followed the swing of the stairway up to the balcony above, in awe of the magnificent sparkling cut-glass chandelier. She envied the luxurious red silk drapes, with swags trimmed with gold tasselling. What she wouldn't give to have some like that, she thought, but knew they would look ridiculous in her small house. Even a cut down version would be silly. Anyway, she didn't even know where she would be living in the future, she reminded herself, so no point in longing for the impossible.

Ellie smiled at her from where she stood with the other servants, looking pretty in her uniform of black dress and crisp white frilly apron and cap.

They waited for the Master and Mistress to arrive, the low murmuring of conversation quickly stilled as the Stauntons appeared from the library.

The large heavy-set man stood in front of them, his rather florid face even redder than usual. Mrs. Staunton smiled, by contrast her pale features were rather pinched. Almost reflecting the pale blue hue of the gown she wore.

'Thank you for coming, and it's good to see all our people together,' he smiled. 'But I'm sorry to say that the situation I wish to talk about isn't altogether a happy one for some of you.'

Fanny twisted her hands together, aware of the tension heightening in the room.

'We've loved living here in *Fairfields*, but both Mrs. Staunton and I have come to a stage in our lives when we wish to live in a smaller house. We have been considering for some years now to live permanently in Monkstown. But it isn't easy to find a purchaser for a house such as this and it is only now that someone has finally made a serious offer,' he hesitated, and looked at his wife. 'This isn't easy for us, but we have to tell you that we will only need a few staff at Monkstown, and unfortunately many of you will have to try to find other positions. Naturally, we will give you all excellent references so that should not be a problem as it is difficult to find good staff.' He seemed to look at Fanny straight in the eyes and she quaked. 'Over the next few days, Mrs. Staunton or I will meet each of you personally. Once again, I want to thank you all for your excellent service over the years.' He nodded, held out his arm to his wife and they returned to the library, closing the door softly behind them.

Fanny looked around her. She didn't know what to do for a few moments, as seemed to be the case with the rest of the staff as well. No one said very much. And only when the housekeeper began to hunt her people back downstairs, and there was a general movement among them, Fanny turned to Seamus and Edward and suggested they go back home.

'Home?' Seamus murmured.

When they arrived at the house, Seamus immediately went to tend to his horses, and Edward took the trap, drove out of the stable yard and disappeared. Fanny was left on her own. It was not what she wanted this evening. She wanted to talk to them. Hear them reassure her that the worrying thoughts in her head didn't amount to anything. How would she feel after they had left the stable yard? Would it be like a death in the family? Would she feel as bad as when Anna had run away, and she had spent her days worrying about what had happened to her. Now she knew she would grieve over every last little thing in this place.

Sunny days in the garden with the sparkling white embroidered sheets belonging to the House floating in the breeze. Her flock of hens, ducks and geese, all of whom she loved. She would miss them sorely. Cooking in her range. Knowing the exact temperature and length of time each recipe required. She walked up the narrow flight of stairs which led to the parlour, her own bedroom and Anna's. On those steps their feet had fallen day after day over the years. She stopped at the return and remembered how it was. It hurt to think she would leave all of those things behind in some vague place of memory. Brightly coloured flashes of days gone by. Her children running in and out of the house playing some game or other. The boys kicking football up against the wall of the stable yard. Riding their own ponies. Anna always in the thick of it all, giving as good as she got when she was young. Fanny had a dread that her memories would fade until they eventually drifted out of her mind and became nothing.

Seamus came in later, and she wondered if he would say anything about what had happened up at the House. But he didn't. He just lit his pipe, and sat staring into the fire.

Chapter Eight

Mike stood at the map table on the bridge examining the charts. They would sail back to Hong Kong at high tide which was just before dawn, and he needed to calculate their bearings. Discussing the navigation with the other officer on the bridge, he took up a pair of binoculars and looked through them at the mainland. A full moon rode high in the sky, sending its bright light across the rolling waves. The grey metal superstructure of the ship glinted, and it had an almost ghostly look about it. There was something magical about this part of the world which got to him. He had done a couple of tours of duty here before he met Anna and enjoyed the life which was so very different to Edwardian England. Although in the Royal Navy it was pretty much stiff upper lip at all times except when he and his fellow officers had shore leave and could make the most of their time in the Chinese cities on the mainland. Shanghai in particular being a most fascinating place.

There was always something happening on board *HMS Minotaur*. It was a floating self-contained city. The hands were kept very active on board ship, cleaning, mending and making clothing. Inspecting and airing bedding. Coaling and oiling. Deep water diving. Landing stores. Inspecting guns. Mike had to keep a log of the movements of their own ships in and out of harbour, those of other navies as well, and personnel who arrived and left the ship.

Usually, in the morning there were *Divisions*. Everyone on board who could attend was meant to, except those on an excused list. At *Divisions* the ship's company falls in, each man according to his own

Division. This morning it was Mike's responsibility to inspect and after standing his men *at ease*, he pronounced *ship's company present,* and a bugle sounded. Mike marched to the quarter-deck and saluted the Commander, who acknowledged the salute. This ceremony harked back to the days of sail and was essential to check the numbers of men on board.

In the afternoon there were *Quarters* for the same reason. The Captain received the Commander's report that all hands were present and ordered the men to take off their caps and bend their heads in prayer in various parts of the deck, led by the chaplain. The band played a hymn, and the men sang, the sound of voices echoing across the harbour.

Today the hands painted the ship, and there was a test of the lifebuoys. Mike was in charge of the firing at targets towed by the picket boats. The next day he was responsible for a party of men who went to Stonecutter's Island for annual rifle practice. He enjoyed the time on the island, and it happened that Johnny was there as well.

'What have you been up to?' Mike asked.

'Stuck here mostly. Although I'm going to be transferred to *HMS Thistle* tomorrow,' Johnny grinned. 'We're sailing to Tolo Harbour.'

'Sweeping practice?'

'Yes.'

'I'm for Mirs Bay. We've to carry out target practice and return to Hong Kong for combined manoeuvres with the Army.'

His schedule was set in stone and there was no changing it. So he got on with it, wherever he happened to be, hoping that time would pass as quickly as possible and that he would be back home in Portsmouth soon.

Chapter Nine

'Any word yet?' Fanny asked Seamus.

He shook his head. It was a dismissive gesture and Fanny said no more. She was nervous, wondering when this meeting with the Master would happen. And whether Seamus might even tell her everything? He had a habit of keeping things to himself. He had no interest in the house, his only love was his horses, particularly their own three. Edward's stallion, the mare for the trap and Daisy, Anna's pony. The other horses in the stables belonged to the Master, but Seamus loved them all.

Fanny jotted down a note on a sheet of paper. There were a lot of questions which needed answers and she could see Seamus being absolutely tongue-tied when facing the Master and in the end finding out nothing about their plans. Her handwriting was very neat but there was no point giving the note to Seamus since he couldn't read it. Maybe she might have the opportunity to talk to the Master or Mistress herself and be able to discuss those things foremost in her mind.

Next she wrote to Anna, explaining that she couldn't go to Queenstown to see her as she had to stay here at *Fairfields* in case she would be called up to see the Mistress. She wasn't going to be given notice of any meeting, she was sure of that, so there could be no gadding about in town or anywhere else for the moment. But she had to clean the house from top to bottom for the party anyway so that would keep her busy.

Tess arrived down that afternoon, anxious to discuss her contribution to the menu.

'I've baked a lovely fruit cake for you, and on Friday I will cook the tarts and custards. Is there anything else you would like? What about a couple of trifles?'

'Thanks so much, Tess. I'm all up in a heap with this business of Seamus having a meeting with the Master, I don't know what he's going to say to him.'

'Everyone feels the same as you do. I had a meeting with the Mistress and she told me I would be going to Monkstown with them, and Ellie too. I feel guilty that I'm leaving the rest of you behind. It's such a pity.'

'You're lucky to be going.' Fanny was glad for Tess. But she would miss her. They had been good friends since both had arrived in *Fairfields* around the same time many years before. Now to face losing all the friends she had made was going to be tough.

'It will be very quiet down in Monkstown with just myself and Ellie, and maybe a couple of maids. We'll be very lonely. Imagine the house with only the few of us bouncing around.'

'It's not that small.'

'No, but compared to *Fairfields* it is.'

'At least you still have a position.'

'I should be glad of that.'

Fanny smiled. 'I wonder how many of the staff will manage to come down to the party.'

'Someone has to hold the fort, although the Master and Mistress will be in Dublin for a few days, so that's one advantage. How many people have you invited?'

'Everyone I could think of,' Fanny said with a wide smile.

'I've to go up to the House later on after I bring the Master back from town,' Seamus announced the following morning when he came in from the stables.

Fanny gazed at him. A ripple of shock swept through her. She twisted the *Claddagh* brooch she wore on her white blouse with shaking fingers but said nothing for a few seconds. 'This is the meeting?'

He nodded, tucking into his breakfast. A large bowl of porridge with buttermilk, followed by freshly baked bread.

'You must remember everything the Master says, I want to hear it all when you come home,' she reminded him.

'What do you think I am, an *amadán*,' he snapped, finishing the last of the bread. 'I'll have another *ponny* of tea.'

Fanny poured. Then she sat down beside him, pulled the list she had made from her pocket and spread it out on the table. 'I've written down a few things,' she said softly. 'First, don't forget to ask about the pension he said he would give you, and how much it's going to be. And when we must leave, that's important.'

'I will,' he grunted, slurping his tea.

She sighed, wondering what he would tell her on his return.

When Seamus pushed open the door later, Fanny stood up immediately and the letter from Anna which she was reading fluttered to the floor. Her eyes stared at him, demanding to know what happened.

He struggled out of his dark green greatcoat with the two rows of brass buttons, and took off his black top hat. He loved his uniform. It was his pride and joy. He was the coachman to the Master. Proud as punch when he drove him into town, in full control of the two greys, or the chestnuts, the status of the Master reflected on him.

Fanny helped him and hung the coat and hat up on the hallstand.

'How much is the pension?'

'He didn't say.'

'And when must we leave?'

'Probably a couple of months.'

She blessed herself. At least it wasn't any sooner than they expected.

'And is there anything we can take with us?'

'He will talk to me again about that.'

Fanny compressed her lips. He was useless. She knew little more than she did this morning, and was vexed with him. She picked up Anna's letter again and continued reading it. But couldn't concentrate.

No one understood how it was for her, nor did she expect that. Not even Anna. If only she had a chance to talk to the Master herself. She would have asked the right questions. Whether she might have got answers was another thing. Servants didn't question Masters.

Chapter Ten

Anna bathed and dressed Bina in her prettiest dress. She had been invited by her Aunt Lizzie, Fanny's older sister, to come and stay in Glounthaune for a night, and take the opportunity while she was there to visit Mike's mother with the children.

'Do you want me to go with you?' asked Meg, combing Bina's curly fair hair.

'No thanks, Meg, it could be awkward as I have to visit Nancy, and there isn't much room in Lizzie's house. I'll be back again tomorrow.' Anna positioned her cream silk hat with the pearl pins which Mike had given her. She wanted to make a good impression when meeting her mother in law. When he had brought her that last time, she felt confident in his presence. She had a status. She was his wife. But on her own it was different. Shyness drifted like sand. It would clog up her ears so that she couldn't hear. Clog up her mouth so her voice was a mere squeak. And then choke her. Maybe she wouldn't go after all? But that thought had to be dismissed, she couldn't change her mind now.

'Are you ready?' Iris put her head around the door. 'You don't want to miss the train. Come on little missie.' She put her arms out to Bina who rushed away from Meg. She hated having her hair combed.

'Come back, you're not finished,' Meg protested.

'She's fine,' Iris laughed.

Anna lifted Eleanor from the crib. 'I hope she stays asleep for a while longer, otherwise I'm going to be mortified on the train if she keeps crying.'

'Bring her downstairs gently,' Meg advised, picking up Anna's bag.

They set off down the hill towards the station. It was a windy day, and the breeze off the sea almost blew Anna's hat off more than once. The sound of the gulls cawing as they ducked and dived into the sea for fish filled her ears. They passed the little jewellery shop where Mike had bought her that pendant all those years ago, the one which Edward had snatched from around her neck and thrown in the fire. She remembered the little man, Albert, who owned the shop and wondered if he was still there. She would have liked to go inside, just to grasp the memory of that day once more. The dusty, moth-eaten scent of old furniture. Wooden cabinets filled with jewellery. Glittering diamonds set in gold and silver. But there wasn't time today. Maybe another time, she thought, before she went home.

Aunt Lizzie was standing on the platform at Glounthaune and immediately rushed forward to greet her, kissing her and then Bina and the baby.

'Let me help you ladies.' A porter came across, and lifted the baby carriage down from the train. Immediately, the child screamed.

'I don't think she likes me,' the man laughed.

Lizzie had suggested they go over to see Nancy as soon as they arrived as she had to pick up some messages and Anna felt very nervous as they walked across the road. She had checked her reflection in the mirror in Lizzie's house before she left and hoped the cream dress with the white trim and matching hat looked well.

Lizzie pushed open the door of the shop and the bell clanged. Inside, the paintwork was dark, and an oil lamp hung from the ceiling, a muted light drifting down from it. Anna shivered. She looked at Lizzie and their eyes met. Eleanor had fallen asleep. Bina gazed around her at the items on the shelves. Particularly colourful were the large jars of sweets. *Liquorice. Sugared Almonds. Raspberry and Custard. Sherbets.* Looking at the sweets even caused Anna's mouth to water.

Suddenly, there was the sound of footsteps and Mike's stepmother was standing in the doorway, a look of surprise on her face. 'Well,' she said slowly.

'Hello, Mrs. O'Sullivan,' Anna said shyly.

'We came over to see you with the children, Nancy,' Lizzie smiled. 'You haven't seen the new baby, she's a lovely little girl.'

'When was she born?'

'In June.'

'Isn't that nice.' She stared into the baby carriage. 'What's her name?'

'Eleanor,' Anna said, but suddenly realised that her mother in law probably wouldn't be happy with her choice of name.

Nancy made no comment.

Anna was about to explain why she chose the name but decided against doing that. It was obvious that Nancy understood.

'And look how big Bina has grown,' Lizzie said. 'Say hello to your grandmother,' she encouraged the child. But Bina was tongue-tied as usual and said nothing. Lizzie continued on chatting, and then asked for the messages which she needed. Nancy busied herself preparing them and then pushed them across the counter towards her. 'Will I put it in the book?'

'Please do, Nancy.'

Anna took the paper bag containing the items. 'I'm glad you've met the children, Mike will be pleased when I tell him,' Anna said.

'He's still away in China?' Nancy's blue eyes bored into Anna's.

They were cold. Always so cold, she thought. 'But he should be on his way home soon,' she said.

'That's good.' Nancy nodded.

Anna could sense it was the end of the conversation.

While initially she had felt nervous and ill at ease, when they arrived back at Lizzie's, Anna was angry. 'My girls are part of her family, her blood, and she was dismissive of them, hardly took the slightest notice.'

'It's her way, Anna. The girls are not her blood if you were to think about it. Perhaps it's the reason she's the way she is with Mike, they never got on.'

'I know that.'

'Don't take any notice.'

'It's hard,' she tried not to cry, but tears welled up. 'I feel so for Mike. If I tell him, he'll be furious.'

'Maybe better not tell him then.'

Anna had to admit that Lizzie was right. She shouldn't have expected much more. Nancy had married Mike's father, a widower, but had never given much time to his son, particularly when their first son had drowned. Her own two daughters took precedence in the family. He hadn't liked his stepmother, but loved his two sisters, although the elder, Maisie, was always on her mother's side. The younger, Vera, was very much Mike's pet.

'When will Mike sail home?' enquired Lizzie.

'He's hoping to leave in a couple of weeks, but I read in the paper that there was a rebellion in China and I worry something will happen to him.'

'Nothing will, don't you worry,' Lizzie said, laughing. 'But let's hope that he'll be home for longer this time. You married a sailor and it's not an easy life.'

'I don't regret marrying him, not for one second,' Anna retorted.

'We all said it was going to be a rough road, but you wouldn't listen to any of us.'

'He's my life.'

'And you are his. He was inconsolable when he lost you that first time.'

'And I him. So I'll put up with the loneliness, Aunt Lizzie. He has no control over where he's sent, it's not his choice. I just hope he'll continue to be stationed in Portsmouth or at least somewhere in England or Ireland for longer this time.'

Chapter Eleven

Fanny worked hard on the days leading up to the party. She had cooked one of her geese, a couple of chickens and a ham, and intended to serve a cold supper. She wanted everyone to be able to sit down to the meal and borrowed chairs and tables from all and sundry. She prayed for a fine September day and put out the *Child of Prague* statue on Friday night in the hope that there would be no rain. So busy, she had tried to forget about leaving *Fairfields* for the moment. Some of the other people in the house had met with the Master and Mistress already and rumours were rife.

On Saturday morning, she was up very early delighted to see the sun shining. Most of her housework was already done but she still had to do some last minute cleaning, and was giving the furniture a polish when one of the boys from the House rushed in and handed her a note.

'What's this?' she asked.

'It's from the Mistress.'

With trembling fingers, Fanny opened the envelope. To her surprise it was a letter requesting her to come up to see the Mistress at ten o'clock. She began to shake. What was this about. God forbid there was no trouble, she whispered a prayer to *Our Lady*. She had invited Mr. and Mrs. Staunton to the party but had already received a note of regret that they were unable to accept because they would be in Dublin.

Fanny changed into a fresh white blouse and black skirt, and made her way up through the trees to the main kitchen door of the House and knocked. It was a while before it was opened by one of the scullery maids and she went inside to see Tess rolling out pastry at the large white deal table. 'I'm not finished yet, Fanny, I'll send them down when they come out of the oven,' Tess said as soon as she saw her.

'I haven't come up for the cakes, Tess, but thanks very much for making them.'

'What then?' Tess looked at her, curious.

'I've got a letter from the Mistress to come up and see her. I'm worried sick. Today of all days. I didn't expect that she would want to talk with me so now I don't know what to think.' Fanny fanned herself with her handkerchief.

'I'm sure it will be all right, go up to the housekeeper and let her know you're here. It's ten to ten already, I'll say a prayer for you.'

Fanny hurried up the back stairs to Miss Lawless's room. She knocked.

'Come in.'

'I've been asked to see the Mistress this morning,' Fanny burst out.

The woman glanced at a list of names on the table in front of her. 'I'll take you up.' She stood. Miss Lawless had only been employed at the House for the last couple of years, and she kept herself to herself, so Fanny hardly knew her at all, although she had included her in the invitation to the party.

She walked ahead and Fanny followed. Nervous now.

'I'm sorry, Fanny, I can't attend the party but it was very nice of you to invite me,' she said over her shoulder as she went up the red carpeted staircase. Her thin white hand slid along the highly polished bannister. She always reminded Fanny of a school teacher she once knew. Sharp and acid-tongued. Now she wondered if she had been wrong. Suddenly the woman seemed more humane, just by saying those few words. Fanny wasn't usually wrong about people, but doubt filtered through her mind now and she questioned herself.

Miss Lawless knocked on the door of the Mistress's morning room, her head bent down as she waited to be admitted. Then Fanny heard a voice, and the housekeeper went in ahead of her. After a moment, she was ushered inside.

'Fanny, it's good of you to come up, particularly as I know you must be very busy today.' Mrs. Staunton's pale blue eyes smiled at Fanny. 'As I am myself. We're leaving just after luncheon for Dublin.'

She was always in awe of the beauty of her employer. Dressed in a pale green morning gown, with white lace trimming, her delicate colouring was a perfect foil for the hue of the silk. A rush of emotion swept through Fanny. She had a sudden urge to throw her arms around Mrs. Staunton and hug her tight. She would miss her so when they left. She had been so grateful for the discarded gowns, blouses and skirts which she had given her over the years. Fanny and Anna would work long into the night re-making the clothes to fit themselves. It meant so much to her, and she had always been very grateful. There were sudden tears in her eyes.

'I regret that we are leaving *Fairfields*. But we've made the decision now and we must stick by it. Both my husband and I feel guilty about leaving our household, all our dear friends who have worked with us over the years and who now have to be uprooted and forced to find other paths in their lives.'

'We'll miss you and the Master,' Fanny murmured.

Mrs. Staunton reached across the table and clasped Fanny's hand for a few seconds.

There was an emotional moment between the women which had never happened before.

'Fanny, I'm so sorry we cannot ask you to come with us, but Mr. Staunton has ordered a new motor car and we will be using that from now on. Although I have to say I'm not too happy about it,' she smiled, a confidential look in her eyes. 'I've travelled in one before with friends of ours, but they go far too fast for my liking. I'm absolutely terrified to be honest with you. I much prefer my carriage, I'm going to miss my horses too, poor things. But Mr. Staunton is absolutely certain of what he wants, so ...' She waved her hands in the air. 'I have no say in the matter.'

'I understand,' Fanny said.

'Now, we'd better get down to business or I'll never see all the people who will be coming into me this morning.'

Fanny waited. Her heart thumping. Her hands clasped tightly in her lap.

Mrs. Staunton pursed her lips. 'Regarding our poultry …'

Fanny thought of her darling hens, ducks and geese too, and felt a terrible sense of loss. She loved them so much. What would happen to them? Would they all fly off looking for new homes, and hate her for not looking after them any longer.

'We won't need so much when we're in Monkstown but the quality of our poultry has been excellent and I don't look forward to purchasing what we need from some other source so would you still be able to raise the flock for us?' She raised her eyebrows.

'I certainly would, but we haven't got anywhere to live yet. Edward is looking out for us.'

'Let me enquire into that for you.' She picked up her pen and made a note on a piece of paper.

'Thank you.' Fanny was grateful.

'And there is something else,' she paused. 'I seem to be asking rather a lot of you, but I always love the way you do the washing and ironing of my own linen, and I wonder if you could continue to do that for me?'

'Yes of course, Mrs. Staunton.'

'Thank you so much. I'll send up one of the girls with it every couple of days and she can pick up the poultry at the same time. And I want you to use whatever you want of the flock, treat them as your own. You can sell the eggs and make some money and also the poultry itself as we won't need a lot. It will be a little business for you.'

'Thank you so much,' Fanny gasped. Unable to believe what Mrs. Staunton was saying. A *little business*. How amazing.

'I shall discuss the terms with Mr. Staunton.'

'That's very good of you, I'm so grateful.'

'At least it will mean we are keeping in touch, and in the meantime I hope to find a place for you. But I would like you to keep our discussions private for the moment.'

Back at the house, Fanny checked her oven. She hadn't expected to be up at the house for so long and was glad to see that her roast chickens weren't burnt black, and was busy sorting everything when she heard voices in the yard.

'Mam, are you there?' Anna called.

Fanny rushed out and threw her arms around her daughter. 'It's wonderful to see you my love.' She kissed her. Both of them in tears then, hugging close.

'Oh Mam, it's so good to be home. I can't believe it.' Anna looked around her.

'Hello my babies?' Fanny hugged Bina, kissed Eleanor, and then welcomed Lizzie, Meg and Iris.

'Can we do anything for you?' Lizzie asked.

'Not at all, I'm well organised and people won't be coming until about six o'clock.'

'It's so good to be home,' Anna sighed. Walking around the kitchen she touched the table, the window sill, the china in the dresser as if to say *hello*. 'I'm going up to my room, I'll take Bina, and Mam, will you keep an eye on Eleanor, please?'

Anna took the child's hand and the two walked up the narrow stairway. On the landing, she stood in front of the door of her bedroom, a mist of tears flooding her eyes. Inside, the room was unchanged. The bed made with the same blue eiderdown. Her little china keepsakes were positioned where she had left them on the dressing table, resting on a piece of white cotton crochet made by Fanny herself. She picked up a little shepherdess, knelt down close to Bina and held it out to her. The child picked it up and stared at it.

'Pretty,' she lisped.

'That's for you, Bina.' Anna wiped her eyes with her handkerchief and sat down on the bed.

'Mammy crying?' Bina reached towards her.

'It's because I'm so happy to be home.'

Bina climbed up on the bed beside her.

'Mammy happy.'

'Yes, Bina.' She hugged her, kissing the top of her head.

Giggling, the child rolled across the bed to peer out the window overlooking the stables. 'Horsies.' She pointed.

Anna followed her gaze and could see her father cross the yard with two horses. One was the mare for the trap and the other was her own mare, Daisy.

'Come on, Bina, let's go to see Grandad.' She took her hand, but as she went on to the landing, was drawn into the parlour. As in the kitchen below her heart thudded with emotion as she was once again in that room where she had spent so much of her life. And there was her beloved piano. She lifted the lid. The ivory keys drew her in. She placed her fingers on them, and played a few notes and chords. Rippling up and down the octaves in a whirl of music. Then there was a loud discordant sound as all of Bina's fingers crashed on to the keys. 'Do you want to play?' Anna asked gently.

'Yes.' The child continued to thump the notes.

'Why don't you sit on the stool, then you can do it properly.'

She pulled out the velvet topped piano stool and lifted Bina up on it. Then she began to sing *Little Miss Moffet* softly, encouraging Bina to join in with her. '*Little Miss Moffet sat on her tuffet eating her curds and whey. Along came a spider and sat down beside her and frightened Miss Moffet away.*' She finished but Bina immediately protested.

'More, more.'

'We'll go to see the horses now,' Anna suggested.

Bina was diverted immediately, and together they went downstairs into the kitchen again where the women sat, chatting amongst themselves.

'Do you think I should go out and see Pa ...?' Anna asked her mother tentatively.

'Yes, why not ...and take Bina with you,' Fanny suggested.

Outside it was quiet. Anna walked to the stables where her own horse

Daisy was usually kept. She pushed open the door but didn't go in at first as she could see her father brushing the horse's coat. She felt there was something between them. A wall of animosity. Her heart beat faster. She wanted to break through it but she was afraid.

'Horsies,' Bina cried, pulled out of Anna's hand and ran in.

Seamus stopped what he was doing and turned to look in amazement at the little girl as she reached to touch the horse's tail. He gave it another brush and the silver grey hair swished out. She held up her hand to him. He handed her the brush, but it was too big for her small grasp. So he let her hold one end and he had the other and together they swept the brush down the shiny tail. The horse whinnied. Bina giggled. 'Horsie,' she cried. Anna drew closer and stood at Daisy's head and stroked her neck. The horse whinnied again and turned to snuggle up against Anna.

'You still know me, don't you, Daisy?' Anna murmured.

'Careful,' Seamus held the horse as she moved backwards. 'Would you like to get up on her?' he asked Bina. She looked at Anna and back to Seamus and nodded with a broad smile.

'First we have to put on her bridle and then the saddle,' he said.

Anna went to where they hung on the wall and lifted them down.

'Your Mam is well able to do this herself but she'll keep an eye on you while I do it today,' Seamus smiled at Anna.

She smiled back and stroked his arm with her hand. It was a moment of reconciliation between them. To her surprise, there were no words needed. No explanations. Suddenly they were back to the way it had always been and Anna was really happy. They went out into the yard. She held on to the bridle and Seamus lifted Bina up. He led the horse forward and she took a couple of steps. Bina screamed excitedly. Then the horse took another step. There were more screams. Anna laughed as they walked the length of the yard and stopped at the gate. Then Seamus took Bina off the horse and held her in his arms.

'Up again,' she demanded.

'You've got plenty of spirit, haven't you Bina?' he laughed.

'More …' she said.

'Tomorrow.'

'This is your Grandad,' Anna said. 'Give him a kiss, Bina, and say thank you.'

The child wound her arms around his neck. 'Thank you, Grandad.'

He put her down on the ground gently. 'Let's go back into the stables and take the saddle off unless your Mam wants to have a ride.' He looked at Anna.

Her eyes widened in disbelief. She had assumed her father wouldn't even let her near his precious horses. She moved closer to him and kissed his cheek. 'Thank you Pa,' she whispered.

'Daisy's been a long time without you,' he said, with a shy smile. Seamus always found it hard to show emotion, and it was only through his beloved horses that anyone could get to the man.

'I might later if there's time, although I want to help Mam.'

'No hurry girl, she'll be waiting for you.'

Back at the house, everyone was busy getting ready for the party. Anna helped too although her mother didn't want her to lift a hand's turn.

'You're the guest of honour, love,' Fanny said.

'There's no need to do anything,' Iris added, taking dishes from the dresser. 'You look after the children.'

So Anna did as she was bid and enjoyed her time spent wheeling Eleanor around in the baby carriage with Bina pointing at this and that, full of excitement.

Anna took them around the stable yard, showing Bina the carriages, the traps, the other horses and out then into the sunlit garden to see the flocks of geese, ducks and hens.

'Don't hurry them, or they'll be frightened,' Anna warned. 'Just look at them.'

Bina watched the ducks waddle into the green-tinged water in the pond and swim around. 'Big feet.'

'That's to help them swim along fast,' Anna explained.

'I want one.' She bent down close to the water and trailed her fingers in it.

'No, you can't have one, they live here.'
'This one is mine.' She pointed.

The house was jammed with people although quite a number stayed out in the yard enjoying the unusually balmy evening. Musicians played in the parlour. Ellie helped Fanny and Tess serve the food. Anna was really happy to see her friends and neighbours once again, and they were all keen to meet the children before they were put to bed.

Later, Ellie and Anna went around to the back of the house and sat on the window sill. Always their choice of place for a private chat.

'It's wonderful to have you back.' Ellie put her arm around Anna's shoulders.

'Like the old days.' Anna hugged her. 'Can you believe all the presents people have given me, including you. I feel embarrassed. There was no need.'

'Your mother tried to keep your return quiet but somehow it leaked out,' Ellie laughed.

'You probably told everyone, you can't keep a secret to save your life.'

'Remember when you ran away? I didn't open my mouth then which was unusual for me I have to admit.'

Anna giggled and hugged Ellie. 'I couldn't have done it without you.'

'I often regretted that I didn't go with you.' Ellie held her hand tightly. 'Then I wouldn't be here now, still in service. My life might have taken a very different turn.'

'But the shipwreck ... would we both have been saved?'

'Mike saved you.'

Anna was silent.

'There's no point in talking about it. I didn't go and that was my own decision.'

'You're right. You don't know how it would have worked out in the end. Now there are more changes in your life, possibly to the good,' Anna encouraged.

'Monkstown here I come. But it's sad we're all going to have to leave here.' Ellie looked around her.

'I've spent my whole life in this place.' Anna ran her hand along the smooth wall of the house.

'I've known you since we were both in school, it seems like my whole life too,' Ellie smiled. 'You're my sister.'

'And you mine. It's strange how both of us have only brothers.'

'I love them too, but somehow between us there is a special bond. I've really missed you since you ran off that day. Things have never been quite the same.' There were tears in Ellie's eyes.

'Remember the old days. The fun we had at school. Going to the dances in the village, musical evenings in our house with all the lads, days in town, and out to Queenstown,' Anna smiled.

'Such laughs.'

'Wish we could go back there.' Ellie was serious. 'But don't mind me, you have your own life now with Mike and the children. It's wonderful for you, but I suppose I'm just feeling a bit lonely.'

'You'll meet a nice man one of these days.'

'I'm on the shelf now, Anna. Not much chance of that happening.'

'You never know who's around the corner.'

Ellie shook her head and laughed.

'I've been so lucky marrying Mike.'

'And having Bina and Eleanor, they're darlings.'

'This could be the last time I'll be here. We don't know when Mam and Pa will have to leave.'

There was a sudden sound of a horse galloping and the girls could hear the rumble of the wheels of a trap approach the gates.

'That's someone else coming.' Ellie stood up and the two went around the side of the house.

Anna's heart thumped with fright when she saw it was their own trap driven by Edward. What was she going to say to him?

Chapter Twelve

Mike's ship steamed into the harbour at Singapore. He had begun his trip home leaving from Hong Kong five days earlier. There had been celebrations on the *Minotaur* in the week before they left. Dining with the Ward Room men on one night, and on the final night they dined with the Gun Room crew.

He shared a three berth cabin with two other naval men who were also on their way home and the three enjoyed their time on the ship, off duty.

He wrote to Anna.

My darling Anna,

I hope you are well and Bina and our new little one, Eleanor. We have just arrived in Singapore, and we're looking forward to spending some time ashore and it will be enjoyable to be on dry land again. The weather is steaming hot with very high humidity. But once we're at sea again it will be more comfortable.

We wandered through the markets today and I bought some embroidered silks for you. You can have them made up into dresses or whatever you want. You will look beautiful, I'm certain about that. We browsed in the gold shops too. Haggling over the prices of items with the little men behind the counters. As you know, I have enough Mandarin to converse, but these traders spoke a language which was unfamiliar to me, but I managed.

I'm looking forward to the next leg of the journey to Columbo. Then on to Marseilles and London. It's bringing you closer all the time. With much love and kisses. Mike. xxxxx

Chapter Thirteen

Anna had an immediate inclination to rush back into the house. She didn't want to face Edward, really terrified at the thought of it. But she couldn't disappear with Ellie standing beside her.

'Hello Edward, how are you?' It was Ellie who spoke first in the jaunty way of hers, like she hadn't a care in the world.

He muttered some words which Anna couldn't catch, and went to push past the two of them.

'It's been a long time,' Anna said with a smile, her eyes meeting his.

'It has,' his reply was blunt. His expression grim.

'I'm sorry about what happened,' she said softly. She felt it was important for her to apologise, even though at the time she had been very angry with him because he had been so much against Mike.

'It was all very well for you to sail off with that ...and leave me to deal with the mess you created. My career was almost ruined you know.' His lip curled.

'Anna, Edward, the very ones. Come inside. We're cutting the cake now and I want to say a few words to everybody.' Fanny appeared.

'Don't ask me to say anything.' Edward's voice was cold. His mouth drawn down in bitterness.

How could he speak so roughly to his mother, Anna wondered, wanting to intervene and tell him off.

'I'll do the talking, don't you worry,' Fanny replied crisply.

'Can I help with the cake?' Ellie asked.

'Would you please?' Fanny led the way back into the house, followed by the girls. There were still a few people sitting outside but most had moved inside as the evening drew in. Fanny had placed the celebration cake on a silver cake stand and Ellie and herself carried it into the hall and put it on a small table so that those who were in the house and those who gathered at the door could hear what she was saying. Everyone clapped when they appeared.

Fanny placed her hands together and smiled. People quietened. 'Thank you all for coming this evening. It's lovely to meet you especially as Anna has come home for the first time in five years.'

There was a big cheer.

Anna could feel herself blush.

'So I baked this special cake for the occasion although I have to thank Tess for making all these delicious tarts and trifles and other sweet things. She is a wonderful baker and we're very grateful to her.' Fanny looked around for Tess. 'She's hiding somewhere I think at the moment but give her a clap anyway.'

There was another round of applause.

'I wanted to say too that this evening is to mark the fact that we'll all be leaving *Fairfields* soon, except a few who will be moving down to Monkstown with the Master and the Mistress. But I want everyone to have a lovely evening, a happy evening. Now I will cut the cake and Ellie will be handing out plates.'

She did that. At first it seemed that there wouldn't be enough to go around but she was economic with their size and everyone received a slice.

It was a really nice evening in spite of the underlying sadness. The music and dancing went on long into the night. Fanny herself was persuaded to play the concertina, and Anna the piano. Edward was the only one who didn't partake. Standing outside with some of his friends, smoking and drinking.

It was late by the time most of the people had departed on bicycles and traps, and left Fanny, Anna, and the others to clear up. 'Right, let's get to it.' Ellie began to pick up dishes and glasses which littered every surface. Between them they had most of it done by the time she had to rush back up to the House, change into her uniform and be ready for work. By all accounts everyone thought it had been a great night. Lizzie slept with Fanny and Iris lay on the settee. Meg was in with Anna and the children. They all got a couple of hours before they were awoken by the work of the stable yard.

On the following day Lizzie, Iris and Meg went home after Mass, leaving Anna and Fanny on their own at last.

'It's so good to have you back.' Fanny put her arm in Anna's as they strolled back from the railway station after seeing them off.

'It's wonderful, Mam, it's been so long.'

'I've counted every second in my heart.' She pressed her hand to her chest. 'Now to have you back again is …' She kissed her.

'Edward still hasn't forgiven me,' Anna murmured, although she felt very happy walking slowly along with Fanny pushing the baby carriage. Eleanor was asleep under the hood, and Bina sat forward, her two legs swinging in their white stockings and white leather ankle strap shoes. Their footsteps followed that same road from the station up to Glanmire which they had always taken since she was a child. It was a beautiful September. The leaves on the trees were turning gold and glimmered in the sunlight, drifting past occasionally and softly landing on the ground, warning of the oncoming winter. As they came to the village, they stopped to talk to people who were anxious to welcome her back. Outside a group of cottages, boys kicked ball, girls played with their *chainies*. They stopped to take a rest on the wall overlooking the Glashaboy River which rushed towards the sea.

Bina climbed out of the baby carriage.

'I'll lift you up,' Anna held her.

'Let me see.' She leaned over the wall.

'Be careful,' Anna kept a tight hold around her wriggling body.

'I want to see the water.'

'No.'

'She's a stubborn girl is our Bina,' Fanny laughed. 'I think we'll go before she jumps in.'

Anna put her back in the carriage, where she kicked her legs against the end of it.

'Don't, Bina, you'll wake Eleanor,' Anna warned.

'Want to go in the water.'

Anna looked at Fanny helplessly.

'Behave yourself, Bina, or else there will be nothing nice for you when we get home,' Fanny said.

The rhythm of the little legs eased as she took that on board. 'Nice?' She stared at Fanny, her blue eyes wide.

'Yes, if you're good.'

'I am good.'

'If you wake Eleanor then that's not being good.'

'Won't.'

'Now look at what's happened, she's awake.' Anna patted the soft cheek of the baby.

Bina leaned back against her sister.

'Don't, you'll hurt her,' Anna admonished.

The baby wailed.

'Now look at what you've done,' Fanny said.

Bina's face crumpled. Somehow she took much more notice of anything Fanny said than Anna.

They arrived home and Fanny began to make the Sunday dinner. Anna helped as well. She peeled the vegetables, while Fanny heated some of the meats left over from the night before.

'We don't need to make anything for dessert, there's still some left.'

'I'll make fresh custard.'

Anna felt nostalgic. She loved Sundays at home. The family around the table in the kitchen. And her mother's cooking. There was nothing like it. Barely home for a day, she was torn in two as she wanted to spend as much time as she could at *Fairfields*, but knew that she would have to go back to Portsmouth soon. Mike was already on his way home.

'How long more can you stay?' Fanny asked.

'A couple of weeks.'
'Is that all?'
'I'm sorry, Mam.'
'I was looking forward to being with you and the children for a while.' Fanny's eyes misted over with tears.
'But at least Father and Edward have agreed that I can come home, that's a huge step forward.'
Fanny patted her hand. 'I know, girl, I know.'

Chapter Fourteen

The journey from Singapore to Port Said took ten days and as they steamed across the Arabian Sea Mike found time heavy on his hands, having no role at all other than that of a passenger. He longed to see the Cliffs of Dover and know that then it wouldn't be long before he would hold Anna and the children in his arms.

He stood at the railing staring across the limitless expanse of empty sea. He took out his binoculars, the ones given him by Uncle George when he was a boy, focused and scanned the horizon, able then to see other ships sailing in the distance. Mike always liked to think that he stood by his shoulder all the time. He had spent his holidays in Portsmouth with Aunt Win and Uncle George and during those years had been imbued with George's love of the sea. Particularly that time when he happened to be there during the Royal Naval Review of eighteen hundred and eighty seven. It had been a wonderful occasion. Ships from all over the world had their bunting and flags flying and bands played. It had been an amazing scene, and George had taken Mike on board *HMS Renown* which was a wonderful experience, even introducing him to Admiral St. Leger. His fate was sealed from that moment.

But it was a hard fight with his father and stepmother. Dan was a schoolteacher in Glaunthaune and wanted Mike to follow in his footsteps enrolling him in the De La Salle College in Waterford where he had spent years training to be a teacher, something he didn't want to do. Qualified, he took up a position in Fenit, Co. Kerry, where the Atlantic ocean crashed up against the shore, beckoning all the time to

Mike. But he had no way out of the bind in which he found himself and hated the system of teaching in the small two-teacher school, the corporal punishment, and even the cruelty at times. It was only on the death of his uncle when he received a letter from his Aunt Win enclosing a box containing all George's seafaring things which he had bequeathed to him. There he found a letter. As he read through it he noticed then that a smaller envelope had fallen into his lap. He opened it, shocked to see some money tightly folded together. One hundred pounds. He couldn't believe it and read again the last few lines of the letter.

All I want, my boy, is for you to join the Royal Navy as I did myself, and then I'll know that my life was worthwhile. You are the son I never had and will carry on my dream.

His uncle's sentiments cut through Mike and on that day he made his decision and gave in his notice to leave the school at the end of the term. After that his life changed radically, and he became a new man. His family life changed too. Only when his father was on his deathbed did he finally forgive Mike for not pursuing a career in teaching. He wasn't sure whether his stepmother ever did.

Chapter Fifteen

Anna hugged the little group on the quayside. 'I'll write as soon as I get home,' she promised her mother.

'Take care of yourself and the children and give our best to Mike.' Fanny kissed them all.

'I should be going with you,' Meg said. 'Remember I promised to come and help when you went home.'

'Thank you, but I'm sure it would be too much hard work for you,' Anna held on to Bina's hand.

'But I'd love to help you look after the children,' Meg insisted. 'What do you think, Mam, can't I go for a while?' She turned to Iris.

'You've enough to be doing looking after us here and trying to find a husband as well,' Iris retorted.

'I don't think that will ever happen,' Meg said sadly.

'Of course it will, I'll look for some nice naval officer for you,' Anna said, smiling.

'She doesn't want a sailor, Anna, she'd never manage living all on her own like you.'

'Of course I could manage,' protested Meg.

'It's a difficult life and it only suits certain women, we've quite a few relations who have married naval men and they know what it's like,' her mother was firm.

'Why don't you come over for a little holiday some time,' Anna suggested, feeling sorry for Meg.

'Can I?' Her face brightened. 'Mam?'

'Does that suit you, Anna?' Iris asked.

'Yes, of course, it would be lovely if Meg comes for a holiday.' Anna couldn't say anything else. She had stayed with Iris and Meg any time she came home, and she owed them a lot for their generosity.

'Have you room for her,' Iris asked.

'We have a small spare bedroom.'

'I don't mind. I'll sleep anywhere,' Meg cried, excited.

A loud horn sounded and in a rush people began to go aboard the ship. Anna kissed Fanny and Seamus once more and lifted Eleanor, taking the two children up the gangplank while a sailor lifted the baby carriage. Another carried her baggage which had increased considerably since she had come home. There had been so many presents from friends and relatives and Fanny just couldn't be stopped buying things for her and the children. There were tears in her eyes as she and Bina waved. The length of time she stood there made the leaving all the more difficult, needing to keep her dear ones in her sight for as long as she could. But the ship began to move away from the quayside. The group below gradually becoming smaller as the ship steamed away, until at last they disappeared altogether. But Anna continued to wave her white handkerchief in case they could still see her, until the harbour, with Queenstown towering above it, the Cathedral topping the hill, all merged into a vague mass of grey, green and blue and was left behind.

Bina tugged at her skirt and demanded her attention, and the baby began to cry.

'I'm cold,' Bina complained.

'We'll go down to our cabin, it will be warmer there,' she said, and lifted Eleanor from the carriage. A steward took her down and she was able to feed the baby. Bina then climbed into bed and they rested there, the two children fast asleep. Whenever she left, she was torn between her longing to see Mike, and the emotional loss of her dear family, even Cork itself.

It was a chilly evening when they arrived home in Portsmouth and Anna took a cab because there was so much baggage. The house was cold and dark and she almost regretted that she had come back at all.

She could have stayed on a few more days, as she wasn't expecting Mike for another two weeks. She took care of the children, reminding herself that this was her home now and would be so for the rest of her life. While Portsmouth was in a different country it really was only a few miles away and she could get back to Cork quickly if she had to. She chided herself for worrying unnecessarily.

Now she spent the time cleaning the house. The presents she received included new antimacassars embroidered by Fanny, lacy sheets and pillowslips from Lizzie, crocheted sets for her dressing table, tablecloths, napkins, and so many other items she had lost count.

The small house had a parlour, dining-room, kitchen, two and a half bedrooms, and a bathroom on the return. Everything was sparkling. She brushed out the back yard and shed too. The work kept her busy and she tried not to be too lonely, missing everyone, even Daisy. For the first time since she had left Cork five years ago she had ridden on her pony. What an experience that was. She hoped that Fanny and Seamus could take Daisy with them to the new house. It would break her heart if she lost her now, particularly as Bina loved her too, and seemed not to have one ounce of fear when she was up on the pony. Living here, there was no opportunity to ride out into the countryside, so she would have to wait until she returned home again.

Portsmouth was a very busy place. Horse-drawn carriages and other vehicles mingled with new motor cars in the streets, the noise and clamour deafening at times. On the docks, it was even busier. A multitude of ships at anchor in the harbour, on the docks sailors of the Royal Navy and other merchant seamen worked alongside each other.

Anna didn't particularly like living here. It had taken her a long time to get used to naval life. When she had been married to Mike at first, he had been stationed here and it made those early years much easier. Life changed drastically when he had been assigned to Hong Kong and contact was by letter only. While she wrote every day, as he also tried to do, sometimes they would each receive a bundle of letters such was the nature of the postal service. Mike's letters were often only quick rushed notes as he hadn't time to write very much. For Anna, it was the most important part of her life and reading Mike's letters, however short, meant everything to her. His last letter had said that he would leave Hong Kong on September fifteenth. In her diary each day she noted his journey. But there would be time spent in the various ports along the way so she wasn't sure exactly when he would arrive. But now her excitement was palpable and she had Bina looking forward to seeing Daddy as much as she was herself.

On the day he was due to arrive she dressed in a new gown Fanny had bought her. It was a rich peach silk creation and set off her dark colouring to perfection. Bina wore a pretty frilled dress in the same shade. But as the afternoon drew to a close, she wondered would he arrive at all. Finally, to her disappointment, she had to put the children to bed at six o'clock, and was sitting in the parlour on her own when, a couple of hours later, she heard the key turn in the lock and rushed down the hall to meet him.

Chapter Sixteen

'I haven't found any house to suit us in the village,' Edward said. 'There are a couple empty but there's no land with them. I'm worried and so is Pa. If we don't find anywhere at all, we might have to move further away. And we haven't heard anything from Mrs. Staunton.' He stared gloomily out into the yard.

'No, but I've every faith in her,' Fanny replied, busy knitting a small white matinee coat for Eleanor. 'She said there's no rush for us to move out yet.'

'The whole place is deserted, not a sinner around,' Edward muttered.

'You don't have to tell me that,' Fanny snapped. She couldn't explain to her son how upset she was that all the friends she had known over the years had left *Fairfields*. She had gone up yesterday to say goodbye to Tess and Ellie who were last to leave for Monkstown. As she waved them off in the trap she burst into tears and had to turn away.

The Mistress had asked her to see that everything was in order before the House was finally closed up, and now she walked in, still going by way of the kitchen and up the back stairs. Although she knew there was no one here, all the time she expected to see the Master and Mistress appear around a corner and tick her off for being upstairs instead of downstairs. Worst of all was the silence. It was eerie and her heart thudded so loud she could actually hear it. As she walked into the Great Hall with its richness of luxurious colour, she asked herself how the voices in this house had fallen so silent. The people who lived and worked here all had such strong personalities, how was it that there were now only empty spaces where they had once been. Doors banged with a weird clanging sound. A breeze whistled through the hallways from a half-open window. Fanny closed it. She felt the place was full of the spirits of the past. All those dead generations calling out to her. She shuddered. It was as if there had been a funeral and all those people who had once lived here had been waked and buried.

She went through every room. The dining room. The banquet hall. The ballroom. And up the Grand Staircase to the upper landings, for the first time having total access to the luxurious master bedroom of the Stauntons. Even though the amazing four poster bed was gone the rooms still had that lived in look. She imagined she could hear the voices of the Master and Mistress softly talking to each other. It was a strange sensation and she wanted to hold on to the moment. This would probably be the last occasion she would ever be here.

As she left the House it was sunset. On the horizon, vivid flames sent streaks of light out into the glowing sky, edged with a glimmering lilac hue, so beautiful she stood still outside the main door and looked around her. The heavens above were so exquisite it hurt, and made this day almost one of the worst in her life.

'Let's hope we'll have somewhere to stable our horses, or else we'll be out on the road.' Edward's lips twisted.

Fanny stopped sewing. To see *Fairfields* become an empty shell in front of her was heartbreaking. She had lived here all of her married life. Her children had been born here. She prayed that she wouldn't have to move too far away. Every few days she went to Caherlag Cemetery and prayed over the graves of her dead babies. Sadly, the ones who died at birth and were not baptised were buried in her own garden. A terrible sense of loneliness dogged her as she realised that she would have to leave her little ones there. Never able to come back to this place again to say a prayer. Herself and Seamus were the only people who knew they were buried there or that they ever even existed.

She wasn't even sure whether Anna or the boys knew about the babies buried in Caherlag, but the babies buried in the back garden were a secret and they had never talked about them.

A few days later, Fanny received a letter from the Mistress, requesting Seamus and herself to go down to Monkstown to see her. Fanny pressed the letter to her chest. Then she rushed out into the yard. When she told Seamus he scratched his head in puzzlement.

'I wonder has she any news about a house or is she going to tell us to leave immediately?' Fanny read through the letter again.

'We'll be camping on the side of the road,' he grunted.

'God forbid that will happen,' Fanny sighed deeply.

'You'd better get down on your knees and start praying.' Seamus bent down to check the shoes on Edward's stallion.

They were down in Monkstown early the following morning, and were happy to see Tess and Ellie again. They had time to talk while they waited, although Fanny was nervous and very uncomfortable, and was relieved when they were called.

'Fanny and Seamus, it's lovely to see you.' Mrs. Staunton shook both their hands. 'Sit down,' she smiled. 'And thanks for coming, I wanted to talk to you face to face rather than write a letter.'

Fanny sat in silence. Her stomach cramped with anxiety. Her hands joined together tightly. She dreaded what was coming next.

Mrs. Staunton smiled at them. 'I'm delighted to say that I've found a house which I think is going to be most suitable for you.'

'Oh thank you, thank you …' Fanny couldn't help herself.

'Thanks, Mrs. Staunton.' Seamus joined in.

'The house is just at the back of *Fairfields*.'

'How wonderful,' Fanny breathed.

'It is *Rose Cottage*, and the home of Tom, the gardener.'

'Tom's house?' Seamus was astonished.

'He has just been offered a post in an estate in West Cork, so he will be moving there shortly,' she explained.

'I was only talking to him the other day and he was worried that he hadn't got a job yet, so he must be delighted,' Fanny said.

'He is, and his wife too, needless to say.'

'It will be a big move for them, all the way to West Cork,' Seamus commented.

'I hope they're going to like it there,' added Fanny.

'They will I'm sure. Now, down to business ...' Mrs. Staunton glanced at the papers in front of her on the table.

Fanny stiffened.

'If you want to move into *Rose Cottage* we will have to charge you rent.'

'Of course.' Seamus nodded.

'But I've been talking to Mr. Staunton and he has agreed that it shouldn't be too high. You will be receiving a small pension, Seamus, so you will be well able to manage to pay the rent out of that.'

'I appreciate it, Ma'am.'

'As soon as Tom and Sally have moved, I will arrange to send you up the keys and you can settle in yourselves. Now there is something else, just give me a moment.' She rang a bell, and after a moment there was a knock on the door.

Ellie appeared, flushed from her run up the stairs.

'Could you please ask Mr. Staunton to join us?'

'Certainly, Ma'am.' Ellie bobbed a curtsy and left.

'He won't be a moment, Seamus,' Mrs. Staunton said.

They sat there quietly, but said nothing. Fanny didn't even look at her husband, wondering what else was coming. When Mr. Staunton came in, both Fanny and Seamus stood up. A sense of propriety in the way they faced their employers.

'Sorry to lose you, Seamus,' the Master said gruffly. 'I wanted to say a formal *thank you* for all your hard work over the years.'

Fanny felt embarrassed.

'We want you to accept this gift ...' He picked up a black box which was on his wife's desk, and handed it to Seamus.

'Thank you very much, Sir.' He bowed.

'We appreciate everything you have done too, Fanny.' He shook their hands. 'And I hope to see you both again soon,' he smiled and left the room.

Fanny didn't know what to say.

'Thank you, Ma'am,' Seamus bowed again.

'It's our pleasure.'

Fanny was walking on air as they made their way to the trap and climbed in. 'Can you believe it, Seamus? We'll be living in *Rose Cottage*.' She was excited. 'And you got a present, what do you think it is?'

'I'll open it when we get home,' he said, grinning widely, lifting his hat to Tess and Ellie who stood at the door waving them off. 'And there's a couple of acres with that house, and fine grass too.'

'And Tom has the garden as nice as *Fairfields* itself.' Fanny was delighted. 'And we'll be able to grow our own vegetables and fruits as well. But I feel guilty taking Tom and Sally's house. They're going to be so lonely.'

'He has to go where there is work.'

'I know, but it doesn't make it any easier for them.'

'We have to leave our house as well, I'm not too keen on that,' Seamus said, his gnarled hands gripping the smooth leather of the reins.

'And your horses.' Fanny was sympathetic.

'Don't want to talk about that,' he grunted

She said no more. Thinking that their lives were so deeply embedded in the earth of the stable yard it might never be possible to uproot.

He was depressed about leaving their home and she could do nothing about that, but he cheered up when he opened the present and saw the gold watch presented to him by the Stauntons.

'It's beautiful,' Fanny breathed, touching the shining glass of the face.

'It is indeed,' he smiled, and turned it over. 'And there's writing on the back. What does it say Fanny?' He handed it to her.

'*To Seamus Dineen, in grateful appreciation from* …' She read out loud, but couldn't even finish, overcome with emotion.

When they received the key from Mrs. Staunton, Fanny persuaded

Seamus to come up to see *Rose Cottage* immediately, so excited when they walked up the path. Opening the front door, she walked along the narrow hall into the kitchen. She always admired Tom and Sally's big black range and wooden dresser, and to her surprise, she saw that the range and other furniture were still there, although empty now of any vessels.

'Some of this furniture must have belonged to the Stauntons, I'll ask the Mistress about it, maybe she might let us have it?'

'We have our own,' Seamus muttered.

'The range is a much bigger one than we have ourselves.' She ran her hand over the gleaming black surface.

'Fanny, we can't throw out our own things, girl, what if we only get a short stay here and have to move on?'

Fanny was taken aback. That could easily happen. 'You're right, anyway, it would take me a long time to get used to a new range, I like my own. But the dresser is nice …'

He didn't reply.

They continued through the house and when they went upstairs she was glad to find that the parlour was completely empty. She was very fond of her pieces of furniture including Anna's piano and had saved long and hard for them over the years, so they would look very well in this room.

'And I'm sleeping in my own bed, Fanny, I'll tell you that,' Seamus said firmly. 'I'm not laying my head down on someone else's mattress.'

Fanny opened the upstairs bedroom door. 'Look for yourself, Seamus, there'll be no doubt about that, this room is empty too,' she said, laughing. Her husband slept in his own bed with Edward, having moved out of hers a long time ago.

Outside, there was a large area at the back of the house where Tom grew vegetables and there were still some potato plants which could be pulled. Two good fields stretched beyond which would be ideal for their own horses, with stables and outhouses alongside. She would get Seamus to fence off an area and build some coops for the poultry.

'Aren't you glad, man?' Fanny asked as she locked the front door.

'At least we've somewhere to live.'
'I hope Edward will be happy too.'
'He didn't really believe the Mistress would keep her word about finding us a house. I was of the same mind myself,' he admitted.
'Oh ye of little faith, men!' retorted Fanny with a toss of her head.

Chapter Seventeen

Anna rushed into Mike's arms.

'How are you, my darling?' He looked down at her. His dark brown eyes warmed through her, and she quivered as he held her in his arms. 'You're looking so beautiful.'

She smiled and tears moistened her eyes.

'I thought I'd never get here, the weather was heavy going once we reached Europe.' His moist lips touched hers, and he kissed her deeply.

She let herself go into his embrace, carried away by the touch of him.

'I've missed you so much.' He kissed her again and again. 'And now all I want is to take you up to bed, my love.'

She blushed and tightened her arms around the heavy uniform overcoat, and let him see that it was what she wanted as well.

'Unfortunately, the cab is waiting outside with all my baggage, so I'll have to let you go for a few minutes. Tell me, how is Bina and our little Eleanor, I want to see them.'

'They're grand but both are fast asleep.'

'I'll look in on them when we go up.' He stood at the door, his arm still around her, and smiled. His skin darkened from the Eastern sun, the whiteness of his teeth and eyes accentuated.

When the baggage was unloaded and brought in, they went upstairs to see the children before he had even taken off his coat. They stood by Bina's bed.

'She's grown so much,' he whispered. 'So pretty, just like you.' He pressed his arm around her waist. 'I'm looking forward to seeing her tomorrow, she's full of personality no doubt.'

'And has her own opinions too, let me tell you,' Anna smiled.

Mike gently tucked the blanket closer around her and they tiptoed quietly out of the room. In their own bedroom, the glow of the lamp cast a warm light. Eleanor lay in the crib. She was awake and he immediately lifted her up and held her in his arms. 'I'm sorry I wasn't here for her birth, you had to endure it on your own. It's so amazing that these two little ones are ours. I can't believe it. And thank you for naming her *Eleanor* after my own mother, that means so much to me.' He put the baby down and covered her with the blue blanket, and as her eyes slowly closed and she slept, he put his arm around Anna and pulled her close.

She cooked dinner and they sat in the dining room, in front of the leaping flames of the fire. He told her about the journey home, every fascinating detail she wanted to know and what it was like on the China Station.

'Chinese cities are just like beehives, masses of people rushing here and there. There's so much colour. Hong Kong is the same, and there are a lot of British and other nationalities working there. The harbour is full of ships and the place has really developed a lot since I was there last. The docks have been extended and new warehouses seem to go up every day. Trade is the big thing. There's money to be made and everyone wants their share. And there are European concessions all over the east.'

'It sounds fascinating,' whispered Anna, eyes wide.

'And there's always something to celebrate. The King's birthday. A visit of important foreign dignitaries. Then the flags are raised, and the bands play. There's so much I could tell you.' He clasped her two hands in his and pulled her on to his lap.

She giggled as he put his arms around her and hugged her close.

'But that's enough about China, now it's you I want. Just you. To hold you in my arms which have been empty for the last year.' He kissed her.

'I've often wondered if ...whether ...' she hesitated.

'What?' he smiled quizzically.

'I read in the paper about the life of naval men when they're away at sea, and how in the ports there are always beautiful women. Daughters of Admirals maybe ...remember that girl in Queenstown you told me about ...Georgina.'

'She's well married by now.'

'You knew her before me,' she insisted.

'I don't think Georgina would go near the China Station although some of the officers' families do go with their husbands for short periods of time.'

'You didn't think of bringing us?'

'It's a very hard place to live, my love. The weather is unpleasant. It's hot and humid. And children often die from strange diseases. Anyway, even if you came you would spend most of the time in Hong Kong with the other families while the men are at sea. We wouldn't hardly see each other at all.'

She nodded. 'I understand all that.' Hoping that she did.

'And as for other women, I have no interest in anyone only you. I'll admit you are right that naval men do take advantage of local women, and have their pick of them. But there are many risks to health and I don't want to fall ill.'

'What illnesses?'

'There are diseases associated with that kind of life. Men can die. Women can die.'

'What are the names of the diseases?' Anna was curious.

'I hesitate to tell you, because they are not names which you should ever repeat, as they are only connected with one thing. Nobody speaks about such things except men.' He kissed her.

'I suppose I shouldn't be asking you,' she admitted, running her fingers through his dark hair. 'My mother would have a fit.'

'Are we not husband and wife?' he asked, tracing the shape of her features with his fingers.

'We are of course.'

'Then there are no secrets between us. Nothing we cannot talk about. And that's the way it should be. We love each other for ever, and your mother has no say in our lives.'

'I'm a mother myself,' she smiled.

'And a wonderful one.'

That night spent with Mike was magical. So used to sleeping alone or occasionally with Bina, the warmth of his body as he curled around her after they had made love brought her back to the way it was when they first met and married and she realised how deeply she loved him. In the darkness of the night, the slightest movement she made received an immediate response from him and his hands would touch and stroke her skin softly. She would do the same and drift off to sleep again.

In the morning, their door was opened and Bina rushed in to climb into the bed beside Anna, a regular occurrence. The little one pressed into her arms and she put her finger against her lips, reluctant to have the child wake Mike. Bina stared over her mother's shoulder at the man who slept beside her, a look of puzzlement on her face.

'Who is he?' she whispered.

'That's your Daddy,' Anna explained, smiling.

'He's not my Daddy,' her voice echoed loudly.

'Remember I showed you his photograph.'

Bina shook her head.

Then Mike's eyes opened and he put his arm around the two of them. 'Is this my little Bina I see here?' he smiled at her.

'No,' she snapped and lowered her head behind Anna.

'This is Daddy,' Anna said.

'No, he isn't.'

Bina slid out of the bed and ran across the linoleum floor and opened the door, standing there staring at them both, a baleful look on her face.

'Come back into bed, Bina,' he called.

But she banged the door and disappeared.

'I'll have my work cut out there I think, although we can't expect her to remember me, it's a long time in a little child's life.'

'She'll know you again in a few hours I'm sure.' Anna was disappointed for him. 'We'd better get up now, I've to feed Eleanor.'

He put his arms around her and gathered her close to him again. 'I don't want to get up, you're so delicious I could stay here all day,' he whispered, and kissed her.

The door opened again and Bina stood there. 'I'm hungry.'

'Wait for me, I'll be down in a minute,' Anna said.

'Shall I get your breakfast, Bina?' Mike asked.

'No,' she snapped and ran out again.

'I'm in the dog house,' Mike grinned. 'Let me take Eleanor up, at least she won't yell at me.' He climbed out of bed and lifted her. 'I hope.'

Anna slipped on her dressing gown. 'I'll take her down with me and get breakfast for Bina.' She held out her arms.

'I'll have to go in to the Admiralty and see what's happening, although I'm due some leave so it will give us a chance to be together for a while.' He kissed Eleanor and handed her back to Anna.

Chapter Eighteen

Fanny stared through the trees at *Fairfields*. It was just one last look she wanted. This place was so much a part of her life she wondered how she would manage to live without everything associated with it. The house had been built over a hundred years earlier, she had once been told by the Mistress, and Fanny loved it. The high windows, the sweep of steps up to the heavy front door, the pillars each side.

She wondered if the new owners would keep the estate as well as the Stauntons had done. Already there was a sense of sadness about the place. There were no gardeners. And she could see signs of neglect already. The smooth cut grass had grown a little, piles of golden autumn leaves had gathered up around the trunks of the great trees and would normally have been swept up and removed by now. The avenue was empty and quiet and there was no clatter of horses' hooves or rumble of carriage wheels as visitors came to call. No butler waiting to open the door in welcome.

Back at the stable yard, it wasn't much better. It too was almost empty. Only a few bags and boxes containing their own possessions stood in the kitchen waiting for Seamus to come back with the trap and make the final trip to their new house. Fanny had stripped her own home of everything. Her precious white lace curtains and pictures were all taken down. Anna's piano and the green plush chesterfield suite in the parlour had been carried in a borrowed dray. Everything was so close to her heart. Anna had taken all of her own little keepsakes with her last time she returned to Portsmouth and that was one responsibility Fanny didn't have.

So much had happened in this house. Fanny thought about her darling Anna, and her three sons. Edward, who was still here with them, and Pat and Jim, who had gone to America and now lived in Madison, Wisconsin. A place she didn't know at all. They had written to her occasionally, although Jim was always the better letter writer of the two and described how it was in America. But for Fanny who had never travelled further than Dublin, it seemed a strange foreign place. Both Jim and Pat were very upset about the sale of *Fairfields*.

Before Seamus came, she went into the back garden and knelt and said a prayer at the graves of her little ones. The flowers which usually grew there had died and she plucked a few dead leaves, picturing little white bones underneath the earth, no flesh left on them now. Tears spurted and she dried them with her apron. But was somewhat comforted when she reminded herself that their holy souls had gone to Heaven and they were with Jesus and Mary, his Blessed Mother. Little angels now.

She said a prayer to them and asked that they would look after her and Seamus when they went to *Rose Cottage*, promising that she would always come back here, even if she had to sneak in without permission.

But would anyone else ever live here in the stable yard? She wondered. Mrs. Staunton had seemed to indicate that the new owners would drive motor cars and that they had no interest in a stable yard. That made it all the more poignant, to think that their way of life would end up on the scrap heap.

'I'll come around later to see if there's anything we've left behind,' Seamus mumbled.

'Let me say a little prayer for good times past.' Fanny knelt down for a moment, then stood up and taking a small bottle from her pocket splashed Holy Water. Blessing herself, she took one last look around her kitchen and shut the door behind her. She climbed up on the trap beside Seamus and stared straight ahead. Outside the stable yard, he stopped and locked the gates. Back in the trap he encouraged the horse to trot as if they wanted to get away from this place they loved as quickly as they could.

As they clattered along, she reminded herself that they were not going very far. They would still see the high wall of the estate from their front door. Maybe it would be comforting of a morning to know that her old home was close by.

So much time had passed in this place. Minutes. Hours. Days. Nights. Hurtling along like a panicked horse. It was only now that she realised that she was swept along too at that frantic pace and regretted the moments lost along the way. Times when she should have stopped to say a consoling word. A gentle touch to reassure. When she was young she had thought her life was endless. It stretched ahead of her, a glowing reality, and she discarded it thoughtlessly, and never valued it.

She threw herself into work. She cleaned *Rose Cottage* from top to bottom and enjoyed arranging all her furniture in the new surroundings. It did her good. Her poultry flock was at home in their new run and she hoped they wouldn't be affected by the move. But they seemed quite happy, although some weren't laying, but that was normal at this time of the year. The dog had settled, and Fanny had brought the cat and her litter of kittens over in a box. But she wasn't sure if they would be as happy and was certain they would be wandering back and forth to *Fairfields* all the time.

'We'll have to keep an eye on the garden in the spring or it will run away on us,' Seamus said.

'Why don't you do that?' Fanny asked.

'I wouldn't know a flower from a weed,' he retorted. 'I only know about good clean grass which will keep my horses healthy.'

'Well, you keep an eye on the veg and I'll watch the plants. We'll put down potatoes, carrots, onions and all the other vegetables. We'll have enough to feed ourselves.'

'And have me breaking my back snagging turnips, and pulling praties,' Seamus grumbled.

'Keep you busy,' Fanny said.

It was strange to be living outside the walls of *Fairfields,* although she saw a lot more of her neighbours who often called for a chat on their way past. There was so much she missed about living in the stable yard. Small things like having a chance to read a few lines in the Master's newspapers in the morning. As he didn't like getting any ink on his fingers she pressed them with her iron before she brought them up to the House. In the meantime, Fred the postman could always be relied on for news.

'The employers up in Dublin are still locking out the workers. People are in a terrible state. They're starving,' he had told her this morning.

'Isn't it awful that the employers won't pay them enough money to live on. We were lucky to be working for the Stauntons, although my cousin Pearl's husband is one of those men locked out of his job, and there's no money coming in to feed or clothe their family.'

As it was now Seamus and herself had to live on his pension which was only a few shillings a week. But she was lucky to have her own little job raising the poultry and doing the laundry for Mrs. Staunton. She had let it be known among her neighbours that they could buy their eggs and fowl from her if they wanted. It would make all the difference to their lives. Edward earned a good living but was never very generous and might not even want to pay anything towards the rent on *Rose Cottage*. She hadn't mentioned it to him yet, but had every intention.

There was a knock on the door, and it was pushed open.

'Ellie ...' She embraced the young woman. It was almost like hugging Anna, both girls always so close.

'The Mistress asked me to bring the washing,' she smiled. 'And she said to give you this letter.' She handed it to Fanny.

'She's so thoughtful, and knew that I'd love to come up and see you.'

'Come in, girl, Fred and I were just talking.'

'Ellie.' He stood up and made a little bow. 'I'm off now on the rest of my round. I'll see you tomorrow Fanny, and thanks for breakfast,' he grinned.

'It's grand to see Fred. The day isn't quite the same without him. When he used to come into the stable yard every day, many's a time I thought he'd never go. Now it's changed. I need him here, to remind me …' Fanny said to Ellie.

'I'm the same. I need to come back. To breathe in this air. I know I'm really lucky to have a new position in Monkstown, but I'll never get used to it.' She looked out the window. 'Even to see the wall is … wonderful.' Her eyes filled with tears, and she held Fanny close. They stood together without another word for a while until Fanny gently disengaged and held Ellie's two hands in her own.

'How is Anna? I had a letter the other day and she told me Mike was coming home soon.'

'I've got a letter too, although I haven't had a chance to read it yet. But I'm hoping all is well over in Portsmouth. It's lovely to see you, and I want you up as often as you can.'

'I have my one day off and I must go home then, but I'm sure the Mistress will let me come up here again.'

Fanny missed all the people who had worked at *Fairfields*. It used to be a hive of activity with the grooms and the boys, always someone to get her water or anything else she needed without a minute's delay. Now she had to do everything herself. But then she rationalised, the busier she was the better. She opened Anna's letter as soon as Ellie had gone. Delighted to hear that her girl was so happy now that Mike had arrived home. But there was little else in the letter. A sense of breathlessness between the lines. She was far too excited to even write a long letter, she said. Fanny was disappointed.

In Mrs. Staunton's letter, she told her that the new people would be arriving in a few days, and she should bring the spare set of House keys and those for the stable yard up to them. The name was Kelleher, and they were a family from County Meath. A husband, wife and three children.

Three young ones, Fanny thought. How lovely it would have been to have children around the House when she was living in the stable yard. Sadly, the Stauntons had no family.

Chapter Nineteen

'How's my little Bina?' Mike smiled and bent down on his hunkers so he could look straight into his daughter's blue eyes. She glared at him, rushed over to Anna and hid behind her.

'I think she must be shy of her Daddy?' he laughed and stood up. 'Maybe it's the uniform?'

'I'll make you breakfast.'

'Just a cup of strong tea, Anna, and some of your own bread if you had time to bake yesterday. It will keep me going on terra firma. I've been so long at sea it seems strange.'

'It's wonderful to have you home. I can't believe it.' She kissed him and he embraced her tightly.

'I've dreamt of being home every night.'

'Your letters told me that.'

'Mammy?' Bina tugged at her skirt.

'Yes love, sit up at the table.'

But she refused to move from Anna's side.

Mike sat at the table and ate his breakfast, all the time smiling at Bina. But all she did was to frown at him.

He stood up. 'I'll be back later, but I don't know what time. I'll unpack my bags then and we'll see what nice things we have for Bina.' He kissed Anna but Bina refused to be kissed.

Mike returned in the late afternoon, and told her that he had a month's leave.

'A whole month?' She hugged him.

'I thought we might go back to Cork and see them all. It's been a long time.'

'Do you know where you will be stationed when you go back to work?' Anna was anxious to know.

'No decision has been reached yet.'

'Will it be Hong Kong again?' Anna asked.

'I hope not. They generally don't assign us to two long terms of duty back to back.'

'That's such a relief.'

'Now, unpacking. I've so much stuff. Let's start with the big trunk.' He bent and opened it, lifted his whites out and put them on a chair. Caps, jackets, boots, and an assortment of other bits and pieces were next. At the bottom, there was a large oblong parcel, wrapped in colourful paper and tied with red string.

'That's for you.' He handed it to her.

'Thank you.' She kissed him and then examined the parcel.

'Open it,' he encouraged. 'Hope you like it. I think I mentioned I had bought it in one of my letters.'

She smiled and undid the cord. The paper crinkled and she unfolded it to reveal some bolts of fabric.

'These are really lovely, Mike,' she murmured, taken aback by the beauty of the Chinese silks. The first one was a simple plain piece in a delicate shade of cream, followed by a blue silk with a pattern of tiny flowers spread over it. The third was a pale green. 'I've enough here for a wardrobe of clothes,' she said, holding up the different pieces until she was surrounded by a rainbow of lovely colours. 'Thank you my love,' she embraced him.

'I'm glad you like them. 'Where is Bina?' he asked.

'She's asleep. But she should be awake soon.'

'I have a doll for her. And a white fur coat.'

'That sounds amazing.'

'And there are some wooden toys as well. They carve some lovely stuff over there. I seemed to spend all my last shore leave shopping for Bina. But I didn't forget you either,' he smiled as he took out a small box. 'Close your eyes,' he said, and moved around, putting something around her neck, his fingers gently closing a clasp at the back. 'Now you can look,' he said.

In the mirror she could see a beautiful pendant, an exquisite aquamarine stone set in gold filigree. 'It's beautiful, Mike, thank you so much.' She kissed him.

'And these too.' He handed her two more boxes which contained a bracelet and earrings to match. She put them on.

'You look beautiful,' Mike smiled at her.

'Mammy?' Bina stood on the stairs. Anna went to her and lifted her down. 'Daddy has been giving me lovely presents, isn't he good?'

'And Bina, I have something for you too.' Mike reached into the trunk and held out a parcel to her.

'No.' She shook her head, her fair curls bouncing.

'Go on over to Daddy,' Anna encouraged.

'Bina?' Mike called her.

She stood sulking.

'Oh well, I'll have to give this present to Eleanor. Do you think she'll like it?' he asked Anna.

'I'm sure she will,' Anna almost laughed at the expression on Bina's face. Her eyes now darting over to the parcel in its red wrapping. and then back to the floor, obviously longing to run and take it from Mike, but reluctant to do so.

Suddenly the sound of Eleanor crying from upstairs could be heard.

'Maybe I'll give it to her,' Mike asked Anna, who had already run upstairs. Bina followed her as far as the first couple of steps of stairs and stood there looking at him, until Anna came back carrying Eleanor. Mike put down the parcel on a chair, stretched out his arms and took the baby. Then Bina suddenly ran across the room, grabbed the parcel and ran into the kitchen with it. Anna and Mike both burst out laughing and although they tried to stifle the sound, there were tears of laughter in Anna's eyes. They followed the child and stood in the doorway watching as she tore off the wrapping, pieces of crinkly paper floating to the ground around her as she tried to undo the string with her tiny hands.

'Let me, Bina.' Anna quickly opened it and finally the last piece of paper fell away.

It was a Chinese doll wearing a typical red satin kimono, and Bina stared spellbound at her.

'I thought it might appeal to her,' explained Mike.

'Do you like your new doll?' Anna asked.

Bina came towards her, and pointed to the face of the doll with its delicate oriental features.

'Isn't she beautiful, Bina?' Anna asked, bending closer.

She nodded silently.

'Say thank you to Daddy. Give him a kiss.' Anna pushed her towards Mike.

She shook her head and turned away, hugging the doll close.

Anna felt disappointed for Mike, but he shrugged.

'I'm sorry about Bina, she's still a bit strange towards you,' Anna said.

'She'll get used to me. Don't worry, my love, come here to me.' He put his arm around her shoulders and drew her close.

'It's so good to have you home. I've been so lonely without you.'

'I'll be with you for a whole month. You'll be glad when I go back to work,' he laughed.

'No I won't. I only hope they won't send you too far away.'

'Hopefully not, it's too hard on you and the children, Anna. I'm so sorry I haven't got a job in an office and come home to you every night.'

'I think it would be too difficult for you to give up the sea.'

'It'll happen some day. My service will be up in nineteen hundred and twenty-four.'

'Will you sign on for more time?' she asked nervously, wondering what he would say.

'I don't know, Anna, it's too far away.'

She said nothing, staring into the dancing flames.

'Don't be worrying about that.' He put his finger under her chin and tipped her face up to him. 'All you need to know is that I love you dearly, you and the children are the most important people in my life. There is no-one else.' His lips touched hers, and immediately she felt reassured.

Chapter Twenty

Over the next few days, there was a succession of drays and some motor vans coming and going to the House. Even Fanny and Seamus were aware although they were on the far side and couldn't see the gates. But all the neighbours were excited that the new people had arrived at last.

On Saturday, Fanny dressed herself in her best clothes, re-arranged her hair, put on her black hat, secured it with her silver hat pin, and walked around to the front gate. Normally, the family who lived in the lodge would keep an eye on who was going in and out, but as they had left, the gates stood open. Fanny had decided it would be better for her to walk up the avenue rather than take the pathway through the trees as she usually would. It was a cool November day. Morning sunshine cast sharp blue shadows on the bright green of the lawns.

Drawn to her old home, she was powerless to stop herself walking towards the stable yard, her feet rustling and crunching through the carpet of leaves which had gathered on the road. Sadly, there was a look of desolation about the place. More leaves had drifted up against the walls and gate and she immediately felt she should be out with her brush. She peered through a gap in the wooden door, but couldn't see anything as her eyes misted over and she was overcome with emotion. Bending her head, she tried to get control over herself. She leaned against the door, one hand touching it, as memories swept through her mind. But she forced herself to leave after a few minutes, and didn't look back.

At the House she walked around and found the kitchen door

standing ajar. She glanced in and immediately smelled smoke. What was going on, she wondered and went in, concerned to see a young woman beating the air with a towel. She appeared to be very flustered, her face rather red with strands of brown hair escaping from the coiled bun at the nape of her neck.

'Are you all right?' Fanny asked, putting her basket on the table.

'I can't get the range to work properly,' she said.

'Do you think it could be the damper?' Fanny asked. 'Is the fuel dry?'

'We had a delivery of coal just yesterday.'

Fanny worked on the damper for a while, and before long flames could be seen leaping through the coals and the smoke eased somewhat. 'It's always hard to get used to something like a range. They have their own personalities.'

'Thank you, I'm so grateful.' The woman tried to tidy up her hair.

'My name is Fanny Dineen, I used to live in the stable yard and I've come up to give your Mistress …'

At that moment a woman came down the stairs. 'Susan, what's happening, there's a lot of smoke in the air.'

'I'm sorry, Mrs. Kelleher, I couldn't light the range but Fanny here was an angel and fixed it for me.'

'How nice of you, Fanny.' The woman came towards her. She was very attractive, with dark hair and wore a grey morning dress.

'There, it's going better now.' Susan poked at it.

'Once you get it going, you'll be away,' Fanny said, smiling.

'I'm Barbara Kelleher.' The woman held out her hand to Fanny.

'I'm Fanny Dineen.'

'It's lovely to meet you.' She shook her hand. 'And what can we do for you, since you helped us so much already,' she smiled.

'Fanny used to live in the stable yard,' Susan explained.

'Why don't we put on the kettle and make some tea, Susan?' Mrs. Kelleher suggested. 'And could you bring it up to my sitting room when it's ready if you don't mind? I'm not sure if we've got anything nice to give Fanny.' She seemed worried.

'I brought up a few things for you. There are eggs, a roast chicken, some cake and apple crumble.' Fanny indicated the basket.

'How wonderful, thank you so much,' Mrs. Kelleher smiled.

'You are so thoughtful. Now, why don't you come up with me and we can get acquainted over tea and your cake, which I'm sure is delicious.'

Fanny was astonished. To be invited up to tea by the Mistress of *Fairfields* was remarkable.

The sitting room furniture was not quite as heavy as the Stauntons had been, and the drapes on the windows were in a soft white material with a trailing pink floral design.

'We've had to leave our own home where we lived for fourteen years and that's been difficult for us. But my husband has bought a company in Cork and we had to move here.' Mrs. Kelleher was very candid in the way she spoke, as if she had known Fanny for years.

There was a knock on the door and Susan pushed it open. Then she picked up a heavy tray from the floor and brought it in.

'Your cake looks absolutely delicious,' Mrs. Kelleher said. 'I'm looking forward to tasting it.'

'May I …suggest something?' Fanny was hesitant.

'Of course,' Mrs. Kelleher agreed immediately.

'There is a dumb waiter here which is very handy if you're bringing up dishes from the kitchen.'

'Sorry Ma'am, but I wasn't sure how it worked,' Susan said, shamefaced.

'I forgot to tell you about that,' Mrs. Kelleher walked on to the landing and opened it.

'I'll use it in future, Ma'am,' Susan nodded.

Mrs. Kelleher laughed and ushered Fanny back into her sitting room. 'Let's sit down before the tea gets cold.'

Barbara Kelleher was a most interesting woman, Fanny decided. A very different person to Mrs. Staunton. Even as they drank their tea she talked avidly. Asking question after question. She wanted to know everything about Fanny and Seamus. How *Fairfields* was run on a daily basis. And she seemed to have no air of superiority about her at all. The fact that Fanny and Seamus would have been on a much lower level socially seemed to mean nothing at all to her.

'The reason I came up was to give you the spare keys of the House and those for the stable yard.' Fanny searched in her pocket and handed them to her.

'Thank you for that, Fanny.'

Mrs. Kelleher looked at them as they lay in her hand. 'There's so much of the past bound up in these keys,' she said slowly, touching them. 'You lived in the stable yard, and there were generations before you. I even feel them around the house here. I sometimes hear footsteps. A door opens and closes. Even voices in the distance.'

'You do, Ma'am?' Fanny was taken aback.

She nodded. 'I imagine the ladies in their crinolines and feathered hats, the gentlemen fighting duels, it was a very different time. I wonder sometimes if the music I hear is that of the musicians playing for the balls which must have been held in the ballroom.'

'When I came here first in the eighteen eighties there were often dances held and great banquets too.'

'So the Stauntons were well known in Cork social circles?' Mrs. Kelleher commented.

'Oh yes, Ma'am.'

'This was a great house, and such a history it must have.'

Fanny nodded. Finding this woman so unbelievably gracious, she had decided that perhaps she might ask a favour. If she refused her then Fanny would have to accept it. Her confidence had grown the more they talked and suddenly she didn't want to delay any longer. Her opportunity was now, and it could be a fleeting one. She might never be in this position again.

'Mrs. Kelleher, if I might be ...so bold ...' she asked timidly.

'Yes?' She seemed interested.

For Fanny, it was a very strange to find herself asking such a woman for a *favour*, like a beggar woman on the street with her hand out.

'Years ago …' Fanny took a deep breath. 'I lost three stillborn babies and …they are buried at the back of the stable yard,' she blurted out, unable to prevent tears moistening her eyes.

'How very tragic for you.' Mrs. Kelleher was sympathetic.

'And I wonder would you mind if I went there sometimes to say a prayer?' Fanny hadn't been able to imagine how she would explain to a stranger this need she had, this promise made to her dead children. And expect this unusual woman to understand what was going on in her own head. Still born babies were not talked about among people she knew, and it wouldn't have happened in upper class circles either. Eyes were averted, mouths closed tight shut. Snap. With disapproval. Like the jaws of a bulldog they once had around the stable yard. After a woman lost a child, she was assured that she would have many more babies. And that the ones lost were for God and not meant for this world.

'Of course you can, Fanny, any time. And if you want to keep the keys of the house you can visit it as well.'

'No thank you, Ma'am. Mrs. Staunton told me to give them to you.'

'We'll hardly be using the place at all. My husband has a new motor car, so we won't need a carriage or horses from now on.'

'I'm very grateful to you, Ma'am. For a lady in your position to be so generous to someone like me is …' She wanted to hug her tight. Just to let her know how much this meant to her.

'We lead a very simple life, Fanny, I don't believe in class distinction. We are all equal in God's eyes and our children are brought up with others in the same way. I'll admit this is a much bigger house then we had in County Meath, but it will give the children plenty of scope. They will go to school in Cork as I don't want governesses or tutors and I particularly dislike boarding schools.'

Fanny listened, astonished. Seamus would never believe it.

'My husband bought this house through an agent, and now I'm wondering if I will be able to run it by myself. It is very large.'

'I'm sure you will, Mam.'

'What number of staff had Mrs. Staunton?'

'Quite a lot. A housekeeper. A butler. A cook. Kitchen maids. Upstairs maids. Footmen. Gardeners …' She rattled off the list, blue eyes smiling.

'And there were only the two of them living there, goodness me,' she said. 'But I will get some staff in time. For the moment Susan and I will manage. The children are with their grandmother for now. Although I do want to have them here soon, I miss them.'

'If I might be so bold …to suggest …' Again, Fanny wasn't sure whether it was in order for her to mention this or not.

'Yes Fanny?'

'Some of the staff are still without positions.'

'Dear me.'

'You may not need a butler and a housekeeper, but perhaps some maids to help with the heavy work?'

'Susan does everything at the moment, but we are not using the upper floors and she can manage.'

'And what about the gardens?' asked Fanny. She was on such a personal level with Mrs. Kelleher now she decided she may as well mention anything which came to mind.

'I think I assumed gardens came with gardeners growing there as well,' she laughed. 'No, it's top of my list, only I haven't attended to it yet.'

'There were three gardeners here, and they looked after the flowers, the lawns, and the walled garden. So you would have all your own vegetables grown here, and fruit as well. The head gardener has obtained a position in Bantry, but the other two are still without work.'

'Thanks so much, Fanny, I can't imagine how either myself or Isaac would be any good at horticulture, so would you mind calling to see me again tomorrow and we can talk some more. My husband will be home later and I shall discuss all you have told me. Now I have quite a lot of unpacking to do so I must say goodbye.' Mrs. Kelleher walked downstairs with her, through that large hallway which Fanny had always admired, opened the heavy front door and took her hand.

'Thank you so much for all your help, Fanny, and I look forward to seeing you tomorrow. Shall we say about twelve?'

'I look forward to it,' Fanny said, and bobbed a curtsy.

'Ah, no bending to me, Fanny, you know I don't believe in that, and do call me Barbara, I hope we're going to be good friends. Until tomorrow, I will have more time to chat to you then.'

'Thank you …Barbara.' She could barely get the name out. 'It's been lovely to meet you and thank you for tea.'

'And my thanks to you for your delicious cakes and the eggs and chicken too,' Barbara smiled and waved goodbye.

Chapter Twenty-one

'What would you like to do now that we're on holiday?' Mike asked over breakfast the following morning.

'We just want to be with you, it's so wonderful to have you back.'

'As I said, we might take a trip home, would you like that?' he asked with a grin, a twinkle in his eyes.

'You know I would,' Anna said excitedly.

'Then that's arranged. I'll get the tickets later. Why don't you walk down with me and we'll bring the children? Or would it be too cold for you?' He looked out the window.

'No, we'll wrap up.'

She didn't want him to go out of her sight. Always wanting to reach out and touch him whenever she felt like it. And proud too that this tall good-looking man was her husband. Suddenly, it made living in Portsmouth tolerable. This was their home and when they closed the door on the naval world then she had him to herself, loving him so much it was as if she had gone back in time to those days when they first fell in love and used to meet at the old cottage in *Fairfields*.

They arrived in Cork a few days later, to be met by Fanny and Seamus. A mix of emotions in Anna's heart when she came through the door of *Rose Cottage* instead of *Fairfields*. While she could see that Fanny and Seamus still longed to be back in the stable yard, she tried to be as enthusiastic as she could about the cottage.

'I can't believe how much Eleanor has grown.' Fanny rocked the child in her arms.

'And me too.' Bina looked up from where she played with the doll Mike had brought her. She was very fond of it now but was still very guarded with him.

'And you too,' Fanny smiled down at her.

'How do you feel since you left *Fairfields*, it must still be lonely for you,' Mike asked.

'I'm getting used to it, but I'm so busy I haven't time to even think. Mrs. Kelleher, or Barbara as she tells me I must call her, has me supplying the eggs and all the poultry for the House when I mentioned that it was my job to do that for Mrs. Staunton. So there's money coming in which is a surprise. I sell some to the neighbours as well and we've bought a cow so that we'll have our own milk and butter.'

Anna was glad to see that her mother and father and Edward seemed to have settled into the new house reasonably well, and that Seamus had even got a job driving a delivery van for the local bread man. It gave him something to do and that meant they didn't have to worry so much about him.

The only shadow on the horizon was that Bina still didn't like Mike. Fanny had never again asked that Bina might come to stay with her, and really Anna couldn't even mention that to Mike as he tried so hard to be a good father to his eldest daughter.

Over the days they visited friends and neighbours. Setting out each day with a definite plan in their minds. Anna dreaded the visit which would inevitably be made to his mother and sisters. She had told Mike that she had called to see her but gave no details of her rather cold attitude.

But to her surprise Nancy was very different on this occasion. Mike had written in advance so Anna supposed that when she arrived unannounced with Lizzie, her mother in law had been taken aback. Now she sat them down to tea. Mike's sisters both took to the children, and even Bina warmed to them. The three year old was happy in the shop helping whoever was serving. If someone came in for a message, she was delighted to hand the parcel to that person in a very business-like fashion. So there was much laughter between them. The elder girl,

Maisie, was betrothed to a young man in the village, but Vera still had to find a boy and couldn't wait to be married and have children of her own. They were all very nice to them, and Anna was glad for Mike's sake. Nancy said little to her, but Anna didn't mind, she would put up with anything for him.

Other visits included a trip to Monkstown where they called into Ellie and Tess. They had time to chat in the big kitchen as Mr. and Mrs. Staunton had gone on their usual visit to Egypt. Then, Mike suggested they have a family photograph taken, and arranged an appointment in *The American Studios* on Patrick Street. So Anna dressed the children in their best clothes, with Mike in his uniform, and went in to pose for the photographer.

'No laughing now …' the man warned after he had spent a lot of time positioning them in front of a draped red velvet curtain. Bina sat beside Eleanor who lay on a big soft cushion on an elaborately carved chair, Anna and Mike standing.

'Anna, put your hand there. Mike, look towards me. Bina, watch the camera.' The photographer fussed. Anna found it difficult not to smile, praying all the while that Eleanor wouldn't cry. But the child was very curious as to what was going on, eyes wide, staring around at everything that was happening.

The photographer took a number of shots. Changing their positions. Anna with Bina and Eleanor. Mike with Eleanor in his arms, and Anna and Mike on their own, standing or sitting. And it was only a moment or two after the camera flashed for the last time that Eleanor let out a loud wail. But it was done by then, and Anna immediately lifted her.

'I don't know how I didn't laugh out loud, you know I hate having my photograph taken,' Anna murmured to Mike after he had paid the man and arranged to collect the photographs before they went back to Portsmouth, ordering extra copies for Fanny, Lizzie and Iris.

On the last day, they all gathered together in the Queens Hotel, with Iris, Meg and Lizzie. As ever Anna felt very lonely when she had to leave Fanny and Seamus and everyone she loved.

'Safe journey, write soon, take care.' They embraced each other.

'Anna, Mam has said that I can go over to you for a holiday, I thought I might come next year, I'm all excited.' Meg held Anna's hand tightly.

'Did I hear right? Is Meg coming to stay with us?' Mike asked as they sat in the lounge on board the ship.

'She wanted to come for a little holiday to help take care of the children.'

'We don't need anyone to help.' Mike wasn't pleased.

'I know, but it's awkward. I feel so thankful to Iris and Meg for letting me stay with them, they were so kind when I had Eleanor and really took care of me.'

'Well, I'm not too keen on her coming over,' he murmured.

'She won't stay very long, I'm sure.'

'I hope not.'

Anna put her hand on his and held tight, praying that when Meg arrived it wouldn't cause a problem between herself and Mike.

Chapter Twenty-two

Fanny's friendship with Barbara Kelleher gave her a sense of still belonging to *Fairfields* and that comforted her. There was something about the relaxed nature of the woman which appealed to Fanny. In and out of the House she often chatted with Susan, swopping recipes for cooking. Seamus was still delivering bread to shops on the outskirts of the city. He was a familiar figure to be seen around Cork once again. But Fanny had to keep a tight rein on him, and warned him to stay sober. If he took to the bottle too often then he would lose his position. In the meantime, Jackeen, one of the stable boys who had worked for them in the stable yard helped Fanny with the poultry and other things which needed doing around the house and garden.

The year came to an end, and they spent their first Christmas in *Rose Cottage*. Lizzie, Iris and Meg came to stay, and it was a very pleasant time. Fanny would have given anything to see Anna and the children, but Mike wanted to spend Christmas with his family, and she couldn't even suggest that they might come over again.

For herself, she wasn't so busy as the Stauntons were still away in Egypt but she was glad to help Mrs. Kelleher. The House was fully staffed now although no-one had moved into the stable yard much to her relief. She couldn't bear it if other people took over her home.

'That lock-out in Dublin is still going on,' she muttered as she poured tea for Seamus and Edward. 'Did you read about it in the paper?'
  They didn't reply.

'I was thinking of bringing some food up to my cousin Pearl, they're in a bad state with Harold on strike, and six mouths to feed. She told me in her letter that they have to go down to Liberty Hall to get help. It's the first letter I've got in weeks as she says she can't even afford a stamp and only found one in a drawer and was able to write to me. It's going on so long she's afraid they'll end up in the Union. And there was talk of sending children to England, but she's not doing that, the priest spoke against it at Mass.'

'Don't go near the place, it's not safe up there, girl,' Seamus grunted.

'No mother,' Edward said sharply. 'It's out of the question.'

'But how are they managing to live up there with the strike and all that?'

'You can't get caught up in it. There are marches being organised by Jim Larkin and the Union. And people are rioting. It's dangerous.'

'I gave some money to the collection at Mass a while ago, but I don't know what use it did. There are a lot of starving children.'

'They've established an army to protect the workers.'

'You said it's called The Citizen Army, is that it?' Seamus packed his pipe.

'They have?' Fanny was shocked.

'And the Irish Volunteers are another army, and there's going to be a group set up down here too. The first meeting ended in disaster when a gang of men rushed up on to the platform, crowd of *langers*.'

'Why did that happen?' his father asked.

'They didn't like what the man from Dublin said.'

'You were there?' Fanny stopped clearing the dishes from the table and stared at him.

'I was just coming from work and was interested in seeing what was going on.'

'You shouldn't have been there.'

'And you mustn't think of going up to Dublin, you might even get caught up with the suffrage.'

'What do you mean?' Fanny snapped.

Edward laughed. 'Women are getting together too, protesting.

Looking for the vote.'

'It's all happening up in Dublin.' Seamus lit the tobacco in the bowl of the pipe and puffed. 'Thanks be to God.'

'And with the Ulster Unionists in Belfast, there could be civil war yet if we are granted Home Rule.' Edward opened the newspaper. 'It says here that ports in Ulster will be watched for arms coming through.'

'There's strife everywhere,' murmured Fanny.

'Give you a laugh, a couple were arrested in New York for kissing on the street on Christmas day, how about that?' Edward roared with laughter.

'And rightly so, disgraceful behaviour.' Fanny nodded.

'And they had to pay a fine of fifteen dollars.'

'They must have had plenty of money,' grunted Seamus.

'Better be careful next time you're doing *Pana* down Patrick Street, no kissing.' Edward wagged his finger.

Fanny tut tutted.

'I'm not interested in that stuff,' Seamus said. 'Isn't there a bit of sport itself in the paper?'

'Not much, there's some English race meetings.' Edward read out a couple of reports for Seamus.

'Will you stay up for the throwing of the bread on the door?' asked Fanny.

'I will not, I'm off to my bed soon,' Seamus announced.

'All the family should be together, well, what's left of us. We have to keep the hunger from the door for the next year.'

'That's only a pishogue,' muttered Edward.

'Am I going to be out there in the cold on my own?' Fanny asked.

'All right, I'll go with you,' Edward offered.

Just before the stroke of midnight, they went outside the house and closed the door behind them. It was cold. A large full moon rode high in the sky and illuminated the garden, frost glistening on surfaces. It was quiet, and they waited to hear the bells ring out the old year and ring in the new. The pealing chimes from various churches drifted on the air and were quite beautiful.

Fanny opened the door and went outside. 'We'll let the *old year out* she said, and closed it again. Then she threw a freshly baked loaf of bread at the door. It bounced against it and then fell downwards and rolled some way down the path.

'God keep us from hunger this *new year*, and pray we don't have a lock-out like they have in Dublin.' She bent her head, took her beads from her pocket and blessed herself with the cross. She knelt on the ground, ignoring the cold damp surface of the hard stones digging into her knees. *'In the name of the Father, Son and Holy Ghost,'* she murmured.

'Mother, get up, you'll catch pneumonia,' Edward urged.

She ignored him until she had finished her prayers. 'You should kneel yourself.'

'And ruin my good suit?'

She didn't say anything, just reached for the loaf of bread and pushed herself up. It was never eaten, but she kept one square for the year and gave the rest to the animals. She went into the hall. 'Now we'll welcome in the *new year*.' Then she closed the door and in the kitchen she took the piece of bread from last year to remind herself that they had been lucky enough to get through the year with plenty to eat and good health into the bargain. Although leaving *Fairfields* had been a dark shadow on their lives she prayed nineteen hundred and fourteen would be a better year.

Part 2

1914

Chapter Twenty-three

Meg arrived in Portsmouth in April and seemed to settle immediately, enjoying herself very much helping Anna around the house, and looking after the children. But as the weeks passed she made no move to return home.

'How long more is Meg staying?' Mike asked Anna.

'I don't know.'

'Well, I'm not happy. We have no privacy at all, Anna. We can't really talk to each other unless we're in our bedroom. I can't kiss you or touch you because I'm so conscious of her watching and likely to talk. It's not the way I want to live. I'm only back from Hong Kong for a few months and I love this chance to be together, I could be back there or some other place next year.' He was cross.

'I did think it was just for a short holiday and now it's too awkward to tell her that she isn't welcome to stay any longer.'

'Do you want me to do that?' he demanded.

'No, please don't,' she begged.

'How long will we give her then?'

Anna didn't know what to say. She couldn't insult Meg, and Iris would be very put out if her daughter arrived home and told her that she was asked to leave.

So she stayed on, and as time passed they included her in the navy social life. Afternoon tea with the other wives. Attending parties and concerts. And she took good care of the children if Anna and Mike happened to be out on their own to meet his friends. But he still wasn't happy about her presence and Anna knew it, but felt guilty that she was the one who had welcomed Meg in the first place.

'Johnny has just arrived back. I've invited him around for dinner when we're both free. Is that all right with you?' Mike put his arm around Anna's shoulders in a gentle embrace.

'Of course it is, maybe Johnny and Meg might …' Anna smiled, and kissed him.

'I don't think she'd suit him.'

'Why not, she's attractive.'

'I don't know, I just have a feeling,' he laughed.

'Anyway, I'm looking forward to seeing him, Johnny is a nice person.' Anna continued to chat about him, but didn't mention Meg again. But she could understand how Mike found her presence irritating, sometimes she felt that way herself. Meg fussed. All the time making suggestions about this and that.

'Will I take the children out for a walk?' She had asked this morning.

'If you like, it's quite mild today,' Anna agreed.

'It's not too cold for them, is it? Maybe I'll put on an extra woolly cardigan on Bina.' She did that. But a little later on she took it off again. 'She's too hot now. Look at her face, it's all red.'

Now she was worried about the baby. 'Eleanor hasn't finished her bottle.' She stared down at her, concerned.

'She'll take it gradually. Don't worry, girl.' Anna tried to calm her down.

'I worry she's not getting enough.'

'She's fine.'

'There, she's taken it now, thanks be to God,' Meg sighed with relief.

It was a constant see-saw of concern for Anna who was caught in the middle. She tried to play a careful game but it was like walking a tightrope, and prayed that Meg would decide to return home soon.

The next day she was very surprised when Meg confided that a man had shown interest in her.

'Where did you meet him?'

'At the party your friends invited me to in Southampton. You know, Charles and Edwina.

'Who is he?' Anna was curious.

His name is David ...' Her cheeks blushed pink.

'Is he a Royal Navy man?'

'He wears a uniform, although it's not exactly the same as Mike's.'

'What rank is he?'

'I'm not sure.'

'I remember you danced with one man a couple of times.' Anna couldn't help smiling.

'He's a wonderful dancer, and the nicest person I've ever met.'

'Has he asked you to meet him?'

Meg nodded.

'You never told me?' Anna was surprised.

'I didn't think he would write.'

'When did you receive the letter?'

'This morning,' Meg smiled.

'What day are you going to meet him?'

'On Friday. He's off duty and wants to take me for a walk in the afternoon.'

'Where is he stationed?'

'Southampton.'

'Maybe we should wait until your mother gives permission?' Anna was uncertain.

'My mother will be delighted,' Meg laughed.

'Do you think he's serious?'

'How would I know?' she giggled.

'We'll have to tell Mike.'

Meg was crestfallen.

'He won't mind, don't look so worried.'

'What if he says I can't meet him?'

'He won't.'

'I hope he doesn't.'

'I'll have to tell him,' Anna insisted.

'Sure he won't be here when David calls, he needn't know anything about him.'

'We're responsible for you since you're living here, Meg, so Mike and I must know what you are doing,' Anna tried to explain.

'I'm not a child, I can do what I want,' she flashed, suddenly angry.

'Of course you're not a child,' Anna reassured.

'Don't treat me like one then.'

'I won't, I promise.'

'And don't let Mike treat me like a child either, I'm over age,' she warned.

'No, neither of us will do that.'

Anna didn't mention Meg's plans to meet the man until she was in bed with Mike that night.

'You remember Meg was dancing with a man at Charles and Edwina's party?'

'I didn't notice, and I'm not all that interested …' He gathered her into his arms and held her close to him, his lips softly pressing on hers. Letting her know that he wanted her.

Later, they lay together, and although she felt the time wasn't right she had to bring up the subject again.

'I was saying earlier about Meg …' she began.

'Oh Anna, don't let's bring Meg into the bed with us, it's bad enough for her to be around us the rest of the time, this is the only place we're on our own.' He lay back on the pillows, with an air of exasperation.

'But I have to tell you …'

'What then?' He closed his eyes.

'This man has asked her to walk out with him on Friday.'

'Who is he?'

'He's a naval man.'

He looked at her, a frown on his forehead.

'Did you meet him during the evening?'

'I think I was introduced but I can't remember his name.'

'He's a friend of Charles isn't he?'

'He has to be.'

'Anyway, she is looking forward to meeting him.'

'I'll have to find out more about him, we can't allow her to spend time alone with a complete stranger.'

'I met you and my family didn't know who you were,' Anna smiled.

'I know, but this is different.'

'She is well over twenty-one.'

'I know that,' he sighed. 'But if this man proves to be unreliable then Iris will have my guts for garters,' he smiled ironically.

'If we could just find out who he is, know a bit more about him,' suggested Anna.

'That's not possible by Friday.'

'We'll have to talk to her tomorrow night.'

'There won't be time, I'm meeting Johnny.'

'Why don't I go with her, and we can take the children as well? He only wants to walk with her.'

'That's a good plan. Then you might find out his background.'

'I'll do that, and it will solve the problem for the moment. But I hope she doesn't mind me being there.' Anna wasn't very sure that Meg would agree. 'I'll explain that we only have her best interests at heart, and I'm sure you'll find that he's a really nice chap. Any friend of Charles would have to be, I don't imagine he'd invite anyone around to his house if that person wasn't of good character,' she said.

'You're probably right …but enough about Meg.' He curled his body around hers and his hands touched her gently. 'Maybe she might run off with this man, wouldn't that be great?' he laughed and tickled her ear with his lips.

'There's something else I want to tell you,' she whispered.

'I love you. Did I say that already? Well, I'll say it again …I love you, Anna O'Sullivan. I love you …'

She turned into him, and they kissed deeply, long, slow.

There was no more talk for a while, but before they went to sleep, she took her opportunity. 'Mike?'

'Forget about Meg.'

'It's not about Meg.'

'Tell me tomorrow, my love,' he murmured, sleepy.

'Must tell you now,' she reached towards his ear and whispered.

'What?' He sat up immediately and smiled broadly. 'Another baby?'

She nodded, delighted.

'That's wonderful, when?'

'I think it will be at the end of the year.'

He held her close for a moment. Then he looked at her with concern. 'How are you feeling?'

'I'm fine, and I'm so lucky not to have any sickness, most women are really ill.'

'I hope I'll be here with you when you have our baby, I always worry about you when you're all on your own.' He touched her stomach gently.

'I'll pray you won't be sent too far away.'

'We'll both pray.' He held her close again, and they lay down, their faces close together. 'You've made me the happiest man in the world, my darling.'

'And you've made me the happiest woman …'

Chapter Twenty-four

Mike ordered a pint of beer and sat on a stool. The tavern was packed with naval men and he talked to some that he knew to pass the time as he waited for Johnny who, as usual, arrived late. Then he felt a thump on his shoulder and turned to see his friend standing behind him.

'At last,' he laughed.

'Sorry, got held up.'

'No excuses. Beer?'

'Thanks.' Johnny slid on to a stool.

'How was the day?' Mike asked.

'Rough. I'll be on the *Vivid* for a few weeks, out on exercises in the bay.'

'I'm glad of the time spent ashore,' Mike admitted.

'Anna must be delighted to have you back.'

'It's wonderful to be home, and to get to know the children, and we're going to have another.'

'You're a lucky man.'

'I am,' Mike agreed. 'One of these days you'll be married yourself.'

'Wouldn't be too sure about that, who knows what will happen as a result of the build-up of arms in various countries in Europe. It's worrying.'

'Lloyd George called it organised insanity.'

'Churchill has looked for more money to increase the number of battleships. Germany is doing the same, France and Russia are building up their armies too.'

'And on the home front, there could be civil war between the North and South of Ireland over Home Rule. If that happens that's where we could be posted.' Mike swallowed his beer.

'What about the strikes and lock-outs over union membership, it's happening everywhere. In Dublin, in London, and in South Africa they even shipped the union leaders back to England.'

'Where did that start?' Johnny ordered another two pints from the barman.

'The gold and diamond mines, the men work in terrible conditions and many of the strikers have been killed.'

'We docked in Port Elizabeth at one time, and a group of us went ashore to see the place. A guide took us out into the bush, and we saw the animals roaming freely. It was amazing. I loved the giraffes, they seemed to float along, and through our binoculars we saw a group of elephants, and a couple of rhino at a water hole. We could have joined a shooting party, but we didn't have time. I've often thought since then that it would have been a hell of a trip.'

'Africa is almost completely colonised by Britain, France, Germany, and Portugal …one of these days some of those animals will be extinct there's so many people shooting them and bringing back their trophies,' Mike mused.

'There's a lot of game out there, it's a massive country, that's hardly likely.'

'It's bound to have an effect as more and more Europeans move there to develop the natural resources. That's why there are strikes, many of the mines are run by Europeans and they pay the workers practically nothing.'

'But the Africans need to be brought into the twentieth century, and civilized,' Johnny said.

'Turned into little Britains and Germans while we take over their homeland?'

'That's the way of the world, the civilized nations teach the uncivilized ones. Look at India. Sure we run the country.'

'And they don't like it,' Mike said.

Johnny took a swig of his beer.

'There have been many uprisings across that continent, one of these years it will boil over. There's an Indian lawyer living in South Africa who's the leader of a resistance movement there. He defied the immigration law which meant that Indians have to stay in the province where they are living.'

'What did he do?'

'He led a march of Indians into another province, I think it was the Transvaal, and he was arrested and sent back. He got a sentence of nine months and because of that there were riots and people killed.'

'What's his name?'

'Ghandhi, he's a social activist.' Mike read extensively and was very much aware of what was going on in the world.

'There are riots everywhere protesting against something or other.'

'Times are changing fast.'

'We're getting morose, cheer up.'

'Well, one of the good things about being in the Navy is the chance to see the world. That's what attracted me. My uncle loved the sea and I suppose I picked up some of his enthusiasm, but, before I forget, Anna and I want you to come over for dinner when we are off together, and then you can meet Meg.'

'This woman you're trying to match me with?' Johnny grinned.

'I told Anna I didn't think she would suit you,' Mike admitted. 'But you can meet her as a first step.'

'Is she as beautiful as Anna?'

'She's attractive.'

'That sounds a bit guarded.'

'Good company, pleasant personality. You could do worse, you don't want to be too old when you get married, you'll never keep up with your children. You're the same age as myself, aren't you?'

'There's a year between us, I was born in eighteen hundred and seventy-nine.'

'So Meg could be perfect for you.'

'She sounds too dull.'

'You don't know what she's like, you haven't even met her,' Mike roared with laughter.

'Matchmaker,' Johnny laughed too. 'You're like my mother. She's always on at me.'

'Anyway, Meg is considering walking out with a man she met recently, so you might have lost the race already,' Mike said with a grin.

'That's my luck,' Johnny laughed.

He enjoyed spending time with Johnny, he was good company. But while he joked about matching Meg with Johnny, having her living with them in their home was becoming more and more irritating and he didn't know how long more he could put up with it.

Chapter Twenty-five

Meg checked her reflection in the mirror. 'Do I look all right, Anna?' she asked.

'You look lovely. That new hat is smart.'

'And the colour matches my blue coat so well.'

'The feathers are cute.'

She turned up her collar.'

'Will I wear my garnet brooch?'

'Yes, it will match your leather gloves.'

'Oh, I'm so nervous. What am I going to talk about?'

'We'll all chat and I'm sure he'll have plenty to say.'

'I'm terrified.' Meg twisted her hands, feeling so scared. She hadn't met a man before who invited her to walk out with him and now she wondered should she even have accepted without thinking, which was exactly what she had done. She tried to remember what he looked like. Not so tall, but good looking, with brown hair, and ...what colour were his eyes?'

'Mammy?' Bina stood at the door.

'Yes, my love.'

'Eleanor is crying.'

'I'll have to go down, Meg, are you all right?' Anna asked as she hurried out of the room.

'I'm as good as I'll ever be, girl.' She looked into the mirror once again. Turned left and right, and finally dragged herself away, picked up her gloves and put them on. The last thing was her small leather handbag, and she checked that she had a handkerchief in it and followed

Anna.

'What if he doesn't come?' Meg murmured.

'I'm sure he will, and if he doesn't then you won't want to have anything to do with him.'

Eleanor was quiet now, and Anna put her in the baby carriage.

'All ready now, Bina? We're going for a walk,' she told her.

Meg hoped that Bina wouldn't be too cheeky. Goodness knows what she might say to David.

They stood in the hallway, and she tried not to appear to be too anxious.

'Relax Meg, he'll come, don't worry.' Anna put a hand on hers.

The grandfather clock in the hall chimed the hour and she stared up at the face, her heart beating fast. One. Two. And then silence.

'He's not coming.' She looked at Anna with a sense of dread.

'We're going out.' Bina went towards the front door, and tried to reach for the handle, which thankfully she couldn't do.

At that moment, there was a knock on the door. Meg stood petrified and was unable to move.

'You go into the parlour, I'll bring him in.'

Meg rushed inside, thinking that she shouldn't have been standing in the hall anyway, that would have looked a bit too eager.

Anna opened the door, smiling as she recognised the man standing outside. 'Come in, David, it's nice to meet you again.'

'Thank you.' He shook her hand and stepped inside.

She led the way into the parlour.

'Meg, how are you?' David went towards her, and handed her a bunch of violets.

'I'm fine, David and …thanks for the flowers,' Meg stuttered a little, even more tongue-tied now. 'Please sit down.' She indicated an armchair. 'I'll put these in water.' She hurried into the kitchen.

'We were going for a walk,' Anna said. 'It's a nice day, would you like to join us, David?'

'I'd like that very much,' he said, smiling.

Meg returned and put the glass vase which contained the flowers on the sideboard.

'Bina is anxious to go out, she hasn't an ounce of patience. Tell them they're going somewhere and they want to go immediately,' Anna laughed.

She led the way down the hall followed by Meg and David. 'We're going, we're going.' The little girl danced around.

'This is Bina,' Anna introduced her. 'And Eleanor is asleep.'

'Pleased to meet you, Bina.' David bent down to her level.

She stared at him, solemn.

'Right, let's go.' Anna opened the door and pushed the carriage through it.

'Let me help you.' David lifted it down the steps.

'Thank you.'

'My pleasure.'

'Where are we going?' Bina ran ahead.

'Let's go to the park. Is that all right for you, David? And Meg?' Anna looked at them.

'Yes, that will be lovely,' Meg smiled as he took her arm.

They chatted as they walked along and then Meg and David fell behind a little.

'You don't mind that Anna and the children have come with us?' she asked tentatively.

'Of course not, I didn't think you would be alone, I don't think your mother would approve of that.'

'You're right.'

'You said you lived in Queenstown,' he said.

'Up near the cathedral.'

'I know it well. I've been in and out of Queenstown over the years.'

'I've only been in Dublin a couple of times,' Meg admitted.

'There's always that bit of competition between Cork and Dublin, particularly in sport. I used to play football, but there's not much time these days, I have a busy life, and mentioning that brings me to something I should tell you. There wasn't a chance when we met.' He looked at her, his eyes sincere.

'What is it?'

'I'm a widower.'

'Your wife died? How sad.' Meg was genuinely sympathetic.

'It was indeed.'

'How long has it been?'

'Just over a year.'

And have you a family?'

'Yes, I have five sons.'

Meg was taken aback. Her glowing imagination had painted David as an unmarried man who would fall in love with her at first sight. Now she didn't know what to say, and stared down at the gravelled path in a confused state.

'I'm sorry to tell you this, but I feel it's only right to be honest. It's not something you should discover from someone else.'

'Thank you.'

They continued on in silence following Anna and the children. Then Bina ran back to them. 'Mammy says to come home for tea,' she announced.

Meg was glad. Her mind was in a turmoil. She couldn't get the fact that David was a widower with a family out of her head. Five children. And all boys as well. Her romantic dream had been demolished. She couldn't even look at him, much less meet his blue eyes.

'What do you think, Anna? Should I have anything to do with him. My God, five sons, imagine.' She was shocked.

'It's a lot to take on.'

'Of course he might never propose marriage. I could be imagining that he's interested.'

'But you do like him?'

'Yes, unfortunately,' she sighed.

'Well, just wait and see what happens.' Anna couldn't think of anything else to say.

'He asked me to meet him again when he's off duty.'

'I don't know, Meg, maybe you should ask your Mam. See what she thinks.'

'God only knows, she could be completely against him, or think I should grab him before someone else does.'

'It's not a good idea to marry someone for the sake of just finding a husband.'

'I realise that.'

'Meet him once more, and you'll be able to know how you feel. If it turns into love then you won't mind how many children he has,' Anna advised.

Chapter Twenty-six

The summer weather was changeable. Some days cold and others warm. While Mike had never mentioned that he wanted a son, Anna knew in her heart of hearts that he did. When she told Fanny that she was expecting another child, her mother immediately said that she must be hoping for a boy. And Lizzie couldn't get off the subject, or Iris either.

Meg was always fussing over her, and really Anna was beginning to feel like Mike did. Claustrophobic almost. And once David appeared on the scene it began to look like Meg might never go home.

'Are you sure that you want to walk out formally with David, Meg?' Mike had asked. 'The fact that he has five children isn't a problem?'

'At first it was. But when I thought about looking after Bina and Eleanor I felt I wouldn't mind a few more. And I do like David,' she admitted.

'He is a Navy man, like me, Meg, you won't see that much of him.'

'If Anna can put up with it then I don't see why I can't,' she smiled.

'It's hard, Meg. You'll be living in Dublin and that could be very lonely,' Anna said gently. She knew what lay ahead for her, but didn't want to go into detail as to how it would be. She would find out herself in time.

But as Anna explained to Mike, this might be Meg's last chance to find a husband, and they shouldn't stand in her way. Iris wouldn't be too pleased if they prevented David from proposing marriage. As far as they knew, he hadn't actually asked her to be his wife yet, and if he did, then the final approval would be Iris's responsibility. In the meantime, they made him welcome in their home.

But suddenly there were worrying reports from Europe since Archduke Franz Ferdinand, the heir to the throne of Austria-Hungary and his wife Sophie had been murdered. There was nothing else in the newspapers. Mike didn't say much although Anna did hear him discussing the latest news reports with David, and Johnny one evening. They immediately stopped talking when Anna and Meg came into the room. But that made no difference. They understood everything, and could follow events in Europe in the newspapers as well as any of their men. When Britain declared war on Germany on August fourth, they were shocked and couldn't believe it was happening.

There were posters on every wall encouraging men to join up and fight for king and country. Young men queued up in their droves outside recruiting offices for the army and navy. Newspaper vendors on corners repeated the news at the tops of their voices. People hurried to buy. Opening their papers immediately and reading as they stood there, being pushed aside by others rushing to find out the latest news. A look of consternation on all faces. And very little being said. Bad news travels fast and everyone wants to know about it. It was like someone had been knocked down by a vehicle on the road, and people rushed to stare, all eyes agog with curiosity.

The women were left at home with their children when husbands and sons just disappeared in a matter of days. Trains chugged out of Portsmouth, hundreds of young men waved goodbye, and no one knew when they would see them again. Mike was involved with the training of those raw recruits on ships at the naval dockyards. He was hardly ever home, and when he did arrive he was exhausted.

'They're mostly young fellows and I can't imagine how they'll ever make sailors, pull a rope, navigate, or anything else. And the Admiral wants them ready to head off for action in a matter of weeks.'

'Will you be going too?' Anna asked tentatively.

'I'm sorry to say that it's likely, my love,' he reached for her hand.

'Oh my God ...' She burst into tears.

He came around and put his arm around her. 'There's no point saying otherwise.' He kissed the top of her head.

'Oh Mike ...' she was distraught. The thought of him leaving to go to war swept through her with a terrible sense of foreboding. 'Don't tell me that, I can't bear it.' She turned her face into his warm embrace crying bitter tears, her hands holding on to him like a person drowning.

'I'm sorry, my love.' He held her tight. 'But they do think that it will be all over by Christmas.'

'But how do they know?'

'I'm sure they have their reasons,' he said gently, drying the tears on her face with his fingers.

'Who are they?'

'The government, the military ... the people who make the decisions.'

'I was hoping you wouldn't have to go, so many men have gone and already there have been many killed.'

'I will be safe, my love, don't worry.'

'How can I help it?'

He held her close. 'War is treacherous,' she said. 'And men are stupid to allow their countries to go to war. It's always men.' She was dismissive of the opposite sex.

'You're right, war is always a mistake.'

That night they lay in bed, arms wound around each other. Anna slept fitfully. In a dream state she could hear the sound of guns firing, explosions going off, and worst of all the screams of the injured. That terrible sound of pain woke her up and she knew there would be no one to soothe the injured men. No one to hold a hand, or whisper a few words of comfort before those young boys drifted out of this world. Tears moistened her eyes and she prayed to God to protect Mike and keep him safe. Turning in the bed she looked at him. He was relaxed in a deep sleep. She stretched out her hand, tempted to stroke his face, but resisted that urge. He needed to rest. So busy all the time now.

But he opened his eyes and reached for her.

'Sorry, did I wake you up, my love.' She kissed him.

'I've been awake for a while thinking about you. I hate the thought of leaving you on your own, it's too hard at this time, although Meg will be company for you now.'

'I'll be all right, it's you I'm worried about.'

'Don't, I'll be fine and I'll be back, never fear.' He placed his hand gently on her. Then suddenly he lifted it again. 'I felt the baby move, my goodness, how amazing,' he said, smiling at her. 'I've never felt it so strongly before.' He put his hand on her again.

'He's growing now, and kicking a lot.'

'He?' Mike looked at her quizzically.

'I want it to be a boy, you know that.' She kissed him.

'Don't be worrying about that. A boy or a girl will be equally wonderful. Number three child, how lovely.' He put his arms around her.

In a few weeks he had gone. Sailing to the North Sea to defend Britain against Germany. Already, almost the entire British fleet had sailed into Scapa Flow, a natural harbour surrounded by small islands in the Orkneys. Forty thousand men on huge dreadnoughts, destroyers, and battleships, a most deadly fleet of awe-inspiring ships with massive destructive force. The plan was to respond to the movements of the German fleet based in the Baltic Sea.

Anna followed the news avidly. Friends in the naval quarters passed newspapers one to the other. Sections of articles underlined if there was particular reference to any of the ships their husbands sailed. Then a shock rippled through when they heard that one of the German U-boats, U21, was first to sink a British warship. *HMS Pathfinder* had gone down amid terrible carnage and two hundred and fifty sailors had died. In Scapa Flow, Britain had no defences against this latest threat.

Mike's first letter arrived weeks after his departure, but said very little. She tore it open excitedly, her hands shaking, tears in her eyes almost unable to see his handwriting. But after a few seconds she managed to calm herself down and began to read.

My darling Anna, and my pets Bina and Eleanor,

I think of you all the time and hope that you are all well, especially you, my love. When your time comes I pray that your delivery will not be too hard on you and that our baby will be born safe and well. Write me soon, as I will be looking forward to hearing from you, although the mails are unreliable and it may take time. I have arrived in ---

I look forward to hearing from you soon. All my love, to my own dearest, your Mike. xxxxxx

She was disappointed that those last lines in the letter had been blacked out by the Navy, but understood that this might happen. It was something often discussed by the wives of Naval officers, and there was a lot of resentment about it among them. The women began to feel that they were considered to be spies by the Admiralty and would tell the enemy where their men were operating.

But Anna was thrilled to receive this first letter from Mike, short though it was, and read it over and over, even bringing it to bed and putting it under her pillow.

Chapter Twenty-seven

'Anna?' Meg burst through the front door and hurried down the hallway.

'Is everything all right, Meg?' she asked.

'Yes, everything is wonderful, David has asked me to marry him,' she announced. Her face pink with excitement.

'I'm delighted.' Anna hugged her.

'I can't believe it, we were in the park and he asked me and I said yes and that was it. He kissed me then. Oh, I'm so happy Anna.'

'And when are you going to be married?'

'He'll be sailing to New York and wants us to get married as soon as he gets back.'

'That's very fast, Meg.'

'I don't mind, I like him so much, Anna, you know what it's like. I suppose I love him ...that's the way I feel.'

'You'll have to ask your Mam.'

'I'm going to write a letter immediately, and David will do the same.' She looked at Anna, a worried expression on her face. 'Do you think she might disapprove?'

'She knows you're walking out, then she must expect that he might propose. Are you sure about him?'

'Of course.' She tossed her head.

'You're not just marrying him for the sake of getting a husband, girl, are you?' Anna wanted to impress her concern on Meg.

'No, I told you I love him, and he is so nice. You like him, don't you?'

'Of course I do, but I'm still concerned that he has five children.'

123

'I've got used to the idea of that now.'

'And I'm sure they're lovely boys.'

'How well did you know Mike when you married him?' Meg asked, a hint of accusation in her voice.

'Not that well, I suppose, but Lizzie knew him and his family.'

'Well, I've accepted him, I love him and I know what I'm doing,' Meg was adamant.

Iris's reply to Meg's letter arrived a few days later. As she read it, the expression on her face became increasingly apprehensive.

'What is it?' Anna asked.

'Mam isn't very happy, and is coming over as soon as she can.'

Anna didn't know what to say.

'What if she doesn't allow me to marry David?' Meg asked.

'That could happen.'

'I don't care what she says, I'm over age,' Meg said.

'You don't want to fall out with your mother, you know how I was barred from home by Pa and Edward for a long time, and that was awful.'

'But you did what you wanted to do because you loved Mike, and all their disapproval didn't mean a whit to you.'

'That's true.'

'Well, I'm going to do the same.'

'There were a lot of arguments when I first mentioned Mike.'

'I'll just have to face that.'

Chapter twenty-eight

Mike's ship, the battleship *HMS Erin* forged through the heavy troughs of water. Grey green waves battered the metal hull and broke in white cascades of water which rushed over the deck and drained off into the sea again only to be replaced by another and another. Mike stared out through the glass windows of the bridge, which were obscured by the heavy rain which pelted down. He held his spyglass to his eye but could see little through it. Then he went to the table where the sub lieutenant worked on navigation calculating their distance back to Scapa Flow.

'How long do you estimate?' Mike asked.

'Twenty nautical miles, sir,' he said, taking a reading from the charts. 'It will be tomorrow in these seas by the time we arrive. That's if the weather doesn't get any worse.'

Sailing in such heavy weather was always a worry. Only a few weeks before a trawler had spotted a German U Boat near Scapa Flow and since then everyone was very concerned that the Germans had managed to penetrate what they considered to be a very safe harbour. Now efforts were being made to prevent the Germans making any further incursions and the Navy were in the process of defending the area by installing underwater nets at entrances and old ships were sunk to prevent access at shallow points.

Mike knew the danger that he and all his shipmates were in. If he was still a single man he didn't think that he would have been so concerned, but now he was married that made a huge difference. He had responsibilities. Anna and the children depended on him for everything. He had to come home for them. He thought of other sailors who had already been killed and how their grieving families would manage to deal with their loss. For Anna to be left alone without him would be heartbreaking for her. But even living in Portsmouth could possibly be dangerous as he wasn't sure what turn the war would take and had begun to think that perhaps she should go home to Cork with the children after the new baby was born.

He decided to write a quick letter when he had a chance later and put that suggestion to her. Although knowing her stubborn nature she would undoubtedly resist, wanting to stay in Portsmouth in case he came home on leave. But as things were developing even that possibility seemed unlikely. If he was granted leave then it wouldn't get him as far as Portsmouth. And it would take time for his letter to arrive. The mail bags were sent in to an office ship at Scapa Pier and then forwarded on by road and train until eventually they were delivered to the naval base in Portsmouth.

He was on duty again at five in the morning, and they signalled the patrol vessel *HMS Duke of Albany*. Over an hour later they passed the outer boom and came to with starboard anchor. The collier and the oiler came alongside and they took on fifteen hundred tons of coal until the bunkers were full, and oil supplies as well. Young naval apprentices on board hosed down the ship, cleaned and scrubbed. Some personnel were discharged and others joined ship.

It was later that night when suddenly there was a huge detonation in the distance and all hands rushed to their positions in response. A ship had exploded. A great orange ball illuminated the night sky and a shower of metal thundered into the sea all around them. The smell of burning carried on the wind was caustic. Immediately, they were ordered to lower boats, and the sailors rowed towards the flaming ship which had already begun to sink. Mike directed operations and they moved through the heaving seas searching for survivors. But sadly at first there seemed to be only dead mutilated bodies which had been sucked down into the green depths and floated back up in the waves, their pale white limbs stretching towards them for help. Here and there they spotted a few sailors who managed to raise an arm to attract their attention and the men hauled them in and wrapped them in blankets. They did what they could for the unfortunate men, but the wounds and burns were terrible, and all they could do was bring them to a hospital ship which had sailed into the area.

For Mike, these times were very difficult, always dreading that moment when he would see the face of someone he knew. Now he doubted that there would be many survivors and wondered if it was a mine which had caused the explosion, or a torpedo, and the resultant concern of all the men on board was that the Germans had managed to get through their defences.

Mike worked four hours on, four hours off, unless they were in action at sea. Then it was all hands on deck. Every man and boy at his station, facing into the icy stinging wind which cut viciously. Winter was something they had to endure. They proceeded out of harbour again, sounded every half an hour, and ran out three hundred fathoms of wire, finding the bottom of the sea at eighty-three fathoms. Marching along the deck, he pounded one hand in its leather glove into the palm of the other in an effort to keep the blood flowing. The weather was still bad although later he grabbed a couple of hours sleep but it was difficult to even stay in his bunk or sleep as the wind got up.

He was worried about the progress of the war. Newspapers came with the post, and men were able to follow daily reports about the terrible carnage in France and Flanders. How long this war would continue was a question which nobody could answer.

It was blowing very hard north westward. Mike noted where they were at this point. The wind was force nine-eleven, the seas eight-nine. By the afternoon, the storm had strengthened. The seas were mountainous. The galley and starboard life-buoys were washed overboard, and other equipment followed. Later the waves were almost forty feet and it was the duty of every man on board to try and save the stores. They fought hard but it was after midnight before the storm eased. Everyone was exhausted but there was no rest that night. By morning they altered course and headed back towards *The Flow* accompanied by other ships as they went.

The next couple of days were spent getting in new stores, and Mike and some of the other officers and men were given leave to go on shore. It was such a relief to be on dry land, and to forget the fear of enemy attack for a short while. The island Flotta was the main British naval base, and where the men were able to find some recreation. This evening there was a number of boxing matches organised, and all the men crowded into the large hut to see those representing their own ship punch their way into oblivion. One of the engineers on board *HMS Erin* was fighting and Mike pushed in with the other men from his ship to get as close as he could to the ring. It was a great night of excitement particularly when their man won his match and they carried him shoulder high in celebration.

That night Mike wrote again to Anna. When they were at sea his letters were by necessity quickly dashed off and there wasn't much opportunity to think of what he might say, but now he had time and was able to write more than usual. Still, he was very aware that letters were read by the censor, and took care not to write anything which would indicate where he was or what was happening around him. Still, it was good to express in his own words how much he loved and missed her and the children, and let her know that he was still alive.

Chapter Twenty-nine

Meg stood on the quayside at Portsmouth watching her mother make her way down the gangplank of the ship. She rushed towards her, arms open wide in embrace.

'Oh what a journey.' Iris hugged her daughter. 'I was lucky to survive.'

'Come on home and we'll warm you up.' Meg took her bags and waved to a cabbie, who helped them up into his cab.

'I'm exhausted.' Iris leaned against the back of the seat, her face pale.

'You poor thing.'

'I could go straight to bed.'

'You can if you want, everything is ready. You're in Anna's room, and she will sleep with me.'

'I don't want to put her out,' Iris immediately objected.

'It's fine, we want you to be comfortable.'

'Thank you, I'm very grateful.'

Meg held her hand and smiled. 'It's so good to see you, I've missed you.'

Iris went to bed for a few hours, and then came down. 'You've a lovely home, Anna, although I'm sorry the children have gone to bed. I was looking forward to spending some time with them.'

'You'll see them tomorrow.'

'I asked Fanny and Lizzie to come with me but neither of them could manage.'

'How is Mam?' asked Anna.

'I was out at *Rose Cottage* last week and they're all grand out there. Have you any news of Mike?'

'I had a letter a couple of weeks ago, but the post takes a long time,' Anna said.

'This war is dreadful, and there are so many men being killed, it's …' Iris stopped speaking. There was a sudden air of tension. She looked at Anna whose eyes had filled up with tears. 'I'm sorry, girl, I didn't mean to say that, I shouldn't have …'

'It's all right,' Anna dabbed her eyes.

'Nothing will happen to Mike, he's going to be fine,' Meg insisted.

'I'm sure he will …' Iris agreed. 'Now …tell me all about this David fellow you've met,' she asked her.

'He's really nice, Mam, I'm very fond of him,' Meg said earnestly, anxious for her mother to understand how serious she was.

'When are we going to meet him?'

'He's going to call tomorrow, isn't that right, Meg?' Anna intervened.

'Does he know I'm going to be here?' Iris interjected, her eyes turning on Meg with a sharp piercing look.

'Yes, I told him. He was going to write to you anyway.'

'Look Meg, is he serious, this man, or does he just want you as a mother for his children?'

'He loves me, Mam.'

Iris raised her eyes up to heaven. 'Love,' she murmured. 'And how do you feel about him, Meg?'

'I love him too.'

'And Anna, what about you?' Iris asked.

'He's a very nice man, we've got to know him quite well.'

'I don't know what to think, but I'll have to meet him before I decide, you do understand that, Meg?'

'Of course.'

'Has he actually proposed to you yet?'

'I told you he has.' A flash of irritation passed across Meg's features. She was on the defensive now and hated that. 'I'm sorry Mam, but it all happened so quickly he didn't think, and neither did I.'

Tension permeated the room, like someone had blown up a balloon until it was too full of air and about to burst at any second.

Anna welcomed David the following afternoon. 'Meg's mother has arrived,' she whispered.

'I'm looking forward to meeting her.' His eyes twinkled as he smiled. 'I brought presents.'

'They'll both be delighted I'm sure.' Anna took his hat and coat and hung them on the hallstand. Then she led the way into the parlour.

'This is David Bradley ...' she announced. 'David, I'd like you to meet Meg's mother, Mrs. Lynch.'

He walked into the room and shook hands with her.

'It's a pleasure to meet you.' Then he turned to Meg, and handed her the present he had brought. 'This is for you, Meg, and for you, Mrs. Lynch.'

'Thank you so much, David,' Iris smiled, obviously pleased.

The conversation was awkward at first, but Iris didn't delay asking David what his intentions were.

'I want to ask you for Meg's hand in marriage.'

Meg stiffened, praying that her mother wouldn't refuse. She glanced at Anna's face and could see that she was terrified of that happening as well.

There was a frown on Iris's forehead. 'What have you got to offer my daughter?' Her voice was sharp.

'I love Meg, and I'll take good care of her. I have a house in Dublin which is comfortable and I hope she'll be happy with me and the children,' he said with a smile. He spoke softly.

'And you have five boys I believe?'

'Yes.'

'She'll have her work cut out for her,' Iris murmured.

'I hope it won't be too hard.'

'You're at sea, and away quite a lot?'

'Unfortunately that is my job. Presently the shipping company is based in Southampton and there isn't always the time to get to see my family. But I am hoping to change to a Dublin based company at some point in the future so it means I will be home more often.'

'If Meg marries you, she doesn't realise how difficult her life would be, although her cousin knows all about it,' Iris said pointedly.

Anna moved in her chair, feeling uncomfortable. There was truth in that remark she had to admit.

'Well, Mr. Bradley, I'll have to reflect on this situation.' Iris looked straight at him and her expression clearly indicated that it was the end of the interview.

'But Mam, won't you please?' Meg exclaimed.

'Meg.' Iris cut sharply across her daughter's words, and she was forced into silence.

David stood up. 'Thank you for considering my request, I look forward to hearing from you when you have made your decision.' He made a slight bow.

'Write to me with a detailed description of your proposal,' Iris said sharply.

Anna stood up as did Meg.

'I will certainly do that. It's been a pleasure to meet you, Mrs. Lynch.' He shook hands with her.

Anna opened the door and the three of them walked into the hall.

'Why is she doing this?' Meg said furiously, tears in her eyes.

Anna didn't know what to say.

'Meg.' David turned to her. 'Don't be so upset, your mother is just protecting your interest in the absence of your father.'

Meg snuffled into her handkerchief.

'I'll write immediately. How long is your mother staying?' he asked Meg.

'Probably another week.'

She took his coat and hat off the hallstand and handed them to him. He stood at the door.

'May I address the letter here?' he asked.

'Yes, do that,' Meg said immediately.

'Of course you can, that would be the quickest,' Anna agreed. 'I'll say goodbye now, David, I hope we'll see you soon,' she said and went back to Iris, leaving Meg and David together.

'I must say you've entertained me royally,' Iris said with a wide smile.

'It's been wonderful to have you, I only wish Mam had been able to come as well,' Anna said.

'You'd never shift Fanny away, sure who'd look after Seamus and Edward, you don't think they could do for themselves?' Iris retorted. 'The pair of them are useless, not worth tuppence around the house.'

'But have you decided about me and David?' Meg asked hesitantly, knowing that his letter had arrived a few days before.

'Yes, I have.' Iris folded her arms.

'And?' Meg's eyes were wide.

'I think he's a very nice gentleman and he seems comfortably off. I think he'll make a suitable husband for you,' she smiled unexpectedly.

Meg jumped up with a scream, and threw her arms around her mother. 'Thank you Mam, thank you.'

'Congratulations Meg,' Anna said, and kissed her.

'I'll have to write to David immediately, although I don't know when he'll get the letter.'

'Don't worry, I've already done so. The address of his shipping company was on the letter he wrote to me.'

'I can't believe this, it's like a miracle,' Meg was astounded.

'So when does David want to get married?'

'Soon ...'

'It can't be too soon, we'll have to arrange your trousseau. And you'll have to come home, you can't be staying here before you're married.'

'You want me to be married at home?' Meg seemed shocked.

'Yes I do.'

'I hope that suits David.'

'Well, he'll have to put up with it, girl, they're my conditions. I'm travelling tomorrow and I want you to come with me, we'll go down to the shipping office and arrange a ticket for you.'

'But I'd like to see David before I leave, explain what is happening.'

'I told you I wrote to him.'

'But there are details …'

'Men don't need to know the details,' she snapped.

'And Anna's going to have her baby, she can't be on her own.'

Iris was suddenly taken aback. 'Oh, yes …'

'I'll be all right, Meg, don't worry,' Anna tried to reassure her.

'No, I'm not leaving you at this time, what if you go into labour in the middle of the night, who's going to run for the midwife?'

There was a moment of consternation between them.

'All right then, but you have to come home as soon as Anna has the baby and is feeling better.'

'Why can't I get married here? It would be so much more convenient,' Meg suggested.

'You have to be married in your own parish.' There was no moving Iris from her point of view.

'That means we can't set a date yet.' Meg was put out.

'What is the hurry?'

'There's no hurry, Mam.'

'Well then?'

'I love David and I want to be with him.'

'You will be with him, you'll be his wife, and stepmother to all those children, although why you want to take on such a big family is beyond me.' She raised her eyes up, incredulous.

'I can't wait.' Meg was excited. 'I'm going to be Mrs. Bradley.'

Anna and Meg began to make plans.

'I'm sorry I can't go shopping with you. I wish I could. But with the baby coming so soon I couldn't walk around comfortably. And it would have been so nice to help you choose your trousseau. There are some lovely things in the shops here.'

'Mam's already said I must have my wedding dress made by Mrs.

Murphy at home. She's going to look for material and discuss it with her as soon as she gets home. I probably won't have anything to do with it, God knows what it's going to look like. It will be all Mother's taste. Imagine. Something out of the ark. Ancient,' Meg screamed with laughter.

'I'm sure it won't be as bad as all that. There will be time for you to choose what you want for yourself.'

'I hope so, or else I'm going to look a fright.'

'You won't, you're going to look wonderful.'

'I hope so.'

'Clothes won't matter to David.'

'Do you really think so, Anna?'

'Of course I do. You're very lucky, he's a lovely man.'

'I am, yes I am,' Meg squealed.

'And you're going to be very happy, I know it.'

'I can't wait. Is it amazing to be married, Anna?' Meg asked shyly.

'Yes it is,' Anna smiled at her.

'Do you enjoy sleeping with Mike?'

'I do …' Anna's cheeks flamed. She seemed embarrassed.

'Tell me what happens,' Meg insisted. Anna was the only person she could talk to like this.

'It's a bit difficult to explain,' Anna was hesitant.

'But how am I going to know?' Meg threw her hands in the air, feeling frustrated. The whole area of marriage was a mystery to her.

'It will all happen quite naturally, it doesn't need an explanation,' Anna said gently.

'Oh …'

'And David will show you.'

'I don't want to be ignorant about it all on my wedding night. What will he think?'

'Men don't like women who know too much.'

'Who told you that? Was it Mike?'

'He didn't exactly say, well, not in so many words …but anyway you don't have to worry about it now, just enjoy looking forward to the biggest day in your life,' Anna reminded. 'It's going to be wonderful.'

Chapter Thirty

It was some time later the following night when Anna felt the first stab of pain, and stifled her involuntary cry. She didn't want to disturb Meg and the children at this stage, knowing from her previous experience that there would be hours of pain before the baby was finally born. She lay back on the pillows and prepared for another pain. On Eleanor, there were long periods of inactivity during which she almost fell asleep and expected things to be much the same this time.

But the pain came very quickly. And a rush of water. It was a sign. It wouldn't be long now. She knew then that there was something different about this baby, he or she wanted out and wasn't going to delay. She pushed herself up and sat on the side of the bed, pulling her dressing gown around herself, reluctant to wake Meg just yet. Her teeth bit into her lower lip as pain whipped through her. If only Mike was here, if only …

A little later, there was a gentle knock on her door.

'Anna? Are you all right,' Meg called from outside.

Anna whimpered, caught in the midst of her agony.

The door opened and Meg appeared. 'Has it started?'

Anna nodded.

'You poor thing. I'll run for the midwife. Can I get you anything before I go?'

'No thanks.'

'I've looked in on the children and they're both asleep. Are you comfortable sitting there, shouldn't you lie down on the bed?'

Anna couldn't say anything. But did as Meg suggested.

'Let me pull the bedclothes up around you, keep you warm.' She drew the blankets and quilt over her gently. 'I'll run as fast as I can for Mrs. Dulcie.' She disappeared.

Sweat gathered on Anna's body as she rolled about on the bed. The pains were whipping through her now, hardly any distance between them. It was just one long pain, and she found it hard to prevent herself from screaming out loud for Mike, her mother and Meg too hoping that she would come back soon with Mrs. Dulcie, the midwife. She didn't want to disturb the children, and pressed her hand over her mouth to stifle her cries, hoping they wouldn't hear her.

She lost track of time, and was only vaguely aware of the sound of footsteps on the stairs and Meg rushing in followed by Mrs. Dulcie. The midwife immediately took over, instructing Meg to boil water and get some towels.

'Your baby is almost here, Anna.' She examined her. 'I can see the head. Now it will only take a few minutes before it's born. So breathe deeply and push.'

'You have a lovely baby girl.' Mrs. Dulcie lifted the child and cleaned her. When Anna heard the little cry of the new born child tears filled her eyes, sheer happiness swept through her but there was disappointment too that she hadn't had a boy. But once she saw the baby all those thoughts left her mind.

'She's a beautiful little thing, she'll thrive well.' The woman put the child in her arms.

Anna smiled. 'Thank you for coming so quickly, Mrs. Dulcie.'

'I'm always ready.'

'She's beautiful,' Meg whispered. 'I love her already.'

'Are the children still asleep?' Anna asked.

'Yes, not a peep out of them.'

'Thank God, I was so afraid they would wake and come in, particularly Bina. How did you even hear me?'

'I left my door open and tried not to sleep too much, I must have sensed it would happen soon.'

'Let's freshen you up, Anna ...' the midwife said.

She felt much better a little later when the bedclothes were changed, and she lay there clad in a clean nightgown, cuddling the baby.

'I'll get out one of the little white embroidered baby dresses Aunt Fanny made and put it on her later,' Meg said. 'She's such a pretty baby. What name will you give her?'

'I think it will be Catherine, it's Mam's second name. She was really happy when I mentioned it. We'll have to wait until next time for another Michael.'

'And it will be a boy, bound to be,' Meg reassured, putting her finger into the baby's hand. 'You have such a grip little girl,' she laughed. 'She's a strong one, Anna, and a beautiful little pet.'

'Meg, come over if you need me.' Mrs. Dulcie put on her coat, and picked up her medical bag. 'Anna, I'll call tomorrow anyway to see you.'

Meg took her downstairs, and returned a little later holding Bina's hand and carrying Eleanor in her arms.

'Here we are now.' She came close to the bed. 'Would you like to see your new sister?'

Eleanor wriggled out of Meg's arms and she put her down beside Anna.

'Look at the little baby, Eleanor, isn't she pretty?'

Eleanor stared at her silently.

Bina stood at the other side of the bed. 'She's very small.'

'She's your sister, but she'll grow much bigger soon and you'll be able to play with her.'

'I don't like her,' Bina said, sulky. 'Can I get into the bed with you?'

'There's not much room,' Anna said, but then changed her mind. 'Of course you can, come up on the other side.'

Meg helped her up. 'Anna, you really should be sleeping,' she advised. 'But I'll make you a nice cup of tea and some fresh bread and butter, or would you like anything else?'

'That sounds lovely, Meg, thank you so much.' Anna leaned back on the pillows. She did feel exhausted now, but wanted to stay awake for the children's sake.

Meg went downstairs.

'What's her name?' Bina asked.

'Catherine.'

'That's very long.'

'Will we make it shorter?'

'Yes.' She nodded her head vigorously.

'How about Cathy?'

'Cathy,' she repeated.

'You like that?'

'Yes, but I don't like her.' She pointed at the baby.

'Why not?'

'Her face is all red.'

'She's a bit warm.'

'Take her out.'

'It's a bit soon for that, but we'll take her out in the baby carriage when she's a bit bigger.'

'I'll get it.' She climbed down.

'No, Bina, she's too small to go out now.'

'But I want to,' she said, petulant.

'I told you she's too small yet.'

'Why don't we have a bath and dress, Bina?' Meg asked, coming in the door. She took her hand and helped her off the bed.

'No, don't want.'

'Come on,' she coaxed.

'No.'

'Then why don't we have breakfast first?' she tried to persuade her.

'Can I have jam?'

'Of course you can.'

'Thanks,' Anna smiled.

'I'll bring up yours now.'

140

Anna was lonely. Her days were long and filled with thoughts of the war. It was all everyone talked about. And the women in the other houses had a stark look of loss in their eyes as they went about the day.

Anna felt the same as all of them. She understood exactly what was going on underneath their skin. Always on the verge of tears. Longing so much to see Mike, particularly as Christmas was coming up. To see his dark eyes gaze into hers telling her how much he missed her. His hands touching her face gently. Drawing her closer to him. His lips exploring hers reminding that he still loved her. That was all she wanted. To know that.

But alongside those feelings was the fear that he wouldn't ever come home. That she would never see him again. In her dreams there was always a knock on the door. Rushing towards it in dread of who she would meet on the doorstep. Her heart almost stopping as she saw the officers outside. They usually sent more than one to impart bad news to the families who lived in the naval quarters. Terror was there all the time.

When she played with the children she saw his likeness in all of them. In the little smiling faces. They were him. And the realisation that she couldn't live without him was something she was unable to avoid.

She lifted Eleanor up and held her close, walking slowly to the window where she stood forlorn, looking out over the sea which was grey and wintry under a cloudy sky with only occasional glimpses of blue. The child pointed, her face animated. Anna followed her gaze to see an officer stride past, his uniform similar to that worn by Mike. For a second, Anna, like the child, thought it might be he. But instantly her sensible side told her that it was impossible. He was somewhere in the North Sea. His ship being battered by monstrous waves. His eyes stinging from the spray. Hands stiff with the cold. She was reminded of the shipwreck of *The Prairie Flower* on which she had travelled from Cork to escape marriage with John Hobbs, and shivered at the recollection of being swept into the sea and struggling in the bulky life jacket until Mike swam from the yacht to save her.

'No, love, it's not Daddy.'

Eleanor bent her head into Anna's shoulder and cried.

'Don't worry, he'll be home soon,' she whispered. While she comforted her children, they comforted her with their innocence.

Later she and Meg decided to walk along the sea front, pushing the baby carriage with the two younger children in it, Bina running on ahead of them. It was windy but she felt refreshed as she pushed against the breeze. The clouds had rolled away. The expanse of the sea stretched out to the horizon, the arc of the blue sky was vast and she was taken across that space to Ireland. To Cork. Home. Suddenly needing Fanny's arms around her.

'We'll have a quiet Christmas ourselves,' Meg said to Anna.

'I should be back to normal by then. I'm getting stronger every day.'

'And little Cathy is growing bigger and bigger. She's a darling.' Meg squeezed her cheeks and she smiled and gurgled. 'I'm envious of you, Anna, with your daughters.'

'But you'll have five sons.'

'I'm scared about that. What if they don't like me?' Meg looked worried.

'Of course they will like you. Sure they're only young.'

'Maybe the smaller ones, but the bigger have their own minds. They could just ignore me, and refuse to do what I say. The worst thing is that I won't know anyone up there.'

'Are you having second thoughts about getting married?' Anna asked, concerned.

'Not really, I love David, it's just being so far away from home on my own.'

'Cork to Dublin isn't as far as here.'

'No, but still …'

'You can visit, and your mother can go up to you on the train.'

'I suppose.'

Meg was quiet for a few seconds, but then brightened up. 'Mam sent me a drawing of the dress Mrs. Murphy is going to make.' She handed Anna the piece of paper. 'What do you think?'

'It's very nice. You're going to look beautiful.'

'I suppose it's not that bad.'

'At least it's already started and that means there will be no delay.'

'You're right. Really I don't care much about the way the dress is made, it's just …I hope David will think I look all right.'

'You will look lovely. It's your special day and the best in your life.'

'Do you always remember your wedding day?'

Anna nodded.

'And I'm looking forward to having a baby too.'

'It will happen.'

'I'd love girls like you.'

'You have your five boys already.' Anna tried to cheer her up.

There was the sound of a baby crying.

'That's Cathy.'

Meg ran upstairs and brought her down. 'Poor thing,' she cuddled her. 'She's hungry.'

'Give her to me,' Anna smiled wryly, and began to feed her.

'I wish I was you,' Meg said enviously.

'It's all ahead of you.'

'I'm looking forward to it, but I wish we were getting married tomorrow. I hate the thought of going home, I won't see David at all before we get married,' Meg was morose.

'The time will fly once we're into the New Year. In one way I don't want to go home either. If Mike is granted leave then I want to be here.'

The week before Christmas terrible news whipped through the naval community. Scarborough had been attacked by German battle cruisers. They fired on the town as they steamed across South Bay. The hotel was hit, the town hall partially damaged, and houses too. Whitby was also attacked, and in Hartlepool the gasworks exploded. Over a hundred men, women and children died, and five hundred were injured.

Anna and Meg were distraught.

'We could be killed ourselves,' Anna whispered. 'The Germans might arrive here and take over.'

'No, that will never happen.' Meg shook her head defiantly.

'All our soldiers are at the front, there's no-one left here to defend us.' Tears filled Anna's eyes.

'Our Navy will do that.'

'How was it that the German ships managed to get through?'

'I don't know, but I'm sure it won't happen again. Our ships will guard us.'

'Mike will be even more anxious for us to go home since this attack. But it will have to be after Christmas.'

'I hope David will be back by then, I really want to see him.'

'I'm sure he will be.'

'We can't let the children see how worried we are.'

They hid their misgivings, and managed to enjoy the Christmas parties which were held by the Navy wives for the children.

Then a large parcel arrived from Fanny containing a goose, Christmas pudding, and presents for both of them and the children. The following day, another arrived from Iris. It kept them going and ensured that they had plenty for Christmas. For the children's sake, they made the very best of it.

Chapter Thirty-one

Christmas on board ship in the Royal Navy was a light duty day for crews if possible. But for Mike *HMS Erin* was on the Northern Patrol line between Britain and Greenland. Their duty was to protect British trade while checking merchant shipping to ascertain what they were carrying in their holds and whether it was bound for Germany.

The mess decks on the ship had been decorated with coloured paper, and the sailors put up photographs of their families just to remind them of home. There was a church service by the chaplains, and an extra tot of rum for every man on board. The chefs worked overtime to make sure everyone was fed a good Christmas dinner, the men being served by the officers. There was much regret among them that they had no piano on the ship. As the squadrons and flotillas had sailed towards Scapa Flow at the beginning of the war, orders were given to throw overboard any fixtures and fittings which were extraneous and inflammable in the event of a major battle with the Germans. But as time passed without that happening, many of the ships replaced the items, but on *HMS Erin*, they still remained without a piano. Regardless, the messes and wardrooms held sing songs, told stories and jokes, and generally the men enjoyed themselves.

Mike went along with the usual celebrations for the sailors, but was aware that there was a plan to launch Royal Naval Air Service aircraft from three seaplane carriers to bomb the Zeppelin sheds at Cuxhaven in Germany over Christmas. He and his colleagues all had the same look in their eyes as they waited for news.

The Admiralty were very concerned about the German airships and it was hoped that this first attack from the sea would at least succeed in destroying some of the Zeppelins. When on land they had to be stored in large sheds because of the effect of the wind on the airships, but regrettably the raid was not successful and did little damage. But the experience made the Admiralty realise that much larger aircraft were needed which could carry a greater payload of bombs.

The weather was cold but the seas were calm. *HMS Erin* patrolled. It was what they did every day. Patrolled. Mostly finding nothing. When he had first been stationed here, he had wanted to fight. Every sailor on the ships in Scapa Flow was enthusiastic about fighting the Germans. This was what they trained for. To destroy the enemy with their superior strength. But with the exception of searching for mines and stopping merchant shipping the men of the fleet remained in their ships. The Germans made brief incursions into the North Sea but usually returned to their ports in Germany without having made much contact with the Royal Naval ships.

Mike was frustrated with the level of inactivity, as were most of the crew. It was strange. He would have given anything to meet the enemy face to face. To feel he was doing something to hasten the end of the war and allow him to go home to Anna and the children.

1915

Chapter Thirty-two

Fanny finished what she was doing, and went out into the garden, finding her granddaughter pushing herself back and forward on the swing.

'Give me a shove, Granny,' Bina called out.

'In a minute.' Fanny picked up a bucket and filled it in the water barrel.

'Go on, Granny, please?' Bina begged.

Fanny went over and stood behind her, gripped the ropes and pushed them away, the wooden seat with Bina astride flying up into the air.

She yelled out loud and threw her head back, her long plaits swinging as she gripped the ropes. Her legs in their black stockings stretched out, her blue skirt billowed up, white frilled petticoat visible.

Fanny pushed a few more times but then ran out of energy. 'That's it,' she said, and the swing slowly lost momentum. 'Are you going to ride Daisy?' she asked.

'Yes,' Bina cried out, excited.

'Come along then, we'll ask Grandad to saddle her, and he will take you.'

Bina jumped down from the swing and went with her, holding tight on to Fanny's work hardened palm.

Seamus helped Bina up on to Daisy's back, and she settled herself in the saddle, gently holding the reins. The horse slowly walked around the field, Seamus holding on to Bina, and Fanny following.

'Can we go outside?' Bina asked.

'No, love.'

I want to.' She patted the horse's neck. 'Daisy wants to.'

'Just ride around the field once and then it will be time for tea …' she said.

'When will Mammy come?'

'Soon love, soon, she's in town.'

'When will the war be over?'

'Nobody knows.'

'I'm afraid of it.'

They continued on, in silence now.

Bina giggled. 'I love to go fast.' She moved up and down on the back of the horse.

'*Stad é sin,*' Seamus said, slipping into Irish. He held on to the reins pulling her back a little. Then drew the horse to a stop, and lifted her down. 'We'll give Daisy a good rub, she needs it.'

'Don't be long, I'll wet the tea.' Fanny left them then. She wasn't very sure about Bina learning to ride and was always worried about her falling off the horse. But it was very hard to say no to the child. So like Anna who had insisted on riding at just about the same age, and never had a moment's fear of anything. But being responsible for her daughter was a very different thing to being responsible for her granddaughter and she worried for her every time she was out of her sight.

The man and the child took the horse into the stable, and Bina immediately began to brush Daisy's coat.

'I'll do her back and you do the rest of her. You won't be able to reach much further.' The man turned to smile at the small child, sharing the love they both had for the horses.

Fanny loved Bina. To have her daughter and her three children living with them in *Rose Cottage* made each day wonderful. Her life had suddenly become so rounded and perfect she could hardly believe it was actually happening. It was as if she had been thrown back in time. To when Anna was a child. Now she had her back. Her darling daughter. Their lives were altered by her very presence. Even Seamus seemed happier. The row between Anna and her father which had erupted when she refused to marry John Hobbs had been forgotten. Fanny could see that he loved Anna like he always did. They had been so close, both loving the animals in *Fairfields,* particularly the horses. Edward didn't say much to Anna and Fanny wondered if he had forgiven his sister.

There was a new sensation at *Rose Cottage*. Days of joy. And all because Anna had come home.

Chapter Thirty-three

Meg raised her arms and twirled around. The hem of the white wedding dress rippled around her and settled in a floating pool on the multi-coloured rug on which she stood.

'It's lovely,' Anna admired.

'Do you really think so?' Meg was uncertain, looking at herself from every angle.

'Yes I do, it's simple, and the white satin flows beautifully.'

'I have to say I like the three flounces in the skirt. Mam has surprised me, I don't know where she got her ideas,' Meg said.

'I'm sure Mrs. Murphy had magazines, and made some suggestions.'

'She must have.'

'Are you happy?'

'Yes, I am, if you like it.'

'I told you I do. And I particularly like the lace panels in the bodice, and the wide belt.'

'Will you put on the veil for me, please?'

Anna placed the headdress of white flowers on Meg's head and the fine veil with the lace border floated to the ground. 'There you are. You will be beautiful on your wedding day.'

Meg turned to look into the cheval mirror, and took a deep breath. 'You really think so?'

'I know so.'

'It's only one week away. I can't believe it,' Meg whispered.

The door opened and Iris came in. 'You're looking lovely, Meg, I never thought I'd see the day.' She burst into tears.

'Thanks Mam.' She embraced her mother.

'Are your shoes comfortable?' Anna asked.

'They're a bit tight.' She wriggled a foot clad in white satin.

'I'm in the middle of icing the cake, I'll get on with that.' Iris disappeared.

'I hope the shoes don't pinch, you'll be standing a lot.' Anna was concerned.

'I'll wear them beforehand, and ease them in. Now it's your turn.' Meg lifted Anna's gown, and held it out towards her. 'Isn't it beautiful?'

'It's gorgeous, if I ever want anything made I'm coming back to your Mrs. Murphy.' Anna took off her skirt and blouse and stepped into the blue satin dress.

'It has a look of my dress with the lace, but isn't identical.' Meg walked around her, adjusting the fall of the skirt.'

'I wish Mike could see us, it's a pity he's missing the wedding,' Anna said sadly.

'David hopes to be in on Wednesday, I have my fingers crossed he won't be delayed.'

'Would you recognise your daughter?' Lizzie asked Iris as Meg came down the stairs on her wedding day.

'I would not. I've never seen you look so well, Meg.'

'You're beautiful, Meg,' Fanny admired.

She smiled, her cheeks pink. 'Where are my flowers?' she asked.

Anna picked up the bouquet of spring flowers and handed them to her.

'Is the sun still shining?' Meg looked out the window.

'How is my hat?' Lizzie stared in the mirror.

'The feathers are waving nicely, go on with you,' Iris laughed.

'And here is your flower girl,' Fanny took Bina's hand and brought her over.

But suddenly Meg's face crumpled and tears welled up in her eyes. 'Oh Mam, I'm never going to be back here again,' she wailed.

'Of course you will, girl, stop snivelling,' Iris snapped. 'Do you want your eyes to be all red. You'll look a fright.'

Meg bawled even louder.

'Oh my God.' Iris embraced Meg. 'You're losing the run of yourself girl, there isn't time for all that now. We have to leave for the church. Do you want David to be wondering whether you're going to turn up or not?'

'We'll be a little late, but that's acceptable.' Fanny tried to calm the emotional atmosphere.

Anna dried Meg's tears with her handkerchief.

'Now we'll go on ahead with the children. And you, Anna and Uncle follow after a few minutes.' Iris directed.

There were a couple of neighbours standing outside the house, all smiles, and they waved as the carriages moved off, the white ribbon bows tied to the bridles of the horses fluttering in the breeze.

'I'm so nervous,' Meg confided. 'What if David doesn't come?'

Anna stared, eyes wide. She pressed Meg's hand gently. 'Don't be silly, of course he will be there.' In her heart, she prayed that he would be. God forbid such a thing would happen.

Anna and Meg waited in the vestibule with her uncle who was giving her away.

'Bina, you walk straight up to the altar. See where the priest is standing.' Anna pointed.

The child nodded.

'I'll be behind you.'

At that moment the sound of the organ filled the church. Immediately Anna was taken back to that first day she went to Queenstown with Mike, and they visited this very church. They were just sitting there when the music began and were transfixed listening to the beautiful strains of the organ. A wave of emotion swept through her and tears moistened her eyes. As they reached the altar she was really delighted to see David smiling at her, very relieved that Meg's worries were unfounded.

The wedding was beautiful, and afterwards all the guests returned to the house for breakfast. Anna helped with the serving and after a couple of hours David and Meg left for their honeymoon. They all crowded outside and waved them off in the cab which would take them to the railway station to catch the train to Killarney.

Anna stood outside and watched until they disappeared.

'You'll miss Meg,' Fanny said from behind.

'I will.'

'And so will Iris.'

'She's got used to her being over with us, it mightn't be so hard.'

'You never get used to it.' Fanny's voice was soft. 'Your children are always your children. I still miss Jim and Pat, and you too when you're in Portsmouth.' Fanny put her arm through Anna's and they walked back into the house.

Chapter Thirty-four

Anna clasped the letter in her hand and kissed the sheet of paper. She was so happy to receive Mike's letters. It had been weeks since she had heard from him and now to receive three together gave her a distinct pleasure as she read each one carefully.

My dearest Anna,

I hope you and Bina, Eleanor and baby Cathy are well. I think of you all the time. Every day, as --- you are the reason why I can face into each day here. Thank you for the parcels you have sent me. The fruit cake and biscuits were delicious, and even more so when I know that they were made by your own dear hand. I shared them with ---------------------------------- and there were many compliments. The socks and scarf you knitted have certainly helped to keep me warm. Thank you, my love. Thinking of you always. Kiss the girls for me. And I will imagine kissing you softly. My lips warm on yours. I can't wait to get home, knowing that you are waiting for me.
I love you always my darling. Mike. xxxxx

Give Meg and David my regards and congratulations on their marriage.

The first letter brought tears to her eyes. The other two were shorter as he had little time to write, but it didn't matter. In all of them, he told her that he loved her and the children and hated the enforced separation between them. Again, some of them had phrases blacked out, and she spent a long time holding them up to the lamp trying to decipher the words, although she had little success.

Fanny rushed in, breathing heavily. 'There's terrible news, Anna.'

'What?' She could feel her heart drop down to her boots. Thinking immediately that something had happened to Mike.

'The *Lusitania* has gone down.'

For a second, Anna didn't know what she meant. 'The *Lusitania*?'

'You know the big liner. There were a lot of people drowned.' Fanny blessed herself.

'Was Mike involved?' Anna's voice was barely a squeak, and as she felt the blood drain from her head, all she could think about was Mike. In her mind, she could see his ship exploding. Flames burning high into the sky. The sailors jumping into the sea to escape as the ship began to sink into the depths. It was like she was drowning herself. Drifting down into the sea. Her arms reaching up to try and swim back to the surface, the light above beckoning to her. But she wasn't able. She was very tired. Unable to breath. Bubbles drifted from her mouth as she searched for Mike in the shimmering light.

'No, it wasn't a Navy ship, there were just ordinary people on it. A lot of rich people from New York,' Fanny explained. 'They were torpedoed by the Germans.'

'My God.' For Anna there was a sense of relief that Mike wasn't caught up in it, but guilt too that she wasn't sympathetic and only thinking of herself and her own family. 'How many people?'

'I don't really know, but there were men, women and children too so I've been told.'

Tears welled up in Anna's eyes. 'That's so tragic. I hope that Martha wasn't sailing, she doesn't always tell me she's coming over. One of these days it could be her or God forbid, Mike.'

'But he's in Scapa Flow, don't be thinking like that.' Fanny put her arm around her shoulders.

Seamus kept an eye on the children while Fanny and Anna went to Queenstown to attend the funerals of the people who had drowned. There were crowds there, and they listened to the conversations which went on all around them. They heard about the two torpedoes which hit the ship as the people were having lunch. It was twelve minutes past two and the ship was only eight miles off the Old Head of Kinsale. Within twenty minutes she had disappeared beneath the waves. Hearing the details made it all the more painful as they walked past the rows and rows of coffins which would be interred in mass graves. The tragedy was enormous and they found it difficult to get their minds around it, particularly Anna. They prayed for the souls of those lost.

'It reminds me of the Titanic going down,' murmured Anna. 'People swallowed up by the sea, their lives snuffed out in seconds, like a flame quenched.' She shuddered, and took Fanny's arm. 'Let's go home, I can't bear it anymore.'

'I wish I could go back to Portsmouth for a week or two, just in case Mike gets leave.'

'I know you want to do that, but is it wise? Mike doesn't want you and the children to travel,' Fanny reminded. 'It's very dangerous these days, if the Germans could sink a huge ship like the Lusitania then what hope have you in a smaller steamer if a torpedo hits you?'

Anna stared at her mother.

'You can't risk your children's lives or your own either.'

'What am I hearing?' Seamus asked.

'Anna was thinking of going back to Portsmouth, but she's changed her mind, haven't you, girl?' Fanny asked pointedly.

'Yes, I have.' She was shamefaced.

'Glad to hear it.' He looked at her. Took a deep pull on his pipe, and the blue smoke drifted upwards. 'I'd miss you and my *peatas*.'

Anna was surprised to hear him say that, and particularly using his soft Irish which took her back in time to when she was a child herself. He always used the word *peata*. It was very sweet she thought, and showed how much he had changed since she had come back.

'Time for the Rosary.' He pushed himself out of the armchair and knelt on the floor, his arms on the cushion, his head down, black Rosary beads threaded through his gnarled fingers.

Fanny and Anna knelt too. Joining in the decades, the last one always in Irish. This moment of prayer every night was offered up for Mike, and the other family members, David being the latest one to be included. Tonight it was even more poignant, so many souls needing prayers.

'Lord, keep our dear ones safe.' They blessed themselves.

The clock chimed nine o'clock. Seamus picked up his candle, and lit it with a taper from the fire in the range. 'Give us a *ponny* of tea, Fanny girl before I go up.'

She poured it for him.

'I'm going to bed as well, goodnight.' Anna kissed her mother and father and left the room, anxious now to go to her children. Mike's children.

'Take a candle?' Fanny said.

'No thanks, it's bright enough.'

Anna stared out of the bedroom window. Moonlight glimmered on the garden, the shapes of the flowers and plants had an air of mystery about them. She felt such a sense of loss in her heart, a physical pain almost, when she thought about Mike and how much she missed him. She picked up a photo of him and kissed it. Staring at his face. His eyes. Reminding herself of how he looked. Sometimes she was frustrated and couldn't quite remember every nuance of his features. The crinkles at the corner of his eyes. Smile lines around his mouth. The shape of his fingers. A mist wafted between them. This war had taken him away from her. So many men had been killed. Every day in the paper they printed the numbers. It was horrendous. And so many men had been injured as well. She had read that casualties in the United Kingdom were almost four hundred thousand at this point in the war. And what would the figure be next month? And the month after?

Chapter Thirty-five

'I'm going to Dublin tomorrow,' Edward announced.

'Why?' Fanny stared at him.

'On business.' He took off his hat and sat at the table.

'Are you doing a job up there? No-one works on a Sunday, it's the Lord's Day.'

'It's not exactly work as such, just an informal meeting, but we might not be back until sometime on Monday.' He ate his dinner quickly. He didn't want to discuss his plans with his mother. He kept his political views to himself, he kept everything about his life to himself. Secret almost. Particularly the fact that he was a member of the Cork Brigade of the Volunteers, although he was only a private. But he believed in an Ireland free of the yoke of Britain, and hoped that Home Rule would eventually be granted, although he didn't agree with those men who joined the British Army and went to fight at the front. Conscription hadn't been implemented yet, and he often wondered whether he would be forced to join the army.

He joined a group of Cork men who were travelling to Dublin the following day to attend the funeral of O'Donovan Rossa. At the City Hall, the great man was lying in state. That famous Irish man, a member of the Irish Republican Brotherhood, had fought against the British, and had been made pay the penalty. Over the years he had been imprisoned in English jails until he left for New York and settled there.

Edward and his brigade waited outside until the hearse began its journey towards Glasnevin Cemetery followed by a large crowd of people. Bands played solemn music as they walked along, the mourners quiet and respectful. It took over four hours to complete the distance. Although Edward and his group didn't get very close to the grave, they did manage to hear the sound of the voice of Patrick Pearse in the distance as he spoke the oration, and the volley of shots in tribute.

There was a lot of talk among the men that Rossa wished to be buried in Rosscarbery where he had been born, and they resented this plan to bury him in Glasnevin.

'He's West Cork through and through. We should have him back. He died in New York but didn't want to lie there,' Edward said vehemently.

'Rosscarbery is such a beautiful place, with the cemetery overlooking the bay, anyone would be glad to be buried in a place like that.'

'This is just like a forest of headstones ...' Edward stared around him.

'He'll always be revered here, God only knows how many more men will lie here beside those who have gone before.'

Edward came back to Cork the next day, fired up with devotion to the cause of Irish liberty.

Chapter Thirty-six

Mike passed the hatch and stopped. There was a roar from the men below deck. He was immediately inclined to go down, but knew that for an officer to catch the hands doing something which was against the rules, then he faced being scorned by the men behind his back. Normally, he was friendly enough with them. Gave them orders. Took no nonsense. But he had known other officers who had taken a stand and lived to regret it.

On this occasion they were playing cards, something which they did when they got an opportunity. He couldn't but sympathise with them, knowing the frustration which everyone on board felt with the level of inaction, just waiting for a chance to fight the Germans. Blow them out of the sea with their torpedoes and cheer as they went down beneath the waves.

There was action in other places. An American steamer was sunk off the Scilly Isles. Another American liner went down in the Atlantic. A HM Auxiliary ship exploded at Sheerness. The liner *Armenian* sank off the Cornish coast. There were Zeppelin air raids on London and the east coast.

But the men in the Royal Navy in Scapa Flow still waited. The Germans had to be watched or they would come out of Wilhelmshaven and take over the North Sea. So while there seemed to be nothing happening, at any moment that could change. Around the coast, there was less protection so the Germans succeeded. Mike would have preferred to be transferred back to Portsmouth and protect the area if he got a chance. But he had to obey orders. There was no questioning an order when you were in the Royal Navy.

The weather was pleasant with gentle breezes. Such a relief from winter in these climes. He had a few hours leave and spent the time in Flotta socialising with fellow officers. But that allowed time to think about home. Longing to be there with Anna and the children. He often wondered if she would still be there for him when this war ended. Whenever that would be. Already he had been away for over two years, with only that short break between arriving back from Hong Kong and being posted here.

He read the papers from cover to cover. The descriptions of war in those far flung places fought by the Allies. In these months, there was the French offensive in Champagne and the British in Flanders, and trouble too in Russia, Greece and Turkey. The violence of this war, spread so far across the world, seemed never-ending.

My dearest darling Anna,

I hope you and my girls are keeping well and enjoying your time spent at home with your mother and father. I only wish I could be there too, I feel lost without you. When I try to sleep, that's the time when I miss you most. The warmth of your body against mine is a reminder of the intimacy between us, something I've only ever known with you. My arms long to enfold you, and my lips to kiss you.

Don't forget me, Anna, although I don't know how you will be able to remember as time stretches between us. ------------------------------- --with the ones we love before much more time passes.

Give all my love to my little girleens, and remember that I love you, and that will never change. Each night, feel my lips soft on yours, and listen for my whispers, and the sound of my heart beating close to yours.

Your Mike. xxxxxx

1916

Chapter Thirty-seven

'We'll collect some kindling for the fire, Bina,' Fanny called to her granddaughter and together they went out into the field. It was Holy Thursday and a pleasant enough day, although there were occasional showers. But now the sun shone brightly and the leaves on the trees sparkled. Beds of daffodils still bloomed, a glorious riot of yellow. Bina ran ahead of her and bent to pick up bundles of twigs to fill the basket carried by Fanny.

'I want to see if the little chickens have come out of their shells yet.' Bina ran on ahead.

'Don't disturb the hatching hen,' Fanny warned, carrying in the basket of kindling.

Bina crept into the hen house, and ran back out to Fanny squealing with excitement.

'Listen Granny …listen. I heard them chirping. Can I have one?' she whispered.

'When they are bigger.'

'Can I feed them?'

'No, not yet, they can eat the yolk of the egg and that'll keep them going until the hen decides it's time to take them out of the nest. We'll put out some water and feed later and then the hen and chicks will have something to eat when they want,' Fanny explained.

'Will the other hens take it?'

'We'll close the door. They won't be able to get in.'
She did that gently, and they went back into the house.
'Is Mammy in the train still?'
'No, she's arrived at Auntie Meg's now.'
'When will she be home?'
'Soon.'
'I want to show her the chicks.'
'And we will.'

Anna had travelled to Dublin earlier in the day with Eleanor and Cathy to stay with Meg and meet her family for the first time. There wasn't room for Bina at Meg's house so the child didn't go, and didn't mind either, always so glad to stay with Fanny. At school, she enjoyed her lessons and was a quick learner. And she also loved music encouraged by Anna to play the piano, Fanny even dipping into her egg money to send her to lessons. And she bought a small sized concertina for Bina and they often played together with Anna.

'Where's my Bina?' Seamus asked when he came in for his tea. Bina immediately jumped up and ran to throw her arms around him. He was followed by Edward who didn't seem to be very keen on having Anna and her brood around. But Bina, being a naturally friendly child, didn't even notice that he found her a nuisance.

'Uncle Edward, what were you doing at work today?' she asked.
'I was drawing a house,' he replied.
'What sort of house?'
'Just an ordinary house.'
'What's ordinary mean?' She stared up into his face.
He didn't answer. But she persisted. 'Ordinary?'
'Like this house.'
'Does that mean nice?'
Fanny caught her eye and covered her lip with her forefinger. But Bina didn't want to understand what that meant.
Edward sighed. 'Yes, it does.'
'That means *Rose Cottage* is ordinary,' she smiled, delighted.

'*Rose Cottage* is much nicer than that,' Fanny laughed.

'Can we see your old house and see if it's ordinary?'

'We can't go there, it's all locked up,' Fanny explained.

'But we looked in the windows before. Can we go again, Granny?'

'I suppose we could.'

'Let's go tomorrow.' She was full of excitement.

Bina was a child who liked to plan things. Tomorrow we'll do this. The next day we'll do that. Time didn't mean a great deal even if it happened to be a month away, to Bina it was always tomorrow.

'Or maybe the next day if we've time.'

She danced around the kitchen. 'Will you come too, Uncle Edward?'

'No.'

Her face was downcast. 'Why?'

'I'm busy, you silly girl,' he snapped.

'I'm not a silly girl,' she retorted.

'Sometimes you are.'

'Leave Edward alone now, Bina, he's been working hard all day,' Fanny warned.

She leaned on his arm again. 'I'm sorry, Uncle Edward.'

'Go on then,' he said, trying to stifle a smile.

As time had passed, there was a gradual change in Edward towards Bina, in particular. He had never quite forgiven Anna for eloping with Mike, and their relationship was cool. As for the other children, he didn't take a lot of notice of them.

Fanny had to keep on her toes. His mood could change suddenly and she had to be ready to intervene at a moment's notice. Edward had no experience of children in his adult life and seemed to have no interest either in getting married, as he had never even mentioned having a girl. Fanny often wondered why this was. His social life was a mystery to her, he wasn't the type of man to come home and tell his mother what he had been doing. Her sons, Pat and Jim, were the complete opposite. Music was one of their first loves, and there were always a lot of girls around, the lads leading the tunes on their accordians at any gathering.

Fanny would have given anything to see them again, but America was so far away it seemed unlikely that they would ever come home again. Anyone who had relatives living there had to depend on letters. It was the only way to keep in touch. Even Lizzie's husband and two sons were in America. Her husband had never kept in contact, but the two sons did write at Christmas and sent a few welcome dollars. She wrote frequently but they never replied other than sending that one card, and she had to put up with that.

'Hurry up, Granny, you're walking too slow,' Bina said, pulling out of Fanny's hand as they walked along the road towards *Fairfields*.

'You're forgetting I'm an old woman, Bina. Look at me, my hair is going grey.' She lifted her hat a little.

'Pull out the hairs.'

'Then I'd be bald.'

Bina giggled. 'You'd look funny if you had no hair like Fred.'

'Behave yourself, we're going in now,' Fanny cautioned. But that made little difference to the six year old. She was so excited. Nothing would have calmed her down today. They had come around here before but for Bina each time was always like the first.

Bina ran over to the stable yard and peered through a gap in the wooden gate. 'I can see the red door and the well. Can we drink the water?'

'No, love, we can't.' Fanny could make out the corner of the coach house, part of the door, and one of the windows of her house, a dilapidated look about it now. There was a sadness about the empty yard. She expected the grooms, and stable boys, the horses and dogs to suddenly come into sight, and in her mind could hear the sound of the hooves, the rattle of the wheels of the carriages swinging in and out, the shouts of the men. She felt lonesome.

'What can you see, Granny?'

'The same as you.'

'But you're bigger than me and you'll see more.'

Fanny was always surprised at the things Bina said.

'The carriages were kept in here.' She pointed. 'And the horses over there in the small red doors.'

'I can't see them.' Bina sounded very disappointed.

'There are no horses there now.' Fanny took Bina's hand.

Around the back the bare gaping windows were like sad eyes looking at her. She lifted Bina up on one of the sills.

'There's all spiders' webs on the glass, I can't see.'

Fanny pulled a bunch of long grasses and handed it to Bina, who rubbed the webs off the glass. Now she peered through. 'I can see the fireplace but there's no fire in it. What's in that other window?'

'The kitchen.'

'Can I look in there?'

They went over.

'It's empty now.' Fanny tried hard to prevent tears flooding her eyes.

'No chairs or table ...' the child said, a sadness in her voice.

'Nothing left at all, Bina ...'

'Where are they?'

'They are in Rose Cottage now.'

'And we sit on them?'

'Yes, the very same ones.'

'It's Easter,' Bina smiled. 'And we'll have Easter eggs.'

'We can eat the lovely *Simnel* cake we made last week, and you can help me with the marzipan.'

'What will we do?'

'You can mix it up, and make little balls to put on top.'

A horse galloped into the yard at a pace. Fanny glanced out the window and saw Edward slide off the back of his stallion, whose coat was shining with sweat.

'Mother?' he shouted, pushed open the door, and stood staring at her, pale-faced and out of breath.

'Is something wrong?' Fanny asked.

'There's ...' he said, agitated. 'It's ...' He gripped the back of the chair with his two hands, his knuckles white.

'Ed, will you tell me what you are saying?' Fanny demanded.

He shook his head, and seemed to change his mind. 'No, it's nothing.'

'Why are you so upset?'

'Don't worry about it. I just rode too hard. Out of breath. Is there a cup of tea in the pot?' He sat down at the table.

Fanny poured one. 'Bread?' she asked.

'I will, thanks. I'll be glad of a bit of butter on it from tomorrow, seven weeks of dry bread, penance.'

'That's what it is,' Fanny reminded.

He gulped the tea, and took a bite out of the bread. 'I could be gone early in the morning,' he said.

'Where? It's Easter Sunday,' Fanny was puzzled.

'A few of us are riding out …'

'Will you be back during the day?'

'I don't know. I may stay with Robert.'

'Your boss?'

He nodded.

'What about your Easter egg, Uncle Edward?' Bina asked.

'Keep one for me, Bina.'

'What colour would you like?'

'You pick.'

'I'll paint your egg a really nice colour.'

'Where's Pa?' Edward asked.

'He's with the horses.'

'I'll go out.'

'Here he is now.'

'I put a blanket on the stallion,' Seamus said, appearing in the doorway.

'Thanks, Pa.'

'You shouldn't ride him so hard,' his father warned, always concerned about the horses.

'I'll have a look at him.' He motioned to his father to follow him outside.

Fanny looked out the window. The two men stood talking. What was wrong, she wondered.

Chapter Thirty-eight

Edward went to the shed at the end of the field and took down a bag hidden at the back which had his uniform and gun in it. He changed there, and put on his overcoat. Then he went into Cork city to meet Robert and a group of other Irish Volunteers. There was a lot of discussion about various orders and counter orders being issued by Tomás MacCurtain. And much disappointment among the men that Roger Casement had been arrested when he arrived at Banna Strand, and that the ship, the Aud, carrying arms and ammunition supplied by Germany, had been intercepted by the British authorities. At that time, the latest orders were that the manoeuvres planned for Easter Sunday would go ahead.

On the following morning, Edward, Robert and their group in the Cork Brigade boarded a train bound for Crookstown. At Kilmurray, they assembled with other brigades of the Volunteers all prepared for a fight. This was it.

Then Tomás MacCurtain and Terence MacSwiney arrived by motor car. The men gathered around them anxious to hear what they had to say. And were stunned into silence when they were told that the manoeuvres had been cancelled. Having travelled from various places in North Cork the brigades weren't happy, a lot of grumbling among them. Edward and Robert marched back to Cork with the others. Caught in torrential rain they were drenched by the time they eventually arrived back in the city, and were ordered to disperse.

'I thought we were going to rise up. Why was it cancelled?' Edward was furious.

'Orders from Dublin.'

'All of our men were ready to blow the heads off the British.'

'Maybe there's some particular reason,' Robert cautioned. 'It might just be delayed until there's more support.'

'But people go off the boil, we won't get the same enthusiasm from the men next time.'

'Sure we will.'

'Who actually cancelled it?'

'Eoin MacNeill.'

Edward stared at him, his hopes for a Republic of Ireland in pieces around him.

Chapter Thirty-nine

Anna and Meg were delighted to see each other, and spent their time sightseeing around Dublin. David was at sea, so the two enjoyed being together after so long. The younger children got on well together, although the older boys hadn't much time for them at all. On Easter Sunday Meg invited the family over, and it was nice for Anna to get to know the Bradleys.

On Easter Monday, they went into St. Stephen's Green. It was a warm day, the sun shone, people strolled arm in arm. Anna and Meg sat beside the pond, and gave the children pieces of bread to feed the ducks. There was much excitement among them, and they screamed and laughed as the ducks rushed through the water, reaching with their beaks for whatever the children threw to them, even fighting among themselves for the food.

Anna opened up her picnic bag, and they shared out the sandwiches and milk she had brought. As they sat there eating, a group of men in uniform rushed up to them.

'You'll have to leave,' one said, waving a rifle at them.

Meg and Anna just stared, their faces pale under the brims of their hats, terrified at the sight of the guns.

'Out, now,' another shouted.

'Yes, yes,' Anna agreed, and immediately ran towards the children. 'Eleanor, Cathy, come now, we have to go,' she lifted Cathy into the baby carriage and took Eleanor's hand.

'Ducks ...' she protested.

'We'll come back later.' Anna ran towards the entrance gate, followed by Meg who had also gathered her brood and was in hot pursuit. As they went through the gate, they saw some other men standing outside. All of them carried guns as well.

'Can I have a gun like that?' little Ray asked.

'No, you can't,' snapped Meg.

'I want one,' he wailed.

'Stay quiet.' She picked him up in her arms. 'Keep up, lads.' The older boys did, the eldest Paddy keeping an eye on the men.

'Who are they, Mother?' he asked, warily.

She didn't answer. They were crossing the road now and turned on to Grafton Street.

'Why have they guns?' he insisted.

'We'll tell you later,' Anna said softly. 'But we have to get home quickly.' She was very nervous.

'There are no cabbies,' Meg said, looking around.

'Not one, where are they all gone?'

'We'll have to walk.' She put down the youngest boy.

'I don't care, once we get back in one piece.'

They hurried down Grafton Street but crowds had gathered at the junction with Dame Street and there were many people outside Trinity College who prevented them from making their way on to O'Connell Bridge.

'What's happening?' Meg asked a woman beside her.

'The Volunteers have taken over the GPO and other places too.'

'A bunch of idiots, are they trying to get us all killed,' a man exploded, his ruddy face becoming even redder. He took off his hat and ran a pudgy hand over an almost bald pate.

'We don't want this. What about our children?' A woman wearing a black shawl held a small child up on her shoulder. 'My son is at the front fighting the Germans, I don't know whether he'll ever come home. Why are they rising up against the British when they're paying us women the separation allowance? If they stop that what am I going to live on?' There was a general air of agreement from the people around, with a few colourful descriptions of the rebels from some of the men.

'Have they taken any other places?' a young rather nervous voice could be heard from the back.

'They're up in Stephen's Green,' Meg said.

The crowd turned almost as one and stared up the street. Fear rippled through them. It was captured on the faces, eyes wide, mouths half open with shock.

'We should get out of here, we might be caught between the two,' the red-faced man burst out to the people beside Meg and Anna wiping his perspiring face with a grimy handkerchief.

Meg gasped, and grabbed Anna. 'What are we going to do? How will we get home? We can't go the usual way. We could be killed if we go near Sackville Street.'

Anna tried to manoeuvre the baby carriage but it was difficult with the crowd of people around them and they were prevented from moving for quite some time. 'We'll have to try and get out of here,' Anna said.

'Why don't we leave the carriage and carry the children?' Meg suggested.

Anna lifted Cathy and Eleanor up. Meg took her youngest in her arms, and the older boys held the hands of their brothers. They turned into the crowd, excusing themselves, but people weren't very accommodating and it took them a long time to get through. To their relief the further they went up the street the less people there were and it became easier to get through.

'We can't go back to Stephen's Green,' Meg said, out of breath.

'I'm tired,' one of the boys complained.

Anna stopped for a couple of seconds, in a sudden panic. She didn't know where she was going. If only she was at home, then she would know every street and lane in Cork, but here in Dublin it was like being in some strange world of unfamiliar names, a maze of blank spaces.

'Let's go down here.' Meg dived down a narrow street of shops which wasn't as crowded as Grafton Street.

Anna glanced at the sign above, it said *Duke Street* but that meant nothing to her.

Eleanor cried. 'I want to go home.'

'We're on our way, pet, we'll be there soon.'

Cathy had cried herself to sleep by now which was some relief.

'We'll make our way to Butt Bridge and try to get across the river, come on boys.' Meg turned and hustled them ahead of her. 'Hold on to each other, I don't want to lose you.'

They turned on to Dawson Street, twisting in and out as they tried to avoid people who were hurrying every which way. They stopped at the end of the street held up by the crowd and it took some time before they managed to find a spot to get across the road.

'Stay here, don't run.' Meg gathered the boys around her. The younger ones held on to her skirt and refused to let go, their faces pale with fright. 'Are you all right, Anna?' She looked back, concern in her eyes.

Anna nodded. 'Where are we going now?'

A couple of young fellows pushed past.

'Look where you're going, you almost knocked us down. I'll give you a right funt if I catch you,' Meg shouted after them but they were quickly swallowed up in the crowds. 'Come on Anna, we'll have to get through here before it gets any worse.' She led the way across the road.

Anna followed along by the wall of Trinity College terrified to even look behind. There was so much noise. People shouting. The rumble of carts, rattle of horses' hooves and the roar of motor car engines. Tears filled her eyes. How would they get back to Meg's home, and how would she protect her little ones?

Westland Row was even worse, and they heard some people shouting that the rebels had taken the railway station. Crowds had gathered at the entrance and were pelting it with stones and yelling insults to those inside. That made the girls hurry all the more hugging the far side of the street, only eventually forced to take a breath when they reached the corner of Great Brunswick Street.

Meg pressed her hand against her chest. 'Have I got all of you,

Paddy, do a count.'

'One, two, three, four …' The others put their hands up.

'I'm not running anymore.' One of them sat on the ground.

Meg dragged him up.

'No, no.' He resisted.

'Let them have a rest,' Anna suggested. 'I could do with one myself.' She leaned up against the railings and they stayed there for a while until Meg persuaded Bert to get going again, and they moved to the edge of the kerb.

'Follow me.' Meg dived across the street with her boys, squeezing between some carts which were heading out of the city, loaded with people and their possessions. Anna followed behind carrying Eleanor and Cathy. They went down a narrow side street on to the quay, and turned up towards Butt Bridge.

'There's a lot of people up there as well.' Meg looked ahead. 'We'll have to try and force our way through, we have no other choice.'

They swung on to the bridge, trying to get the attention of those who were there. They were mostly men but also a lot of women who shouted invective, and flung all manner of refuse at whoever was at the far side of the bridge. Meg and Anna pushed their way through, mostly given access by men.

'You shouldn't go through ma'am,' one of them warned. 'It's dangerous.'

'We have to get home,' Meg said.

'With all those childer?'

'If we stay here it could be worse,' Anna added.

'Right, ladies. Let's get these little lads up on our shoulders.' He hoisted Bert up. 'Let's try and get them over, although there's a big crowd around Liberty Hall. Where are you going, Missus?' he asked Meg.

'Fairview.'

'There's trouble over there too, I'd watch yourselves.'

Meg stared at Anna, her face pale.

His friends lifted the other boys on their shoulders and shouting at the crowd ahead forced them to part and let them through. Anna followed.

The group of men were good natured and brought them over the bridge and on to the quay on the other side.

'We'll go by the back streets.' Meg was out of breath.

The men put the boys down on the ground.

'Thank you so much.' They were very grateful.

'Mind yourselves, ladies.' The men disappeared back into the crowd.

'Are we near your home now?' Anna asked Meg anxiously.

'Much nearer. I know where I'm going now. I walk into town a lot with the boys and I usually take the back streets just to familiarise myself.'

It was quieter now, and they didn't feel the need to run at such a pace. The evening had clouded over and it was chilly, but the boys didn't complain as much as they walked along.

'I'm hungry,' one of them said.

'I'm sorry but I haven't got the picnic bag, I must have left it in the Green,' Anna said.

There was disappointment on the boys' faces.

'We'll have to wait until we get home to have something to eat.'

They said no more, sulking.

'How long do you think?' Anna asked Meg.

'Shouldn't be too long,' Meg smiled at Anna for the first time. It was the most relaxed Anna had seen her since they had left St. Stephen's Green.

'If we don't dawdle then we'll be eating much quicker,' Meg said to the boys.

They grinned at each other.

But it didn't deter the children from stopping every now and then and what should have been a fairly short journey turned into a very long slow one. It was getting dark when they came close to Fairview Strand and they stopped suddenly as they heard a pop-pop-popping sound in the distance.

'What's that?' Meg whispered, her face white with fear.

'Gunshots,' Anna whispered nervously. Knowing the sound from home when her father had gone out shooting rabbits or scattering crows.

'My God,' Meg blessed herself.

Two women came rushing towards them, holding up their skirts, their shawls flying behind them. 'You can't go down that way, they're fighting on the bridge.' They were breathing heavily.

The girls stared at them.

'Not with those childer.'

'But we live on Annesley Place.'

'That's far too close, you'll have to go somewhere else.'

'Maybe we can stay with Hannah.' Meg looked at Anna.

'Good luck, girls.' The two women hurried off.

By a long roundabout route they arrived at Hannah and Kevin's house. They could still hear the sound of guns shooting in the distance which was frightening although they both tried to hide their worries from the children.

'This isn't the way home,' one of the boys piped up.

'We're going around to see your Auntie Hannah and Uncle Kevin,' explained Meg.

'We'll get some apple tart there,' the lads grinned at each other.

Meg knocked at the door. There was no answer.

'Maybe they've gone away,' Anna was disappointed.

'Probably to avoid the trouble.' Meg knocked again.

'What are we going to do?' Anna asked.

Chapter Forty

Having stayed overnight with Robert, it was late on Easter Monday when Edward arrived home in Glanmire, and by then he had the news that an uprising had already happened in Dublin. In Cork, a group of the Volunteers held the Volunteer Hall in Sheares Street, and a cordon of barbed wire had been erected by the army around the building.

'Edward, where have you been?' Fanny asked the moment she saw him come in the door.

'I told you I'd probably stay with Robert.'

'I painted your egg blue, Uncle Edward.' Bina rushed over to him, the egg wobbling on her palm.

'Thank you, Bina.' He picked it up.

'It's time for bed Bina, you stayed up late to give Edward his Easter egg, let's go up now,' Fanny said and they went upstairs.

'There's been a rising in Dublin,' Edward said to his father.

Seamus stared at him.

'The Volunteers have risen up against the British. And the Citizen Army as well.'

'You're serious, man?'

'I am. We heard the word this evening. Patrick Pearse, Connolly, and a group of men went into the GPO and took it over. Other battalions hold various points in the city. MacCurtain and McSwiney had mobilised the Cork Brigade as well but we were stood down yesterday.'

'I didn't think the Cork Brigade intended to rise up, or the Dublin Brigades either, I thought you said we were going to wait until Home

Rule was granted, didn't you tell me that?' Seamus asked.

'Yes, I did, but ...'

'But?'

'It was looking as if we might get it before the war began, but now God only knows when it will happen. All of us were for rising up against the British.'

'Why are you going with them? What's all that about?'

'I'm part of the Cork Brigade, I can't just stand back and refuse to take part. I want an Irish Republic as well as the rest of the men, when we were stood down I was ...' He lowered his head, reluctant to admit to Seamus how strongly he felt.

'You say they've risen in Dublin?'

'And maybe in other places as well.'

'It could be the ruination of us.'

'What could be the ruination of us?' Fanny asked coming into the kitchen.

'You may as well tell your mother,' Seamus said.

'What?' Fanny demanded.

'There's been an uprising in Dublin,' Edward said slowly.

'A what?'

'The Volunteers have taken the city.'

Fanny eyes were wide with shock. 'My God.' She blessed herself. 'What about Anna and the children?' She sank into a chair.

'Don't worry, Mam, she'll be all right,' Edward reassured.

'But we don't know what's going to happen up there.'

'It will be all over in a few hours, believe me, probably already finished by now.'

'I hope so.' She took her beads from her pocket and began to pray.

'Hopefully we've caught the British unawares, they might have to trade with us, and that's to our advantage,' Edward grinned.

'Anna and the children could be caught in the middle of it all.' Fanny dabbed her eyes with the edge of her apron.

'They're staying out with Meg and she's not living near the GPO.'

'I hope so.'

'Isn't she coming back tomorrow anyway?' Seamus asked.

'Thanks be to God. I won't sleep a wink tonight thinking about them.'

'What time does the train come in?'

'Two o'clock.'

Chapter Forty-one

'Knock a bit harder,' Anna urged.

Meg did.

Eleanor cried.

'I'll see if there's a window open.' Meg hurried around the back, and the boys followed her.

Anna felt exposed even though there was nothing happening on the street. Her heart beat loudly, and the sound of the guns echoed so loud her ears popped.

'Are you all right, Eleanor?' She put her down on her feet, but she immediately raised her arms up again.

Meg came back. 'It's all locked up.'

'Is there anywhere else we can go?' Anna asked anxiously.

'We could go to another brother of David's, but we would have to go over the bridge, they live on the other side.'

'Let's try that. We can't keep the children out all night.'

'But they could be holding all the bridges.'

'They're so tired and hungry,' Anna whispered.

'Then let's go towards the next bridge and see if we can get across.'

It was almost dark now and Anna was very nervous, feeling that people were watching. Out of the corner of her eye, she could sense curtains being twitched and glimpsed a flash of lamplight every now and then. As they walked along, the shadows of people hurried across the streets ahead and disappeared into the deepening twilight. She didn't mention her misgivings to Meg reluctant to cause her any further worry, but knew that she must be just as afraid as she was herself.

'Listen, there's someone coming.' Meg pulled up sharply. The boys huddled behind her.

Anna could hear the footsteps come closer, and peered into the shadows, her heart beating rapidly.

A man appeared. 'Mrs. Bradley, there you are. Hannah and Kevin asked us to look out for you, they've gone to her family in Marino.'

'Mr. Toner?' Meg was surprised.

'You're in danger, the Volunteers have the bridge and the British aren't too happy about it,' he said, with a grin.

'We can't get home,' Meg burst out, tears in her eyes.

'Come with me.' He led the way towards his own house. 'Your childer must be right worn out.'

'It took us a long time to get through the city …' Anna explained. 'We went into St. Stephen's Green but the men made us leave, and there were so many people around …'

He stopped outside a door, and pushed a key into the lock. 'I told the missus to lock the door and take the spare key out so that I could get in again. Betty, it's me, and we have visitors,' he called out.

Mrs. Toner immediately took care of them. A big pot of tea on the table, milk for the younger ones, and thick wedges of bread and jam. 'Sit yourselves down, we were wondering what happened to you,' she said. 'This is a terrible situation, and having to listen to those guns is frightening.' She glanced at her husband. 'I hope it doesn't go on for too long, otherwise we could really feel it in our pockets if you can't go to work.'

'I thought the plan to rise up against the British was all cancelled, the notice was in yesterday's paper, but now that I find it has happened I'm going to join my friends, they're at the GPO,' Mr. Toner explained.

'You didn't tell me about this plan,' his wife said, a sharp reminder.

'I didn't think it was happening, so there was nothing to tell.'

There was tension between them.

'Sorry, I haven't introduced you. This is my cousin, Anna, from Cork and her two girls, Eleanor and Cathy,' Meg said.

'I'm glad our lot are in bed by now,' Mrs. Toner said. 'But yours seem to be pretty tired.' She looked at the children, a couple of whom had their heads lying on their arms.

'I don't know where we're going to sleep tonight,' Meg was as tired as the children herself. 'But if we could just rest in a chair it would be all right.'

'I'll move some of ours in together and there will be a big bed for you, and I have a couple of mattresses for your smaller ones and night clothes as well.' She went upstairs, and returned a short time later. 'Come on, bring them up.'

Meg had to wake the boys and get them to walk upstairs, not without a few protests from the ones who had been heavily asleep. Anna lifted Eleanor and Cathy up in her arms, and followed. When she put them down on the mattress they were asleep immediately, hardly aware that they had been moved.

Meg and Anna came back downstairs after settling the children. At that point, Mr. Toner was explaining to his wife what he had seen and heard earlier. 'All hell's broke loose. We've taken O'Meara's and the Manure Works. We have to get the arms stored in Fr. Matthew Park up to the GPO and the other posts we are holding, some of the fellows turfed people out of their motor cars and carts so that we could move the stuff. You should have seen them run. 'Now I've to get my uniform and gun.' He hurried upstairs and was back in a few moments.

'But you could be in danger,' Betty burst into tears.

'We're fighting for Ireland.'

'What if something happens to you?' she wailed.

'I'll be all right, woman, don't worry.'

'I can't believe this, it's like a nightmare.'

'Just stay inside, and pull something over the windows, I'll get a message to you if I can. You know I have to do this. I can't turn my back on Pearse and Connolly. Now I've to meet the boys.' He disappeared out the back.

Meg and Anna stared at one another in shock.

'We should block the window, Mrs. Toner,' Anna suggested.

'Maybe move the dresser over it,' Meg said.

'Help me girls, I'll have to take my china out.' Betty began to hand the girls plates, saucers and cups and after a few minutes they pulled it over. Then she led them into the parlour. 'Is there anything else we could use to block this window?'

'Mrs. Toner, could we pull over the table and turn it on its end?' Meg asked and they helped move it.

'And girls, call me Betty, we're all in this together, no need for formalities.'

During the night the gunfire gradually diminished and they managed to get some badly needed sleep. But they were awoken very early by a loud crash. Some of the children began to cry. Anna and Meg stared at each other in shock.

'What was that?' Meg asked, her face white. They blessed themselves. There was a knock on the door and Betty appeared, wearing her dressing gown. 'Are you all right, girls?'

'That was like an explosion, do you know what has happened?' Anna asked.

'God only knows, I'm afraid to think on it.' She shook her head.

'I'd give anything to have David home with us.' Meg shivered.

Betty handed her a jug. 'There's hot water for washing,' she said, 'And nappies for the baby.' She put them on the bed. 'I've made some breakfast, so don't be long.' She went downstairs, her slippers making a clatter on the lino-covered steps.

'We can't stay here eating these people out of house and home. If only we could get back to our house, we've plenty of food there.' Meg poured water into the bowl on the washstand.

'We should offer to go out and see what we can buy, there's a shop down the road.'

'It doesn't look like we'll be able to get home, it's too dangerous,' Meg murmured.

'Let's wash and dress quickly and get the children up.'

'They're all still out for the count.' Anna looked at them.

'Betty, thank you so much for letting us stay, I don't know how we'd have managed without you.' Meg was grateful.

'Thanks too for sharing your food with us. We were thinking of going around to that shop and see what we can get,' Anna said.

'There's no need for you to go around, I'll slip out myself.'

'We'll have to try and get home later.' Meg made the boys sit down quietly.

'You can't, listen to the guns, they've started shooting again.'

Anna could hear the shots which sounded like whips cracking, and a ripple of fear swept through her.

'What are we going to do?' Meg asked.

'I don't know.' Anna shook her head. 'I was meant to go home today, but …'

'Stay here with me girls, I'd hate to be on my own now that Mr. Toner has gone.'

Chapter Forty-two

On the following day, Seamus drove Fanny and Bina to the railway station. It was just before two o'clock, and Fanny hurried on to the platform, holding Bina's hand. There were a few people standing there, but she didn't recognise anyone. She stared along the line, but there was no sign of the train in the distance. Seamus joined her and they waited. Fanny impatient, moving from one foot to the other.

'Let go, Granny, I want to look for the train.' The child pulled away.

'No, stay with me, girly,' Fanny kept hold of her. 'What time is it?' she asked Seamus.

He pulled his pocket watch from his dark green waistcoat. 'I think it's after two, isn't it?' He pointed to the minute hand which marked five past the hour. He was never too sure about the time.

'Yes it is. That train is late and it's unusual.'

'Can I look at your watch, Grandad,' Bina asked, always fascinated by the beautiful timepiece.

'There ...' he held it out.

'Let it swing.'

He did and she put out her hand and touched it. 'See how it shines.' Her face was alight.

'Something may have delayed it, particularly if there is trouble in Dublin.' Seamus put the watch back in the small pocket of his waistcoat.

'Pray that it's all over by now, Edward seemed to think that it wouldn't last.'

'I'm sure he's right, girl.'

At ten minutes past two Fanny went into the ticket office. 'Dick, we're waiting for the Dublin train. When do you think it will arrive?'

'Fanny, that train is cancelled.'

'What?' Fanny was shocked. Her heart thumping.

'There's trouble up there, you've heard about that I suppose, Fanny?' She nodded.

'The rebels may have taken the station.'

'How much do you know?' Fanny pressed him.

'We have no information yet.'

He seemed impatient with her, and she hurried back on to the platform, telling Seamus what he had said.

'Is Mammy not coming?' Bina asked.

'No my love, not today. But I'm going to write and tell her to get back as quick as she can.'

The following morning Fanny brought Bina to school, milked the cow, fed the poultry, and then got on with the latest batch of linens which had arrived from Mrs. Staunton. It was hard work. Scrubbing the whites on the wooden board. Up and down. Up and down. Her hands and arms red from the water. Then she squeezed the clothes out, and folded each one. Feeding them through the rollers of the mangle until almost all of the water had been wrung out. The weather was good today, and she hung some of the smaller items on her line, and spread the larger over the bushes.

Then it was time to iron the batch washed the day before. She put the heavy metal iron on the range until it had heated to the temperature she needed. On her table she spread an old folded sheet and placed a table napkin on it. She dashed some water on the napkin. The hot iron hissed and she quickly followed the shape until she was happy with the final result, folding it over the way Mrs. Staunton liked them to be presented at table. She checked outside every now and then for rain but to her relief the day continued fine, the sky a clear blue, not a cloud in sight.

She continued on. Each napkin was pressed and folded with precision. Next, the pillow slips with their lace insets and ruffles.

These were more difficult, requiring a smaller iron to smooth the frills. Working her way in and out until there wasn't even the slightest crease in the crisp white cotton. Bolsters were much the same. And then the large sheets, and heavy bed covers. She enjoyed ironing, something so satisfying about piling up the folded items when she was finished. She ran her hand down the smooth edges loving the soft feel of the linen.

Later she went to the school. When she arrived there, it was Bina's turn to dust the schoolroom and she still hadn't finished. Fanny waited at the door. 'You're doing a good job. When you're a bit older you'll be lighting the fires as well.'

'I'll be in Book Two then.' She rubbed the chalk from the blackboard energetically.

'And very good you are too. Come home now and do a bit of dusting for me.'

'But I was going to ride Daisy …' Bina was taken aback.

Fanny smiled and when Bina had put away her dusting cloths, they went home together. As it was, Fanny shepherded most of the children home, at least those who lived nearby. It wasn't easy, as they ran about, screaming and laughing, and refusing to stay close to her.

'Hold my hand, Bina,' she insisted, and was glad that she didn't run off with the rest of them. 'Keep me company, won't you?'

'Yes, Granny, I will.'

'You're a good girl.'

'Will Mammy be home today?' She looked up at her grandmother with such a trusting look Fanny felt guilty that she couldn't tell the dear child that she didn't know when her mother would be able to come home.

Edward had brought the newspaper home the day before but there was no mention of any trouble in Dublin or anywhere else around the country. This evening she went to the village herself and bought *The Evening Echo,* finally seeing a report about a gunboat which sailed up the River Liffey and shelled Liberty Hall in Dublin. Continuing down the page she read that rebels held various places in the city and soldiers were arriving from England to put down the rising. In Cork the British army were going around searching houses for arms, and men were arrested in the city, in Queenstown, and in other places on suspicion of being involved.

'What's wrong, Granny?' Bina looked into her face.

'I'm just …' She snuffled into her handkerchief.

'Don't cry.'

'I won't, don't mind me, I'm only being silly,' Fanny tried to smile at her.

Bina giggled. 'Big silly Granny.'

'That's me.' She dried her tears and kissed Bina.

When Edward came in, she suggested that they had better hide their guns. He agreed, and they went out to the shed. Seamus and Edward often went out shooting with the dogs, and came back with plump birds for the pot, or maybe a rabbit or two. But if the army came searching and found their guns would they be arrested?

Edward hid them under the hay in the stables, and Fanny felt a little better about it.

Chapter Forty-three

Over the next couple of days, as the shop down the road wasn't open, Betty Toner, Meg and Anna managed to ration out the food which Betty had in her larder. There was a good stock of flour, buttermilk and oatmeal, so they were able to make porridge for breakfast and bake bread every day. As regards meat or vegetables, all she had was a piece of bacon, potatoes, carrots and parsnips. Along with that were a few sausages, and they cooked a big pot of coddle. They were even able to give some of their food to the elderly couple who lived next door. Meg being the one who offered to dash in to them. The girls were so grateful to Betty who shared everything she had with them, even her clothes and her children's clothes.

As the week went on the cracking gunshots diminished, but every now and then there was a loud barrage which frightened the life out of them, particularly the children. There were fourteen in the house and it was difficult to keep them occupied. So noisy all the time the women felt they would never escape it. But the shouting abruptly stopped when the gunshots echoed and then the crying started, particularly from the younger ones.

'I wish I could stay outside for longer than just taking a quick run across the yard to the privy,' Anna giggled. 'I'd love a few minutes of peace and quiet.

The back yard was surrounded by high walls, and they considered it safe enough to run across. Ironically, the weather was very pleasant during the day although the temperature dropped in the evening and it became quite cold.

'It would be good to stay outside for a while and breathe in the fresh air. It's terrible to be forced to stay in the house all the time.' Meg flicked through the pages of the book she was reading.

'You know what is the worst thing for me, it's the darkness. We've covered all the windows and I hate that.' Betty cast stitches on to her knitting needles in the light of the lamp.

'Still we're lucky to be able to stay inside and keep ourselves safe. God forbid one of us would be shot.'

They blessed themselves.

'But how long more will this go on? We'll run out of food eventually.'

'Our families must be up the walls worrying about us,' Meg sighed.

'Mam won't know when I'm coming back. She was expecting me on Tuesday.' Anna sipped black tea, her two hands around the cup.

'She'll understand, there must be reports in the papers.'

'Won't stop her worrying. And I'm so glad I didn't bring Bina,' Anna admitted.

'I don't know whether the children will get over this. Look at Ray, he just won't let go of me.' She held him close.

'Your Eleanor is like a little captain. Bossing all the boys around.'

'She doesn't seem to mind the sound of the shooting once she's playing some game or other.'

There was the sound of a scream as one of the boys fought with Eleanor.

'Your children are very good to let ours play with their toys,' Anna was grateful.

'I've always impressed upon them to share their things with others,' Betty said. 'But it doesn't always work.' She put down her knitting needles, and went over to them. 'I'll take this now, and I'll only give it back when you promise to play with it together. All right?' She put the little train engine in her pocket.

'Mine.' Her four year old son reached for it. 'Want it.'

'I told you to share it, and not to be fighting with a little girl.'

He made a face at Eleanor who had a very cross look on her face. She stuck her tongue out at him.

'Eleanor, that's very rude, you shouldn't do that,' Anna spoke sharply to her.

She pouted.

'I'm very sorry, Betty,' Anna felt embarrassed.

'No doubt he deserved it.'

'It's not ladylike.'

'None of them are behaving very well. It's not normal for children to be confined to the house like this, they're always out playing.' Betty didn't seem to mind.

There was a crash against the door and a football shot through from the hall.

'Don't hit it so hard,' Meg warned.

One of the boys ran in, picked up the ball and rushed out again.

'I'm sorry, your house will be wrecked,' Meg apologised.

'What else have the older lads to do, at least it keeps them occupied.'

'I wish this would end,' Anna whispered. 'I wish …'

'We all wish …' murmured Meg.

Saturday dawned. The food was running out. There was only a small amount of bread left. The children were hungry now and didn't understand why.

'What will we do?' Anna asked Meg.

'I don't know.'

'Do you think it will be safe to go outside. There isn't much shooting now.'

'We can't take a chance.' Meg's face was ashen.

'I've a headache.' Anna pressed her hand on her forehead.

'When did you last eat?'

'Yesterday morning. I gave mine to the children today.'

'You shouldn't have done that, we must all keep our strength up for as long as we can.'

'They're so hungry, it breaks my heart to see them.'

The day crawled by. Everyone was very tired now. The children hadn't any energy to play, and the football didn't bounce up and down the hall quite so often.

'I counted the shooting this morning, there was only a few shots,' Betty murmured. 'It's been quiet for a long time.'

'We can't go out yet,' Meg said.

'Let's go to bed early,' Anna suggested, going to get the children ready.

'They're almost asleep.' Meg looked at them sitting around listlessly. 'It will make the time go faster.'

On Sunday morning, there was a loud knocking on the front door. Betty went down the hall. 'Who's there?' she asked, her voice quivering.

'It's me, Joyce.'

She opened the door. 'Get in quick, you shouldn't have taken a chance by coming out.'

'It's over,' she said excitedly.

Betty stared at her neighbour, her mouth open.

'They've surrendered,' Joyce explained.

'Thanks be to God. But are you sure about that, there were a couple of shots this morning …or maybe that was yesterday? I'm all confused. I don't know what day I have. Are they all right? The men I mean?'

'I don't know, Betty, I only hope ours are safe. One of my neighbours sent his young fellow in to tell me.'

'I can't believe it,' she said nervously.

'Well, now you can relax, it's been quiet most of the day.'

'What is it?' Meg came up behind her.

'The fighting is over,' Betty said.

'That's wonderful …' Meg rushed back inside.

'Thank you so much for telling us,' Betty gripped the other woman's hand.

Still afraid, they didn't move out of the house immediately.

'I believe Joyce but I'm not sure that they wouldn't start shooting again, who's to say?' Betty said.

'We'll wait until we see some activity outside.' Meg looked around the side of the dresser to try and see into the street. 'There are people out there,' she gasped.

'I can see them too,' Anna was on the other side.

'Do you think it's really over?' Betty rushed into the parlour and pushed over the table a little.

'It seems to be,' they shouted to each other.

Meg threw her arms around Anna and hugged her. Betty joined them, all three dancing around in a circle, surrounded by some of the children who screamed, 'It's over, it's over.'

Chapter Forty-four

Worried about Anna and the children, Fanny wasn't able to sleep very well, and instead of lying there in the bed staring into the darkness she always got up and did some baking or other work which needed doing around the house. Today being Sunday she couldn't do anything which would be considered servile work so she went out into the garden and watched the dawn come up. It was a beautiful morning, and a chorus of birds sang a cascade of music. She sat on a seat under the apple tree near the house. Its twisted branches spread wide from the old knotted trunk and were clustered with pale white blossoms, which drifted in the breeze and caught in her hair. She reached with her hand and touched them, loving the velvety softness of the petals. She thought of the wonder of God and how he had created such beauty, and she prayed to Him, suddenly more hopeful that He would keep Anna and her grandchildren safe. He had to listen to her prayers. She couldn't lose them. They were her life.

She woke Bina later.

'Do I look nice?' she asked Fanny. The blue cotton dress with the white trimming was pretty.

'Of course you do, my love.'

'Is my bonnet straight?' She pulled a face.

Fanny adjusted it.

There was a shout from outside.

'That's your Grandad.' Fanny picked up her handbag.

Bina ran ahead of her and opened the front door. 'We're coming.'

'Hurry up or we'll be late for Mass,' he growled.

She climbed up into the trap beside him and leaned forward to stroke the rump of the mare.

'Don't dirty your gloves Bina,' Fanny warned as she sat into the back seat.

They arrived at the church, and before Seamus had even pulled up the mare, one of his friends rushed alongside. 'It's over.'

Fanny stared down at him. 'The fighting in Dublin?'

'Yes, they surrendered yesterday.'

'Who told you?'

'A friend of mine drove down early this morning with the news.'

'That means Anna will be able to come home.' Fanny was overjoyed.

Bina jumped out of the trap and reached up to take her grandmother's hand.

'Let's go into Mass and say a special prayer of thanks.' Fanny stepped down.

On Thursday, Bina, Fanny and Seamus met the train from Dublin, rushing along the platform searching for Anna and the children among the large crowd.

'There's Mammy.' Bina pointed to where Anna was coming towards them with the children.

'Anna?' Fanny ran forward and threw her arms around her. 'It's so good to see you, my love, was it terrible?'

'Not so bad, Mam.'

'Mammy?' Bina screamed.

'Bina, my pet?' Anna reached for her as Fanny took Cathy.

'Where's the baby carriage? Is it still on the train?' Fanny asked.

'I had to leave it behind on Grafton Street, I'll tell you what happened later.'

'Let's go home, Seamus is outside with the trap.' Fanny couldn't believe she had Anna and the children home at last. But she didn't ask Anna what had happened in Dublin until the children were in bed that night, and she could find out what her daughter had endured during the week.

'We heard that all of the Volunteers were arrested, and Betty was very worried about Mr. Toner,' Anna explained.

'Weren't they very good to take you in?'

'We were so grateful to them.'

'You poor things.'

'And the noise of the gunfire was horrible. I don't know how the children will get over it. Now if they hear any loud noise they jump with fright.'

'We'll get them over it, don't you worry, Anna. A few days in the quiet of *Rose Cottage* and they'll forget all about it.'

'I don't know, Mam.'

'If those Volunteers hadn't risen up against the British then you wouldn't have had to go through such a terrible experience.' Fanny was suddenly angry. 'And to think that Edward is involved as well …'

'But Mr. Toner went off with his gun without a thought for himself.'

'None of the people around here thought they should have risen up. Many of our friends have husbands and sons at the front fighting for England and here you have these men fighting against them. A lot of people can't understand that.'

'And Mike is in the Royal Navy. He won't approve of it either. Are there any letters?' Anna asked.

'No.'

She was disappointed.

'And David is in the Merchant Service, and he'll feel the same no doubt,' Fanny added.

'Well, we couldn't help being drawn into it.'

'No.' Fanny patted her hand. 'Of course you couldn't, put it out of your head.'

'But you have to admire the men. To have the courage to stand up against the British Army was amazing. So few men fighting against the thousands of troops they brought over.' Anna pointed out.

'I know that.' Fanny had to agree.

Edward came in.

'Isn't it great that Anna got home safe with the children?' Fanny asked.

'I'm glad to hear it,' he said. 'Were you close to the action?'

'It was right over our heads, Meg lives near Annesley Bridge and there was a lot of shooting there.'

'Annesley Bridge? There wasn't much going on there.'

'We didn't know exactly what was happening, and it was only afterwards we were told that the Volunteers were only there for the first couple of days, and then they left, but there was still sniper fire during the rest of the week. We couldn't even get back to Meg's house and had to stay with a neighbour.'

'And here the men who were in the Volunteer Hall refused to give up their guns,' Fanny added. 'And the Bishop was trying to persuade them to give them up.'

'We should have risen up in Cork as well,' Edward grunted.

'There were rumours that some men gathered in Macroom but then it was cancelled.' Fanny looked at him keenly.

'I didn't want that,' Edward retorted.

'Were you involved?' Fanny asked sharply.

'No, I told you, it didn't happen.'

'That doesn't mean you weren't involved. Have you joined those Volunteers?' she snapped, terse.

'So what if I have?'

'My God.' She blessed herself.

'We have to fight for Ireland, I'd have been up in Dublin if I had a chance.'

'What will your father say?'

'He'd fight too if he wasn't so old. Sure he speaks the Irish, more than most. I have hardly any words.'

'What would your boss Robert say if he knew, you could lose your job. Did you think of that?'

'He's a member as well.'

'When did you join up?' Fanny was angry with him.

'In nineteen hundred and fourteen, when the Volunteers were established. Although most of the people I know want to achieve Home Rule and that won't happen until after the war, but we're still prepared to fight for Ireland.'

'I'm shocked.' She lowered her head.

'It's over now, Mam, don't worry,' Anna intervened.

'It will never be over until we have freedom. Did you see the Proclamation which Patrick Pearse read outside the GPO?' Edward asked.

'I read it.' Fanny went over to the press and pulled the newspaper from it. 'There it is.'

'Anna might be interested.' Edward handed it to her. 'That's what we want for our own country, the Republic of Ireland.'

Silently, Anna read the Proclamation. Very impressed by the words written there.

'What will your husband think of that?'

'I don't know, Edward.'

'He won't like it, take it from me. He's in the Royal Navy. A Britisher. You only have to listen to him speak, he has lost his Cork accent. And Bina speaks with the same English accent, it's quite noticeable.'

'No, she doesn't,' Anna denied.

'She bloody does, don't argue with me.'

'Edward.' Fanny blessed herself.

'And I wonder what he'll say when he hears that the British have executed three of our leaders.' He threw the newspaper on the table.

Fanny and Anna just stared at him, and neither of them were able to say a word.

'Who were they?' Anna asked after a moment.

'Pearse, MacDonagh and Clarke …'

'I can't believe they would do such a thing,' Anna burst out.

'That will make people sit up and change their attitude towards the British, I'd say,' Edward said, a bitter tone in his voice.

Chapter Forty-five

On the morning of the thirtieth of May, nineteen hundred and sixteen, Admiral Jellicoe, the British Commander in Charge received intelligence that the Germans were assembling in the sea between southern Norway and the coast of Denmark threatening merchant ships and the Royal Navy patrols.

With smoke pouring from the funnels of the *HMS Erin* she weighed anchor and put to sea. All the men, including Mike, were excited at this unexpected turn of events. Now they were going to see action, and at last, the fleet would engage with the enemy.

In convoy, the battle cruisers turned south-south-east, at twenty-five knots, and it was almost five o'clock when the forces attacked the Germans. Mike was on the bridge watching the progress seeing artillery fire between the scouts of both navies. Explosions and subsequent fires lit up the sky, and he could see a number of ships hit by shells, and eventually sink beneath the waves. He took instructions from his superior officer and checked the navigation charts as the force turned north in an effort to bait the Germans and entrap them within the cordon of the Grand Fleet. Then orders were issued by the Admiral to bring their ship in line with the other ships. It was after seven by now and with the amount of smoke and fire in the air, visibility was poor. The noise thundered in their ears, and when a ship right beside them took a direct hit and exploded, almost taking them too, Mike thought that this was it. The ship had detonated in a few seconds, water surged and rushed over the gunwales and across the deck. Two of her funnels collapsed. Their own gunners fired at the enemy ship which they could just see in the distance. And it was only through making a sharp turn to port that they escaped being hit by their return fire. They were not able to pick up survivors at that point but as the German ships disappeared out of range, they turned back. There were a lot of men killed, and those they managed to rescue from the sea had severe injuries and burns. Some of these didn't even survive because of the length of time they had been in the water, although the medical staff tried to do what they could. It was a horrifying sight. So many of their ships were on fire, and many of them were already sinking. He couldn't imagine the toll of men dead and injured.

Their own ship was damaged and they had to sail into the Firth of Forth for repairs. That they had so far escaped death themselves was a miracle.

To Mike's surprise he was granted leave while the ship was in dry dock and was delighted to be given four days. With some of his fellow officers, he took the train down to Edinburgh, and they spent the time there. He could have gone all the way to Portsmouth but without Anna and the children there seemed little point. And it was impossible to travel to Cork in the short time he had.

While he was there, he heard news that Lord Kitchener was dead. The cruiser *HMS Hampshire* had struck a mine off the Orkneys and all men on board had been lost. A pall descended on Mike and his friends, and they wondered if the battle they had fought was the start of their war. During those four days of relief they had been able to put the danger of serving in the North Sea out of their minds temporarily, but now it came back and lashed at them, and they didn't know what would face them when they sailed once again out of Scapa Flow into the unknown.

Chapter Forty-six

Anna was very disappointed to hear from Mike that he had four days leave and hadn't managed to come over to Cork. But she was glad that he had a chance to take time off. But by now he was already back in Scapa Flow facing into the war once more.

His most recent letters were very short. Barely a few lines. His last one still had a line blacked out, and she was angry about that.

My darling Anna and my girls,

I have little time to write these days as --------------------------------- ---------- but believe me, you are all in my mind constantly. Remember that I love you all and never forget me. You are my life.
All my kisses xxxx Your Mike.

'Will the war ever be over, Mam?' Anna asked her mother.

'I don't know, love, we just have to leave it with God.'

'He's not helping much,' she said with bitterness. 'They said it would last six months when it began, now it's two years.'

'All we can do is pray that we will beat the Germans.'

'There are so many countries involved now I wonder is that ever going to happen.'

'Don't worry so.'

'I can't help it. I have no life. I never see my husband.' Anna ran her hand through the silky coat of the dog. He turned his head and pushed his cold nose into her hand and licked it. 'I must see if the farrier is finished shoeing Daisy.' Anna stood up. 'And I might ride out for a while, will you watch the children for me?' A short time later, Anna was astride Daisy and riding along the road, following the high wall of *Fairfields*. She trotted along, until she came to an old door and stopped. Mike used to come through this door to meet her. She leaned forward and touched it, but it wouldn't move. There was a bolt on the far side and she had often replaced it after Mike had left and now had a crazy hope that it would have been forgotten and that she might be able to get in. But the door remained stubbornly closed against her. 'There is no chance of getting in, girl,' she whispered, stroking the horse's neck. 'Let's go.' She trotted for a while, and then broke into a canter as she rounded the corner following the wall along the top of the estate. There were high wrought iron gates here similar to those at the main entrance but she knew that they were never used. She pulled the reins and Daisy slowed down and stopped. She stared into the thickness of the trees which grew in profusion around the bars, breathing in the scent of the foliage. Reminded of those first days when she knew Mike and they met secretly in this place. She pulled a leaf from the branch of a beech tree and took a deep breath. Closed her eyes. Wishing so hard that Mike was here with her now. Holding her close to him. His skin against hers. The taste of him so sweet as he kissed her. Whispering words of love over and over. Tears moistened her eyes and drifted down. She could feel their saltiness. He always caught her tears with his finger and smiled. *Little pearl drops,* he would say softly.

After that she rode more often to this place in the early morning. It helped her to relive the memories as autumn slowly crept in. But it rained almost every day. The water fell through the trees, trickling with a soft sigh on to the drying leaves, pools gathering in the cupped shapes, and then overflowing on to those below. It was as if the trees were crying, and she was crying too for her love. He had left her. She might never see him again.

In spite of the rain she still rode out. Fanny didn't approve, warning that she would catch cold. And when Anna did begin to cough, her mother tried to persuade her to stay at home.

'You'll have to take better care of yourself.' Fanny was gentle.

'It's only a cold, this will clear.' She dismissed her mother's concerns.

'I'll make a hot toddy for you tonight going to bed. And I'll have one myself as well just in case what you have is catching,' Fanny laughed.

'I hate whiskey, Mam, you know that,' Anna protested.

'You know I swear by a toddy, it keeps me well,' Fanny laughed.

'You and Lizzie, there's a pair of you in it,' Anna teased.

'We're not that bad. A little tipple won't do us any harm.'

'All right,' Anna gave in.

But the cough persisted and it was almost Christmas before it eased. Fanny made up various herbal potions which helped but didn't clear up the cold completely, and Anna had to stay home.

Bina looked after her. 'Mammy, have a drink so you won't cough so much.' She handed her a hot lemon juice prepared by Fanny.

'Thank you, Bina.'

'When is Santa coming?' she asked for the umpteenth time that week.

'Soon,' Anna put her off.

'I want to see Santa,' Eleanor demanded.

'Thanta …' Cathy's voice joined in.

'He'll come to see you all,' Anna said.

'When?'

'Christmas Eve.'

'When is that?'

'It's a secret, sshhhh,' Anna whispered, covering her lips with her finger.

'Thecret,' Cathy lisped.

'Yes, my love,' Anna laughed.

To their delight, a large parcel arrived a couple of days before Christmas.

It was from Mike and according to his letter he had been in Edinburgh on a two day pass and did some shopping. There were presents for everyone. Anna received a beautiful pale pink silk blouse which was much admired. Fanny had some pretty handkerchiefs, Ed and Seamus tobacco, and there was a doll for each of the girls.

Everyone said it was a wonderful Christmas, but all Anna wanted was to see Mike come in the door and her happiness would have been complete.

1917

Chapter Forty-seven

In January, nineteen hundred and seventeen, the Cunard liner *Ivernia* was sunk by a German submarine in the Mediterranean, and over one hundred people were drowned. Later that month in the Atlantic, *HMS Laurentic* hit a mine. In February, another Cunard liner, *Laconia*, was lost, and the survivors landed in Ireland. On April sixth, America entered the war. And by June the first American troops had landed in France.

Mike had got hold of a newspaper which had done the rounds of the Officers' Mess, and was reading it as he drank a cup of tea during *seven beller* - how naval men described afternoon tea. The door was pushed open, and a whirl of cold wind swept through as a couple of men came in.

'O'Sullivan,' one of the officers called. 'Report to the Captain.'

Mike stood up immediately. To find when he arrived that he was being transferred to another ship *HMS Princess Royal*. He gathered his belongings and the next morning he was steaming towards the ship. He wasn't so happy about the move. He had got used to the *HMS Erin*, and knew the officers and a lot of the men too and would miss their company. He settled into his quarters and later, having been introduced to his fellow officers, he checked the lists to see if there was anyone else he knew on board. To his delight he saw Johnny's name there and went looking for him.

'Hey man, what are you doing here?' Johnny gripped his hand, hard.

'Just been transferred.'

'I heard *Erin* had been damaged?'

'And I had a few days leave.'

'We were involved in the Heligoland Bight and Dogger Bank but got through that without too many scars, although no-one knows who won in Jutland.'

'At least we sent Germany back to Wilhelmshaven with its tail between its legs.'

'But there was a huge loss of life and ships,' Johnny said. 'And really nothing much accomplished.'

'The Germans are using aeroplanes to drop bombs now, much more effective than the Zeppelins.'

'We'll have to improve our own flying capabilities to withstand the Germans in the skies.'

'A lot of our people don't believe planes will ever be better than artillery or ships, though I wouldn't be too sure about that. They didn't send over that many planes but they wreaked havoc on London.'

'What's it like serving on *Princess Royal*?' Mike asked.

'Not bad. We're overcrowded and have to eat in relays as there isn't enough space. Sleeping too is a problem with limited cabins and some of us have to sleep in hammocks.'

'It was the same on *Erin*, we'd take it in turns,' Mike laughed.

'But we try to entertain ourselves if there is no action. Singing a few songs and telling stories keep us sane.'

'No doubt the men enjoy a game of cards too.'

'You can be sure of that,' Mike nodded.

'How is that beautiful wife of yours, Anna?'

'Very well as far as I know, although I haven't seen her since the beginning of the war.'

'Is she still in Portsmouth?'

'No, she went home, I was concerned for her safety in England with the children, we have three girls now.'

'Three, you have been busy whenever you did get leave,' Johnny roared with laughter.

'What about you?' Mike asked.

'What about me?' Johnny repeated with a grin.

'And women?'

'Sure what chance have we got to meet women stuck up here? I'll probably always be a bachelor.'

'Never say no, you'll meet *Miss Right* one of these days. Could happen anywhere,' Mike cajoled.

'If this bloody war would end there might be some chance.'

'Can't go on forever.'

'Talking of wars, what do you think of the uprising at home?' Johnny asked.

'Crazy, and the executions of the leaders were quite unnecessary, Maxwell is a cruel bastard, although that's between you and me, don't repeat it,' Mike warned.

'Can we expect more of the same in the future then?'

'Most of the Volunteers and Citizens were interned in Wales and various other prisons, but almost all of them have been released by now, although I wouldn't think they have disbanded.'

'As regards Home Rule nothing will happen until the war is over.'

'And the King ordered the royal family to drop their German titles.'

'About time. Although dropping the titles doesn't mean a lot.'

'All those royal families have connections, the Greek king was forced to abdicate, maybe our lot will find themselves in the same position before long.'

Mike glanced at his watch and stood up. 'I'm on duty.'

'And I have to see the Engineering Officer.' Johnny walked on to the deck with Mike, the two almost blown off their feet by the strength of the wind off the sea. 'We're weighing anchor at five …'

Chapter Forty-eight

The only thing that kept Anna and Fanny going during those slow grinding months of the war were the letters they received. Anna kept up a constant correspondence with Mike, Meg in Dublin, her brothers in America, her friends Martha and Gladys in New York, and Edwina and Charles in Southampton.

While they followed the course of the war, reading every article they could find in the newspapers, there was so much happening in the world, they could hardly believe some of the things which were reported. They felt so protected here in *Rose Cottage*. A darling idyll which put its arms around them and held close.

'I think our little ones are turning into right Corkonians,' Edward laughed. 'Good to hear Bina is losing her British accent.'

It was a bit strange for him to make a joke, Anna thought. He was always so taciturn.

'We are Cork girls,' Bina retorted.

'Yes, you are, indeed, and all the better for that.'

'You're in a good humour today, Edward,' Fanny commented, putting on crubeens to boil.

'We're thinking of tendering for the work on the Ford plant, it would be a great contract if we could get it.' He had a self-satisfied look on his face.

'That'd be worth a lot of money to you.'

'And there will be lots of jobs going. Particularly for the soldiers when they come back, if this damned war ever ends.'

'But the racecourse is going to be knocked down to make room for that factory, why did they have to do that?' Seamus grumbled.

'It's a big site, near the city and the river, perfect.'

Horses were Seamus's life, and the idea of progress never appealed to him.

'I'll take you down to the last race meeting, Pa, it's on Easter Monday.'

'The last?'

Seamus wasn't happy about that.

It was good news for Edward, but the next day they were shocked by the tragic news of the death of a neighbour's son in France.

'It's so hard,' Mrs. O'Connor wept when they called. 'The army has said that he has died but they say nothing about sending him home. Don't you think that's odd, Fanny?'

'It is.' She wasn't quite sure what to say and always found it hard to try to find the right words when someone died.

'If they bury him out there in France we won't be able to find him. What will we do then?'

'They'll be able to tell you where he is. Don't worry.' Anna put her arm around the woman.

'I shouldn't be telling you all this, your man is out there as well, Anna. I'm sorry.' Mrs. O'Connor was very upset.

'Let us know if you hear anything more,' Fanny said. 'Come in to us if you'd like, just to talk.'

'Thank you Fanny, I would …'

'Maybe we'll see you later, Mrs. O'Connor,' Anna wanted to impress upon her that they really did want to see her, any time. Although deep down it wasn't what she wanted herself. To share the other woman's grief would only remind her that she could be going through the same sense of loss one of these days. It was one of the most difficult things she had to bear.

Ellie came to visit as often as she could, and Anna was always glad to see her.

'I had to come up,' Ellie hugged Anna.

'Has something happened?'

'Well, yes, you could say that,' Ellie smiled coyly.

'What is it?'

'I've met a boy.'

'Who is he?' Anna was excited.

'An American.'

Anna and Fanny's eyes were wide with amazement.

'One of those sailors on the ships?'

She nodded.

'But there's been a lot of talk about them, and all of the women who go out to Queenstown to see them on the *Dove* train. You didn't go out on that train surely, did you?' Fanny was shocked. 'A lot of those women are of a very low character, Ellie.'

'No, I didn't take that train, what do you think I am? I met him at a dance in town with my friends.'

'And I've heard that they're always fighting outside the pubs, they sound …very rough,' Fanny said slowly. 'You must be very careful.'

'Don't worry, Mrs. Dineen,' Ellie said, smiling.

'Well, tell us, is he nice?' Anna asked.

'Of course he is. Tall and fair haired. And he's so generous. All of the men have a lot of money, but they can hardly go out with the children running after them begging.'

'What's his name?' asked Anna.

'Howard.'

'Do you walk out with him?' Fanny asked.

'Yes, sometimes, on my day off.'

'What does he do?' Anna asked.

'At home he works in his father's company and he just joined up when America came into the war.'

'Do you really like him?' Anna asked, smiling.

She nodded, blushing.

'Has he proposed?'

'Not yet, but I'm hoping …'

'I'm delighted for you.' Anna hugged her.

'I never thought this would happen, can you believe it?'
'I knew it would.'

In the evenings, Fanny caught up with her knitting and the needles clicked as she worked on a cardigan for Bina.

Anna read the paper for Seamus.

'There's nothing good in it any more. Just give me a bit of sport, what matches are on?' Seamus demanded.

She went on to tell him about the hurling and football. That kept him happy. He was right. There was nothing positive in the paper, it was all negative, and didn't do them any good. She put it away, and took up her crochet. The white thread was fine, and she worked close to the oil lamp to be able to see the tiny stitches in the collar she was making for Eleanor, and tried to put the war out of her head.

1918

Chapter Forty-nine

In the spring, Anna began to ride again. Today the weather was pleasant. Bright sunshine. Blue skies. Although an east breeze kept it cool, and she wore a warm coat. But she needed to get out of the house. Clear her head in the fresh air and let the pale sunshine warm her winter cold body. Daisy took her away from thoughts of the telegram boy. He brought bad news. Always bad news. That small piece of paper with those brief, desperately brief words, which would impart good news or bad. It could be either. Even though she knew if anything happened to Mike, the Royal Navy would send officers to speak the dreaded words. But even so her heart tumbled inside any time she saw the boy on his bicycle.

Bina sat in front of her on the horse and together they trotted around the high walls of *Fairfields.*

'Let me hold the reins,' Bina demanded.

'We'll hold them together.'

'No, I want to do it on my own.'

Anna didn't answer. She wasn't in the mood for an argument. And Bina could argue. On and on.

'When you're bigger.'

'What age will I be then?'

'Maybe twelve.'

'When will that be?'

'You're eight now, add that up.'

'Eight, nine, ten, eleven, twelve …yes, twelve,' she exclaimed, her face brighter.

Anna wondered would Mike even be home when his eldest child was twelve. Or would all of his children be grown up by the time the war ended.

'The war has to finish soon, it's been four years.' Anna was despondent. 'I won't know Mike when I see him.'

'Of course you will,' Fanny reassured.

'I'm weary of it.' Anna bent her head.

'We all are.'

'God isn't listening.'

'He will, girl.' Fanny put her hand on Anna's head and stroked her soft dark hair.

'But when?'

'When he decides.'

'At least the countries are talking peace,' Fanny said.

'Who are?' Seamus asked.

'The governments.'

'And there was an announcement that Britain is ready to talk about granting Home Rule.'

'Edward will be glad.'

'But it mightn't include the whole country.'

'He won't be pleased about that. Better not mention it to him, we don't want to put him in bad humour,' Fanny said.

'Is that the first time they've talked about peace?' Anna hadn't remembered anyone else even mentioning the word.

'Is it in the paper? Read it to me,' Seamus demanded.

'Can I see it, Mam?' Anna asked.

'Here.' Fanny handed her the page.

Anna read some of the items in the article. 'There are fourteen points.'

'Fourteen? Don't bother then.'

'Well, they're talking, that's something.'

'The Germans should go back to their own country, that's what I think. Anything else in the paper?' he asked.

'There's a bit about rationing of food.'

'We can grow our own so we're lucky,' Fanny said.

Anna continued reading, hugging that word *peace* in her heart, praying that it would finally happen this year and that all this horror would end. But as time passed, there was no agreement between the various countries and no progress made.

But God had other plans. He swooped on his people and ambushed them.

'Iris says there is Spanish Flu in Queenstown. Some of the American sailors have it.' Fanny read down the closely written page of the letter she had received today.

'I hope Ellie's boyfriend doesn't catch it. Did it come from Spain?' Anna asked, suddenly worried.

'I don't know, it's in other countries too.'

'We'll have to be careful. Wrap the girls up when they go out.'

A week later a rumour went around the village that a number of people had gone down with the flu.

'How many of the children are sick?' Anna asked the teacher.

'A few of them, we're thinking of closing for a week or two until the epidemic is over,' she explained.

'I think you should close today, it's too risky for the rest of the children. They could all catch it from each other.'

'I haven't got authority yet.'

'Well, I won't be sending Bina or Eleanor in for a while ...' Anna went out into the yard of the school where the children were playing.

'Mammy?' Bina rushed over.

'Are you feeling all right, Bina, love?'

'Yes, Mammy.'

'Where is Eleanor?'

'She's in the privy.'

Anna went over behind the school into a shed where a bench with a number of holes in it was erected over a stream.

Eleanor was sitting there.

'Are you all right, love?'

She shook her head. 'I'm sick, Mammy.'

'My love.' Anna reached for her.

'Eleanor isn't well, Mam.' Anna rushed in the door, carrying her.

Fanny's face paled.

'What's wrong?' Bina asked, following behind.

Anna put her sitting in a chair. 'Baby, where does it hurt?'

'My head, and here …' She pointed to her throat.

'Her face is flushed.'

'She has a fever.' Anna put a hand on her forehead.

'We'll get her into bed straight away. I'll fill a hot water jar.' Fanny went to get it.

'Come on baby.' Anna brought her upstairs. Quickly put on her nightdress and drew the bedclothes over her.

Fanny put the jar wrapped in a cotton bag at her feet.

'How is Cathy?' Anna asked.

'She's asleep.'

'Bina, love, are you all right?' she asked.

'Yes, Mammy.'

'I'll go for the doctor,' Anna said. 'Will you keep an eye on Eleanor, Mam?'

'I will, don't worry.'

Anna rushed downstairs, and without even putting on a coat, she took the bicycle from the shed, rode out the gate and down the hill. She knocked on the door of the doctor's house. It was opened by his wife.

'Mrs. O'Malley, is the doctor here?' Anna was out of breath.

'I'm sorry, Anna, he's out on calls, there are a few people sick in the village.'

'Is it the flu?'

'I'm not sure, he's been gone all day and I don't know when he'll be back. I'll give him a message if you like?' she asked.

'Please would you tell him that my daughter isn't feeling well, she's five, and I'd appreciate if he could call up as soon as he can.'

Anna stared straight ahead, cycling furiously, praying that no-one would stop her to talk. But the road up the hill back to the house was strangely quiet, only one old man walking slowly, leaning on his stick. She knew him and just waved as she passed but kept going. The realisation that this flu may have already arrived at their door was terrifying.

Anna sat by Eleanor and Fanny cooled her head with a damp piece of cloth and gave her a cold drink of water every now and then.

'I'd give her a hot toddy if you'd let me …' Fanny said softly.

'Do you think we should?'

'I always gave it to you when you had a dose and it usually worked.'

'But what if it's the Spanish flu?' Anna whispered. 'That's really serious.'

'It's probably not much different to ordinary flu.'

'I don't know what to do.' Anna pushed Eleanor's curly hair back from her forehead. The movement disturbed the child and she began to cry.

'I'm sorry, love, ssshhhh …'

'I'll mix up that little drink for her.' Fanny went downstairs.

In the kitchen she took a small bottle of whiskey which she had hidden behind the bag of flour. Then she poured a little into one of the baby cups the children used, spooned in plenty of sugar, some herbs she had collected the day before, and finally added hot water. She left it cool, stirring it slowly and then went upstairs again.

'It's just a hot drink, Anna girl, with a little whiskey in it.'

'What if it makes her worse?'

'I don't think that will happen.' Fanny sat by the bed.

'But how will we get her to drink it? She's half asleep.'

'Wake her up a little,' Fanny suggested.

Anna put her arm under Eleanor's head. 'Baby, will you wake up for me?' she whispered.

She protested, moving from side to side.

'I don't know whether we should give it to her, Mam.' Anna was worried.

'If she doesn't take it quickly it will be cold.'

'Eleanor, Granny has something nice for you,' Anna whispered.

The little girl looked at Fanny.

'Would you like something sweet?' Fanny asked. She dipped a spoon in the cup and brought it close to Eleanor's mouth.

'It's lovely, open up. Come on, good girl,' Anna encouraged.

The child's mouth opened but it was really a cry and gave Fanny a chance to spoon the mixture into her mouth. She made a face and then closed her lips seeming to enjoy the sweetness.

'I'll give her some more. Have another drop, pet.'

Unexpectedly she nodded, and Fanny managed to give it all to her.

'There, did you enjoy that?' Anna asked.

'It should bring down her fever.'

Anna kissed her. 'Go to sleep now, my love.'

Anna continued to sit by her, while Fanny looked after Bina and Cathy and to their relief so far they both seemed well.

'I'm worried,' Anna said. 'There's no sign of the doctor.'

'He's probably very busy.'

'We should keep Eleanor on her own. If it is this flu, we don't want the others to get it.'

It was almost eight o'clock when the doctor knocked on the door. Anna brought him up to see Eleanor who was sleeping.

He examined her.

'Is it the flu?' Anna asked anxiously.

'I don't know. Has she got a sore throat?'

Anna nodded.

'Is she coughing very much?'

'No, but she's been sleeping most of the day since I brought her home from school.'

'Keep her in bed, and give her drinks every now and then.'

'We were doing that,' Fanny explained.

'Then see how she is tomorrow and let me know.' He picked up his large doctor's bag.

'Can you give her any medicine?' Anna asked.

'I'm sorry, but I haven't anything to give you, there is no medicine for the flu other than to stay in bed. How are the other children?'

'Bina and Cathy seem to be all right. I'd be glad if you would have a look at them?' Anna asked.

'I will.'

He examined them and advised Anna to watch them during the night.

'We will, doctor,' Anna agreed.

'Just remember that this flu can pass from one person to another. And for yourselves, try not to touch each other, a lot of adults have contracted it, even more than children. And don't go to gatherings of people if you can help it.'

'What about Mass?' Fanny asked. It was very important to her.

'My suggestion is perhaps to go during the week, but not on Sunday when there are a lot of people there.'

'But that's a sin,' she was shocked.

'I understand, but I must give you advice about your health.'

'How much do we owe you, Doctor,' Fanny asked. It was a long time since she had called the doctor, always relying on her own remedies.

'I will send you the bill, Fanny.'

She nodded, wondering how much it would be. This doctor was new to the village, and the previous man who had retired never charged much at all, and sometimes might even accept something which she had baked instead of money.

'He didn't give us anything for Eleanor, I was sure he would have some medicine.' Anna was disappointed.

'I think we'll have to stick with the old ways. I read in the paper that if you make a drink of bread soda and sugar in hot milk it might help. So we'll try that. There were other things in the article, but they all sounded a bit strange. But I might put onions at the windows, that can help to get rid of the germs,' Fanny suggested.

'Oh no, I hate the smell.' Anna shuddered.

'If it helps, it's worth it. My mother always did that.' Fanny went out the back to the shed where she kept them, a sense of purpose about her.

Anna gently put her hand on Eleanor's forehead. A few days had passed but her baby still had a fever. She sighed and whispered a prayer. God forbid something would happen to her darling.

'How is she?' Fanny tiptoed into the bedroom.

'She seems a little better. Less flushed and not so hot.' Anna looked up from where she sat by the bed.

'Here is another hot drink.' Fanny carried it over.

'Thanks.' Anna put it on the bedside table. 'I'd prefer to get her to eat something. She hasn't had much since she fell ill.'

'She likes anything sweet.'

'But it will have to be plain.'

'How about some semolina with jam?' Fanny adjusted the bedclothes.

'She might eat that.'

'I'll make it straight away.' She hurried downstairs, and Anna heard her footsteps coming back up. 'Why don't we give her an egg flip in the meantime, the semolina will take time in the oven.'

'Thanks Mam.'

As the child had been sleeping for quite a long time, Anna decided to wake her up. 'Eleanor?' she whispered, touching her cheek. 'Are you going to wake up for me?' The dark eyelashes fluttered slightly. 'Come on baby.' She held her hand.

The door opened and Bina came in. 'Is Eleanor better?' She peered over the wooden bed end.

'Bina, please go out, you might catch this cold. Go on now.'

'I won't.'

'Do what I tell you.' Anna found it hard to control her annoyance. She had hardly slept the last few nights and was very tired by this stage.

Bina wandered over to the door. 'I never see you,' she grumbled.

'I have to look after Eleanor, and you must look after Cathy.'

'She takes all my toys,' she sulked.

'You have to share your things with your sister.'

'I don't want to.' She hung out of the brass handle of the door.

'Go downstairs to your Granny.'

'What's she doing?'

'She's in the kitchen making something for Eleanor.'

'Will she make something for me?'

'I'm sure she will.'

'Will you come down soon?'

'When I can.' Anna nodded.

The door closed with a thump.

Anna sighed. She did not want Bina around the sick room at all, but it was very hard to force her to stay downstairs.

'Mammy …'

Anna looked at Eleanor, delighted to see her blue eyes staring sleepily into her own.

'My little pet? How are you feeling? Is your throat still sore?' She cupped her face in her hand.

She shook her head.

Anna was very relieved.

'Have you a pain?'

'No.'

My God, she thought, our prayers have been answered.

'I'm hungry,' the little child complained.

'Granny is making something sweet for you now.'

Fanny appeared at the doorway carrying the glass of egg flip and Anna sat Eleanor up and held it to her lips. 'Is that nice?'

She nodded.

Whatever Fanny was putting into the drinks seemed to be doing the trick, Anna thought. She had decided she wouldn't ask what exactly it was. Fanny had foraged in their own garden and in the hedgerows at the side of the road too for various herbs and plants. Old remedies which had been handed down in her own family had been tried. Anna was sure the little drop of whiskey had been added to whatever she concocted and while she didn't approve of alcohol if it helped Eleanor to get better then she would turn a blind eye.

The doctor had called a few times over the past couple of weeks and he felt that Eleanor was slowly improving, but that she still needed a lot of care.

Anna hadn't told Mike that Eleanor was sick. He knew about the Spanish flu epidemic and had mentioned it, but that none of the men on their ship had caught it. Now that Eleanor was getting better she told him, but he was so far away there was nothing he could do and she felt he didn't need any extra worry.

After a couple of weeks, they allowed Eleanor to get up for a short time each day as she definitely seemed to have more energy, but still kept her away from the other two children. The spread of the epidemic had halted somewhat, and reports of illness and deaths were less and less, and slowly Eleanor recovered and was back to her usual self, full of vitality once more.

The weather was more pleasant as they headed into the summer months, although newspaper reports of the murder of the Russian royal family were horrific, while at the same time the Allies were making greater inroads on the Western Front, and there was hope that the end of the war might finally be in sight. In September the Allies broke through the German lines and they were in retreat at last, and there was joy among everyone when finally the war ended at eleven o'clock on November eleventh, nineteen and eighteen. Although it was the following day when word came through, Fanny screamed for Anna and they held each other close, tears coursing down their cheeks.

'Mike will be coming home,' Anna cried, hardly able to believe that she would see him for the first time in four years. They rushed out to find Seamus, and men thumped each other in celebration, running from one house to another to tell their neighbours the good news. But it was bittersweet for Mrs. O'Connor who had lost her son, and for others who were in the same position.

Ellie came up to see them on her day off.

'I'm so excited it's over, and …Howard has asked me to marry him, can you believe it?' She was radiant.

'That's wonderful, Ellie.' Anna embraced her.

'Congratulations girl, I hope you'll be very happy.' Fanny kissed her.

'So when is the wedding?' Anna asked.

'Before he goes back, and he's not sure about that yet, but he's going to ask permission and then we can set a date.'

'I'm so happy for you.'

'At long last I've met a man …' Ellie giggled.

'You'll have to live in America, how do you feel about that?'

'That's the sad part, I'm going to miss everyone so much.'

'It's like myself, but you'll get used to it.'

'I hope so.'

'It was meant to be. Destiny …' Anna hugged her tight.

Chapter Fifty

'The Armistice has been signed at last.' Mike thumped Johnny's shoulder when they met in the Mess.

'Can you believe it?'

'I wasn't sure it would ever happen, while I knew there were talks going on it was never certain.'

The men in the Mess roared, an extra tot of rum issued to them in celebration.

'What are the terms?'

'It's not clear yet.'

'Is this the end of the fighting I wonder,' Johnny asked.

'Let us hope that it is. Such a death toll, it's hard to imagine.'

'It could still come unstuck, you never know.'

'I hope not. I'm looking forward to getting home to see Anna and the children.'

'It's leave I want too. A decent few weeks.' He raised his glass as did Mike.

On the twenty-first November, nineteen hundred and eighteen the war ended at sea. In the dimness of early morning, their ship raised steam, let her moorings slip, and joined the ships of the Royal Navy Grand Fleet as it left the Firth of Forth and sailed out into the North Sea. Battleships, cruisers and destroyers.

Mike watched from the deck, almost overcome by the sight of the great gathering of ships. This was Operation ZZ. Under the terms of the Armistice the German fleet was to sail out into the North Sea and give themselves up to the British Royal Navy in Scapa Flow.

'Admiral Beatty has ordered us to be ready for action.'

'He doesn't know what's going to happen when the Germans surrender.'

'We have to be prepared for anything.'

In the North Sea, the Royal Navy ships sailed in two convoys at a distance of about six miles from each other in company with American and French warships until they finally saw the Germans and moved in closer to escort their enemies which were led by a British cruiser *HMS Cardiff*.

Hours later, the German fleet had anchored off the Isle of May imprisoned by the allied ships. That night, the sailors cheered, it was the final action of the war, the surrender.

On duty in different areas of the ship, Mike and Johnny happened to meet as they walked towards each other on a companionway. They gripped hands and held strong, wide grins on their faces. There were no words exchanged. None needed.

Part 3

1924

Chapter Fifty-one

After the war, life changed for Anna and Mike. He was posted to Devonport in England and was appointed to a shore position training new recruits, attached to *HMS Indus*. Anna loved Devonport and was especially happy when she gave birth in nineteen hundred and nineteen to her first son, Michael. And two years later Joseph followed.

But Bina had stayed with Fanny and Seamus when Anna and Mike returned to England after the war, although they would have loved to have her home with them, her love for Fanny and Seamus and the country life persuaded them to let her stay in Cork. Although they missed her very much, for Anna and Mike life was almost perfect.

'My love.' Mike put his arms around Anna and held her tight. 'Are you feeling all right? You look pale.'

'I'm fine.' She hugged close to him.

'Daddy?' Michael rushed down the hall, and threw his arms around Mike's legs, followed by Joseph. He grabbed them both and put them up on his shoulders. Michael took hold of his cap and it swirled down to the floor with a swish on the linoleum.

'Anna, can't you control these boys?' Mike asked, laughing, as he ran along the hall with the boys screaming and shouting and beating his back like he was a horse.

'Don't hit Daddy,' she laughed too, and reached upwards in a vain effort to catch hold of one of their hands, but they were so excited it was impossible.

'Daddy?' Eleanor and Cathy ran in from the yard screaming his name.

'Where are my girls?' he shouted, grinning down at them. But Michael and Joseph continued pulling out of him and it took some time before he managed to lift them down.

Eleanor immediately held his hand, looking up at him, tears in her eyes, and Cathy took his other hand. He knelt down and gathered them in his arms, holding them tight. There were tears in Anna's eyes as well to see how much her children loved their father. He had only been in London for a few days, but no matter how long or short his absence the children always missed him sorely.

'I've some news, Anna ...' Mike said, after they had finished tea and the children had been put to bed.

She looked at him, surprised. 'What news?'

'I don't know how you'll feel about it, I'm not even sure how I even feel about it.'

'Mike, what are you talking about?'

'I've been discharged,' he said slowly, head down.

'Oh my love, how awful.' She took his hands and held them tight.

'It's not a strict discharge but as I've come to the end of my engagement they haven't offered me another.'

'Why?'

'It's to do with the Irish situation.'

'But you love the Royal Navy, can't you talk to them, try and persuade them to give you another engagement?' Anna asked.

'I've tried these last months.'

'Why didn't you tell me?'

'I didn't want you to worry.'

'I wish I'd known.'

He shook his head. 'It's over now.'

'You can't do anything about it?'

'No, they've made their final decision.'

'I'm sorry, love.' She kissed him.

'I thought we'd go home, you'd like that, wouldn't you?' He cupped her face in his hands.

She nodded. 'You know I'd like to go back home, but I don't want you to leave the Navy although I often hoped you'd be transferred back to Queenstown.'

'Well now we're going home. All of us.'

'But you're not happy, I know you're not.'

'I can't say I'm happy, I'll admit that it is a disappointment.'

'What will you do at home?'

'I'm not sure.'

'You'll have to get a job.'

'I have plans,' he grinned.

'Doing what?'

'Well, I had a choice. Take the full pension or a lump sum and a smaller pension. So I decided to accept the lump sum. It gives me the opportunity to go into business.'

'Business?' Anna seemed astounded.

'Yes, I was thinking I might open a shop.'

'Selling?'

'Of course selling.'

'What?'

'General goods. Sugar, flour, grains and then things like sweets for the children and tobacco for the men, I should have enough to rent somewhere in town.'

'I'm not so sure about it.' Anna was doubtful.

'I'll have to do something.'

'Will you have enough money?'

'I hope so. I'll have to buy stock and cover the rent until we get going, and once we make a profit we'll be flying high.'

'I've heard Martha say it's very hard to make a profit particularly when you start out.'

'This will only be a small business venture with low costs, it's not like Martha. They're into business in a very big way, there's no comparison.'

'When will you be free to leave?'

'Three months from now, at the end of May.'

'I can help in the shop,' she offered, smiling. 'I'd like that.'

'Let us wait and see, we have to find a premises first.'

'I'm excited about going home. How wonderful it will be to see Bina and Mam and Pa, it's been so long. But I feel guilty feeling so happy.' She held his hand tight.

'You're entitled, and don't feel guilty, it will work out well for us, I'm certain of it.'

When Mike and Anna came home with the children, Fanny invited everyone she knew to welcome them back and there was a big party at *Rose Cottage* on the night after their arrival. They all stayed at the cottage for the first few days, although Mike wasn't too keen on that as Edward's attitude towards him was cool to say the least. While the civil war had ended and the Treaty agreed between Britain and Ireland, there was still much bitterness among the people. Edward was against the Treaty which divided Ireland, the British still holding six of the northern counties. And his old antipathy towards Mike because of his Royal Navy connections was inflamed again and it became very tense at *Rose Cottage*.

So Anna and Mike found a couple of rooms in a house on South Mall and they moved into the rather cramped space immediately. Fanny wasn't very happy about it, hoping to have Anna and the children around her for a time, but there was no changing Mike's mind.

There was much to-ing and fro-ing between *Rose Cottage* and their new home. Fanny persuaded Seamus to help her transport furniture and other bits and pieces which she didn't need down to Anna and Mike's new home.

'It's a bit small, but sure you might be able to get something bigger soon,' Fanny said, staring around.

'I don't mind.' Anna shrugged.

'Where is Mike?'

'He's talking to some people about renting a shop and then bringing the children out to see his mother.'

'It would be far better if he got himself a job, Anna, what does he know about shop keeping?'

'He had to help his mother in the shop at home since he was a child.'

Fanny sniffed, and didn't seem to be impressed. 'I just feel it's a very uncertain thing to be doing when you've a wife and five children.'

'I'll be helping him,' Anna insisted.

'He's going to put his wife behind the counter?' Fanny was horrified.

'I offered.'

'Well, I don't approve of that. I didn't bring you up to be a shop girl, it's way below you,' Fanny retorted.

'I have to help my husband,' Anna replied softly.

'I don't know why he gave up the Navy, at least he had a wage, even if he was away most of the time.'

'I wanted to come home,' Anna said hesitantly. Mike had not wanted her to tell anyone that he had not received another engagement and so the reason why he had returned home with Anna and the children was because he wanted to please her.

'And Mike gave up his position because you wanted to come home?' Fanny was astonished.

'Well …yes, he could have taken up another engagement, but decided against it.' Anna went to check on Joseph who was sleeping.

'I can't believe it.' Fanny shook her head.

'Don't worry, Mam, everything will be all right.'

'I suppose we'd better get on with our work, or Seamus will be back in on top of us.'

They worked hard, moving furniture around the rooms. Placed dishes into the dresser which Mike had bought. Made up the beds.

Hung up all the clothes.

'You'll need something to divide the bedroom.' Fanny stared around, hands on hips. 'I have it. There is a large grey quilt I brought over, it's under those things on the settee.' She went searching. 'What do you think?' She held it up.

'It looks all right. Thanks for bringing it.'

'How will we hang it?'

'Mike will put up something.'

'This isn't the way I want you to live. Surely you could have found a better place?' Fanny asked.

'Mike needed to find somewhere quickly, he didn't want to put you out by staying at *Rose Cottage* any longer. He felt it was an imposition.'

'And Edward didn't make it any easier.' Fanny twisted her lips bitterly.

'Is there any cord?' Anna looked around.

'There was some tying the bed linen I brought, I wonder would it be long enough.' Fanny picked it up and handed one end to Anna. 'Hold that.' She stretched it out.

'It won't cross the whole room.' Anna stood at the wall.

'But it will cover the length of the bed and you'll have some privacy. In the meantime, I'll look for a longer piece at home. Get Mike to put a couple of hooks in the wall.'

'Thank you Mam, you're so good to me …' She hugged Fanny. And then suddenly began to cough.

'You've been coughing a lot lately, girl, we'll have to get you something for that, I don't like the sound of it. Maybe you should go to the doctor? Do you know if there is one living close by?'

'It's only a cold.'

'I'll make you up a mixture.' Fanny went around the room tidying things.

'And it will probably taste horrible as usual.'

'There's no harm in taking it, and I'll make up a mustard plaster as well, that will help.'

'Don't bother with that,' Anna protested.

'Well, try the herb mixture.'

'I will.'

'I'll make it up and bring it in tomorrow. Bina will come with me. But...did you want her to stay here with you?' Fanny asked hesitantly.

'I'd like that but there isn't enough room, she is fourteen.' Anna looked around.

'To be honest I'd miss her terribly,' Fanny admitted. 'She's been with me in *Rose Cottage* since you came back to live with us during the war and now I don't know how I could get on without her, my own darling girl.'

'And I did say I'd leave her with you, I remember that.'

'When you have a bigger place to live, you and Mike can decide. For the moment, Bina can stay with us.'

The door opened and Seamus put his head around it. 'Are ye ready?'

'I'll come in tomorrow. And look after that cough, go to bed early and maybe take a hot drink, it will do you good.'

'I will, Mam, don't worry so much. I'll be all right.'

'Maybe I'll come back in with that herb drink to you this evening? The quicker you start taking it the better.'

'No Mam, I don't want you to go to so much trouble. There will be plenty of time tomorrow,' Anna persuaded.

'Well, all right then.' Fanny gave in.

'I've found a shop, Anna,' Mike yelled as he came in the door, followed by the children.

'Where is it?'

'Oliver Plunkett Street. It's just a small place, but it will do us fine.'

'That's great, love.' She hugged him.

'Mammy, there's going to be sweets and all.' Eleanor was full of excitement.

'And we can eat them,' Cathy giggled.

'You cannot, they're for the customers,' Anna retorted. 'Where is Michael?'

'He's out throwing ball with the lads next door,' Mike pulled a newspaper from inside his jacket.

'Eleanor, will you get him in, he's too young to be out at this time of the evening,' Anna asked.

'He won't come in for me,' she said, her expression sulky.

'Of course he will, tell him the tea will be ready soon.'

She went slowly across the room.

'I'll get him,' Mike smiled.

'He does tease her, you know what he's like, full of mischief.'

'Don't our rooms look good?' she asked. 'Mam was here today and brought lots of stuff she doesn't need.'

'I'd prefer to buy our own,' Mike said.

'Do you not like our rooms now?'

'I do, the place is grand. Fanny and Seamus are very generous, and I appreciate all their help.'

'It's only for now.' Usually Anna made her own decisions about what she did about the house when they lived in England and he was home so seldom he never even noticed the changes. Now she hoped that he would be more relaxed as he definitely hadn't been too happy living in *Rose Cottage*.

Immediately the tea was over, all of the children went to bed, Anna cleared away the dishes, and then sat by the range doing some mending. Mike was at the table working on his accounts for the business.

'Did you talk to your Mam about the shop? What did she think?' asked Anna.

'She thought I was mad. Says I'll never make a penny. Certainly not enough to feed the family.'

'But she runs your shop in Glounthaune, isn't it successful?'

'My father worked as well so the amount of money we made in the shop wasn't so important. She says she didn't make much over the years, and even now it would be hand to mouth only that Maisie is teaching and can earn some money to keep them going.'

'But you'll be in the city. Surely that will make a huge difference and there will be many more customers every day?' Anna tried to be enthusiastic.

'I hope so. Anyway, I've made an arrangement with the owner. It's just a weekly rent and I'll be collecting the keys tomorrow,' he said, with a wide grin. 'So the first step will be to give the place a good clean and paint it. I want it to look really attractive to customers, and hope they'll be persuaded in to spend their money with us.'

'I can help with the cleaning, and serve behind the counter.' She kissed him. 'This is exciting, a new challenge.'

'Let's hope it's a success, my love, I'll be using all of my lump sum.'

'Of course it will be a success, I know it.' She couldn't help but be enthusiastic.

'I was talking to Con today when I went to Glounthaune, and he gave me the name of a carpenter who might be able to do the work on the shop. We'll have to put in shelving, and build a counter and I'm sure there will be other things too. I can do the painting myself.'

'When will we open?'

'As we must pay the rent immediately I want to open as soon as we can.'

'Where will we buy the things we will be selling?'

'Mother gave me the names of some people she buys from so I'll call on them.'

'Maybe your mother could help you,' Anna suggested, but even as she said it, she realised that if Nancy became involved in their business it might not bode well for their own relationship.

'I was surprised to find she was in very good humour today. She didn't even seem to mind the children running around the place.'

'Did you call over to see Aunt Lizzie?'

'While I was talking with Mother I sent the children over, otherwise we wouldn't have had a moment's peace.' He stood up and replenished the fuel in the range.

'It's cosy here,' Anna murmured. 'Just the two of us. I can't believe I have you to myself all the time now.'

'You're looking tired, my love, how is your cold today?'
'It's almost gone.'
'You should see a doctor.'
'Mam is bringing me some medicine.'
'Which doctor have you gone to before now?'
'I haven't needed to go to a doctor in Cork. I've never had anything wrong with me. I'd have told you if I had.'
'I know you would.' He kissed her. 'But I don't want you to be ill, my love, I worry about that.'

Chapter Fifty-two

Mike lifted a bag of provisions out of the dray and carried it on his shoulder into the little stock room of the shop. Anna lifted another smaller bag and followed him in.

'Can I carry something?' Eleanor tagged behind her.

'I want to help you, Daddy?' Michael put his hands up.

'Come out to the dray and I'll give you a bag.'

There was great excitement among the children as the shop was now ready to open after a couple of weeks of hard work, cleaning, painting and making the place look attractive to customers. On the outside it was painted a rich dark green, with their own name *O'Sullivan* in white lettering above the door. This colour scheme was repeated inside with the lower half of the wood panelling also green, and the top white. The shelving was white so it had a bright open look. There were two windows and a space before each to display their products. Flour and dried fruit in hessian bags, sugar, tea, spices, and a host of other products, were stacked at the back. Fanny brought in her spare hen and duck eggs. She always had more than she could sell. On the counter were round ropes of twist tobacco which Mike would cut with a very sharp knife and pare off shavings. Old men would chew it and spit out the brown gobs. In glass display cases were slabs of chocolate and toffee on trays, and on the shelves behind were large glass jars of coloured sweets. *Bulls Eyes. Rhubarb and Custard. Satin Cushions. Sherbets. Acid Drops.* And other flavours too which the children couldn't wait to taste.

Michael sidled around the counter, his hand raised. 'Want one.'

'Not yet,' Anna said with a smile. 'You can all choose something before we go home, that's for all your hard work.'

She was giving the windows a last polish. 'And tomorrow is our first day of business.' She looked around. 'Is everything ready?'

Mike put his arm around her. 'Thanks for helping, my love. I'm really proud of my team,' he laughed.

'When will we get our pay?' Eleanor asked.

'Each one of you can choose a couple of sweets.'

Michael pointed to a jar, a wide smile on his face.

'I want a *Satin Cushion*,' Eleanor said. 'Please?'

'And that was very polite of you, Eleanor.'

'Can I have a *Raspberry and Custard?*' Cathy asked.

'And what else do you say?' Anna opened the jar and shook out a couple of sweets into one of the little quills of newspaper which the children had made earlier with painstaking care.

'Please?'

'There you are.' Anna handed it to her. And then continued to give each child what they wanted.

Eleanor threw hers on the weighing scales on the counter with a loud clanging sound.

Michael offered his quill to Anna, a wide smile on his little face. 'Mammy doesn't have any.'

'You keep them.' Anna cupped his cheek and bent to kiss him.

'What about Daddy?' Mike asked from where he knelt behind the counter putting items on the shelves below.

Their hands reached out towards him.

He laughed. 'No thank you.'

Delighted that the sweets wouldn't be shared, they continued sucking.

Those first days of shopkeeping were exciting. They were open from seven in the morning to ten o'clock at night and they all helped. Anna and Mike wearing white coats as they served behind the counter. Bina, Eleanor and Cathy wore white aprons made by Fanny when they came to help after school.

Mike wasn't home until quite late in the evening although Anna waited up for him, keeping his dinner warm.

'That was so good, my love. The apple tart was delicious.'

'Maybe I might bake a few for the shop?' Anna suggested.

He looked at her, surprised. 'It would be a lot of work for you.'

'I wonder if they would sell?' Anna was enthusiastic.

'But if you find it too tiring then you have to stop. Thank you, dearest.' He kissed her.

Anna had brought her old bicycle from Glanmire and every day she cycled over to the shop from South Mall with Michael and Joseph on the carrier as soon as the girls had gone to school. From the beginning her apple tarts had sold very well, and she often had to go back and start baking again during the day. Following on from that were requests from customers for other cakes, and Fanny offered to make lemon madeira, apple upside down cake, fruit log and iced fairies, and all of these were an instant hit.

'We should have opened a cake shop and sold nothing else,' Mike said when she arrived with a half dozen more tarts and he put them in another glass display case he had bought. Fanny arrived shortly afterwards. And as they put a sign which Mike had made in the window - *Fresh cakes just arrived* - the women began to push their way in.

'I worry about Mike, it's just bed to work ...' Anna confided in Fanny.

'Don't you work just as hard? You should get out to me more often, or he should visit his family, breathe in the fresh air in Glaunthaune, and it would do you and the children so much good too.'

'It's awkward with Edward.'

'Come out this Sunday, and don't mind him.'

'Mike won't come. Anyway, Sunday is the only day off and he's usually working on his accounts then.'

'He doesn't get a chance to meet his friends, does he?'

'No, his best friend in the Navy, Johnny, is in China and he only gets an odd letter from him. And his friend Con in Glounthaune is busy in the pub all of the time so unless we visit he doesn't see him. But he's happy with the shop.'

'All this hard work is taking its toll on you also, Anna, you haven't got rid of that cold yet. Did you take the mixture I gave you?'

'I did.'

'But you're still coughing, I don't like it, I think you should go and see the doctor,' Fanny insisted.

'Mike wanted me to go, so maybe I will later.'

'Why not go around now, I'll watch the children,' Fanny suggested.

'And Cathy and Joseph have colds too.'

'It's this weather. So changeable.'

'I'll just make the tarts,' Anna shook flour into her mixing bowl. Then cut up the margarine.

'Here, let me finish those. How many will you make out of this?'

'I'll get three out of it and with what I've done already there will be enough.'

'I have to say your tarts are really tasty, I trained you well,' Fanny smiled.

'Thanks so much, you're wonderful to help us like this.' She looked over at the box which contained the cakes Fanny had made.

'Go on around to the doctor, would he be there at this time?'

'Yes he is. I looked at the sign on the gate.'

She went to the surgery and when she met the doctor she explained about the cough and he examined her. He asked her a few questions and then gave her a bottle of medicine. She was glad to go back to Fanny and show it to her, knowing she would stop worrying about her, and Mike as well.

As Christmas approached, they widened their range of cakes to include Christmas fruit cakes, and puddings as well, and both Anna and Fanny were kept very busy as people placed their orders. Even Bina helped Fanny, and Eleanor helped Anna. Beating flour and sugar, eggs, cleaning and stoning the fruit. They all worked hard.

Anna felt very tired as she put the last tart in the oven, and had to sit down and rest. There were two puddings boiling, and she would have to stay up to keep an eye on the level of the bubbling water, and top it up when it was necessary. Lately, she found the long hours extremely exhausting and tonight she pressed her handkerchief to her forehead to wipe away the perspiration which had gathered. There was a slight pain in her chest and she found it difficult to breathe, hoping that she wouldn't begin to cough and wake the children who were already in bed. After a while, she managed to force herself up and tidy away the mess after her baking. There was flour spread on the table, and she had to wash it down as well as clean the bowls and other vessels she had used. Then everything had to be put away, and the floor brushed. Mike would be in soon and she didn't want the room to be untidy when he came in. For his dinner, she cooked some meat and potatoes, and put them in the oven to keep warm. Then she went to bed, asleep almost immediately. But she woke again a half an hour later with a fit of coughing, reaching for the bottle of medicine the doctor had given her which she always kept by the bedside. She sat up and sipped it until slowly the cough diminished, and she could lie down again, and sleep.

Chapter Fifty-three

'Time for bed, Bina,' Fanny reminded, darning a pair of grey woollen socks belonging to Seamus. Her eyes peering intently at the stitches under the oil lamp which hung over the table.

'Can you see, Granny?'

'Of course I can see,' she retorted.

'You're squinting.'

'The light's bad.'

'I could do them. You said my darning was good.'

'And it is too, but I must finish these tonight.'

Bina stood up and put away the copy of *Great Expectations* by Dickens. It was her favourite book. As she leaned to kiss Fanny, she whispered. 'I'm glad I'm staying here with you, Granny.'

'If you weren't here, I'd have no one to look after me.' She dropped her darning in her lap and put her arms around Bina. There were tears in her eyes.

'Now I can ride Daisy, and look after her, and we can walk into the woods, and I can play with my friends. But I like going into the shop to see Mammy and Daddy, will we be going tomorrow?'

'I've a big wash to do for Mrs. Staunton so when I'm finished maybe we'll go in. I'm just hoping that it won't rain so that I can get the bedsheets dried.'

'I'll say a special prayer.' Bina took a candle from the shelf.

Fanny lit it for her, and then she went upstairs to bed, waving over the bannister. 'Goodnight Granny.'

'Don't read too long,' she warned.

'I won't.'

On Christmas Eve, Fanny and Bina tied the curtains back from the front window, and Bina lit the Christmas candle and placed it in a hollowed out turnip on the sill. Then Fanny and she both knelt and said a prayer for Mary and Joseph who were making their way to Bethlehem.

'All the candles which everyone has lit will help them,' Fanny said as they stood up.

Bina ran outside and waved at her through the window. 'It looks lovely.' She came back in. 'Let's put the decorations around the room.' She picked up bunches of greenery they had collected earlier and draped them over the pictures in the kitchen and parlour.

'Don't forget the ivy,' Fanny handed it to her. 'And the holly.'

'Where's the crib?'

'I have it here.'

Seamus had made the crib from old packing wood many years before and they arranged the figures carefully among the straw. Mary and Joseph, and the Infant Jesus in a stable. Bina smiled, positioning the donkey, the cow and the sheep.

'And the three kings,' Fanny added.

'We'll put them at the back.' She did that. 'I love the crib.'

'Now we know it's Christmas.'

Later they had supper. It was traditional for the Dineens, Seamus and Edward especially, to eat pigs' trotters on Christmas Eve night. Fanny had a small slice of spiced beef, and a nip of gin. Bina was allowed a slice of Christmas cake. When they had finished it was time to hang up their stockings at the ends of their beds. Although Seamus and Edward weren't very enthusiastic about that particular ritual they went along with it for Bina's sake.

All up early on Christmas Day, Bina rushed downstairs still in her nightdress. 'Look what Santa brought,' she cried with great excitement.

'And what did he bring?' Fanny asked.

'A book called *A Christmas Carol*, I've never read that one.' She leafed through the pages. 'And some lovely ribbons, and hankies, and an orange.'

'Now isn't Santa so good,' Fanny smiled.

'Yes he is, and what did he bring you?'

'I got an orange and hankies as well. And Seamus and Edward got oranges too.'

'I'm looking forward to eating it.' She held it in her hand. 'Isn't it beautiful?'

'You can have some later. Now there is another surprise for you.'

'Where is it?' Bina asked excitedly.

'Let's go up to the parlour and see.'

Bina led the way.

'Now girl, what do you think of that?' Fanny asked.

Bina stared.

'It's one of those gramophones ...' she gasped.

'Yes.'

'It's beautiful.' Bina touched the shining wood.

'Now I wrote all the instructions down.' Fanny took a piece of paper from her pocket and read from it. 'First we open it up.' She raised the lid. 'Then we put one of these black things called a record on to the turntable. We wind it with the handle here and then bring this over to the edge of the record. There's a little needle sticking out and we press this button.'

They waited until they heard a tinny sound coming out of the horn.

'Listen, it's like you playing your concertina.' Bina breathed.

'I thought you might like this one, but I bought another record which plays songs,' Fanny smiled.

'It's not very loud.' Bina was disappointed.

'I forgot to open the doors.' She did that and the sound magnified.

'That's much better, thank you, Granny.' She hugged her.

'I kept it hidden until now, so that we can enjoy our Christmas.'

'Did it cost a lot of money?' Bina put her ear to the horn.

'It did indeed, and it will take me a long time to pay for it, girl.'

'I love it,' Bina was enthralled.

'We'll put it away now.'
'I can't wait to play it some more.'
'We'll have to get ready for Mass.'
'I'm wearing my new dress.' Bina ran into her bedroom.

Fanny put on her coat and hat, as did Bina, and they went outside while Seamus brought around the trap. Fanny always felt there was something very special about Christmas morning Mass in Riverstown Church. Both she and Bina joined the choir, singing carols before and after the Mass, the harmony of all the voices so uplifting.

After they had finished their own Christmas dinner, Edward went over to see some friends of his, and Seamus, Fanny and Bina went down to South Mall in the trap to visit with Anna and Mike.

There was great excitement when they arrived, and they were welcomed, hugged and kissed.

'Here, Mrs. Dineen, have my chair,' Mike offered.

'No, I'll squeeze on to the settee, let Seamus sit there.'

Mike led Seamus across the room nearer the range.

'Do you like our Christmas tree, Bina?'

Eleanor and Cathy took her hand and brought her over to where branches of laurel stood in a pot of sand, with colourful decorations hanging on ribbons.

'We made the little figures and things, aren't they pretty?' Eleanor fingered some of the paper images.

'See they're all different colours, I made that one.' Cathy reached up. 'And that, and that.'

'We cut them out of pieces of cardboard and painted them,' Eleanor explained. 'And see these golden ones, they're from Daddy's tobacco,' she said proudly. 'And we put the holly and ivy around the room, look.'

'Santa brought me this little train.' Michael held it up to show her.

'That's lovely.'

Bina went over to Anna to where she was sitting with Joseph on her lap.

'How's my big girl?' Anna hugged her.

She laughed.

'First, a Christmas drink.' Mike went to the table where he poured a glass of whiskey for Seamus, and a small gin for Fanny.

'Ah you've got my favourite.' She sipped it. 'Ah that's grand, warms the cockles of my heart. Are you having something Anna? Mike?' she asked.

'No thanks, Mam, but I'm sure Mike will.'

He poured a glass of whiskey and raised it to Seamus and Fanny. 'A Happy Christmas to everyone.'

'Happy Christmas,' they chorused.

'Let's give out the presents, and then we'll have a singsong, I brought the concertina,' suggested Fanny.

They gathered around, and she opened her bag. 'Now Bina will hand them out. This is for your Mammy.'

'Happy Christmas, Mam.' Bina gave it to Anna with a wide smile. 'I wrapped it especially for you.'

'Thank you, love, and Mam …and Pa.' She opened the soft brown paper and took out a pair of soft black leather gloves with tiny white stitches at the sides. 'These are beautiful.' She put them on. 'What do you think?'

'They're lovely on you, Mam.' Bina kissed her.

'And now for your Daddy.'

Bina handed him his package which was an oblong box and there was much guessing as to what it was. 'Now I'm going to open it, last chance to guess what you think it is?' he smiled at them.

Michael giggled.

'It's sweets,' Cathy said.

'Daddy doesn't like sweets.'

'I think it's a box of cigarettes,' Eleanor intervened, insisting on her turn. Very grown up.

'All right, it's opening time.' Mike undid the paper to reveal a box containing a pipe. 'Now how about that, none of you were right.'

'Let us see it,' Eleanor said.

Mike put it in his mouth and posed, grabbing his naval cap from the back of the door, pulling down the brim slightly and winking at them.

'You're very smart, so handsome,' Anna smiled at him.

'I'll enjoy a new pipe. Thank you, Fanny and Seamus and Bina.' He bowed formally.

'A pipe smells nicer than cigarettes,' Eleanor smiled up at him.

Bina gave out the rest of the presents. Then it was Anna and Mike's turn, and there was much merriment among them.

'And Granny bought us a lovely present,' Bina announced.

'And what is that?' Anna asked.

'A gramophone,' Bina said, excited.

'How lovely. You'll be able to listen to music whenever you want.'

'Will you come over to hear it?'

'Of course we will.' Anna put her arm around Bina and drew her close.

Anna served tea later. What was left of the goose was carved up. There was spiced beef and drisheen.

'I'll have some drisheen,' Fanny said with a smile.

'You can have as much as you like.' Mike sliced it for her.

'I'll have spiced beef,' added Seamus.

'Everyone help themselves, this is Christmas. We're celebrating. And I have good news.' Mike walked across to Anna and took her hand. 'We're going to live in a new house,' he announced.

'You are?' Fanny was taken aback.

'Yes, I applied for it when I came back but I kept that a secret, I didn't want you all to be disappointed if we didn't get one. The Corporation are building new houses up on the North side of the city.' Mike had a very satisfied smile on his face.

Anna jumped up and threw her arms around him. 'That's wonderful, my love. Tell us where it is?'

'It's on Hillside Terrace, but I haven't got the exact address yet, they'll write to us.'

'When can we go to live there?'

'It will be a few weeks.'

The children rushed towards him, all asking questions.

'Will we have a garden like Granny?'

'No, but we have a big yard at the back for you to play in.'

'How lovely,' Fanny was so glad.

'How many rooms?' asked Bina.

'It has three bedrooms, a parlour and a kitchen and an indoor toilet.'

They skipped around, delighted.

There was plenty to celebrate then, and Fanny took out her concertina and played a few tunes. The children had their favourites and called out the names. They insisted on singing then. They loved to do that. Standing in a row their clear voices echoed in harmony around the room. Then Anna sang her favourite song, *Carrigdhoun*, and the children joined in. Fanny sang *Why did they sell Killarney* but the children thought that was really funny and laughed and giggled.

'Play dee-die-diddle-dee?' Cathy cried excitedly.

'The *Swallow's Tail*,' Eleanor said. They all jumped up as Fanny played the reel and they danced around the room holding hands.

'Play the *Boys of the Lough?*' Eleanor asked again, she could remember the names of all the tunes Fanny played.

'I'll play the *Woman of the House*.' Bina took the concertina and even Seamus and Fanny got up and Mike too all of them dancing around the room until there was a sudden bang on the wall.

'We'd better quiet down,' Mike said, with a wide grin. 'The neighbours are complaining.' They all burst out laughing.

'And another surprise. As a special treat you are all going to *Miah's* next Saturday,' Mike announced.

They had gone to the cinema once before and had such fun watching the antics of Charlie Chase and the Keystone Cops. When it was over, they hadn't wanted to leave, so to think they would be going again filled them with excitement.

'Wasn't it a lovely day?' Fanny put her arm around Bina in the trap and they hugged together behind Seamus, the horse clip-clopping along the streets. There was hardly anyone around on this Christmas night, most people at home enjoying themselves, and just one carriage to be seen in the distance up ahead and a motor car which passed both vehicles, all noise and belching smoke. The weather was very cold, a bright moon high in the dark sky above which was scattered with twinkling stars. There was a sheen of white frost on the roofs of buildings, fences, and gateposts.

'It's real Christmassy, isn't it,' Fanny said. 'Are you happy, Bina? Did you enjoy yourself?'

'Yes, it was lovely.' She reached for her muff and pushed her hands into it.

'It was nice to be all together, indeed it was,' Fanny said, seeing Anna in her mind's eye. She had grown thinner, and her face had hollows which hadn't been there before. Always thin, but never quite as thin as she looked now, Fanny thought. While Anna had got medicine from the doctor, she didn't think it had done her much good.

But Fanny felt that it wasn't her place to interfere in Mike and Anna's life. They both worked so hard perhaps that was the reason she was so thin. But this new house might make a difference, it sounded like it would be much more comfortable than the two rooms they had on South Mall, and warmer too, she hoped.

On St. Stephen's Day, the *Wren Boys* arrived at *Rose Cottage*. A group of fellows dressed in raggy clothes stood outside, carrying a sprig of holly with a dead bird hanging from it. The traditional story was that the bird betrayed the hiding place of St. Stephen, the first Christian martyr.

The wren, the wren, the king of all birds. They sang the verses of the song loudly. *Up with the kettle and down with the pan, give us some money to bury the wren.*

Bina opened the door and looked out, followed by Fanny.

The boys began singing again.

'Have we money, Granny?' Bina asked.

'Let me find something.' She went back in and took a small cup from the shelf over the range, and picked a couple of coins from it.

'Sing again,' Bina clapped and encouraged the boys.

Fanny came out and dropped the coins into a cap.

They gave them another verse. and then wandered off down the road. Bina followed them for a bit, and would have loved to join in with their singing she enjoyed it so much. The visit of the *Wren Boys* always rounded off Christmas.

1925

Chapter Fifty-four

Fanny continued to bake cakes for the shop and went in every day with Bina who sometimes helped Mike attend to customers. Although there was a lot of jealousy between the three girls as they competed for the chance to ask the first person if they could help them.

'Thanks so much for baking the cakes and for coming in so often, Mam, we're both very grateful to you,' Anna said, anxious to let her mother know how much it meant to herself and Mike.

'I enjoy it, you know that, and Bina wants to come in, so if I leave the tea in the oven for your father and Edward, I needn't rush back.'

'Iris was in today and bought a cake. She was telling us that Meg is coming down for a visit with some of the children and I'm looking forward to seeing them,' Anna was excited. She hadn't seen Meg in such a long time.

'That's wonderful.'

Meg and her two younger boys came in to see Anna on the day after they arrived. It was a Sunday, and Anna was glad of the chance to welcome Meg into her home, such as it was.

'Is David at sea?'

'No, his ship docked the other day and he's looking after the older boys. I'll be sorry to miss some of his leave, but he should be at home for another couple of weeks when I get back.'

'Your boys have grown so big, I can't believe it. Although I'm sure you must be disappointed that you haven't had a baby yourself yet, I know you would have loved a little girl,' Anna said softly.

Meg nodded, a look of sadness on her face.

'But maybe it might still happen?' Anna suggested hopefully.

'I say a prayer every day.'

'All we can do is hope about such things,' Anna was sympathetic.

Mike had gone out to see his mother so it gave the girls a chance to chat.

'A pity it's such a wet day, it would have been nice for the boys to go outside and kick ball in the back yard.' Anna looked towards the window which was lashed by heavy rain.

'They seem quite happy looking through the girls' books.'

'Mike is always buying books for the children. He reads a lot himself.'

'The girls are lovely. So pretty.'

'You should meet Bina, she's really grown up now.'

'She stays all the time with Fanny?'

'Yes, there isn't space here for her, and she wouldn't like sharing with her sisters, three girls in a bed is a bit tight,' Anna had to admit.

'You must miss her,' Meg said.

'She's in and out a lot, almost every day after school, and loves to serve the customers.'

'I'll come in tomorrow with Mam.'

'It's only a small place, but it's enough for us, and Mike seems to enjoy it.'

'I envy you having all your family around you, it's lonely in Dublin.'

'But David's relations are nice, aren't they?'

'Kevin and Hannah are, but his mother and the rest of them don't take too much notice of us.'

'That's so sad, Meg. I don't know what to say.'

'Don't worry, Anna, it's just good to talk to someone about it, I can't mention it to my mother, she would be too upset if she heard that.'

There were tears in her eyes, and they held hands.

'Mam, don't be crying.' Meg's youngest came over and put his arm around her shoulders.

'I'm not really crying, just laughing at something Anna said.' She forced a smile. 'Go back to the girls ...'

He did as she asked.

'He's the softest of all of my boys, always so concerned for me. It's lovely really.'

'You're lucky to have them.'

'I know, they keep me going.'

'Why don't you come down more often to see us?'

'It's a long journey and I have to watch my money you know. But I'll try, maybe in the summer.'

'Or we could visit you, although we're so busy with the shop we only have Sunday to relax at home and one day just doesn't give us enough time to go very far.'

'I'm sure you're enjoying having Mike back all the time, it must be wonderful.'

'It's made such a difference, but he works hard too and doesn't get home until very late each evening.'

'He's there when you need him and that's everything.'

'I hope we can survive and that the failure of the next harvest doesn't move to the rest of the country,' Mike said that evening. 'In the west people are finding it very difficult since the harvest failed last year. The weather has been terrible and the potatoes rotted in the ground. It reminds people of the last famine in the eighteen forties, some of the papers are even saying that. Although the government is denying that it even happened.'

'To think people haven't enough to eat is really dreadful and here we are making cakes and people can actually afford to buy them.' Anna was sympathetic.

'Now that we're into our second year we will have to make sure we attract people with money to our shop. Your baking, and Fanny's too, has made a big difference, but some of our other products haven't sold well and are just sitting there. The men aren't interested in changing their habits, and continue to go back to their usual shops for their tobacco, probably Lampkins, so we'll lose money on that. Sweets are slow as well. Parents won't give the children the money so the only ones sucking sweets are our own. There's a lot of people out of work, no-one has money for luxuries.' He threw down the newspaper, and took out the journal, looking at the columns of figures which he carefully wrote up each evening.

'I'll stop them eating the sweets. Make sure they keep their hands out of the jars,' Anna said firmly. 'But sales were very good at Christmas, weren't they?'

'The cakes and puddings sold but we probably didn't charge enough and that's the reason why we're not showing a profit. They were much cheaper than the other cake shops. And people haven't paid what they owe anyway. They run up a bill but then I can't get the money out of them. It's awkward trying to remind someone that they owe me, if I say too much then they probably won't come back. That's something which I didn't really expect.' Mike wasn't very optimistic. 'And the gifts we gave customers at Christmas had to be given to some of the ones who don't pay which was ridiculous. And on top of that, the rent in the new house will be higher than here, so we'll have to watch our own spending. We can't spare any money for new clothes or shoes, we'll have to make do with what we have already. My pension is small so we must rely on that for day to day things, there will be no money out of the business after the rent and other expenses are paid. It's even hard to cover those costs with what we are taking in every day now.'

'I thought it was going well,' Anna said slowly.

'If I could get in all the money owed, it would be.' He leaned his head on his hand with a defeated air.

Anna had never seen him like this. His initial enthusiasm for business had waned, and she could see that he was very worried.

She put her hand on his. 'It will work out, my love,' she said, determined to do as much as she could to make the shop a success. 'And we're all really looking forward to moving to our new house. It's going to be lovely.'

'Some space at last,' he said with a grin.

'I wanted to ask you about Bina, do you want her to live at the new house with us?'

'If she wants to.'

'She loves living in the country with Mam and Pa, and I did promise to let Mam raise her, she missed me so much when I went away.'

'Let her stay with Fanny if that makes her happy.' He totted up the column of figures in the accounts book. 'Sure she's in and out of the shop all the time anyway.'

Anna felt relieved. She knew Fanny loved Bina and if she was all alone with Seamus and Edward and had no child to love at *Rose Cottage* it would surely break her heart.

She coughed, took her handkerchief from her pocket and covered her mouth.

'That cough is getting worse. You'll have to go back to the doctor and get something else,' Mike insisted, changing the subject. 'How do you actually feel, my love?'

'I'm a bit tired,' Anna admitted.

'All the work is too much for you. Won't you please go around to him tomorrow.'

'All right, I will.'

'I'm sorry that I can't go with you but I'll have to be in the shop. And don't bake any tarts tomorrow, just rest.'

'I'll go over in the afternoon when Mam comes and she will look after the children.'

The doctor examined Anna. Using a stethoscope to listen to her chest. She gripped her hands tightly, praying that he wouldn't say anything bad.

'You seem to be run down,' he said after a few minutes. 'Have you lost weight recently?'

'I'm not sure, I've always been this size.'

'Have you been coughing up any blood?'

She shook her head. There had been a couple of flecks of blood on her handkerchief once or twice but she had explained that away to herself. It was just because she was coughing too hard. That was the reason for it.

'You need a lot of bed rest, you shouldn't work too hard,' he said. 'A few weeks in hospital would do you good.'

'No, I can't go into hospital,' Anna said immediately.

He looked at her quizzically.

'I have five children, well, four living with us, and we're moving into a new house so I have to be home,' she explained.

He nodded.

'Can you give me something for my cough? The last bottle of medicine didn't seem to work.'

'Yes I can, but bed rest is very important.' He went to a press behind his desk and took out a large bottle.

'Take this three times a day, just one teaspoon. It's stronger.'

'I will and I'll rest as often as I can,' Anna promised.

'You're quite flushed.' He put his hand on her forehead.

She didn't reply.

'I'll take your temperature.'

She was suddenly nervous. He picked up a yellow tube and pulled a smaller white glass one from it.

'Please open your mouth.'

She only managed to open her lips a little.

'A bit more.' He pushed the thin cold tube under her tongue.

Immediately, she almost choked and had to suppress a cough.

'Relax,' he said. 'We'll just leave it there for a short while.'

She nodded. Trying to control the urge to cough she stared at his chest. He wore a white coat over a black suit and a shirt which had a wing collar and a black bow tie.

While he waited he took up her wrist and held it in his hand. After a couple of moments, he took the tube out. Then he shook it and stared at the numbers written along the side. 'Mrs. O'Sullivan, your temperature is raised so we must watch that.'

'Is it bad?'

'It's not good,' he said firmly.

Her teeth gripped the soft skin of her lip. 'What can I do?' Anna asked.

'I told you, bed rest.' He stretched out his hand and shook hers. 'Look after yourself.'

'How much do I owe you?'

'I'll send the bill. Give me your address.' He waited, pen in hand, and wrote it down.

'We'll be there next week.

He noted that.

Fanny appeared at the door the moment Anna turned the handle. 'How did you get on with the doctor?' she whispered, glancing back into the room, closing over the door and standing on the landing.

'He gave me more medicine.' Anna was breathless after the climb up the stairs.

'And what did he say about your cough?'

'It should go away if I take the bottle.'

'Well, I hope so. Did he say anything else?'

Anna shook her head.

'You're quite thin, did he mention that?'

'No,' Anna denied.

'You should go to bed early.'

'I will.'

'I've given the children the soup that was there, and I've been keeping it hot for you.' They went inside.

The children ran over to her.

'Bina's reading us a story about Oliver Twist,' Eleanor shouted.

Anna kissed and hugged them.

'Sit down and have that, it will warm you up.' Fanny poured out the soup.

'Thanks Mam.' She watched the children as they gathered around Bina again.

'The shop is very quiet,' Fanny said. 'When I was down yesterday, there wasn't one person there. Not one in all that time. The girls were very disappointed.'

'This year hasn't been busy,' Anna had to admit.

'How are profits?' Fanny always had a good grasp of money matters.

'I don't know,' Anna was deliberately vague. 'Mike deals with all of that. But we have money to pay the rent here and feed ourselves so I suppose we must be doing all right.'

'But he has to pay the rent in the shop as well?'

'Of course ...'

'I wondered what sort of business man he'd turn out to be in the beginning, I'll tell you I wasn't very confident about his ability, but maybe he's making a good fist of it after all,' Fanny murmured.

Anna hugged her mother. But she didn't dare tell her how worried Mike was about the business. If she had opened her mouth and told anyone how bad things were, she knew he wouldn't have been a bit pleased.

Anna told Mike that the doctor had given her a bottle of medicine, but made no mention of his other instructions. There simply wasn't the time now as they were moving over to the new house in a matter of days. And he was concerned about the shop too and she didn't want to worry him.

As soon as they had the key of the house, Seamus came over in the trap and Fanny and Anna bundled all of their belongings into it, making more than one trip with furniture, bedding, clothes, crockery and other bits and pieces piled on top.

The children were delighted. The fact that they had so much space to run around filled them with excitement. There wasn't that much furniture so nothing to prevent them jumping and tumbling to their hearts' content.

'Money is a bit tight at the moment.' Anna was forced to explain to Fanny why she couldn't buy curtains for the windows.

'I have some you can use,' Fanny offered.

'Thanks Mam.'

'They mightn't be exactly the same size but we'll get around that by altering them.'

'It's just temporary, we're waiting for money to come in, but please don't mention that to Mike.' She felt embarrassed, and realised that she shouldn't have said anything to her mother. Mike didn't want the family to know that they didn't have much money. Although she had tried to cut back as much as she could, even food was reduced and there was nothing fancy bought any more. She remembered the threats that she would rue the day if she married Mike which her father and Edward had made, and even Fanny too, and while now they had these problems there was never a day, or an hour, or even a second, when she regretted choosing him as her husband. She loved him more than her own life.

Chapter Fifty-five

Anna was so happy to be settled into their own home at last. She was up at five every morning with Mike, and on a Monday morning, her washing day, she rose even earlier so that she could get it done before she began to bake for the shop.

It was hard work as Anna boiled a large pot of water, poured it into the tub, and began to scrub the cottons on the washboard. First the whites. Then the colours. Rubbing with carbolic soap and then pulling them inside out. It was hard on her thin hands and exhausting. But it had to be done. She was glad it wasn't a wet day, there was nothing worse than having to hang the clothes over the range, and around the kitchen to dry. While in the South Mall, she had to go up into the attic where there were long lines and hang the clothes up there. Now she could hang them out in the back yard to blow in the breeze if it wasn't raining, and she loved the fresh scent from the outdoors when she brought them in.

She was breathing heavily when she went out into the yard to pull the clothes through the mangle and force the last of the moisture out of them. It was as she was pegging up the different garments on the line that she began to cough. Harsh phlegmy coughs which cut through her. She stopped what she was doing and a white petticoat belonging to Cathy fluttered to the ground. She pulled her handkerchief out of her pocket and held it against her face, moving towards the wall, her hand stretched out against it for support. She was racked with a bout of coughing which caused her to bend over, weakened so much she couldn't even stand.

Slowly, she staggered towards the open back door and managed to sit into the nearest chair, continuing to cough, suddenly aware of a large stain on her handkerchief. She stared at it, horrified to see that it was saturated with blood.

She burst into tears at the sight.

'Mam?' Eleanor leaned over her. 'What's wrong? You're bleeding …'

Weakly, Anna opened her eyes. She must have passed out for a time as she couldn't remember what she had been doing.

'It's very cold, I'll close the door.' Eleanor pulled it over.

'The washing …' she just about managed to say the word.

'What Mam?' Eleanor moved closer.

'The washing …,' she whispered.

Eleanor went outside, and then reappeared a moment later with the basket and put it down on the floor. Then she picked up a towel and ran to Anna, wiping the blood off her face. 'Are you all right, Mammy?'

'Yes, I am.' She nodded weakly.

'Will I get Daddy?'

'No, you will have to help me make the tarts today.'

'But I have to go to school.' Eleanor loved school.

'Cathy will tell the teacher you have to stay with me. Now, run and wash first, and then dress.'

Anna stood up, unsteady on her feet, walking slowly up the stairs after Eleanor. In her bedroom she poured water into the bowl and washed her face. Taking a glass of water and rinsing out her mouth. The taste of the blood was unpleasant and she washed her teeth. Scrubbing her hands and arms then to make sure they were really clean. It was important when she was baking to make sure that everything was spotless.

After the others had gone to school, except Joseph, Eleanor scooped the required amount of flour from the big sack.

'Right, a little sugar, a little salt.' Anna put that in. 'And then mix the margarine, and add water.' She stood back and let Eleanor do that part of it, watching as she moved her hand around the bowl and formed a round lump of pastry.

'That's very good. Now slide it out of the bowl on to the board.' Anna flicked flour over the board before the pastry landed.

She felt a little better now and when they were finished baking, Anna put the box of tarts in the basket on the bicycle. Eleanor sat on the carrier, with Joseph in front of her, and they rode over to the shop.

There they found Mike talking animatedly to a man in naval uniform. 'Look who's here, Anna,' he said with a wide smile.

'Johnny?' Anna gasped.

'Just been transferred back here for a month or two.'

'How was China?'

'Grim, as usual. I'm glad to be back home for a while.' He stretched his hand out and took Anna's. 'It's lovely to see you again.'

'This is our second eldest daughter, Eleanor.' Mike introduced her proudly.

'What a lovely young lady, I'll have to be on my best behaviour.' He saluted her.

Eleanor giggled, and saluted him back.

'Madame.' He stood to attention.

They laughed, and Anna began to place the tarts in the glass case on the counter.

A woman came in then, and Mike excused himself to Johnny and served her.

'I'll have one of those nice apple tarts,' she pointed.

'They're freshly made this morning,' Anna said.

'You're a very good baker,' she said.

'Thank you.'

'They're always so tasty.'

Mike took the book out from under the counter. 'Will I put it down for you?'

'Please.'

Anna handed it to her. 'Thank you.'

There were a couple of other women in after that, and they all bought but didn't pay. Not a penny came over the counter.

'Mike, why don't you and Johnny go out and have a chat somewhere, Eleanor and I can manage here, can't we, love?'

'Yes, Mam.' The girl nodded.

Anna went into the back and put on her white coat, and Eleanor tied on her apron. 'All ready, pet?'

'We might do that for a while,' Mike said. 'Thanks for letting me off.' He kissed Anna.

'You don't take much time off, my love,' she said to him. 'Mike works almost around the clock you know, Johnny.'

'I know him well, he never rests,' he laughed.

'Enjoy yourselves,' Anna said.

'Why don't you come up to us and have supper, Johnny?' Mike asked.

'I'd like that, but I wouldn't want to put you out.'

'No you won't, although I don't know what you might get to eat this evening,' Anna laughed.

'Don't worry about that, I'll treat Mike here to something in town.'

'We'll be back soon, Anna.' Mike turned to Johnny. 'Give me a minute, I'll just take off my coat.'

The two went off. Anna was so pleased. Mike had only one friend, Con, and he didn't get out to Glounthaune very often to see him, so for Mike to get the chance to meet Johnny made Anna really happy. They stayed at the shop for the next couple of hours and then Mike and Johnny arrived back.

'He insisted on buying me lunch at *The Imperial*.' Mike clapped him on the back.

'It's the least I could do.'

'As I'm not home until late every night, I invited Johnny to come out to us some Sunday, it really is the only day we have free,' Mike suggested.

'Thank you, I'd be delighted.'

'Let us know when you'll have a Sunday off.'

'I'll have to look at the roster, I haven't got it yet.'

Meeting Johnny again gave Mike a definite lift, and his mood improved. Anna was so happy for him, and knew that he had missed the Royal Navy. It was understandable, although he hadn't told her how he was feeling since they had returned from England, but she knew he had to be missing the life at sea, loving it so much since he was a boy.

In the weeks following, Anna's health improved and when Johnny arrived out she was able to cook one of Fanny's chickens with vegetables for the dinner, apple tart and hot custard for dessert.

They sat down together at the table, and there was much laughter as Johnny teased the children about all sorts of things. The little boys particularly enjoyed listening to his stories about the places he had served all over the world. He gave Michael his cap and Joseph wore Mike's. They were rather too big for them but the two little faces peeped out from under the brims and grinned at everyone definitely having a good time. Johnny could tell a good story, she had to admit, and when Mike joined in, the two batted off each other constantly.

Afterwards they went out into the back yard and kicked a ball around with the two boys. And that was Johnny's suggestion of course as Mike had no time to play with his sons these days. It turned out to be a very enjoyable afternoon, and Anna couldn't remember when they had such a good time.

She made tea later, and they sat chatting. It was then that she began to feel unwell. Suddenly, she couldn't quite get her breath, and a fit of coughing racked her. She stood up unsteadily, trying to excuse herself but not having much success as she went towards the door, and had to hold on to the wall to keep her balance.

'Anna?' Mike was beside her immediately. 'What's wrong, love?'

She shook her head and went out the door into the hall.

Eleanor appeared beside her holding a cup of water. Mike took it and held it to her mouth, but she was coughing so much she couldn't swallow.

'Hold the cup, Eleanor,' Mike said and gave Anna his handkerchief but as she put it to her mouth it was suffused with blood. He put his arms around her, carried her up the stairs to their bedroom, and lay her on the bed, pulling up the pillows behind her and supporting her with his body. But the coughing fit continued, the bleeding a frightening stream from her mouth.

'Eleanor, get a towel for Mam.'

The girl ran out and returned in a moment. Mike held it against Anna's mouth and raised her up gently until the bleeding diminished. 'You'll be all right love, just rest here and close your eyes.'

She nodded, her face chalk white. But then gripped his hand.

'Apologise to Johnny please?' she whispered, embarrassed that she had to leave the room so abruptly.

'Of course I will.'

'Go down and tell …him.'

'I will …but first let me ease the bedclothes from under you, then I can cover you up. Eleanor?'

'Yes Daddy?'

'Pull out the blanket and the eiderdown from under Mam.'

He held Anna up in his arms as she did that. Then let her down again on the sheet, and drew the bedclothes over her.

'Thank you.'

'Are you warm enough?' He put his hand on her forehead.

She nodded, feeling cold and hot at the same time. She couldn't breathe very well and the pain in her chest was uncomfortable, but she said nothing to Mike.

'I'm going to go for the doctor,' he said.

'No don't, I'm all right …' She didn't want to see that doctor again and was afraid that he would put her in hospital.

'You must see him, it's not an ordinary cold any more Anna, it's serious, that bleeding …' He stared down at her, so worried.

She nodded, having no energy to argue with him.

'Eleanor, will you look after Mam?'

The girl stood at the top of the bed, smoothing the pillow nervously.

'Yes, Daddy.'

Mike rushed down the stairs and went into the parlour. 'Johnny, Anna isn't well and I need to go for a doctor.'

'Let me do that, you stay here. I'll get a cab,' he offered.

'Would you?'

'Of course, where does the doctor live?'

'He's on South Mall, but I can't remember the number. There's a plate on the railings. Thanks mate.'

'I'll be as quick as I can and hope that I'll have him with me.'

'Daddy?'

'Yes, love?'

'Where's Mammy?' Cathy asked.

'She's in bed.'

She ran upstairs.

The two young boys stared out the window. 'Is Johnny gone?' Michael asked, a look of disappointment on his face.

'No, he'll be back.'

Mike went up to Anna, sitting at the end of the bed with Eleanor, and Cathy, the three silent, watching her sleep.

'What's wrong with Mam?' Cathy asked softly.

'She has a cold.'

'She was sick another time as well,' Eleanor said slowly.

'What do you mean?' Mike asked.

'The same, there was blood in her mouth and she had to sit in the chair.'

He stared at her.

Chapter Fifty-six

Fanny and Bina arrived on their bicycles outside the shop, and unloaded the boxes of cakes which had been tied to the carriers. In the shop Mike was staring at his accounts book, a frown on his forehead.

'Here we are,' Fanny said brightly.

'Daddy, you've sold all the tarts already.' Bina peered into the glass case on the counter.

'No, we didn't have any today, Anna isn't well.' He didn't raise his head.

Fanny looked at him, puzzlement in her eyes. 'What's wrong?'

'It's that cough …' he said slowly.

'That's been going on for too long, she should have gone to the doctor again.' Fanny took the cakes out of the box and put them on the counter.

'He came last night, we were lucky, it being a Sunday.' Mike was very downcast.

'What did he give her?'

'Another bottle of medicine, but he said she must stay in bed and that's the only way she'll get better.'

'She's been working too hard,' Fanny murmured.

'Probably.'

'She can't be baking any more tarts, I'll make a few extra as well as the cakes, at least I have plenty of apples left in the store room.'

'Thank you, Fanny, I appreciate it. You've been a great help, but to be honest things have been very slow lately. There doesn't seem to be much money around.'

'Is Mam going to be all right?' Bina asked, arranging the cakes in the glass case.

'Of course she is, girl, don't you be worrying.' Fanny hugged her. 'Mike, we'll go up home to see her.'

He nodded.

Fanny took Bina's hand and the two left together, the bell on the door clanging behind them.

They rode up to the house as quickly as they could. It was a tough climb, but Fanny was anxious to get there. She was very worried about Anna, disturbed by the look on Mike's face when he spoke about her. And she hoped that he had told her everything, God forbid, it wasn't any worse than a bad cold. He had said very little, but that may have been because Bina was there.

They arrived in. The house was quiet, the younger children sat in the kitchen while Eleanor read a book. As soon as they came in, the three rushed over and threw their arms around Fanny and Bina.

'Mammy's sick.' Michael's lip trembled, and large tears drifted down his cheeks.

'She'll be better soon.' Fanny comforted him.

'Eleanor says we mustn't go up, Mammy is in bed,' Cathy said with a cross look at her sister.

'Daddy told me to let Mam sleep and not to make any noise,' Eleanor said.

'You must all be very good. Did you bring Mam anything to eat?' Fanny asked.

'I asked her but she said no. I left a cup of tea there a while ago.'

'We'll go up now and see how she is,' Fanny said, and taking hold of Bina's hand, they both walked upstairs, and Fanny rapped gently on the door. There was no response so she went in. Anna lay in bed, her eyes closed. She was extremely pale and wan. Fanny went across to the bedside, and adjusted the blanket, but she didn't wake.

Bina's face was as pale as Anna's.

'What's wrong with Mammy?' she asked.

'She has a bit of a cold, but she'll get better soon.' Fanny comforted her.

'Is it like the flu Eleanor had?'

'It is, indeed.'

'She got better after a while.'

'And Mam will too, don't you worry.'

They stood looking at Anna.

'We'll go back down, we don't want to disturb her,' Fanny decided.

In the kitchen, she cleaned up and prepared a meal for the children. There was some chicken and potatoes there so she heated that up for them. They all tucked in and while they kept their voices low they chattered away as they usually did, obviously reassured by her and Bina's presence.

She went back upstairs after a while and sat at the side of the bed, her hand holding Anna's, and then, to her surprise she opened her eyes and looked at her. 'Mam?'

'How are you, my love?' She cupped Anna's face in her warm hand, shocked by the dark shadows under her eyes.

'I'm all right, I'm better than I was last night.'

'That's good. Can I get you anything? A drink maybe? Something to eat? There's a little of the chicken left.'

Anna shook her head. 'I'm not hungry.'

'You must eat, girl.'

'Maybe tomorrow, I'm sure I'll feel better then.'

'A hot cup of tea, how about that?'

Anna nodded. 'Just a half cup then,' she smiled weakly.

'I'll be back up in no time.'

She kissed her and let her hand rest on her arm for a moment, but said no more.

Downstairs, she made fresh tea and was looking into the cupboards for milk when she noticed that there was actually very little food on the shelves. No butter, only margarine. A square of bread which was obviously Saturday's. Of course, Anna had no chance to shop for food today, or bake either, although usually there was plenty in the house and Fanny never noticed bare shelves even when they were living in the house on South Mall.

While Anna had said she couldn't buy new curtains, she never mentioned that she couldn't buy enough food either. Fanny was shocked. Things were obviously much worse.

She went out the back to bring in coal for the range which had gone down, but again found that all there was in the coal house was a small heap of slack, which she would use to keep the fire going overnight. But it was never enough to keep the fire lit during the day. Now she had to use what was there, and immediately decided to send Seamus down the following day with some of their coal and logs.

She brought the tea up to Anna, who sipped it.

'You're looking more lively now, girl. A little colour in your cheeks.' She wanted to cheer her up.

'Thanks Mam. Are the children all right?'

'They've all had something to eat so don't be worrying, and I'm making some soup from the carcass of the chicken so that will have to do Mike when he comes home. But I'm going back to the shop just in case he needs help, and I'll come back later and put the children to bed. Bina will stay to look after them.'

Back at the shop, Fanny found Mike still staring at his accounts book, no one else in the shop.

'Mike, I came back to talk to you …and …left Bina there.' She was breathing heavily when she came in.

'Sit down, Fanny.' He pulled out a chair from the back.

'Thank you, while it was all downhill I was peddling so fast I've caught my breath.'

'You shouldn't have come back, there are very few people coming in, as you can see, not even a few children looking for a pennyworth of sweets.'

'I want to talk to you about Anna, I realised that you didn't say much when Bina was here. Now, tell me what the doctor said?'

He sighed. 'He told Anna that she has to rest, and not work so hard. Eat good food and take care of herself. But as I went outside the door with him, he told me that …' Mike bent his head.

'What?' Fanny was impatient.

'He thinks she may have consumption …'

'Oh my God …' Fanny blessed herself. 'How bad is it?'

'Bad.'

'My darling girl …' she burst into tears.

For a moment they were silent. Mike put his hands into the pockets of his coat and walked to the door. Staring out into the street beyond which was thronged with people walking past.

Fanny tried to control the well of emotion within her. How could this have happened? She asked herself. What had caused this awful disease?

'Does he …think she will …get well?' she stuttered after a while.

'If she looks after herself, although he would prefer if she goes into hospital.'

'If she goes there she might never come out,' Fanny retorted. It was what she always thought, the same as anyone else she knew.

'She refuses to go, you know how stubborn Anna is. She must look after the children and won't leave them on their own, and then she wants to bake the tarts as well.'

'There's no need for her to bake, I can do that.'

'I was actually going to say to you that maybe we shouldn't bother selling cakes from now on.'

'But I thought they went well,' Fanny was surprised.

'I don't get paid, Fanny, so it's a waste of time.'

'I know some shopkeepers find it hard to get people to pay up, although we make sure we pay all our bills on the dot every Friday, otherwise the shopkeepers are gone out of business.'

'That's exactly what has happened. For the last while I haven't been able to pay the rent and the owner of the shop has been in and out wondering when he's going to get it.'

Fanny stared at him, astonished. 'You must have money to pay the rent, and you'll have to insist on getting paid every time a person buys something.'

'That's all very well, but it's not the way things are done, and anyway if I put my foot down they'll all just drift away. They know well we're new in business and are probably taking advantage. Look at the accounts ledger, sales are much less than previously, I only sold half a dozen items today.' He waved towards it.

'And you don't know anyone in town. With us it's different. In the village, we know every shopkeeper's family, and if we don't pay, then we will see the results and poverty in their wives and children.'

'I suppose it's a bit like that with my stepmother, although she did warn me that I'd never make a penny. I can't believe it has collapsed, I was so full of optimism that we would be able to run our own business and have a good standard of living. And now we've lost all that money, or I've lost it I should say.' He bent his head.

'Pity you left the Royal Navy,' Fanny murmured, slightly under her breath.

He didn't respond to her remark.

'You could teach, perhaps?'

'I couldn't see myself standing in front of a class again. Anyway, I hated it.'

'You might have to bottle that up, your wife and children are more important.'

'Who'd employ me?'

'I'm sure someone would,' Fanny tried to be positive.

'It's different in the Free State.'

'Perhaps.'

'I have to look after Anna now, that's the only thing that matters.'

She stood up. 'We'll do that together.'

'Thank you.' He nodded.

'But consumption is …one of the children could catch it, couldn't they,' she hated saying that to him, but was well aware that whole families had been stricken down with the awful disease.

'Yes. But the children have been exposed to it for a good length of time and the doctor feels taking them away wouldn't be advisable now. Anyway, even if they went somewhere else you can't expose other people.'

'So I, or Seamus or Bina, …any of us could …' Fanny's heart beat loudly, she could hear it in her ears.

'Or myself.'

'Maybe I should keep Bina at home?'

'Perhaps, although she will want to see her mother.'

'Just for a while until Anna gets better.' Fanny was trembling.

Chapter Fifty-seven

Anna put her feet on the cold lino. She had stayed in bed most of the time over the last few days and actually felt better. The cough had eased a little and she was taking the bottle the doctor had given her. Fanny had made a couple of meat pies for them and delicious broth which Anna had managed to eat. Yesterday Seamus had brought in a load of logs and some coal as well so there was plenty of heat in the kitchen and a fire in her bedroom. She was worried about having enough money to buy what they needed, but when she mentioned it to Mike, he just told her not to be concerned, everything would be all right.

She made a list of prices and sent Eleanor down to the nearest shops to buy pigs feet, tripe, and other offal instead of more expensive meats. Milk was four pence a quart, and sugar two pence a pound. The last time she bought potatoes they were one shilling and four pence a stone, but Fanny brought in her own which she had stored over the winter.

But when Mike saw the pile of fuel in the coalhouse, he wasn't a bit pleased. 'I will look after you and the children, you're my own family, my responsibility,' he said bluntly.

'Mam noticed how little coal we had and …' she tried to explain.

'They're very generous, although I must pay for it.'

'I don't think they expect that, they might be insulted.'

'I can offer at least. I don't expect them to pay for our fuel out of their small money.'

She said no more.

Fanny's pies and vegetables kept them going during the week, and every day Anna went downstairs for a short time and peeled and cooked the spuds in the kitchen, and baked bread as well. That done, she made a cup of tea for herself and went back to bed. Fanny had taken a bag of washing home with her the day before and Anna was worried that Mike might even object to that. But when she brought it back a couple of days later, all neatly pressed, Anna was grateful. She had said nothing to him so wasn't even sure if he realised that it had happened as he didn't say a word. She sighed with relief when he put on a clean collar the following morning and didn't ask who had washed it.

'Mam, I'll get Eleanor to do the washing next week, you've enough to do as it is with Mrs. Staunton's linen as well as your own. And I'm feeling a lot better already so I'll be back to normal by then,' Anna said when Fanny called.

'But I thought the doctor said you were to stay in bed for a few weeks?' she asked anxiously.

'I'm going to be completely well soon,' Anna insisted.

'That cough is still bad and your chest is wheezy,' Fanny pointed out.

'Don't worry about me, Mam.'

'It's hard not to.' Fanny held her hand tight.

'Once I take my ease and don't do so much I'll be all right. By the way, we want to pay you for the coal and logs. Mike said he'll do that soon.'

'What?' Fanny was surprised.

'You know how he is, so independent,' Anna tried to explain.

'Tell him not to even think of it. You're our daughter. If you need something then we'll give it to you. What's wrong with that?'

'I understand, and I'm very grateful, but Mike thinks differently.'

'I don't know what Seamus is going to say, he'll be right put out if Mike comes to him and says he wants to pay.'

'We always like to pay our bills,' Anna explained.

'And we don't want a repeat of the row which went on between

Seamus and Mike's father. That split the two families for years, do you remember?'

'Don't remind me, Mam, but I want to thank you so much for all you've done for us, all the cakes you've baked and everything else, we're so grateful.'

'But you gave me all the flour and stuff needed for the cakes, I just had the few apples and baked them,' Fanny pointed out.

'And that took time and you brought them into the shop as well every day, but Mike has decided that it's not worth selling the cakes any longer.' She pressed her hand on her chest in an effort to breathe. 'Sorry …'

Fanny sighed. 'Stop talking so much, it doesn't do you any good.' She looked into her bag. 'Here's the *Liberty* magazine for you. You'll have something to read while you're lying there. Have a look at the latest fashions.' She flicked through a few pages. 'I was horrified at what they call the *flappers* – the girls who wear those short dresses. Would you look at them.' She opened a page and held it out to Anna. 'And the hair is cut short too, they call it the *bob*. I can't believe it.'

'I think I read that the skirts had gone up a couple of inches but not that much.'

'I'm certainly not going around like that,' Fanny laughed. 'If I had a little hole in my stocking then everyone would see it. As it is there is one at my ankle.' She pushed her foot out and raised her skirt so Anna could see the hole. 'I'll have to get some soot from the fireplace to fill that in.'

'I wouldn't mind the bob style for my hair, it's so long it takes ages to arrange every day.' Anna admired the photo. 'I wonder is Jim's Edith a *flapper*?'

Fanny raised her eyebrows.

'Ask him in your next letter, just for the fun of it.'

'I will indeed,' Fanny laughed.

'And I'll tell Mike that I'm going to be a *flapper* when he comes home.'

'He probably doesn't know what it is.'

'I'll shock him,' Anna smiled at the thought. 'But I'll have to pick the right moment.'

'You're supposed to be reading, not talking. Shush now, pet and be quiet while I do a few things downstairs.'

Anna and the children were all in bed when Mike came home that night, although Anna heard the key in the door and raised her head when he came in.

'How are you, my darling?' he said softly as he sat by the bed and kissed her.

She hugged him. 'Your dinner is warming. I made a stew with the meat you brought home yesterday.'

'It wasn't the best cut of meat, just a few scrag ends, but they probably made up a good stew.'

'It was very tasty.' Anna reached for her dressing gown which lay across the bed. She didn't like to tell him that the meat had diminished a lot in the cooking, and she and the children hadn't eaten very much, keeping most of it for him.

'Don't get up,' he said.

'The children will hear us talking.'

'All right, let me help.' He put his arm around her.

'I can manage,' she protested.

'And deprive me of the chance to hold you close?' he smiled and kissed her again.

She giggled and let him lift her up and put the dressing gown on her. It wasn't often they had the chance to be together without the children being around. And at night, he generally didn't wake her when he came in.

'You're very late, my love, why don't you come home and do your work here?' she asked, watching him ladle the stew on to a plate.

'I don't want to do that, I need to forget about it when I'm home.' He came over to the table and began to eat, dipping her freshly made soda bread in the soup.

'How was it today?'

'Not much better. My ladies who bought the cakes have all but disappeared, and haven't paid their bills either. Coughlan arrived this evening again, he threatened that he'll put us out if we can't pay the back money. I have until next week. What did I say a minute ago, I wasn't going to bring the shop home and here I am already talking about it,' he smiled wryly at her, his brown eyes full of regret.

'We must talk about it, I want to know,' she insisted. 'But finish your dinner first.'

She sat watching him eat, and could see that the problems of the shop were lying heavily on him. There was a heaviness about the slope of his shoulders, and his features were gloomy, it was something which he couldn't obviously hide.

'That was really nice, thank you my love.' He reached his hand out and covered hers.

'I'll make you tea.' She leaned on the table with her hands and tried to push herself up, wishing she had more energy. But it was like trying to shift something very heavy and she couldn't manage.

'Let me.' He went over to the range.

'Thanks.'

When he had brought the teapot over and poured, she sipped the hot tea and was revived somewhat. He packed tobacco into the pipe and smoked. The aroma curled around them and as always, she was reminded of home and her father.

'Tell me again what Coughlan said?'

'Next week he's coming in and will evict us if we can't pay the back money.'

'That's awful.' She was horrified.

'It's a terrible blow. I was so sure that we'd do well and never have to worry about money for the rest of our lives.'

'Isn't there any way we could get some money to pay it? How much is it altogether?'

'Eight pounds ten shillings and that includes next week, our last week.'

She stared at him. 'That's an awful lot.'

He nodded.

'Could we sell something? Maybe my jewellery?'

'I gave you most of the pieces you have and you're not selling. We could never replace them.'

'What about my fob watch?'

'No.' He shook his head, adamant.

'What are we going to do?' She felt helpless. Wanting to help him in some way. Wishing he would let her.

'We'll have to close. If we go on we'll only build up more debt.'

'People are dreadful, why can't they pay their bills?' Anna was angry.

He shrugged.

'You must be so disappointed. You really enjoyed the shop. And so did I.'

'Well, we have to close now before we lose any more money. I've been able to pay for all the goods we have in the shop out of the money I got from the Navy so I don't owe anyone other than Coughlan. There is some stuff we can use ourselves like flour but in a way I'd prefer to sell as much as I can, that money might go some way towards the rent.'

Chapter Fifty-eight

Having no other option, the following week Mike printed a large sign and put it in the window - it announced a *Closing Down Sale*. Suddenly it was busy again, and he was amazed at the amount of people who came in to buy the last of their produce. Old men grinned at him with toothless gums, obviously delighted to get their tobacco at such a bargain price. Even some of the people who owed him money came in and cleared their accounts which he couldn't believe actually happened. By Saturday, he had amassed seven pounds, three shillings, sixpence halfpenny, and a couple of farthings.

When Coughlan came in Mike had already counted the money which was all coin and offered him the whole lot, each value done up in packets, pounds, shillings and pence.

'There is a list.' Mike passed the sheet of paper over to him.

The man looked at it. 'You owe me more than that,' he said sharply.

'I realise that and I'll give you this amount.' He indicated the money packets neatly stacked on the counter. 'But I'll still owe you one pound, six shillings and three pence halfpenny.'

Silently, Coughlan stood there looking at the money, his moist lower lip sticking out.

'I wondered if we could do a deal?' Mike asked.

Coughlan's head jerked up. 'What sort of deal?'

'Have you any use for the counter and the shelving which I erected, if another shopkeeper comes in perhaps you could sell it to him?'

Coughlan looked around the shop.

'You have to admit that the shop is in a much better condition now than when I came in. It's clean and was freshly painted inside and out. You could maybe get a bit more rent from someone because of that, and they won't have to spend money doing it up. They just have to paint over our name.' As he said that, Mike's stomach took a dive. That was something he hadn't thought about and now the realisation of what it meant cut through him.

'I might and I mightn't.' Coughlan grunted.

Mike didn't say anything, his heart beating like a drum. His pension was due the following week and he couldn't afford to take the balance owed to Coughlan out of it. How would they manage, he wondered?

'You owe it to me one way or the other.' Coughlan pushed a thick finger on to the list with the balance owing clearly written at the end.

'Yes, I know that.' Mike swallowed. It wasn't going as well as he had hoped.

'And you'll have to pay it. I'll have some boyo in here and he'll be trying to do deals as well, and probably will care less about the paint and all of that.'

'Could I pay it every month …a small amount?' Mike asked. It was his last option.

The man's mouth fell open. 'D'you think I'm a right gom?'

'Well, I don't have it to give you.' Mike raised his hands.

'Damn and blast you.' Coughlan spat on the floor.

'You can't get money when there is none,' Mike said.

'How much are you offering?' he asked, gruff.

Mike was frantically trying to calculate how much he could spare out of his pension, and afraid to give him too much he decided to go low.

'I could give you …eh …sixpence a week.' He stared at him.

Coughlan laughed out loud. 'What do you take me for?'

'I have a family and it may take me some time to get a job.'

'I'm not going to finance your crowd of brats.' He spat on the floor again.

Mike winced.

'It will be a shilling a week and if you miss a week then there will be interest added on at the end. You could be paying for a long time.' He turned on his heel and went out the door, then swung back. 'I'll give you until tomorrow night to be out of here.'

Mike nodded.

He returned home very late, having spent the time clearing away what was left of the stock and packing it. In the back room which he had jokingly called his office his papers were bundled up too. Then he took out the tools he had brought in with him and began to dismantle the counter. He didn't see why he should leave it there for Coughlan. The wood was good and he thought perhaps he might be able to use it for something else at home. But he had to get everything out of here and as he literally didn't have a penny, he couldn't hire a vehicle to carry it as he had done when he was opening the shop.

It was after twelve and Anna was fast asleep. He sat in a chair beside the bed, noticing that her thin body hardly made any impression on the bedclothes. The hollows in her face were shadowed and it was only now that he realised how ill she must be. She never complained of feeling pain or anything else. Always a smile when she dismissed his queries. How would he look after Anna and the children he asked himself, feeling so helpless. He was a failure. His money was all gone. And he had to force his family to live on a pittance.

In the morning, he brought Anna her breakfast. Tea and bread and butter was all she wanted.

'How are you feeling, my love?' He helped her to sit up, re-positioning the pillows behind her.

'I'm all right, thank you, love,' she smiled up at him, and he kissed her. 'What happened at the shop, did you meet Coughlan last night?'

'Yes.'

'How much money came in yesterday? Did we have enough to pay him?' she asked anxiously.

'No, but we weren't that far off the total amount, one pound, six shillings, and three pence halfpenny short to be precise,' he tried to smile.

'How will we find that much?' Her face paled even more.

'I've arranged to pay him a shilling a week until I clear it.'

'That should be all right, we'll just be very careful,' she said. 'Where are the children? I don't hear them making a racket as usual.'

He went to the window and looked out. 'The girls are playing *picki* and the boys are playing *cat and dog* with two sticks,' he smiled down into the back yard.

'It looks like a lovely day,' Anna said.

'It is. Would you like me to bring out some chairs and we can sit in the sunshine? The fresh air would do you good.'

'I might, later.'

She seemed very tired, he thought. 'But there is something I have to ask,' he hesitated.

'What is that?'

'I know I said that I didn't want help from Fanny and Seamus, and that embarrasses me. But I'll need to borrow the trap to take the stuff out of the shop, I have to clear it by this evening. Do you think they'll let me have it?' He found it difficult to ask the favour but he had no other option.

'Of course they will, Mam and Pa will do anything for us.'

'Hopefully they're not going anywhere today, but first I'll take the kids to Mass. Will you be all right until we get back?' he asked.

'I'll be fine. I'm only sorry I can't help but I'd probably be useless to you.'

'There isn't much left in the shop so it shouldn't take too long.' There was a trace of bitterness in his voice.

Mike knocked on the door of *Rose Cottage* which was ajar. When Fanny appeared, she stared at him with a look of shock on her face.

'Anna's all right, there's no problem, don't worry,' he said immediately.

'Then what?' She ushered him inside.

'Daddy?' Bina ran over, her arms outstretched.

'How are you, love?' He hugged her, smiling.

'Why are you here? Is Mammy with you and everyone?' She stared up into his face and then past him to the door.

'No, I'm on my own.' It was only then he saw that Lizzie and Iris were sitting by the range.

He went forward and shook hands.

Fanny pulled out a chair. 'We'll be having dinner soon, will you stay?'

'No thanks, I must get back, but there is something …'

'How is Anna?' Lizzie asked.

'She's getting a little better,' he said.

'Thanks be to God,' Iris blessed herself. 'I'm doing a Novena for her.'

'Should we go up to see her?' Lizzie asked.

'She's resting a lot at the moment, and I try to keep her from talking too much, her chest is bad.'

The two women nodded, understanding.

'I posted a letter yesterday, so she should get it tomorrow,' Iris added.

'Thank you, she'll be happy to hear from you.'

'Mike, would you even have a cup of tea?' Fanny asked.

'No thanks, Fanny, I came over because I hoped that Seamus might let me borrow the trap.'

'Why do you need it?' Fanny was always straight.

'Can I go with you?' Bina interrupted.

Fanny put a finger over her lips and gave her a warning look.

'I've closed the shop and I must clear it by today.'

'What happened to it?' Bina burst out again.

'I'm very sorry to hear that, Mike, Anna must be upset.'

'She is. It's a big disappointment to both of us.'

'Do you think you will be using the trap today?' He stood up again.

'We have to take Lizzie and Iris to the train later,' Fanny explained.

He was taken aback and his heart somersaulted.

'But it won't be until six o'clock,' she smiled.

'So do you think Seamus would let me have it for a few hours?'

'I'm sure, go on out and ask him.'

Bina went to the door.

'Fanny, I'm very grateful.' He shook hands with her and with Lizzie and Iris. 'Enjoy your dinner.'

'Tell Anna we were asking for her.'

'I will. Goodbye Fanny and thank you.' He followed Bina and outside saw Seamus brushing the mare. 'Seamus?' he called.

'Ah Michael a mhic,' the man stopped what he was doing and smiled.

Mike shook his hand. 'I was just in with Fanny and I asked her if I could borrow the trap, although I probably should have asked you first but …'

'What are you blathering about, you're all of a dither man,' Seamus laughed, standing with his hands on his hips, a wide grin on his face.

'Right, I'll come to the point, could I borrow the trap today? We're closing the shop and I have to move everything by this evening or else the owner will throw it on the street, mind you, it isn't much but I don't want that at least …' his voice tapered off.

'Once you're back in time to take Lizzie and Iris to the train.'

'I will of course, thank you.'

Seamus went into the stable, unhooked the tack and began to harness the mare.

They arrived at the shop and Bina tethered the horse to a lamp post. Inside, Mike lifted the boxes and put them in the trap. Then the lengths of wood were put in as well as various other bits and pieces. Bina carried the empty jars.

'Daddy, there's a sweet at the end of this jar, look, it's a raspberry and custard.' She stared into it. 'Can I have it?'

'Course you can.'

Eventually, the place was cleared and he stood there staring around him. All this week he had known this was coming, but hadn't expected to feel quite so bereft. Once again, he felt such a failure. All his hopes had been tied up in this business venture. And the loss he felt now was as bad as when he left the Navy. He stood outside. His name *O'Sullivan* over the door reminding him of his uselessness as a man, and as a husband too. Every time he passed this way in the future he knew he would feel the same.

'It's sad we're closing our shop, Daddy, isn't it?' Bina said.

'It is, Bina.' He locked the door.

'I liked serving the customers.'

'And you were very good at that.' He put his arm around her shoulders.

'I'd like to have my own shop one day.'

'And you will, girl.'

Mike climbed up into the trap, followed by Bina, and they turned for home. All the time he was thinking about Anna and how he had let her down. She had consumption and he knew very well that the money difficulties they had experienced in recent months may well have caused her illness. The thought of that twisted his gut and now he simply didn't know where he would get enough money to pay the doctor and buy the best of food for her. It was the only way she would get better. He had read enough of the terrible disease and how it passed from one family member to another, and that if she didn't get the right care then he might lose her. He couldn't get his head around that possibility.

When they arrived at the house, Bina went up to see Anna, and the other children helped him unload the trap. Before he left he hurried up to see her.

'How are you, darling?' He kissed her. 'Did Eleanor bring you something to eat?'

'Yes, Mam's broth, tea and bread and butter, it was lovely,' she smiled at him.

'Did you have enough?'

'Plenty,' she laughed.

'I'm taking the trap back to Seamus, and I will probably bring Lizzie and Iris to the train to save him the trouble, so it will be a couple of hours. Come on Bina.'

'Get back as quick as you can, I miss you.'

It was a little after five when he arrived in Glanmire and Lizzie and Iris were ready to leave.

'I'm sorry to be so late, but it took me longer than I expected. I'm sure you were wondering would you catch your train.'

'We were,' they laughed.

'Now, I'm going too,' Fanny said. 'I made a steak and kidney pie and boiled a nice piece of bacon. And there's a few other things as well, so they'll keep you going for the week. Will you carry these out to the trap?'

'You really shouldn't, Fanny, this is too much.' He stared at the two boxes which were on the table. 'I'm so grateful.' A wave of emotion swept through him, and he put his arm around her.

'None of that, boy.'

'We're going to miss our train. Come on now,' Lizzie fussed, so he gave one box to Bina and took the other himself.

Outside, Seamus was harnessing up the other horse. 'The mare is a bit tired and as it's a warm ould day, Daisy will take us the rest of the way.'

'It's a bit of a squeeze,' laughed Bina as they all got in.

They arrived just in time for the train and after they had waved Lizzie and Iris off, Fanny turned to Mike.

'We'll take you home, Mike, can't have you walking all that way.'

'There's no need, it will be too late for you.'

'I want to see Anna,' Fanny said, climbing in.

There was no arguing with her, so they set off. Eleanor and Cathy were playing in the yard with their dolls and rushed to meet them when they arrived. Inside, Anna sat near a low fire in the parlour, and was really happy to see them all.

'You shouldn't be up, love,' Fanny put her arm around Anna's thin shoulders.

'I'll be too weak if I stay in bed all the time, Mam, and it's quite pleasant here. Now, sit beside me and tell me all.' Anna waved to the chair near her. 'Can I get you anything?'

'Not at all. Thank you, love.'

'Pa?' Anna asked.

'I'm happy with my pipe,' he said.

'Girls, help Bina put all the things we brought into the press,' Fanny said.

'Yes, Granny.' They took the boxes and afterwards they ran in and told Anna everything that Fanny had brought.

They chatted and laughed, and Mike could see that Anna was in very good form, and was so glad of that. For himself, he made an effort to hide the sadness of losing the shop, and joined in the talk.

'Thank you, Mam, for bringing all the lovely things to eat, you're so good, we really appreciate it. We won't know ourselves this week.' Anna held her hand.

'And my thanks as well, Fanny and Seamus, for lending me the trap.'

'We'll be over again during the week,' Fanny promised. 'And you take care of yourself, Anna, and don't be doing too much. Are you still taking that bottle the doctor gave you?'

'I am, don't worry,' Anna smiled.

'Granny, we're going to walk in the *Corpus Christi* procession next week.' Eleanor came close to her.

'Are you? Isn't that nice.'

'I'm wearing my Holy Communion dress,' Cathy said.

'And what about you Eleanor?'

'My Communion dress is too small.' Her eyes filled with tears.

'We'll get you a new one,' Anna said. 'Don't worry.'

'Why don't you borrow one of Bina's dresses, you wouldn't mind, would you Bina?' Fanny asked.

'I have a couple of white dresses that would be nice.'

'Right, we'll pick one and bring it over next week,' Fanny promised.

'Thank you, Bina. Thank you Granny.' Eleanor kissed them both, delighted.

Anna was grateful to her mother.

'You didn't mind Mam bringing all those things, did you, Mike?' Anna asked softly when they were in bed that night.

'I suppose I have to admit that providing for my own family is important to me but I have to be grateful, I can't do it myself now.'

'Your pension will be coming in next week.'

'Thanks be to God for that, but between now and then I don't know what we'd have done for food, I gave Coughlan every last penny I had to reduce the amount owing.'

'Are you very disappointed about it?' Anna curled into him.

'Of course I am, after all the effort it's terrible to see nothing out of it.'

'I'm sad too, I had hoped that it would be a good business and something for the children's future, but now ...'

'We have to survive on my pension which is only a pittance. My decision to take a sum of money from the Navy wasn't a good one. I hadn't anticipated failure,' he sighed.

'People don't have so much money nowadays, and everything has got much dearer.'

'We're living in The Free State, and I suppose it will take some time for our government to begin to run the country properly.'

'It wasn't your fault that people wouldn't pay.'

'I hadn't considered that either,' he admitted. 'Not at all.'

Chapter Fifty-nine

Mike spent his time looking for a job. Out early every day, in and out of companies offering his services. He went to the docks in Cork and Cobh too but had no luck. Weeks passed, and it was a struggle to survive on his pension. Without the help of Fanny and Seamus, Anna just didn't know how they would have managed. Fanny was the one who brought the good food, and fuel too, and even suggested that Anna should come out to stay in *Rose Cottage*. But she wouldn't leave Mike and the children, and worried that he might go back to sea, the thought of that just too much for her. She couldn't lose him again.

Leaning up against the pillows, she closed her eyes and drifted off to sleep. That was happening more often and she hated to be asleep when someone came into the room.

'Mammy? Are you awake?' Eleanor was the first.

'Yes I am of course, I just closed my eyes for a minute. I'll go down now and heat up the dinner, I'm sorry love, I should have done it already.' She sat up and swung her legs out of the bed.

'Here's your dressing gown, I'll help you with it.' Eleanor did that and Anna forced herself up into standing position.

'Can you walk, Mammy?'

'Of course I can.' She put her hand on the bed end and slowly walked to the door. 'You can just help me go down the stairs, you know how wobbly my legs are.' She made a little joke and held on to the bannisters for support. But by the time she reached the end she was already having difficulty breathing.

The child stared into her face, worried.

'Where are …' She fought for breath, wondering where Michael and Joseph were.

'Are you all right, Mammy?'

She couldn't reply.

There were tears in Eleanor's eyes.

Anna wasn't able to say anything. She pulled a handkerchief from her pocket and pressed it against her mouth.

'Mammy, you're bleeding again.' Eleanor was horrified.

The other children dashed in the door and when they saw Anna they all burst out crying.

'Mammy, Mammy …' The boys hung out of her.

Cathy just stood there, tears rolling down her face and screamed.

Eleanor took a towel, and wiped the blood which had drifted down Anna's chin and neck. She still coughed and fought for breath which was painful. A wave of nausea passed over her and the room seemed to drift away in a fog, the children's faces were vague and she couldn't tell who was who. Then everything went black.

'Anna, Anna, wake up.' Mike stroked her cheek gently.

She opened her eyes.

'Thanks be to God, you've come back to us,' he smiled at her.

Anna tried to smile at him but wasn't able to. She still struggled for breath and could hear loud hoarse sounds, puzzled as to what they were.

'Mammy?' Eleanor held her hand.

'Will you have something, my love,' Mike asked. 'Some water or a cup of tea?'

She shook her head.

'I've sent for another doctor, he'll be here soon and will be able to give you something,' Mike reassured Anna. 'You're going to be all right, my darling.'

She loved him so much. Thoughts drifted around her head. Mike. Mike. She was back in Queenstown with him. He was buying her something in a shop. She didn't know what it was at first but then he put a gold chain around her neck and she looked down and saw that it was a pretty locket. She pressed her hand against her neck and could feel it still snuggled there on her ruffled nightdress.

A man came later. He wore spectacles and carried a large brown leather bag which he put on the end of the bed. She didn't know what he was doing here. Then he put a cold thing on her chest and made her sit up and did the same on her back. Patting her skin with his fingers. He pushed one of those glass things into her mouth and she found it very difficult to breathe. But she had to leave it there for a few minutes and was glad when he took it out, feeling annoyed with him. And who was he anyway?

She lay down and closed her eyes. The trees of *Fairfields* were all around her. The sun sparkled through the leaves and there was a pattern on the rug on the ground where Mike lay. The walls of the ruined cottage hugged around them, and there was no sound only the whisper of a gentle breeze drifting through the branches, and the singing of the birds. She turned to Mike and his arms tightened around her. Their eyes met.

'I love you, Anna, love you, love you …' His lips touched hers, his tongue caressed, and she leaned into his embrace.

'I love you, Mike.'

Fanny and Seamus were there now, and all the children. How lovely, she thought. Mike dabbed her forehead with something cool. Thank you, my love, she tried to say but couldn't. The man with the glasses was there as well. Fanny came close and held a cup to her lips. She said something.

'Thank you, Mam,' Anna whispered. Music filled her head. Her brothers Jim and Pat were playing their accordians and Fanny played her concertina on her knee singing. 'Come on, Anna, play us a tune,' someone called, and other voices joined in. The keyboard of the piano wavered in front of her. She put her fingers on the keys and pressed down her foot on the pedal. The sound was beautiful, and she played again her most favourite tune, *Carrigdhoun*, the music echoing all around her as she sang the words.

'Anna, Anna …' Fanny called her from very far away.

Mike's face was close to her own now. His lips gentle on her cheek. 'My darling …'

Bina held her hand.

She could hear Eleanor and Cathy crying.

Michael and Joseph stared at her from the end of the bed, coming and going like little ghosts, white faced.

She remembered then something she must do. She tried to speak.

'What is it, my love?' Mike came close again. His ear close to her lips. 'Tell me?'

'Mrs. Walsh,' she managed to whisper.

'You want Mrs. Walsh?'

She nodded.

'Eleanor, go over for Mrs. Walsh, quickly …' She could hear his words.

Someone murmured prayers. That was nice, she thought. Why were they praying? It must be the Rosary she thought.

They all went away then and left her on her own. She put out her hand to see if she could feel them, but couldn't.

She drifted, and only awoke when she felt a cool hand on hers. She opened her eyes. It was Mrs. Walsh. She was so glad to see her. 'Please forgive me. I saw your children wearing those lovely clothes you got from America for the Corpus Christi Procession and I had no money to buy my children anything new and I was envious of you, so envious, please forgive me ...' she gasped with difficulty.

Mrs. Walsh patted her hand. A great sense of relief swept through Anna.

Mike came close again. He was wearing his naval uniform, brass buttons shining, and his peaked cap with the white top. He sat beside her and they looked out over Queenstown Harbour. People walked on the promenade. The band played on the bandstand. The breeze whipped Anna's hair under her hat, and a strand crossed over her face. She wore her pale grey suit, with the matching fur muff. She pressed her hand against the fur but couldn't feel its softness.

Mike held her close to him, but there was a mist between them and everything was very quiet. She felt herself slipping out of his arms and being drawn away towards a bright twinkling light. She stretched out her arm and tried to hold on to him, but the distance between them grew wider and she couldn't see him any longer, she couldn't see her children or Mam and Pa - she was all alone.

Chapter Sixty

The day was bright outside, but the parlour was in shadow. Mike had drawn all the curtains and covered the mirror over the fireplace with a white pillow slip. Anna's wooden coffin was laid between two chairs in the parlour. Flickering candles at each end. She lay there, so still, her skin like porcelain. Bina, Eleanor, Cathy, Michael and Joseph stood around it, their faces white, tears on their cheeks. Joseph and Michael had their arms around Eleanor, Bina and Cathy hugged each other. Fanny, Seamus and Edward sat on chairs on the other side. Fanny was quite inconsolable. Lizzie and Iris were beside them, the two women keening some old lament of long ago. Mike's mother and his two sisters were there as well.

On the mantle was a tray of cigarettes, matches, a box of snuff. People helped themselves. In the kitchen Fanny had made sandwiches and Mrs. Walsh presided over a large tea pot and poured cups of tea for anyone who wanted one. Mike had bought porter for the men. He had to borrow the money needed for the funeral from his friend Con in Glounthaune and had promised him he would pay it back as soon as he could. Johnny had also given him money towards the cost, insisting there was no need to repay it.

Flanked by his two friends, Mike stood in the hall and welcomed people as they came in. Shaking hands. Listening to the sympathetic murmurs extended to him.

Mourners walked around the coffin one by one, blessing themselves and murmuring prayers. They made the sign of the cross on Anna's forehead and some kissed her. Others patted the children on the shoulder, or hugged them. Mike, Fanny, Seamus, Lizzie and Iris sat up with Anna all night praying for her soul. Fanny wanted to keep Anna with her as long as possible and didn't close her eyes once.

The following day, there were more people in the house and at about four o'clock Mike stood over the coffin. There was a tense silence, and even Lizzie and Iris were quiet. He leaned over and slowly took Anna's face in both of his hands and kissed her lips. It was a terrible moment. Then he covered her hands with his. Tears welled up in his eyes, and drops of moisture fell on to her white skin. He blessed himself.

Fanny sobbed then, unable to control herself, and the children too as Mike lifted the top of the coffin and secured it down with help from his friends Johnny and Con.

The funeral hearse arrived. It was drawn by four black horses with black plumes on their heads. The people all gathered outside the house, as Mike, Seamus, Edward, Johnny and Con lifted the coffin on their shoulders and carried it into the hearse. Then Mike joined the children and walked behind as it moved off, the family and friends following slowly behind.

Anna reposed overnight in the North Chapel, and early the following morning, Mike, Seamus and Edward went to Caherlag Cemetery to dig Anna's grave with the help of other neighbours. They took shovels out of the trap, and went inside. The grave was only a short distance inside the gate and Mike dug the first grassy sod and he and the men shovelled the earth in a heap on one side.

It reminded Mike of his own father's burial which was the only other time he had helped dig a grave. It was hard work. They took a break. Mike had brought a bottle of whiskey and the men shared it amongst each other. As he stared down into the earth, his heart began to thump violently at the thought of putting his darling into the darkness below.

After the Mass, they made that sad journey from the church to the cemetery. The wind whipped around them, gusting with rain every now and then. Mike and the men carried the coffin from the hearse and it rested on one side until they wound ropes around it and slowly lowered it into the ground. Mike then gathered the children beside him. Fanny had tried to persuade him not to bring the two boys to the funeral, but he was adamant that they should be there to say goodbye to their mother.

The priest said the prayers, and the people joined in a decade of the Rosary. Mike took a handful of earth and threw it on top of the coffin, the sound of the stones loud as they scattered on the wood. It was the final farewell to Anna, and each of the children did the same. People began to move, although the family stayed there even after the priest had left. But noticing the pinched white faces of the children, Mike ushered them away and Fanny took charge.

He turned back then, and from behind the wall the men took their shovels again and began to move the mound of earth back into the grave. The first shovel full of earth and stones rattled harshly on the wood of the coffin and slowly the sound grew more faint as the grave was filled up. Mike struggled to stay controlled, feeling such heartbreak inside him he thought he would begin to scream at any moment.

They smoothed the mound, and then the men climbed into the trap. Before they went too far, Mike excused himself and went back to the cemetery saying that he had left the shovel behind. He had deliberately let it fall among the grasses at the head of the grave. All he wanted was a few minutes with Anna before she drifted out of his mind, a terrible worry that he would forget her blue eyes, her smile, her touch and eventually lose her altogether.

Part 4

1929

Chapter Sixty-one

Bina picked up her diary. Fanny had given it to her at Christmas, telling her that it would be nice to start keeping a diary as she was going to be nineteen on the sixteenth of January, and was a young woman now.

She opened the little book and looked at the first page. The name *Charles Letts's* was printed there and the words *Tempus Fugit* underneath. She thought it was so pretty and turned over the page. There was a calendar on the left hand side and on the right a space to write her name and address. Her pen was on the dressing table and she dipped it in the ink bottle. She wrote carefully in the little space.

Bina O'Sullivan, Rose Cottage, Glanmire, Co. Cork.

These were the first words she had written in her first diary. She was looking forward to filling in the little section for each day. She smiled to herself.

Reading on, she found a section called *Personal Memoranda,* where she neatly inserted the size of her gloves - *six and a half,* and her shoe size - *three and a half.* Her hat size was next, and then her dress size. After that, she entered her w*atch number.* The times of the bus service into the city and home again, three times a day there and back. And how much money she had saved went into the cash account. It wasn't much, just seventeen pence. There was also a little pad on which she could make notes and rub them out if she changed her mind.

In the evening, Seamus, Fanny and herself rode in the trap up to Hillside Terrace. When they arrived, Bina ran on ahead, pushed open the door, and in the parlour was immediately surrounded by her sisters and brothers. They threw their arms around her, and then hugged Fanny and Seamus when they appeared.

'Good to see you, Fanny, Seamus, won't you sit down.' Mike stood and carefully put a bookmark in between the leaves of the book he had been reading and replaced it on the shelf. Everything was very precise where Mike was concerned. Books in alphabetical order according to the author. He ran the house like he was still in the navy. His motto - *A place for everything and everything in its place.*

'Seamus, some tobacco?' Mike offered.

'Thanks, Mike.'

'You're looking lovely, Bina, is that a new coat?' Eleanor admired. 'But you've already one like that in blue, haven't you?'

'Granny bought them for me.'

'I'd love one.'

'I'll let you have a lend.' Bina unbuttoned it.

'Will you, when?'

'When you can fit into it. Try it on now.'

Eleanor did, but it was quite long on her as there was a noticeable difference in their heights.

'You've a few more inches to go,' Bina said.

Eleanor looked disappointed.

'It won't take that long, and I'll give you a lend.'

'Make your Granny and Grandad a cup of tea, Eleanor, and Bina if she wants one,' Mike said.

Eleanor went out, Fanny, Bina and all the children followed.

'What's for your tea?' Fanny asked sixteen year old Eleanor.

'I made bread.' She took out the loaf of soda bread from the cupboard.

'Well, that looks really nice, aren't you a good girl. And have you anything to put on it?'

'Just margarine, your jam is all gone.'

'Aren't you lucky I brought you some more?' Fanny smiled and produced a pot from her bag.

Eleanor was delighted. 'Blackberry and apple, lovely.'

'And here's a few other things.' Fanny always brought food. Although she was quite aware of Mike's fierce independence and knew he never wanted any help, she felt food didn't fall into that category. He had got a job in a shipping company some months after Anna had died and managed to feed and clothe his family, although all of Bina's clothes were passed on to Eleanor and Cathy.

Bina wandered back into the parlour and sat on the arm of Seamus's chair.

'Well Bina, now that you're finished at the College for Young Ladies, are you going to look for a job?' Mike asked.

'No, Granny says I don't have to work.'

'Your sister works helping a woman make hats. Why should you do nothing? There is a mill near Glanmire, you might find a job there.'

'Bina, would you carry in the tray for me?' Fanny asked from the door.

She did as she was asked and then went back into the kitchen with her sisters and brothers disturbed by what her father had said.

'How are things with you at *Rose Cottage*?' Mike asked Fanny and Seamus.

'Good, Mike, we're managing,' Fanny replied.

'That's good to hear.'

'Mike, there's something I've been wanting to ask you.'

'Yes, Fanny?'

'Would you think about getting married again?' Fanny asked softly. 'It's been years since Anna died and the children need a mother, particularly the girls.'

'Anna was the only woman for me, Fanny, you know that, how can I ever replace her?' He looked at her, a wounded look in his brown eyes.

'I know we can never replace her.' She bent her head.

'And you know my own mother died when I was young, and I had a stepmother …I don't want that for my children.'

'But I'm sure Nancy was a lovely mother to you,' Fanny said.

'She didn't like me, Fanny. We never agreed on anything. That's the problem when another woman comes into a household.'

'But maybe you might find someone nice, there's a lot of women who would be only too glad to marry you.'

'I don't want a woman who's looking for a husband,' he snapped. 'Then she comes in here to take care of my children because she has no other choice, and treats them in a despicable fashion when I'm out of sight.'

'What about Meg, sure she took on David's family and there's never been a problem.'

'No one will replace Anna, Fanny, no one.' He seemed irritated with her.

'But it's so hard on the children.'

'We're quite happy here together.'

'Sure Eleanor hasn't been in school since she was twelve, and has had to be a mother to the other children. Doing everything for them. Cooking. Cleaning. Washing, ironing and sewing. That's too much for a young girl, she's not much more than a child herself. And now she has taken on her job making hats for that shop in town.'

'I help her, we do things together,' Mike said.

'I know you do, but …'

'Look Fanny.' He softened his tone. 'Things are not going to change. I'm not going to bring another woman into this house. A stranger who doesn't know my children, or even how we live. As it is, we all get on fine, and we have you and Seamus helping us as well, you know I really appreciate what you do for us.'

'Mike, I'm getting old, I haven't the energy I used to have, as it is I need Bina to look after me.'

'Would you like to see one of the little hats I make for the shop in town?' Eleanor asked Bina.

'Yes, I would.' She was enthusiastic.

'I'm not that good yet, I'm only at it a few weeks.' Eleanor searched in a box and took one out. 'Fit it on.'

'It's lovely, let me look at it.' Bina ran across to the mirror.

Eleanor came behind. 'You wear it pulled down on one side, it's really nice on you.'

Bina adjusted it and turned back to Eleanor. 'It's lovely.'

'Let me try?' Cathy pushed in.

Bina handed it to her.

'Do you like the little flower, isn't it pretty?'

'I must have one of these,' Bina said. 'How much are they?'

'Two shillings and eleven.'

'I'm saving up but I haven't got that much.'

Cathy stared at herself in the mirror pulling the hat in all different directions.

'Did the woman in the shop give you a hat for yourself?' Bina asked.

'No, the pieces of fabric are all cut out and I have to bring back the same number of hats, otherwise I don't get paid.'

Bina was really keen to have one of those hats but knew that it would take her a long time to save up enough money, unless Fanny gave her a present.

'I might put some money down on one, and pay it off.'

'You could do that …' Eleanor whipped the hat off Cathy's head.

'You'll have to save up as well, Cathy,' Bina laughed.

'I'll make my own,' she retorted.

'Won't be as nice.' Eleanor folded the hat in the box. 'And you'll have to ask for permission to use my machine.'

Cathy grimaced.

Fanny appeared. 'We'll go home now, Bina. Would you get our coats?'

'All right, Granny.' She took them off the hook behind the door, and helped her on with it. Then Seamus appeared and she did the same.

'Thanks girl.'

'Will you buy me one of Eleanor's hats for my birthday?' Cathy begged Fanny.

'A hat?'

'Yes.'

'Why doesn't Eleanor make you one?'

'She won't.'

'You know I can't give you one of these,' Eleanor exploded.

'Don't be arguing, girls, work it out between you without fighting. Otherwise, your father will be on the warpath.'

The girls looked at each other. 'No, Granny, we won't.'

'Promise?' she smiled.

They nodded.

'Daddy was saying he wants me to go to work,' Bina said as they started out on their journey home.

'Work?' Fanny was surprised.

'Yes, he mentioned the mill.'

'Of all places.'

'I'd hate to work there, it's awful,' Bina grimaced. 'And I must be at home to help you with the washing and ironing for Mrs. Staunton, and the fowl, and the work around the place.' She was the only one who realised how tired her grandmother could be. And how she had to take a stretch in bed every afternoon so she could get through the day, and went to bed as early as Seamus did. The nights of music when Bina played the melodeon or piano with Fanny joining in on her concertina were not quite so frequent, and she missed that. But she told no one how Fanny was these days.

Chapter sixty-two

Bina sat in the church, her hands clasped together nervously. It was the First Friday tomorrow and she always went to Confession with Fanny on the day before.

The man ahead of her came out and left the door of the Confession box swinging open. The darkness inside beckoned and for a few seconds she couldn't even stand up. But Fanny touched her arm and murmured that she was next so she had no choice but to go in. Closing the door after her the darkness became dense, and she knelt down and stared at the mesh, which divided the penitent's section from where the priest sat. It was claustrophobic, and she could hear her heart beat loudly, and hoped the priest wouldn't notice. The shutter snapped open. Her mouth was dry and she couldn't speak immediately, but finally managed to blurt out *Bless me father for I have sinned*. She continued on, mentioning some small sins like losing her temper, and telling a lie, but couldn't even remember when she had committed them.

As it was, her whole being was suffused with thoughts of Garda William Gleeson whom she had met just after New Year. She remembered that day so well. She had been walking down Patrick Street, and coming in the opposite direction was a Garda. He was tall and handsome in his uniform she thought immediately and wondered how it was she hadn't seen him before. They passed each other and she kept her eyes straight ahead too shy to even look at him. But then she couldn't resist glancing around and found herself looking straight into his face as he did the same thing. She blushed and turned her head, hurrying through the crowd of people on the path anxious now to get away as quickly as possible.

But she wasn't going to tell the priest any of that.

She waited for him to say something, but to her relief he didn't, and went on to murmur the Latin words of Absolution. Her penance was an Our Father and three Hail Marys. She opened the door quickly, and Fanny was next. After she had said her penance she wondered what Fanny was saying to the priest as she was in the confessional for so long. It was Fr. O'Hagan and she couldn't imagine telling him a big sin. How embarrassing that would be particularly when they might meet him walking down the road, or if he happened to call to *Rose Cottage*.

Fanny came out at last and it took a few minutes more for her to say her penance before leaving.

Bina had no anticipation of meeting the Garda she had seen on the street again, and couldn't believe it when he happened to be at a dance she went to with her friends the following week. After dancing with her for the evening, he asked if she would meet him again, and could he ask her parents for permission to walk out with her. She was thrilled, and agreed. He wrote to her the following day.

'Who's writing to you, Bina?' Fanny immediately wanted to know when she saw the letter.

'It's from a man.'

'What man?' Fanny turned on her.

'I met him at a dance, he's a Garda.'

'And who is he?'

'William Gleeson is his name but he said everyone calls him Will.'

'And where is he from?'

'Tipperary.'

'Don't let Edward know he's writing to you.'

'I won't,' she laughed. 'But he wants to walk out with me and to meet you and Grandad.' Bina handed her the letter.

'I suppose we could invite him to tea, I want to have a look at him anyway, see what sort of man he is.'

He was coming over on the following Wednesday and Bina was beside herself with excitement. On the day, she changed her clothes more than once never satisfied with how she looked.

After he arrived and they sat down to tea, Bina was a bundle of nerves but she could see immediately that Fanny and Seamus liked him and was so relieved. But then Edward arrived home and Will was introduced. The chat continued around the table but Edward was quiet. So happy, Bina didn't notice, as he was aloof at the best of times.

But after Will had gone home, Bina helped Fanny to clear up and Edward sat there reading the paper as was his usual habit. But then he put down the paper.

'Bina,' he said her name in a sharp flat tone.

'Yes, Uncle Edward?' She was filling the dresser with their best china.

'This man you've met.'

'Will?' She stopped in the act of putting the plates into position.

'How old is he?'

'I don't know.' She hadn't asked him his age. 'What does that matter?'

'He's too old for you.'

'He isn't.' She turned around.

'Anyway, regardless of age, he's not suitable.'

'Why not?'

'I'll choose the man you'll walk out with.'

'Why should you do that?'

'Because I'm the head of the family.'

'Granny, you like Will, don't you?' Bina appealed to Fanny.

'Yes, I have to say I do, he's a very nice young man.'

'Well, regardless of that, Bina, I say you're not to see him again.'

She stared at him, disbelieving.

'Edward, she's only just met Will,' Fanny said.

'I've made my decision.' He left the room.

Bina burst into tears. 'Granny, why has Uncle Edward said I mustn't see Will again?'

'He's just being a bit cranky.'

'But he can't do that, I'm nineteen now, I can do what I want.'

'It would be better if you were over twenty-one.'

'I'll have to wait that long?'

'I don't know, to tell you the truth, pet.' Fanny seemed as upset as Bina was.

'And this is what he did to Mammy, he didn't want her to marry Daddy and she had to run away in the end because he wanted her to marry John Hobbs.'

'And I was guilty of encouraging that match as well,' Fanny admitted.

'What am I going to do?'

'We'll work something out,' Fanny said.

'How?'

'Maybe you could meet him somewhere …'

'Where?'

'Let me think about it.'

It was Fanny who came up with the plan. When Will arranged to call, Bina and Fanny would go for a walk in the evening and they would meet Will on the road to Mayfield. Then Fanny would go to the *Rambling House* in the village where she would spend time with her neighbours for a while, and leave Bina and Will together.

He wrote every day and Fanny always received the post, keeping Edward unaware of the correspondence between the two.

Today they set off in the evening and following the narrow road watched out for Will who should be waiting for them around the next bend. Bina could hardly stop herself running with excitement.

'Don't be so anxious to see him, be more decorous, young ladies don't rush like that. Didn't you learn anything in that college I sent you to,' Fanny warned her.

'They told us what we should do, but I'm looking forward to seeing him so much all that goes out of my head,' Bina laughed.

They rounded the corner but as the road ahead was bordered by high trees they couldn't see him.

'He's not here,' Bina was disappointed.

'He'll be here any minute.'

Bina couldn't believe he was late which was unusual for him, always so prompt.

Suddenly up ahead they saw a light flash.

'There he is,' Bina cried.

'Run on then.' Fanny let her go.

'We thought you weren't coming.' She burst out when she reached him.

'Why would you think that, have I ever let you down?' he laughed.

They turned back towards Fanny.

'Mrs. Dineen.' Will shook her hand.

'I'm right glad to see you, boy. Now, I'll head back to the *Rambling House* and chat with a few friends for a while. I'll come back a bit later and pick you up, Bina.'

'We'll be watching out for you here,' Will said.

She waved and headed back to the village.

Will turned to Bina and took her arm. 'I've missed you.'

'It seems so long since last week.' She looked up at him.

'Let's hurry, we don't want to meet Edward.'

She smiled.

They walked along to an old house which stood just off the roadside. It hadn't been lived in for some years and Will pushed open the door. Inside he shone the torch around the dim interior.

There was a scent of dampness in the place, and often the flutter of the wings of a bird high above.

'I always think this place is so scary.' Bina hung on to him.

'Are you warm enough,' he asked putting his arm around her.

She had brought a rug and now put it down on an old settee. They sat on it, and the springs squeaked loudly. 'This will collapse one of these days,' she laughed.

'And the two of us in the middle of it.' He kissed her and she let herself melt into his arms.

They talked for a while as it grew darker. She felt completely safe with Will in this dark space, never a worry that anything would happen.

'There is something I must tell you,' he said later.

'What is it?' she asked, suddenly worried.

'I'm being transferred.'

'Where?'

'Dublin.'

Her heart twisted.

'But why are they transferring you?'

'I'm not sure. They don't usually tell us.'

'How often will I see you?' Bina was upset, thinking immediately that she would lose him when he went to the colourful life in Dublin.

'As often as I can.' He moved closer to her and she could feel his lips soft on hers. Every time he held her close, she nearly fainted with longing. The closeness of his body on hers was intoxicating. The touch of him. The scent of his skin. He was the only man who had ever touched her so intimately and she knew without a doubt that she loved him.

'When do you have to go?' she asked hesitantly.

'I've to be on duty on the first of March, but I must leave a week before so that I can find digs.'

'That soon?'

'I'm sorry.'

'I'll miss you,' she whispered, hating the thought of losing him.

'And I you.'

'When will I see you again?' Tears filled her eyes.

'As soon as I can.'

So relieved, she put her arms around him and held him close.

Chapter Sixty-three

Bina and Will met at a dance in Mayfield for the last time before he went to Dublin. She had gone with her friends and watched the men who gathered on the gallery above just in case Edward happened to be there, but there was no sign of him.

When Will arrived she waved and quickly moved through the crowd towards him.

They clasped hands.

'Dearest,' he whispered in her ear.

'I don't see Edward up there,' she smiled at him.

'Then let's dance, my love.' He swept her on to the floor. The music soared and the band played a quickstep, *Sunshine* by Irving Berlin. She loved to dance with Will. He held her in his arms and they danced as one. What joy. She imagined she was a flapper. Although the hemlines of her skirts were just below the knee nowadays, she felt she was as fashionable as any of them. Next it was a slow number, and they swayed together, his cheek against hers, his arms around her body. Telling her that she was his. Then the tempo increased, and they danced a Charleston, *Everybody Loves my Girl.* She was delighted to be wearing her new shoes with the ankle straps, knowing she looked exactly the part. The next was a waltz, *Come let us dance,* and she sang along with the words - *Why is the day brighter, why is my heart lighter, when I'm looking at you.*

'Let's go out for some fresh air,' he suggested later.

There were other couples standing outside, and they went around the corner of the building where it was quieter.

'I'm going to miss you so much,' Bina whispered.

'And I you, but we'll keep in touch, I'll write every day if I can.' He kissed her.

'And I will too.'

'There's something I want to ask, Bina …'

Her heart thumped.

He let go of her hand and moved suddenly.

She stared at him, puzzled as to what he was doing, only then noticing that he had gone down on one knee.

'Bina, will you marry me?' he asked softly.

She was not even sure she had heard him correctly and didn't answer at first, in shock.

'Bina?' he smiled.

'Yes, yes …' She leaned forward and put her arms around his neck.

He stood up, held her close to him and kissed her. 'Thank you,' he yelled out loud, held out his hand to her and on his palm was a small brown leather box.

She stared at it, her eyes wide.

'Open it, Bina.'

Her fingers trembled as she pushed up the lid, and she couldn't believe her eyes when she saw the exquisite diamond ring.

'Try it on, I hope it fits you.'

She picked it up and slid it on to the third finger of her left hand. 'It's beautiful, thank you, I love it.' She hugged him.

But then, suddenly, out of the corner of her eye she saw Edward get out of the trap, tie up the horse, and walk straight towards the entrance door.

'Oh my God, Will, he's here,' she said.

'He won't see us.' He put his arm around her and they turned away. But that movement caught Edward's attention and he looked in their direction.

Bina almost fainted as he made his way over.

'I told you that you were not to meet this person,' he said angrily.

'Look, Edward …' Will began to speak.

'Shut your mouth. Who do you think you are?' he demanded.
'What's wrong with dancing?' Bina asked.
'Go home,' he said, bluntly.
She looked at Will.
'Better do as he says, Bina,' Will said. 'I'm leaving now anyway.'
'Go on.' Edward pushed Bina in front of him.

At home, Bina climbed out of the trap and went into the house. Fanny and Seamus were both in bed. He followed her into the kitchen. She turned, determined to face up to him.

'What do you mean by meeting with that …' he shouted.

'Why were you so rude to Will?' she attacked him, suddenly not caring what he thought.

'He's not good enough for you.'

'Why should you decide whether he's good enough for me?'

'In this family, I make the decisions and you obey them.'

'I won't obey you,' she retorted.

'You have no choice.' He moved closer to her, threatening.

She hated him then.

Fanny appeared in the doorway, clutching her dressing gown around her. 'Edward? Bina? What's happening?'

'She is not to meet that man again, I caught them outside the dance hall and you wouldn't believe what I saw,' he shouted.

'We were just …' Bina didn't know what to say.

'Look, Bina, if I talk to your father, then he will be of the same mind as myself. This man isn't for you.'

'My father loved my mother and they ignored you. He'll understand about Will and me. I'll talk to him myself.'

'Talk away, you'll be wasting your time. You'll marry whomever we decide.' His expression was bitter. 'Get out of my sight,' he muttered.

Fanny put her arm around Bina and took her upstairs to bed. 'He saw you at the dance?' she asked when she closed the bedroom door.

'Yes, but I have something to tell you,' Bina said, with an excited giggle.

'And what's that?' Fanny asked.

'Will and I are engaged.'

'To be married?'

'Yes. Look at my ring, Granny, isn't it beautiful?' Bina stretched out her fingers so Fanny could see it.

'It certainly is,' she admired. 'I'm delighted for you, girl.' She hugged Bina.

'I was almost going to tell Edward on the way home.'

'You'll need to get around him, and that won't be easy.'

'I'll persuade him.' Bina was so happy she couldn't see how anyone would stand in her way.

'Seeing as Will is going to work in Dublin then there is plenty of time. When are you thinking of getting married, I presume it won't be this year?'

'We haven't decided on a date, he just asked me tonight.' Her heart beat like a butterfly's wings.

'Well, he's done the honourable thing and hasn't left you here wondering,' Fanny said. 'But you can't wear the ring, you know that?'

Bina stared at her. She hadn't realised. Hadn't thought it through at all.

'Until you get permission to marry him you have to keep that ring a secret. Hide it somewhere in your room,' Fanny instructed. 'And tell no one, you understand? If Edward finds out, you'll never get him to agree to a marriage, so we have to step carefully and work our way around him.'

Bina looked at her ring. So disappointed that she couldn't wear it. She wanted to shout to the world and tell everyone that she loved Will and that he loved her, and she was going to be Mrs. William Gleeson.

Chapter Sixty-four

And Will did write every day. And Bina wrote every day. Their letters full of love and the everyday inconsequential things too. Each evening she took out her ring from its little box, kissed it and put it on her finger. So sad then to hide it away again.

One evening, as Fanny and Bina were sewing, Fanny put her hand on her stomach and gave a little scream.
 Bina looked at her. 'What's wrong, Granny?'
 'It's just wind, love, just wind,' she dismissed it.
 'Can I get you anything, maybe some soda?'
 'No thanks, girl, I'm all right …'
 And she was for another week, until it happened again.
 'Granny, you must go to the doctor.'
 'I told you it's just wind, Bina,' Fanny resisted.

My darling Will, I'm worried about Granny. Something is wrong but she won't go to the doctor. And she's very tired all the time, although I try to do as much as I can for her, she still needs more. We don't go up to Hillside so often because she just cannot manage the journey. And she's got so thin I hardly recognise her. I hope you are well. All my love. Bina. xxx

His return letter was full of concern, and he told her that he would come down to Cork the following week on the train. Bina was so happy, counting the days until she would meet him again. But to her disappointment, Fanny wasn't strong enough to walk to the *Rambling House* on that night. Bina was reluctant to leave Fanny alone, but she persuaded her to go on ahead and not to worry about her.

She left before tea time, hoping that Edward wouldn't get home too early. It was a bright July evening and she quickly ducked into the old house hoping no one had seen her. She pulled over one of the window shutters and stood behind it until she heard footsteps on the road outside and peeped out. 'Will?' she called.

'Bina?'

'I'm here.'

He came in, and immediately stretched out his arms and she ran to him.

'God, it's so good to hold you. It's been too long.' He looked down at her and lowered his head to kiss her.

She pressed herself closer to him and they stood there for a moment in silence. It was almost a month since they had been together and she needed to know him again. Just to remind herself of everything about him. See his eyes, feel his hands, hear his voice. 'Thanks for coming, Will, I wanted to see you so much.'

'They've kept me working. I've been on night duty, and if I get a chance of overtime I take it so that I can save as much as I can for our wedding. And I didn't want to turn up here and upset things with Edward either. How is Fanny?'

'She's not well and couldn't come this evening.'

He was concerned. 'Give her my best wishes, will you?'

Bina nodded.

'Do you know if she mentioned anything to Edward about our engagement?'

'I don't think so.'

'But when will we be able to get married? I'd marry you tomorrow, and then you could leave here and we'd live together in Dublin. It would be a perfect solution.'

'If only I could.'

'Let's hope that Edward will come around one of these days,' he said.

'I hope so.'

'Let's not talk about him, I don't want to waste our precious time. I have to get back on the seven thirty train.'

She clung to him.

Arriving home, she was surprised to see that the kitchen was empty. She ran up the stairs and gently opened Fanny's bedroom door.

'Granny?' She went over to the bed. 'Are you all right?'

'Bina, I'm not good at all, that pain is at me again.' She pressed her stomach. 'Oh it's terrible,' she groaned.

'What can I get you, Granny?' Bina asked, desperately worried. Fanny looked very pale and drawn.

'I'm going for the doctor,' Bina said.

'No, no, this will pass, it always does.'

'But you're not well,' Bina said, touching Fanny's forehead gently.

'I'll be fine by tomorrow morning, don't you worry. I'll just stay in bed this evening. Can you make something for Seamus and Edward? Use the eggs there and fresh ...' she gasped as another pain swept through her.

'Can I get you some gin, Granny, a little tot might help.'

'Do girl, thanks.' She turned her head into the pillow.

Bina ran downstairs and picked up the little bottle from the press. Then she poured some water into a cup and ran upstairs with both.

'Will I put a drop into the water?' she asked Fanny who took a while to answer.

'Just a little, Bina.'

She did that and brought the cup over to Fanny.

'Can you sit up, Granny?'

'I don't know that I can, girl.' She tried to raise her head.

'Let me help you.' Bina put the cup on the bedside table and helped Fanny into a sitting position. Then she handed her the drink. Fanny sipped it slowly, just a little at a time.

'Is that doing any good for you?' Bina asked anxiously.

'I'm sure it will.' Fanny lay back on the pillows, exhausted.

'Mam?' A voice called from below.

'Oh that's Edward, he'll be wondering about his tea.' Fanny seemed worried. 'Go down quick, don't keep him waiting, you know what he's like.'

'I'll get it for him, you just relax there.' Bina went down a couple of steps and met Edward on the way up. 'Uncle, Granny is sick, she has that terrible pain again.'

'I was wondering where she was,' he said and went into the bedroom. 'Mother, how are you?'

'It's not that bad now, Bina will make your tea, go on girl, get it ready.'

'Would you like something to eat, Granny?' Bina asked.

'No girl, no, just a cup of tea maybe. This little tot has helped.'

After they had finished tea, a couple of local men came in to play cards with Seamus, and Edward went off into town as was his usual habit in the evening. As she didn't want to stay in the kitchen with the men, Bina went back up and sat with Fanny. Now she slept but Bina stayed there watching over her. All the time she was thinking of Will. Imagining him sitting in the train. The carriage with the low light. The velvet covered seats. The pictures on the wall. The sound of the metal wheels on the railway tracks. Clickity-clack, clickity-clack. It would be after eleven when he arrived at Kingsbridge station, and by the time he walked to his digs in Kilmainham probably heading for twelve. She felt very lonely after him.

She slept with Fanny that night, just lying near the edge of the double bed so that she wouldn't disturb her. But Fanny slept well through the night, and in the morning the pain had eased.

'There, I'm much better, didn't I say as much?' Fanny smiled at her.

Bina hugged her. 'But you shouldn't work so hard today just in case it comes back.'

'I won't, girl.'

'Daddy, Eleanor and Cathy and the boys are coming out tomorrow,'

Bina reminded.

'That's right, I forgot, now I must get baking.'

'I'll do it for you.'

They were back to normal, and Bina was very relieved. As the days shortened, Fanny was quite well, but was still very tired. Eleanor and Cathy and the boys came out to see their Granny more often now, usually on a Sunday. Mike came as well, although as time passed he expressed concern about Fanny.

'I'm sorry to see you looking so poorly,' he said that last evening. Eleanor, Cathy and the boys were already out in the paddock with the horses.

'I'm not that bad, Mike, anyway, I have Bina to look after me.'

'She's a good girl,' he smiled at her.

'There's something we have to tell you, Mike,' Fanny said. 'We'll talk now while the children are outside.'

Bina stiffened.

He waited.

'Bina has met a young man.'

He stared at her.

'Who is he?'

'He's a Garda, Will Gleeson.'

'Where's he from?'

'Tipperary.'

'And when did you meet him?' He turned to Bina.

'After Christmas.'

'And I'm only hearing about it now?'

'When she met him first, Edward refused to allow her to walk out with him,' Fanny explained.

'Edward?'

'Yes.'

'He isn't Bina's father, it's not his place to allow her walk out with this man or not.' He was suddenly angry.

'In this house he is the boss, Mike, so we have to go along with whatever he decides,' Fanny explained, pressing her hand against her chest as her breathing became difficult.

'Granny, are you all right?' Bina was concerned for her.

'I'm all right, girl.'

'Where is this man stationed?' Mike rapped.

'Dublin.'

'What are his intentions?'

'We write every day and …' Bina was about to say they were already engaged but then decided not to mention that.

'So you don't see him that often?' He seemed a little calmer.

She shook her head, thinking in her heart that she would give anything to see Will more frequently.

'Well, I suppose you are nineteen and growing up, I'm sure you've met other boys already,' he conceded.

'We sometimes talk of how it was with you and Anna, Mike, and how Edward refused to allow her walk out with you.'

'The whole family came between us. Both families.' Anger grew in Mike again, and his eyes darkened.

'I have to admit that.' Fanny bowed her head.

'You'll have to keep it a secret until we can tell Uncle Edward, Daddy. Please?' Bina begged. 'Grandad doesn't know, or Eleanor or Cathy, no one knows.'

'I haven't a wide circle of friends so I suppose I can keep a secret. Your mother certainly could.' A look of bitterness flashed across his features. 'God rest her.'

'If Mammy was still here I know she would really like Will.' There were sudden tears in her eyes.

Eleanor dashed in. 'Are you coming out to the horses, Bina?'

'Go on out, Bina, enjoy yourself,' Mike said.

'Thanks, Daddy.' She kissed him.

'I can't believe it, you've told your father?' Will threw his arms around her.

'Granny did.'

'And what did he say?'

'Not much really, he wasn't too pleased he's only being told now. He was angry.'

'But is he going to talk to Edward?'

'We asked him to keep it a secret.'

'Did he agree to that?'

'Yes,' Bina laughed.

'Then we're on our way, fifty per cent of the way,' he laughed as well. 'And I'm saving as much money as I can.'

'I don't have any to save really,' she had to admit. 'All I have is eleven pence.'

'Don't worry, I just hope we'll have enough money to get married, that's if the Wall Street Crash doesn't affect us over here too much and the banks don't collapse and take all our money with them. One of these days, we could all be standing in a queue outside hoping to withdraw whatever we have saved.'

'I've been reading about that in the paper, it's a terrible thing, all those people who committed suicide because they lost all their money. I hope your money is safe.'

'It's our money now, Bina,' he reassured.

Chapter Sixty-five

At the beginning of December, Fanny took a bad turn and Bina insisted on Seamus taking her into the Victoria Hospital. She had her well wrapped up against the cold but was very worried about her when the doctor insisted on keeping her in.

'We think it is gallstones and we may have to operate,' he explained after she had been examined.

Tearfully Bina held her Granny's hand.

'You do whatever you have to do,' Fanny smiled. 'Just get me better so that I can go home.'

Bina visited Fanny every day, but she didn't seem to be improving and there was no more talk of the operation. As Bina was leaving one evening, the doctor called her aside.

'You know your grandmother is quite ill,' he said.

Bina nodded.

'Is there anyone else in the family I can talk to?'

'My grandfather or my uncle.'

'When will they be in?'

'I don't know.' Bina could feel herself begin to shake.

'Well, you had better tell them. Your grandmother should be taken home.'

Bina stared at him. 'Why? What about the operation?'

'I'm sorry to tell you she's going to die,' the doctor said abruptly.

Bina burst into tears, rushed out of the hospital and ran to her uncle's office where she told him what the doctor had said.

Edward grabbed his hat and the two of them went back to the hospital where he insisted on seeing the doctor again. But in spite of all his questions, the explanation was the same. Fanny was going to die.

'When?' Bina whispered.

'I'm not sure,' the doctor said.

Bina and Edward looked at each other in horror.

They brought Fanny home just before Christmas.

'I'm so happy to be back at *Rose Cottage*,' she said, smiling, touching the door as Edward carried her in. Just a light bundle these days. 'Sit me down in my kitchen,' she said.

He did as she asked.

'Granny, I'll make you something to eat,' Bina offered. 'I did some baking, a fruit cake and an apple tart, would you like a slice?'

'Thank you Bina but I'm not hungry, girl, just sit here with me for a while all of you. Seamus, why don't you smoke your pipe?'

'I will to be sure.' He packed the bowl and lit the tobacco. The smoke drifted, a fragrant scent in the air.

'Ah, I love it,' Fanny smiled and closed her eyes.

They sat there in silence. It was so quiet Bina could hear herself breathe. She reached and held Fanny's hand, so happy when her hand gripped hers. Tears welled up in her eyes but she didn't want to take out her handkerchief and just let them drift down her cheeks, able to taste the salt as they trickled on to her lips.

'Bina, maybe you'd play me a tune on my old concertina?' Fanny asked softly. 'I'd love that.'

Bina went to the parlour to get it, drying her tears as she climbed the stairs, and hoping that she could stop crying. But it was very hard to keep a smile on her face as she came back and played some of Fanny's favourite tunes.

The music echoed around the room and Fanny tapped her little feet on the floor in time to the rhythm, a smile on her face as everyone kept time to the beat. Bina tried to prevent herself bursting into tears praying she wouldn't upset her darling Granny.

Christmas was quiet. Mike, Eleanor, Cathy and the boys came over for Christmas dinner. Lizzie and Iris were there as well. Fanny wasn't able to go to Mass, but when they arrived back, Edward carried her down and she sat in her favourite chair. Bina cooked a goose, and spiced beef. Fanny had made the pudding and cake back in October, and at the end of the meal Edward poured whiskey on top of the pudding and set it alight. But Fanny wouldn't eat anything and only sipped a glass of water every now and then for them, however much they coaxed her. Bina played the concertina for her and she seemed to enjoy listening to the music, but she grew tired quite quickly and Edward brought her back to bed.

They sat with Fanny. Lizzie and Iris chatted about times past. Swopping stories of their lives when they were all young growing up in the woollen mill at Castlelyons.

When the girls were together they cried, but didn't let Fanny see how they felt.

Bina wrote to Will to tell him how bad Fanny was, and putting it in writing seemed to cut her heart to pieces. It was suddenly real. Happening now. Her dear Granny was dying.

Fanny didn't get up again after Christmas. She slept a lot and when she did open her eyes she didn't seem to know who was there. But suddenly one evening, she squeezed Bina's hand.

'Granny?'
'Bina love?' she whispered.
'Yes Granny?'
'Look after my little ones for me will you?'
Tears welled up in Bina's eyes.
'Of course I will.'
'Say a prayer for them.'
'I'll never forget them.' She kissed Fanny.

On New Year's Eve, Eleanor and Cathy came over and together they threw the bread against the door as Fanny had always done. They stayed with Bina after that, and on New Year's Day, Lizzie and Iris came back up again. They took it in turns to sit with Fanny keeping a vigil during the day and right through the night. Now she had slipped into a deep sleep and didn't wake or move at all. They knew that it would be soon.

Bina was terribly upset, and couldn't imagine how she would live without her darling Granny.

1930

Chapter Sixty-six

On Friday night they were kneeling by Fanny's bed saying the Rosary. She hadn't opened her eyes or spoken to them at all over the last few days, and they were taken aback now when she suddenly opened her eyes.

'Granny?' Bina whispered.

Fanny looked at her and smiled. 'Don't forget my little ones,' she said. Her last words quite clear.

Then she closed her eyes again and her head fell gently to one side.

They were silent for a moment.

'She's gone,' Lizzie touched her hand.

Bina burst into tears. She bent over Fanny and kissed her cheek, and then stood back and let the others say their goodbyes.

Eleanor and Cathy held each other close, sobbing, inconsolable.

'What are we going to do without her,' Cathy murmured.

'Mammy gone and now Granny too.' Eleanor dabbed her eyes. 'On Christmas Day she was tapping her feet. How could she be dead now?'

So full of emotion, Bina wasn't able to utter a word.

Later she took out her diary and as she opened the page teardrops fell and obscured her first efforts to write the words. She crossed them out and tried again.

Jan 3 Fri Granny died this evening at 10.20. R.I.P.

Together, the girls washed Fanny, and dressed her in a brown habit. Until the undertakers brought the coffin, Seamus and Edward put her lying on an old door on the bed over which they put a white sheet. Lizzie and Iris covered the mirrors with white pillowcases and opened the windows a little. Seamus lit four white candles, one at each corner of the bed, and all of them knelt and prayed for Fanny.

Bina sent telegrams to Will, Mr. and Mrs. Staunton and Tess in Monkstown. Fanny's relatives in Castlelyons. Seamus's family in Knockraha, as well as Meg in Dublin. Then she went up to *Fairfields* to tell Mrs. Kelleher and Susan.

All the neighbours and friends crowded into the house and waked Fanny. Singing the traditional mournful songs she always loved. Bina, Eleanor and Cathy made food for the mourners, and Edward kept the men happy with porter and whiskey.

In the small hours, the three girls put on their coats and took a walk outside.

'She loved her garden,' Eleanor murmured.

'Green fingers. Anything she put down grew …she had the touch.'

It was a cold night, the sky clear and studded with stars.

'How old was Granny?' asked Eleanor.

'Seventy-one,' Bina told them.

'You'd never think she was that age, she was so full of life.'

'She could do anything. Our Granny was wonderful,' Bina said softly.

'She was always there for us, especially when Mammy died.' Cathy wiped her eyes.

Edward hurried out of the house towards them.

'What is it?' Bina turned.

'Stop singing,' he hissed.

'We're not singing.'

'Someone was singing, I could hear it. Some sort of weird screeching.'

'It must be Lizzie or Iris keening, it wasn't us.'

'No, it's not them, they're praying now.' He went back inside.

'If we weren't singing then who was?' Eleanor asked.

'My God, it must have been the *banshee*,' Bina whispered.

Their eyes grew wide with shock and they rushed back into the house.

'The *banshee* always comes when someone has died.'

'Auntie Meg saw Mammy at the end of her bed when she died,' Bina whispered.

'Did she?' Cathy was astonished.

'So she told me.'

'Let's go back to Granny, I don't want to hear the *banshee*.' Bina led the way upstairs.

Fanny was taken to the chapel in the hearse just before six o'clock that evening. The girls wore the black mourning dresses they had for Anna's funeral, although they didn't really fit terribly well.

'How do we look?' Bina asked.

'At least the hems have gone up, otherwise the dresses would be a disgrace.'

'And I'm wearing this black coat belonging to Granny. I like wearing it just because it's hers.' Bina smoothed the soft wool fabric.

'Is there another one I could wear?' Eleanor searched in the wardrobe. 'This one looks all right.' She slipped it on. 'What do you think?'

'It will be fine for the funeral. You can alter it afterwards.'

'Granny was never the same after Mammy died. She was broken-hearted after her,' Bina said.

'They're together now,' Eleanor whispered. 'In Heaven.'

The girls hugged each other.

The following morning the telegram boy arrived. When he had gone, Bina looked through them and took the one addressed to herself.

'Give them to me.' Edward held out his hand.

She handed the others to him.

'All,' he said.

Bina struggled to build up the courage to refuse.

'This is addressed to me.' She tossed her bobbed hair.

'Give it here.' He took a step closer.

'No.'

'Bina, I won't repeat what I've said.' He was angry now and she could see it in his eyes.

The door opened and Seamus walked in.

'Grandad, Uncle Edward won't let me read my own telegram.' Tears clouded her eyes, all the pent up emotion about to explode.

Seamus looked at them both, his features white and drawn. 'Can't you let the girl be, Edward?' he asked, tiredly.

'I read all telegrams which come into this house.' He stood over Bina, belligerent.

'Your mother is going to be buried today, just let her rest in peace.' It was unusual for Seamus to argue with his son. 'Leave be, Edward, it's none of your business.'

'What do you mean?'

Seamus muttered something in Irish.

Edward turned and flung out of the door.

Bina's hands trembled and she smoothed the creases in the envelope. She opened it. Will's few brief words of sympathy made her cry all the more and she ran upstairs to Fanny's room and threw herself on the bed and screamed. Burying her head in the softness of the white pillow, the last place her darling grandmother had laid her head.

At one o'clock, they went to the church and after Mass Fanny's coffin was carried out to the hearse. It took Bina back to Anna's funeral and it made it all the harder, the loss of the two people she had loved most in the world. But Will had come into her life and she knew she would never manage to survive without him.

The funeral procession wound its slow solemn way along the narrow road. Tears drifted down Bina's cheeks. It was a sharp cold January day, the wind pulling and dragging at their clothes, their breaths solidified like puffs of steam in the icy air. The sound of the clip clop of the horses' hooves, the occasional twist of leather and clink from the reins merged with voices in prayer.

They arrived at Caherlag. Branches on the trees twisted and turned wildly in the wind. Bina looked over the wall. The open grave was just a short distance away. It had been dug by Edward, Seamus, Mike and other family members earlier in the day and she dreaded moving closer, the thought of seeing her mother's coffin deep within the earth was terrifying.

She watched the men lift the coffin from the hearse and awkwardly carry it through the gate. The mourners pushed from behind and she walked in and found herself at the end of the grave, but to her relief she couldn't actually see the top of Anna's coffin.

Bina put her arms around Eleanor and Cathy as the men lifted it. There was a slight unevenness in the ropes and the coffin swung slightly. Seamus's grip was not quite as strong as the other men. For a moment Bina wondered if she could help him and was about to move forward when she realised that he would be ashamed if he couldn't lower his own wife's coffin into the grave, and it wouldn't do for a girl to help anyway. But he managed to get control of the rope and slowly the men lowered the coffin into the grave and it disappeared from sight. At last they're together again, Bina thought.

The priest murmured some prayers and splashed Holy Water. Seamus bent down and dug his hand into the pile of earth on one side and flung it on top of the coffin. Bina hated the harsh rattling sound. It seemed so final. But she had to bend down to take a handful and throw the earth and stones on the wooden top as did the rest of the family. Then the men took their spades and filled in the grave and Fanny was hidden from Bina. She would never see her again.

It was lonely when they went back to *Rose Cottage*. Mike had taken Eleanor, Cathy and the boys home, and all the other mourners had left.

Lizzie, Iris and Meg stayed and they sat there, saying little, all of them still thinking about Fanny.

'Who would like a drink?' Edward asked, picking up a bottle of gin from the table.

'I'll have a small gin, thank you,' Lizzie accepted.

'And me as well,' Iris said. 'I'd like to raise a glass to Fanny, she enjoyed her nip of gin.'

'And a little toddy too betimes,' Lizzie added.

'There you are, ladies.' He poured. 'Meg?'

'No thank you, Edward, I don't partake.'

He poured a whiskey for himself and Seamus, and they all raised their glasses.

'To Fanny.'

There was a knock on the door. They stared in its direction, a look of curiosity on their faces.

Edward went out to answer it, and came back with a telegram in his hand. He opened it and read the contents. 'It's from Jim, he's coming home from America.'

'When?' Bina burst out, excited. While she had never met her uncle, his letters to Fanny always seemed so interesting she was delighted to know that he was coming home at last.

'Tomorrow week.'

'I'm so looking forward to seeing him, but it's sad he couldn't get here in time to see Granny,' Bina whispered. 'She used to pray that she would see him again before she died.'

'She would have loved to see Pat too,' Lizzie sipped her gin.

'A pity I have to go back to Dublin, I'd like to meet him again. It's a long time since I saw him,' Meg said.

'Come back when he's here,' suggested Iris.

'David will be gone back to sea next week so I won't be able to come down again.'

'Bring the younger ones with you, sure the older can look after themselves.'

'And have the place wrecked while I'm away?' Meg laughed.

'Football in the parlour? Anyway, I'm hoping you can come up to see me soon.'

'We'll try, won't we Lizzie?' Iris promised.

'Maybe you might come as well, Bina? It would do you good.'

'Thank you, Auntie Meg, I'll write and let you know.'

'I look forward to hearing from you, I'm going to miss Fanny's letters.'

'I'll definitely write to you, every week.'

'Thank you, Bina.'

They said the Rosary for Fanny, and just before Seamus went up to his bed he pulled a letter from his pocket and handed it to Bina. 'Your grandmother asked me to give you this.'

'What is it?'

'I don't know.' He shook his head.

Bina stared at Lizzie in puzzlement.

'Well, open it,' she said. 'Go on, girl.'

She pulled open the flap and took out the letter, slowly opening it. Tears filled her eyes.

'What does it say?' Lizzie asked.

Bina began to read aloud, her voice quivering.

Saturday 28th December 1929

I give and bequeath to my granddaughter Abina O'Sullivan –
Sewing machine. Gramophone. Dressing Table and Chest of Drawers with Mirror and the China Clock. (All my clothes to my granddaughters Abina, Eleanor and Cathy O'Sullivan.)
I also recommend Abina to my son's generosity in recognition of her kindness to me to give her at least £10.00 ten pounds out of my money at present in the bank. And I direct that this must be given when wanted.

Fanny Dineen
Mary O'Connell
Ignatius Crean

Bina burst into tears.

'She always appreciated everything you did for her, Bina girl.' Lizzie put her arm around her.

'I can't believe she's given me all her precious things, and especially the china clock, she knew I loved it.'

'And ten pounds too, that's a lot of money, Bina. You'll be set up.' Iris was pleased for her.

'But I'd rather she was still here with us.'

'Of course we would, but maybe she's in a happier place now, God rest her.' Lizzie blessed herself.

'And she wrote it just a week before she died,' Bina said slowly. 'So she must have known she was going to die.'

'Don't dwell on it, Bina love, Fanny wouldn't want that.'

Bina wasn't consoled and later, when all of the others had gone to bed, she went out into the stable and groomed Daisy in the light of a lamp. The wind whirled around the building, and it creaked and moaned as if it was in mourning too. Edward's new stallion and the mare were uneasy, moving in their stalls. Suddenly, the door opened and her heart almost stopped as she stared at it wondering if there was someone there. Then she thought she heard a voice calling and turned sharply. The door rasped and banged closed again caught by the capricious wind.

'Granny?' she whispered, her voice shaking.

Was she still with her, Bina wondered. Fanny had believed in the spirits. Believed in another world.

She put her arms around Daisy's neck. The mare was old now and Seamus had warned her that she might not live through another winter, and Bina was fearful that she would leave her too. She cried hot tears then, and wondered how she would bear the loss of all those she loved so much.

Chapter Sixty-seven

Bina recognised her uncle immediately when she met him at the railway station. He was handsome and tall and wore a dark suit under a heavy grey overcoat and immediately she was able to see Seamus's likeness in his face. He wrapped her in a big bear hug.

'Granny would have loved to see you.' She was in tears.

'Shucks, I'd give anything to have her here.' His own eyes were moist too.

'She died on Friday week last.'

'Thanks for sending the telegram and letting me know.' He picked up his suitcase and they made their way out of the station.

'I didn't think you'd be able to come.'

'I'm only sorry it wasn't sooner.'

'You're here now,' she smiled at him.

'We'll take a motor cab up to the house.'

'So this is *Rose Cottage*, isn't it pretty?' He stood outside in admiration. 'And I know it was a comfort for Mam and Pa to be so close to *Fairfields*.' He looked over towards the high walls.

'I'll take you in to Grandad, he's not been the same since Granny died.' She led the way up the path and into the house. 'Jim is here, Grandad,' she called out, taking her coat off, and going into the kitchen where Seamus sat by the fire, his head bent.

'Pa?' Jim took off his hat and stood in the doorway, his broad shoulders filling the space.

Seamus looked up at him.

'Do you not know me, Pa?' Jim went towards the old man, his hand stretched out.

'It's Jim, Grandad,' Bina said.

'Ah, Jim, *mo chroi.*' Seamus took his hand and held tight.

'It's been a long time, Pa.' Jim pulled a chair over to where Seamus sat and patted his shoulder.

Tears filled the old man's rheumy blue eyes and trickled down through the ridges on his face.

Jim put his arms around Seamus and held him close. They sat like that for a while, not a move out of either.

The door opened and Edward appeared.

Jim stood up. 'It's great to see you, Edward.'

'And you too,' Edward smiled.

They wrapped their arms around each other.

'I'm sorry I missed Mam's funeral, it took time to book passage. But we'll have a chance to catch up on things now. How's life been for you?'

'Good enough.'

'Why don't you take your coat off, Uncle Jim, and sit by the range, it's a cold night,' Bina suggested, beginning to cook something for them to eat.

'It's nothing like Madison, always snow in winter, and pretty chilly too. This is like springtime over here,' Jim laughed.

'How are Edith and Paul?' Bina asked.

'They're in great form.'

'A pity they couldn't come over too.'

'Paul is in school.'

'Granny always said she would love to meet them, if only she...' Bina murmured.

Jim looked over her shoulder. 'Shucks, is that drisheen you're cooking?' he asked, with a laugh.

'Course it is.' Bina put the plates in front of the men, cut bread and poured hot tea.

They tucked in and there wasn't much talk for a while. When they were almost finished, Bina sat down herself and ate bread and jam. She hadn't been able to eat much at all since Fanny had become so ill, her stomach in knots. 'You must meet Daddy and Eleanor, Cathy and the boys, they'll be delighted.'

'We'll go over to see them one of the days,' Jim promised. 'I'm looking forward to visiting. I want to see everyone, Bina, you and I will make a vacation of it.'

Bina giggled. She loved Jim's broad American accent and the unusual words he used sometimes.

'How long will you stay?'

'I sail back on the eighth of February.'

Bina was glad to hear that Jim was going to be home for so long. Now she might have a chance to talk to him about Will.

'How's the old house in the stable yard, Pa?' Jim asked Seamus.

'The place is empty,' he grunted.

'There's no one living over there?'

'No. It's like a morgue.'

'I get it. Maybe I'll wander over there.'

'All locked up.'

'Mrs. Kelleher might lend us the key,' Bina suggested.

'What a swell idea,' Jim smiled. 'We could all go over.'

'I'd love that. Granny and I used to go around the back and look in the windows, but it used to make her sad.' Bina was excited. She had never done more than that, or peer in through the cracks in the door.

'I'm not for going over,' muttered Seamus.

'Me neither,' Edward added.

'But it will be all right if we ask for the key, Uncle?' Bina appealed to him.

'I suppose ...if you want.'

'How well do you know the people in *Fairfields*?' Jim asked.

'Granny knew Mrs. Kelleher quite well, she supplied her with eggs and fowl, and did some laundry for her. And I know her too from going up and down.'

'Then I guess it will be ok to ask. We'll go over together.'

The following evening Eleanor and Cathy came over to *Rose Cottage* to meet their Uncle, and it was a rowdy gathering with much laughter. The girls brought Bina a present of a bottle of lavender perfume for her birthday which would fall in two days' time.

'Happy Birthday to you, Happy Birthday to you ...' they sang together.

'Thank you,' Bina was so pleased. 'I love lavender.'

'You're going to smell really nice,' Eleanor said, and the girls giggled.

Bina opened the bottle, and put perfume behind each ear and on her wrists.

'We must celebrate your birthday,' Uncle Jim said. 'We'll go into town to have tea, how about that?'

'Thank you, Uncle Jim.' Eleanor and Cathy cheered.

'And invite your Dad and the boys as well.'

'Daddy is never home until late,' Eleanor explained. 'So I don't think he'll be able to go. And I've got a job in the Sunbeam factory, I start next Monday,' she announced proudly.

'Congratulations, Eleanor, now we have two things to celebrate.'

'We'll have to ask Daddy first.'

'I'm sure he'll say yes.'

Jim didn't seem to think there was any problem there, Bina thought, he was so confident about everything.

'Where would you like to go?' Jim asked Bina.

'I don't mind.'

'The Tivoli,' Eleanor suggested.

'Lovely,' Cathy smiled broadly. 'Tea and cream cakes for all of us.'

That night, Bina decided to talk to Uncle Jim about Will. She would be twenty on Thursday and grown up. It was time. The following morning, after Edward and Seamus had gone to work, and she had cooked breakfast for Jim, she sat down opposite him at the kitchen table, and took a deep breath.

'Uncle Jim?'

'Yes, Bina?'

He was immediately interested in anything she had to say. She loved that about him, so different to Edward.

'I have a boyfriend,' she said, shyly, her cheeks pink with embarrassment.

'A boyfriend?' he asked, with a wide grin. 'How is it I haven't heard about him before? Mam never mentioned anything about boyfriends in her letters.'

'We have to meet secretly because Edward doesn't like him,' she explained all about Will, and how she would go out with Fanny and they would meet him at the old house.

'That seems ridiculous. What has Edward against him?'

'He doesn't approve of me marrying a man who wears a uniform. It's just like Mam, he didn't want her to marry Daddy either.'

'I heard all about that.'

'But we are very fond of each other, Uncle Jim, and he gave me …' She stopped speaking, wondering if she should continue.

'And?' he encouraged.

'I've something to show you.' She ran upstairs to her bedroom and under the loose floorboard she took out the two boxes. Kissed both of them and ran back down and handed them to Jim.

'You open them,' he said.

She smiled, opened up the small brown leather box and took the ring out. 'Do you like it?'

'It's beautiful, Bina. Let me see it on you.'

She slipped it on to her ring finger. Loving the look of it. The five little diamonds sparkling on the gold band.

'And you don't wear it at all?'

She shook her head, a mist of tears in her eyes. 'And he gave me my watch at Christmas, but I have to hide it too.'

'That's a shame, we'll have to do something about it.'

'But what can I do?'

'Why don't I write a letter to Will and ask him to come down. Then we'll see.' He patted her hand.

He did that straight away, and on their way into town they posted the letter.

On Bina's birthday, Will sent her a lovely birthday card, and there was a small box in the envelope as well. Her heart leapt with excitement when she opened it, thrilled to find a beautiful pair of gold earrings nestling in a bed of black velvet. She put them on immediately, and decided that if Edward made any comment she would just come out straight and tell him Will had given them to her.

They all met at the Tivoli later, although Mike didn't come. For the first time since Fanny had died Bina felt able to smile properly, and even enjoyed eating the delicious sandwiches and cakes which her uncle ordered for tea.

Jim's visit was a whirlwind of visiting family and old friends. And Bina went everywhere with him. To Knockraha where Seamus's family lived, Glounthaune to see Lizzie, and Iris too in Cobh. Many's a night there were parties, and on one occasion they didn't get home until six thirty in the morning.

When she brought Jim up to meet her father the two men talked together for a long time sitting by the fire in the parlour. She left them and stayed in the kitchen with Cathy, Eleanor and the boys.

But she overheard Jim's booming voice mention her name and curious to hear what they were saying, she stood by the parlour door and listened. Eleanor came over beside her.

'They're talking about me,' Bina whispered.

Eleanor's eyes widened.

'Listeners never hear good of themselves,' Mike said, suddenly appearing around the door.

The girls looked at each other but said nothing.

'Bina, come into the parlour, I want to talk to you.'

She went in.

'Jim tells me some man wants to marry you and that you're actually engaged. As usual I'm last to hear anything in this family.' He seemed cross. 'I thought the man was supposed to ask the father for permission to marry his daughter?'

Bina's heart dropped into her stomach. She didn't know what to say.

'Is this the same man you were writing to?' he asked.

'Yes. Will gave me a ring but I wasn't able to wear it. So I didn't tell anyone.'

'He should have come to me before he ever gave you a ring,' Mike said.

Bina was silenced.

'And what if I say *no*?'

'I love him, Daddy, and he feels the same, surely you can understand that?'

'Get him up here to see me.'

'I will.'

'And I suppose if he's a Garda he can support you?'

'Yes he can, and he's coming down to Cork next week.'

'I'll see him then.'

Jim smiled reassuringly at Bina.

Chapter Sixty-eight

'To be walking through the gates of *Fairfields* takes me back.' Jim gazed around him with an air of nostalgia as they went over to the stable yard. 'It looks unkempt. Pa wouldn't have kept it in this condition.'

'He's so lonely, he's never come back here, not once,' Bina said, sorry too that it looked so bad. Leaves and branches gathered in heaps. Ivy grew around the walls. Even the roof of the house looked as if it needed repair.

'To see it like this tears at my insides.' Jim seemed to shudder.

'Let's go up now and ask for the keys.'

'Do you go up to the front door these days?' he asked.

'No, never. Granny and I always went up through the trees to the kitchen door if we were taking up the fowl, or the laundry.'

'Who's doing it now?'

'We still supply the eggs and fowl for them, but Mrs. Kelleher told me I didn't need to do the laundry when Granny was ill. But I'll probably start again soon.'

'Mam was lucky to have you to help.'

'Granny and I did everything together. I feel lost without her.' Tears flooded her eyes.

They arrived at the back door and Bina knocked.

'Hello Bina, what can I do for you.' Susan appeared.

'This is my Uncle Jim, home from America.'

Jim shook Susan's hand and Bina went on to explain about the key to the stable yard.

'Of course you can, just let me find it.' She went to a kitchen cupboard and opened it. Hanging on various hooks were a number of bunches of keys and it took her a moment or two to identify the particular one. 'There it is.' Her hand rested on the bunch and she lifted it off and handed it to Bina.

'We only want to visit for a short while and I might take a few photos with my camera,' Jim explained.

'I'm sure that would be fine.'

'Should we check with Mrs. Kelleher?' Jim asked.

'I could ask her if you like,' she offered.

There was no problem about seeing the stable yard and the following morning they went back to *Fairfields*.

'This is so wonderful,' whispered Bina.

Jim pushed the big key into the lock and turned it. Then he put his weight against the wooden gate and it moved forward scraping the flagstones which had become overgrown with weeds and grasses over the years.

On the left hand side were the red painted stable doors and at the other end their family home and the carriage houses.

'I was twenty-three in nineteen hundred and seven when Pat and myself left from Queenstown. Mam, Pa, Anna and Edward, came down to see us off. They were all very upset, although Pat and I were so excited, two young fellows off on an adventure. We thought we'd never get to America and to make some money we cut men's hair on the journey over, we were very good with the scissors,' he laughed. 'Unfortunately, we didn't appreciate how lonely they were at home until Mam wrote later and told me.' He lifted the heavy wooden top of the well and lowered the bucket. Bina listened until they could both hear a splash and Jim brought up the bucket brimming with sparkling water. There was a small cup attached to it and Jim scooped water and offered it to Bina.

She sipped. 'It's so cool and fresh.' She handed the cup to him.

He refilled it and took a long draught.

'Nothing like spring water from home,' he smiled broadly. 'I've been longing to taste this.' He put the bucket back into the well and closed it. 'Let's go inside.'

The front door of the house opened without too much difficulty, and the hallway brightened as daylight flooded in.

'It hasn't changed at all.' Jim gazed around.

'Let's see the kitchen.' Bina went inside. The room was completely empty now. Faded marks on the walls where the range and dresser had stood and shelves had been fixed.

'I hadn't imagined it quite so bare,' Jim said.

'Granny used to tell me what it was like living here. She always had the range lighting as she had in *Rose Cottage*. A kettle boiling on the hob. A pot of soup or stew on for the dinner. New bread baked in the oven. Granny would never offer day old bread to anyone, even the tramps who called selling stuff. She would be ashamed to do that.'

'She never changed.'

They climbed the narrow stairs up to the parlour.

'We used to sit up here when Mam let us, and we'd play our accordians with Anna on the piano. Those were great nights filled with music.' There was a slight catch of emotion in his throat.

'And your accordians are still at home,' Bina said. 'Granny always kept them under the bed. Did you ever get another one?'

'I sure did.' His loud voice boomed around the room.

'And do you play much?'

'As often as I can.'

'With Uncle Pat?'

'I don't see much of him, he lives in New York now, but I get together with friends of mine and boy, we make music.'

'Do Aunt Edith and Paul play?'

'Edith plays the piano and Paul likes the accordion too.'

'I play Mammy's piano and the concertina and the melodeon.'

'This was a wonderful house of music. We missed it sorely when we left.' He put his arm around Bina and hugged.

She opened a door. Winter sun slanted through the window across the brown painted floorboards, the shadows of the panes reflected on the white wall. 'This was Granny's room.'

'And we were downstairs, and I can remember many a pillow fight between the three of us. Jumping on the beds. Shouting. Screaming. Until Pa or Mam would let a shout at us. Then it would be quiet for a while until it broke out again. We had such fun in those days.'

They stood in the hall again. 'I hate leaving.' Jim looked around. 'I can hear the voices in my head.'

'I'm sure we could borrow the keys again before you go.' Bina was hopeful.

'I'll drop a note to thank them anyway and ask. Shucks, I almost forgot to take the photos.' He took a camera from a leather bag which was slung over his shoulder.

They went into each room again, and then outside.

'Pose for me at the well, Bina. You'll look right pretty there.'

She did, smiling at the camera.

'Now, let's see where the carriages were kept.' Jim strode over to the large wooden building and pushed open the door. To their surprise, one of the carriages was still there.

'I can't believe this.' Jim was taken aback, as was Bina.

'Granny and Grandad never knew this carriage was here, they thought everything had been taken out of here.'

'Isn't it beautiful.' Jim ran his hand across the black surface, cutting through the coating of dust. 'It just needs cleaning.'

Jim pressed a silver handle and opened the door.

'It's so beautiful inside.' Bina touched the blue velvet seats.

'Sit in,' Jim suggested.

'Should I?'

'Sure, I'll sit beside you.'

'All we need is a couple of horses and we'd be away,' he laughed. 'Better than any of those automobiles we have now. The days of the horse and carriage have sadly gone.' He stepped out and took another photo of her.

'I'm dying to tell Grandad it's here. Maybe he'll come over to see it with us,' Bina was excited, thinking that it might give Seamus a boost, he was so down since Fanny had died.

Lastly they went into the stables where the beautiful wrought iron stalls still stood.

'Look at the tack,' Jim yelled, pointing to the leather bridles which hung around the walls. He took one down and examined it, blowing the dust off until the brown leather shone through.

'You know, Bina, I used to polish this tack every day, it was our job to do that after school, me and Pat and Edward too. And if it wasn't up to Pa's standard he would crack the whip and woe betide us if we didn't get it shining by the next morning.' He took down a saddle.

'And there's a brush,' Bina said, excited.

'We kept the Staunton horses in perfect condition. They were the best of quality and we had the use of them all the time. I met this American man at a race meeting and he offered both Pat and me jobs on his ranch in Wisconsin. We couldn't refuse the chance as he paid our fare, although we had to pay him back out of our wages. When we had done that we moved into the city where we did much better, but we missed the horses. Always missed them.' He took a riding crop, swished it, and then put it back on its hook. 'When I tell Pat this place is still here untouched he'll definitely come back on vacation. He was sorry he missed Mam's funeral, as I was myself.'

'I didn't think Granny would die so quickly. It was a terrible shock when the doctor told us to take her home from the hospital.'

'She told me in her last letter that you were looking after her really well.'

Bina was quiet for a moment. The loss of Fanny was still very raw. 'There's something else I want to show you,' she said, leading the way around to the back garden. 'This is where Granny and Grandad's little babies are buried.' She bent down and put her hand on the withered flowers.

'I never knew …' Jim seemed shocked.

'She told me about them when I was young and we used to visit and say a prayer.' Bina blessed herself. 'It was the last thing she said before she died …*don't forget my little ones.*'

Jim knelt beside her and blessed himself also. They were quiet then for a little while.

'How many babies?' he asked softly.

'Three here and two more in Caherlag.'

'I knew about the two boys up there, but not about these ones buried here.'

'Two girls and another boy. They didn't live at all.'

'We lost two children as well.' He was cast down.

'I'm sorry to hear that.'

'But we have our son Paul and we're so very glad about that. We love him dearly.'

'The flowers have died now but they'll bloom again in spring and summer.'

'I'll have a special Mass said for these little ones,' Jim said.

'I pray for them every night, and come over here as often as I can.'

'It must have been very hard on Mam and Pa to lose five children,' he said slowly.

'They never talked about it.'

'Thanks for telling me.' Jim blessed himself.

Bina received a letter from Will by the midday post, thrilled when he told her that he was coming down on Monday and would arrive on the Dublin train at two fifteen.

She went to the railway station to meet him. They had tea in town and she told him about Jim, and how thrilled she was that he was on their side. It was Will's birthday and they went shopping, and she bought him a new pair of shoes as a present. Since Fanny had died, Edward allowed her to keep the egg money and she saved as much as she could.

Later, she brought Will up to meet her father.

'He can be a bit abrupt, but don't mind that.' Bina warned as they went in, and squeezed his hand.

Eleanor and Cathy and the boys were well behaved when they met Will, and then Bina introduced him to her father. They shook hands.

'I'll talk to Will, Bina, you stay in the kitchen with your sisters,' Mike instructed.

Dread swept through Bina. What would her father say to Will? Would he refuse his permission for them to marry?

'Is he your boyfriend, Bina?' Eleanor asked, excited.

'Yes.'

'He's nice,' Cathy said.

'He's very tall.' Michael ran into the hall.

'Don't go into the parlour, Daddy is talking to him.' Bina pulled him back into the kitchen.

'Hey,' he protested.

'Keep quiet.' She pressed her finger against her lips.

They waited. Unable to hear what was going on in the parlour as the door was firmly closed.

Bina said a decade of the Rosary as she stood there. Her hands clasped.

'Are you praying, Bina?' Cathy asked.

She nodded.

'What are you praying for?'

'Stop talking, Cathy,' Eleanor whispered, having the sense to keep quiet.

They sat on the form at the table.

The clock on the wall ticked. The time passed. So slowly Bina could hardly keep her patience.

Then Mike called her in.

'Good luck,' Eleanor said.

That was repeated by the others, giggling.

She went in and immediately looked at Will, relieved to see that he was smiling.

'Will has told me ...himself ...that he wants to marry you, Bina. At last I've got it from the *horse's mouth* for a change and not through third parties. So, we've had a long chat and I've agreed that you may marry him. He seems a sensible man so he should be able to curb you excitable nature.'

'Thank you Daddy, thank you.' She rushed over to him, flung her arms around his neck and hugged him tight. He smiled wryly.

He asked all the children in then, and announced that Bina and Will were getting married. There was great excitement and he offered Will a glass of whiskey to celebrate. Then, Bina asked them all out to Rose Cottage for a party on the following night, as Uncle Jim would be sailing for America soon.

When they left later Bina felt like she was walking on air. 'I can't believe Daddy agreed that we can be married, what did you say to him?'

'We just had a man to man chat, and it really didn't take much persuasion. I think he'd already made up his mind.'

'I'm so happy, Will, we can make all the arrangements for our wedding now.'

'I'm so glad you're as happy as I am.' He held Bina's hand tight.

Will saw her home and went back to Cork to stay the night with friends.

The next evening he came out to *Rose Cottage* and met with Jim. It was a cordial occasion, the two men getting along tremendously well. Mike, Eleanor and Cathy arrived, as well as Lizzie and Iris, and other relatives and friends. When Edward arrived home and met Will he had no other choice but to shake hands and be pleasant.

'These two young people are engaged to be married, Edward,' Mike said, smiling. 'And I don't think anyone should stand in their way.'

Edward's face was a picture of resentment.

'So raise your glass and join with us in a toast to them.' Jim handed him a glass of whiskey and they raised their glasses to Bina and Will.

Much to Bina's relief, he joined in.

'Every happiness to you, Bina and Will.' Mike kissed her and shook Will's hand. 'May you be as happy as your mother and I were.'

It was a great night of music and celebration and went on until the small hours. Bina only wished that her Mam and Granny could have been here to share it with her.

On Jim's last morning, he and Bina had a last nostalgic look around the stable yard. It meant a lot to both of them.

At Queenstown, it was sad to watch him stand on the deck of the tender waving at them.

'I wonder when we'll see Jim again,' Bina asked no one in particular.

'He said he might bring Edith and Paul next time,' Seamus answered the question.

But no one said anything else as the tender slowly left the quayside on the way out to the liner which was at anchor in the roads off Cobh.

'There he goes.' Bina waved her scarf vigorously.

'Bye Jim,' Lizzie shouted.

'Slan leat, a mhic.' Seamus was emotional as he waved goodbye to his son.

While Bina hoped to see Jim again, she thought Seamus must be wondering if he would still be alive when he returned?

Chapter Sixty-nine

Because the family were all in mourning after the death of Fanny, and still wearing black, Bina and Will decided to wait until the autumn to get married, finally deciding on the twenty-first of October, nineteen hundred and thirty.

She still raised the poultry and did the laundry for both Mrs. Staunton and Mrs. Kelleher and the work helped her to save money for getting married. She was kept very busy, continuing to do all the chores Fanny used to do. Milking the cow. Cooking. Washing. Ironing. And gardening too.

Today she was making butter. Pouring in the cream, and straining off the milk, energetically dashing the plunger up and down in the churn until the butter had formed and she moulded it into shape with the butter pats. Later, she planned to bake bread and scones, and spend the evening darning her grandfather's socks, and lastly to write a letter to Will.

She chose the design for her wedding dress and Eleanor's bridesmaid's dress from a magazine with the help of the dressmaker, finally deciding on a soft pink silk full length dress with wide sleeves, a white cape and shoes, and a cute cloche hat in white with silver trim.

Eleanor would wear a white scalloped skirt with a pink top, a white cape and a pretty organza cap. The groom and best man would wear grey suits, white wing collars and pink bow ties, with white carnations in their button holes.

Lent drifted past, and she was particularly careful to stick with the rules which Fanny had always done. Eating only one main meal and two small collations every day. Black tea and dry bread. She had also given up sweets for Lent as a special penance. In memory of her Granny, she went to the Mission in the church, as they had always gone together.

Will took an excursion train from Dublin whenever he could, and Bina went to Dublin in June and stayed with her Auntie Meg. She had a wonderful time with Will, and now she counted down the days until they would be married.

Almost every night he drifted into her dreams. Last night they were in the old house. In the velvet darkness he told her that he loved her. Mysterious whispers. You are mine. I am yours. Always. His hands moved slowly through her hair, and softly cupped her face, his lips were on hers, moist, warm, promising so much. Through the skylight window she saw the stars in the sky above. Twinkling. Will's body inclined closer. She felt the slight roughness of his chin on her face. Tenderly his hands touched. A cloud passed. The three-quarter moon was revealed. Bright. Too bright. She closed her eyes and felt herself float like driftwood in a slow sultry stream ...

'Uncle, do you think you could get Granny's money out of the bank for me?' Bina asked, feeling awkward about approaching Edward on such a matter.

He didn't reply.

'It's the ten pounds she left me, remember, I'll be leaving on Friday and I'll need it.' She twisted the band of her engagement ring around her finger.

'So soon?' Seamus grunted from where he sat at the range.

'I'm getting married next Tuesday,' she said, and then regretted that she sounded sharp. She hadn't meant to upset her grandfather. She went and sat by him, her arm around his shoulder. 'Remember I told you, Grandad. I'm sorry it's come around so fast.'

He nodded.

'Why don't you just take some of it? You must be careful and no splash it on foolish things,' Edward said.

'I'd prefer to have it all, then I'll put it in a bank in Dublin.'

'I'll see if I can get the time.'

Bina stared at him. Was he ever going to give it to her? What would her Granny think if she knew?

These last weeks she had done a lot of shopping. Cathy came with her after school some days and they enjoyed choosing the various things she needed for her wedding and honeymoon.

'I hope Uncle Edward will give me the money,' she confided to Cathy.

'He'll have to give it to you, it's yours.' Cathy was angry on her behalf. 'Why don't you ask Daddy to talk to him?'

'I might have to do that, although he's always so busy at work he mightn't have much time to go out and see Uncle.'

But it wasn't necessary. The following evening when Edward came in, he handed her an envelope.

'As I said, don't splurge it all,' he warned.

'I won't,' Bina smiled at him. So relieved that he had given it to her at last.

Every day presents arrived at *Rose Cottage* from friends and relatives. Sets of china. Irish linen pillow and bolster slips. Bedsheets. Tablecloths. Cutlery. There was even a beautiful lace bedcover from Ellie, a friend of her mother, who used to work with the Stauntons in *Fairfields* and now lived in New York with her American husband and children. Bina had written to Ellie to let her know that Fanny had died, and since then they had kept up a regular correspondence. Bina was amazed at her generous wedding gift.

There was so much to bring up to Dublin she had to buy two more large suitcases and even then some of the heavier items had to be left behind to be brought up at a later time. She was so excited to be bringing so many lovely things up to Dublin, and couldn't wait to see how they would look in their new home.

On Wednesday, Bina cycled up to Hillside Terrace. Eleanor was to be her bridesmaid and Bina brought up her own wedding dress, and Eleanor's skirt and top, with the capes and hats. Both dresses carefully folded in cardboard boxes and tied on to the carrier securely.

'Fit on your dress, Bina, and Eleanor too, we want to see how you will look on your wedding day,' Cathy beseeched.

They went upstairs and reappeared a short time later.

'You're beautiful.' Cathy was in awe.

'Eleanor, take care of your dress when you travel up and keep it in the box, you don't want it creased in the suitcase,' Bina warned.

'I'm so looking forward to the wedding.' Eleanor touched the soft silk of the skirt. 'And it's going to be lovely to wear bright clothes, I'm so tired of black, although Daddy wants us to wear it until Christmas.'

'I feel the same, but we have to mourn Granny.'

Mike walked into the parlour. 'You both look lovely,' he smiled at them.

'Why can't we all go to the wedding, Daddy?' Cathy asked.

'I'm sorry, Cathy, but I'm too busy.'

Tears filled her eyes.

'We want to go too,' Michael shouted.

'And me,' Joseph added.

'I'll send you a photograph,' Bina promised.

'That won't be the same.'

Bina regretted that all her family wouldn't be at her wedding. But both she and Will had felt that to be married in Cork and have to face Edward's opposition, which still simmered, their wedding day might be spoiled.

'When are we going to see you?' Cathy asked.

'I'll come and visit.'

'When?'

'Don't worry, it won't be long.' She hugged her.

'Can we go up to Dublin?' Joseph asked.

'When we get a bigger flat. We've only a small place now.'
Their faces were sad.

Before she left, Eleanor walked over to Bina carrying a large brown box tied with a red ribbon.

'Happy Wedding Day,' they all shouted.

'Open it up,' Cathy said, excited.

Bina did and was delighted to see a white china dinner service with a lovely design of tiny gold flowers around the edge of each piece. 'Thank you, it's beautiful.' Bina was emotional.

'You can have lots of parties,' Cathy added.

Bina kissed them.

Eleanor took a little box from her pocket. 'Now, something borrowed. I want you to wear the silver bracelet Granny gave me.'

'Thank you, Eleanor.' Bina took it and slipped it on her wrist. Reminded of Granny, tears moistened her eyes.

'And something blue.' Cathy handed her a lace garter.

Bina laughed. 'Thank you, Cathy. Tuesday will be the most wonderful day in my life and I'm sorry you won't be there.'

Chapter Seventy

The following morning she was delighted to receive a letter from Will.

My own darling pet,

Here goes for my last letter to you as a lover. Next time it will be as a husband which will be just a week from today. I hope that you will like the room I have found for us. It is a nice one on Fairview Avenue, the only thing that is wrong is that it is dear, fourteen shillings a week, but we will have the use of the kitchen, and I will tell you all about it on Friday night. Of course there is nothing final arranged until you come up, except that there will be a small party on Monday night. It looks as if they are expecting a great burst up, but we are not going to spend money on drink to give them all a gay time because when it is over we are the ones who will have to pay the piper.

I will leave everything alone until I see you on Friday. Noel and myself are going to be great swells as we will be dressed the same so that you won't know which of us you will be married to.

I must finish up now and I am saying goodbye to you for the last time on paper. Did we ever think it would come so easy in the end?

All my love and all my kisses to my own dearest and say goodbye to Grandad for me until we see him as one.

Ever your own Will. xxxxx

Bina took out her writing pad and replied immediately.

My dearest love,

Just a few lines in a hurry for the last time single from Rose Cottage, so here is the last.

I just received your loving letter containing the details. I'll be taking the four o'clock train tomorrow, so be at the station at seven thirty will you, and wait by the engine, and I will see you. I don't want to leave the carriage before I might lose anything. I'll be wearing a fur coat and a navy blue hat and I won't get on to the platform until the people are nearly gone.

I will have to finish up now, I am feeling very lonely. It is my last day at Rose Cottage and my poor grandfather feels terrible. I have promised to send him a new pipe and tobacco for Tuesday morning next, so he is expecting a good smoke.

Goodbye now my own sweet love until we meet tomorrow night. The worst part is still to come when I am leaving and have to say goodbye for a while to Grandad.

All my love and all my kisses to my own darling Will.
I am forever and forever your own loving Bina. xxxxx

Seven thirty on tomorrow evening love.
I'll be with you again with God's Help.

She folded the sheet of paper carefully, and slipped it into the envelope, closing it with a kiss. Then she wrote Will's name and address at his digs for the last time.

That night, quite a few neighbours and friends called. Bina was taken aback as she hadn't expected to see anyone, embarrassed that she hadn't baked anything tasty which she could give to the visitors, except some apple tart and scones she had made for Edward and her Grandad.

But Mrs. O'Connor was one of the first and brought sandwiches and fruit cake, and Edward always had some porter and a bottle of whiskey in the house so there was enough to go around. Bina didn't feel quite so lonely surrounded by her neighbours and friends. Even Susan and Barbara Kelleher came down to say goodbye. To her surprise, Mrs. Kelleher gave her a set of beautifully embroidered table napkins, and Susan's gift was a lace dressing table set. Bina was overwhelmed.

Chapter Seventy-one

Bina's last day at *Rose Cottage* dawned. She woke up to the sound of the birds singing. The cock crowing. Although there was very little poultry left now, only a few hens and the cock, just enough for her grandfather and Edward.

She cycled up to Caherlag to Anna and Fanny's grave. It was a bright day, and the sun shone high in the sky, although a cool breeze whistled through the trees which sheltered the last resting place of her dear ones. The cemetery was very old. Wild grasses grew tall around headstones, many of which stood crookedly, the names of those buried there illegible. She wished that a headstone had been erected for Anna and Fanny instead of the metal cross. But it wasn't her place to do that, although she wondered about asking Will if they could do it sometime in the future.

On the grave, she put a fresh bunch of pink roses which she had cut in the garden. Among the last few roses still blooming, they had a beautiful scent and were Fanny's favourite. She knelt and cried bitter tears, prayed for their dear souls, and those of the babies buried here as well. Sadly, she said goodbye, and then went over to *Fairfields*, peering through the crack in the wooden gate of the stable yard like she used to do with Fanny when she was a child. Still crying, she went around to the back garden and whispered a little prayer for the souls of the lost babies. Although she had told Uncle Jim about them, she wondered would anyone else ever say a prayer for them until she returned?

Lastly, she went out into the stables and said goodbye to Daisy, wrapping her arms around her, desperately aware that she might never see her again.

In her own bedroom, she packed the last of her precious things. Then took her two diaries from underneath the loose wooden floorboard. Some photos of Anna, Fanny, Seamus and herself when she was a child. A small blue bag in which she kept a length of one of her own dark curls which Fanny had first cut when she bobbed Bina's long hair.

Having already packed her clothes, and cleared the furniture of her possessions, the room was so bare she found it hard to even look around. The only items lying on the bed were her dress, coat and hat which she would wear when she travelled to Dublin. There was a mist of tears across her eyes as she went into Fanny's room. But it wasn't the same any more. Edward slept there now and it was austere and held no memories of her darling Granny.

In the parlour, Bina wound up the gramophone and put on one of the big records. The music of the flute players and fiddlers echoed through the house and she remembered the times they danced around this room. But she couldn't listen for long, and lifted the needle and put the record back into its paper sleeve. She would bring it up to Dublin as soon as she could. She stood for a moment staring around her, and ran her hand along the back of the green chesterfield suite, so soft she wanted to let the scent cling to her skin and always be with her, so that she would never forget her dearest grandmother.

The sound of a motor car approached the house and she went out to see who it was.

'I came home to bring you to the station, there's a lot of stuff and Pa won't be able to carry it all,' Edward said gruffly.

'Thank you, Uncle.'

Bina regretted that he had come home. She wasn't ready to leave. Would she ever be ready to leave?

'I'll have to check if there's anything I've left behind,' she said quickly. A desperate anxiety to go around the house again, just one more time.

'I'll start taking your suitcases out to the motor car,' Edward said.

She was already in the kitchen. Imagining Fanny cooking on the range, or baking, or scrubbing. She reached out her hand and touched the table. 'Granny,' she whispered.

'Bina, I want to take a snap of you.' He appeared in the doorway.

'But I'm only wearing my house skirt, I'll have to change my clothes.'

'You can do that in a minute.' He picked up his camera and fiddled with it for a few minutes. 'Come outside and sit on the bench, it's sheltered there and not too cold.'

She followed him.

'Put your hand under your chin, and give me a nice big smile,' he instructed.

For Bina, it wasn't easy to smile.

'Is that everything? Pa is already in the motor car.'

'Yes I think so.' She picked up a small navy blue travelling bag and her handbag and followed him slowly out of the door, closing it gently behind her. Hearing the click of the lock had a terrible finality about it. She walked down the path. At the gate she stopped and looked back at the cottage. Sunshine sparkled in the windows, and there was a rich green sheen on the leaves of ivy which clustered around the door and up as far as the roof. But it had such an air of loneliness without her darling Granny standing in the doorway, she had to turn away, tears in her eyes.

As if he understood she was leaving, the dog followed her out. She bent to pat his head, and ruffle his coat. Then, biting her lip she climbed into the motor car and sat down, reluctant to let her uncle and grandfather see how upset she was. As the car moved off, she stared straight ahead and whispered goodbye in her heart.

At the station, it was very busy, people rushing along the platform to find a place on the train, but Edward managed to find Bina a seat in the first carriage near the engine and loaded on her luggage.

It was almost time now.

She put her arms around her grandfather. 'Goodbye dear Grandad, I will be back to see you as soon as I can.'

Seamus seemed unable to say anything, tears slowly drifting down his rugged cheeks. Bina gently dried them with her handkerchief.

She hugged Edward then, and he pushed a ten shilling note into her hand. 'Watch that money now, don't go wild.'

'Thank you, Uncle.' She tried to control the rush of emotion which threatened to overwhelm her.

'And here's a photo of *Rose Cottage* I took.' He handed it to her.

'Thank you.'

'Bina, Bina …'

She turned around to see Cathy, Michael and Joseph running towards her, and held her arms out wide to gather them close. 'Thanks for coming to see me off.'

'We had to, couldn't let you go on your own, girl.' Cathy embraced her tightly. 'I'm going to miss you something terrible.'

Michael and Joseph hugged her, tears on both their cheeks.

'Daddy and Eleanor said to say goodbye too but they couldn't come.' Cathy hugged her again.

The guard's whistle blew. She said goodbye one last time and went into the carriage. As the doors were banged closed one after another she leaned out the window and waved to them as the train pulled out of the station. Thinking there was nothing so sad as that sight of her grandfather standing there, his shoulders bowed, staring after the train, a shaft of sunshine bathing him in light, his figure casting a dark shadow on the platform. Then the others surrounded him, all waving to her, and slowly the little group became more indistinct as the train drew further away and they eventually disappeared.

Chapter Seventy-two

October 1930

17 Fri *I left home for Dublin to get married and caught the 4 o'clock train. Arrived in Dublin at 7.30. Everyone was very lonely after me. Met Will at train station in Dublin and stayed in Fairview with Auntie Meg.*

18 Sat *We went around shopping and bought all sorts of nice things for our wedding breakfast. Then we went to Confession to Fr. Masterson.*

19 Sun *I went to Mass and Holy Communion with Auntie Meg. Will came over about 4 o'clock and I was very excited to see our flat. It's very nice, and while it isn't Rose Cottage it is a start. This was a very wet day.*

20 Mon *Will was on holidays. We went to buy my wedding ring and had a great day out. Eleanor arrived on the train from Cork at 7.40 and we all came back and had a great party until 2 o'clock. We really enjoyed ourselves and I met some of Will's friends.*

21 Tues *My Wedding Day!*
We were married at 11 o'clock in St. Agatha's Church, North William Street. We all came back to Auntie Meg's and had a

lovely breakfast. They gave us a great send-off and we left for our honeymoon about 4 o'clock and took a cab to the Meath Hotel.

That was the last entry in Bina's diary she chose to share.

TO MAKE A DONATION TO LAURALYNN HOUSE

Children's Sunshine Home/LauraLynn Account
AIB Bank, Sandyford Business Centre,
Foxrock, Dublin 18.

Account No. 32130009
Sort Code: 93-35-70

www.lauralynnhospice.com

Acknowledgements

As always, our very special thanks to Jane and Brendan, knowing you both has changed our lives.

Many thanks to both my family and Arthur's family, our friends and clients, who continue to support our efforts to raise funds for LauraLynn House. And all those generous people who help in various ways but are too numerous to mention. You know who you are and that we appreciate everything you do.

Grateful thanks to all my friends in The Wednesday Group, who give me such valuable critique. Many thanks especially to Muriel Bolger who edited the book on this occasion also, and special thanks to Vivien Hughes who proofed the manuscript. You all know how much we appreciate your generosity.

Special thanks to Martone Design & Print – Brian, Dave and Kate. Couldn't do it without you.

Thanks to CPI Group.

Thanks to all at LauraLynn House.

Thanks to Kevin Dempsey Distributors Ltd. and Power Home Products Ltd., for their generosity in supplying product for LauraLynn House.

Special thanks to Cyclone Couriers, Southside Storage and Transland Group.

Thanks also to Irish Distillers Pernod Ricard. Supervalu. Tesco.

And in Nenagh, our grateful thanks to Tom Gleeson of Irish Computers who very generously service our website free of charge.

Rose O'Connor, Walsh Packaging, Nenagh Chamber of Commerce, McLoughlin's Hardware, Cinnamon Alley Restaurant, Jessicas, Abbey Court Hotel, and Caseys in Toomevara.

Many thanks to Ree Ward Callan and Michael Feeney Callan for all their help.

And much love to my darling husband, Arthur, without whose love and support this wouldn't be possible.

MARTONE DESIGN & PRINT

Martone Design & Print was established in 1983 and has become one of the country's most pre-eminent printing and graphic arts companies.

The Martone team provide high-end design and print work to some of the country's top companies. They provide a wide range of services including design creation/ development, spec verification, creative approval, project management, printing, logistics, shipping, materials tracking and posting verification.

They are the leading innovative all-inclusive solutions provider, bringing print excellence to every market.

The Martone sales team can be contacted at (01) 628 1809 or sales@martonepress.com.

CYCLONE COURIERS

Cyclone Couriers – who proudly support LauraLynn Children's Hospice – are the leading supplier of local, national and international courier services in Dublin. Cyclone also supply confidential mobile on-site document shredding and recycling services and secure document storage & records management services through their Cyclone Shredding and Cyclone Archive Division.

Cyclone Couriers – The fleet of pushbikes, motorbikes, and vans, can cater for all your urgent local and national courier requirements.

Cyclone International – Overnight, next day, timed and weekend door-to-door deliveries to destinations within the thirty-two counties of Ireland.

Delivery options to the UK, mainland Europe, USA, and the rest of the world.

A variety of services to all destinations across the globe.

Cyclone Shredding – On-site confidential document and product shredding & recycling service. Destruction and recycling of computers, hard drives, monitors and office electronic equipment.

Cyclone Archive – Secure document and data storage and records management. Hard copy document storage and tracking – data storage – fireproof media safe – document scanning and upload of document images.

Cyclone Couriers operate from
Pleasants House, Pleasants Lane, Saint Kevin's, Dublin 8.

Cyclone Archive, International and Shredding, operate from
11 North Park, Finglas, Dublin 11.

www.cyclone.ie   email: sales@cyclone.ie   Tel: 01-475 7000

SOUTHSIDE STORAGE
Murphystown Road, Sandyford, Dublin 18.

FACILITIES

Individually lit, self-contained, off-ground metal and concrete units that are fireproof and waterproof.

Sizes of units : 300 sq.ft. 150 sq.ft. 100 sq.ft. 70 sq.ft.

Flexible hours of access and 24 hour alarm monitored security.

Storage for home
Commercial storage
Documents and Archives
Packaging supplies and materials
Extra office space
Sports equipment
Musical instruments
And much much more ....

Contact us to discuss your requirements:

01 294 0517   -   087 640 7448
Email: info@southsidestorage.ie

Location: Southside Storage is located on
Murphystown Road, Sandyford, Dublin 18
close to Exit 13 on the M50

Transland group

Transland Group is one of Ireland's most reputable and innovative transport and logistics companies. We provide a daily pallet distribution service within Ireland through our membership of PalletXpress, and a consistently reliable UK and European import / export service through Palletways, Europe's largest pallet network. Our palletised distribution network offers unbeatable coverage in over 20 countries.

Transland Group is committed to creating innovative, technology-driven supply-chain solutions. Our pioneering low-cost online booking facility enables customers to avail of special discounted rates for early booking, saving them time and money. Customers can also track their consignments online from collection through to delivery, and receive POD information automatically upon delivery. This facility is especially beneficial for small to medium sized companies, who can manage all their transport requirements through one system.

Customer satisfaction is at the core of Transland's business. Our mission is to provide the highest level of service to our clients in all areas of our operation, and respond proactively to customers' requirements.

Transland has offices in Ireland (Dublin) and the UK (Lichfield), and is a member of the IIFA, BIFA and CILT. For more information, please visit www.translandgroup.com.

THE MARRIED WOMAN

Fran O'Brien

Marriage is for ever ...

In their busy lives, Kate and Dermot rush along on parallel lines,
seldom coming together to exchange a word or a kiss.
To rekindle the love they once knew, Kate struggles to lose
weight, has a make-over, buys new clothes, and arranges a
romantic trip to Spain with Dermot.

For the third time he cancels and she goes alone.

In Andalucia she meets the artist Jack Linley.
He takes her with him into a new world of emotion and
for the first time in years she feels like a desirable beautiful woman.

Will life ever be the same again?

Available now online
McGuinness Books
www.franobrien.net

THE LIBERATED WOMAN

Fran O'Brien

At last, Kate has made it!

She has ditched her obnoxious husband Dermot and is reunited with her lover, Jack.

Her interior design business goes international and TV appearances bring instant success.

But Dermot hasn't gone away and his problems encroach.

Her brother Pat and family come home from Boston and move in on a supposedly temporary basis.

Her manipulative stepmother Irene is getting married again and Kate is dragged into the extravaganza.

When a secret from the past is revealed Kate has to review her choices ...

Available now online
McGuinness Books
www.franobrien.net

THE PASSIONATE WOMAN

A chance meeting with ex lover Jack throws Kate into a spin. She cannot forgive him and concentrates all her passions on her interior design business, and television work.

Jack still loves Kate and as time passes without reconciliation he feels more and more frustrated.

Estranged husband Dermot has a change of fortunes, and wants her back.

Stepmother, Irene, is as wacky as ever and is being chased by the paparazzi.

Best friend, Carol, is searching for a man on the internet, and persuades Kate to come along as chaperone on a date.

ARE THESE PATHS TO KATE'S NEW LIFE OR ROUNDABOUTS TO HER OLD ONE?

Available now online
McGuinness Books
www.franobrien.net

ODDS ON LOVE

Fran O'Brien

Bel and Tom seem to be the perfect couple with successful careers, a beautiful home and all the trappings. But underneath the facade cracks appear and damage the basis of their marriage and the deep love they have shared since that first night they met.

Her longing to have a baby creates problems for Tom, who can't deal with the possibility that her failure to conceive may be his fault. His masculinity is questioned and in attempting to deal with his insecurities he is swept up into something far more insidious and dangerous than he could ever have imagined.

Then against all the odds, Bel is thrilled to find out she is pregnant. But she is unable to tell Tom the wonderful news as he doesn't come home that night and disappears mysteriously out of her life leaving her to deal with the fall out.

Available now online
McGuinness Books
www.franobrien.net

WHO IS FAYE?

Fran O'Brien

Can the past ever be buried?

Jenny should be fulfilled. She has a successful career,
and shares a comfortable life with her husband,
Michael, at Ballymoragh Stud.

But increasingly unwelcome memories surface
and keep her awake at night.

Is it too late to go back to the source
of those fears and confront them?

Available now online
McGuinness Books
www.franobrien.net

THE RED CARPET

Fran O'Brien

Lights, Camera, Action.

Amy is raised in the glitzy facade that is Hollywood. Her mother, Maxine, is an Oscar winning actress, and her father, John, a famous film producer. When Amy is eight years old, Maxine is tragically killed.

A grown woman, Amy becomes the focus of John's obsession for her to star in his movies and be as successful as her mother. But Amy's insistence on following her heart, and moving permanently to Ireland, causes a rift between them.

As her daughter, Emma, approaches her eighth birthday, Amy is haunted by the nightmare of what happened on her own eighth birthday.

She determines to find answers to her questions.

Available now online
McGuinness Books
www.franobrien.net

FAIRFIELDS

1907   QUEENSTOWN   CORK

Set against the backdrop of a family feud and prejudice
Anna and Royal Naval Officer, Mike, fall in love.
They meet secretly at an old cottage
on the shores of the lake at Fairfields.

During that spring and summer their feelings for each
other deepen. Blissfully happy, Anna accepts Mike's
proposal of marriage, unaware that her family have a
different future arranged for her.

**Is their love strong enough to withstand
the turmoil that lies ahead?**

Available now online
McGuinness Books
www.franobrien.net

THE PACT

THE POINT OF THE KNIFE
PRESSES INTO SOFT SKIN ...

Inspector Grace McKenzie investigates the
trafficking of women into Ireland and is
drawn under cover into that sinister world.

She is deeply affected by the suffering of one
particular woman and her quest for justice
re-awakens an unspeakable trauma in her own life.

CAN SHE EVER ESCAPE FROM ITS
INFLUENCE AND BE FREE TO LOVE?

Available now online
McGuinness Books
www.franobrien.net

1916

On Easter Monday, 24th April, 1916, against the
backdrop of the First World War, a group of
Irishmen and Irishwomen rise up against Britain.
What follows has far-reaching consequences.

We witness the impact of the Rising on four families,
as passion, fear and love permeate a week of
insurrection which reduces the centre of Dublin to ashes.

This is a story of divided loyalties, friendships,
death, and a conflict between an Empire
and a people fighting for independence.

Available now online
McGuinness Books
www.franobrien.net

Love of her Life

A man can look into a
Woman's eyes and remind her of
How it used to be between them...
Once upon a time.

Photographer Liz is running a successful business. Her family
And career are all she cares about since her husband died, until
An unexpected encounter brings Scott back into her life.

Is this second chance for love destined
To be overcome by the whims of fate?

Available now online
McGuinness Books
www.franobrien.net

CUIMHNÍ CINN
Memoirs of the Uprising

Liam Ó Briain

(Reprint in the Irish language originally published in 1951)

(English translation by Michael McMechan)

Liam Ó Briain was a member of the Volunteers of Ireland from 1914 and he fought with the Citizen Army of Ireland in the College of Surgeons during Easter Week.

This is a clear lively account of the events of that time. An account in which there is truth, humanity and, more than any other thing, humour. It will endure as literature.

When this book was first published in Irish in 1951, it was hoped it would be read by the young people of Ireland. To remember more often the hardships endured by our forebears for the sake of our freedom we might the better validate Pearse's vision.

Available now online
McGuinness Books
www.franobrien.net